BRIGHT STAR

The debut novel by
Dallas Anne Duncan

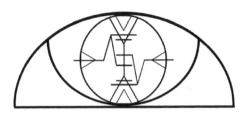

BRIGHT

STAR

THE MERIDIAN TRILOGY • BOOK ONE

DALLAS ANNE DUNCAN

Dallas Anne Duncan, LLC
>> A Creative Publishing Co. <<
Athens, Georgia

Library of Congress Cataloging-in-Publication Data

Names: Duncan, Dallas Anne, author.
Title: Bright Star / Dallas Anne Duncan. — 1st ed.
Description: First edition. | Athens, Georgia : Dallas Anne Duncan, LLC, 2021.
Identifiers: Library of Congress Control Number: 2021920329
ISBN 9798985012101 (hardcover) | ISBN 9798985012118 (ebook)
ISBN 9798985012125 (paperback)
Subjects: High fantasy, fiction, fantasy fiction

Books published by Dallas Anne Duncan, LLC may be purchased in bulk for promotional, educational, or business use. Please contact your local independent bookstore for details.

The text of this book is set in 11-point Baskerville.

First edition: 2021. First paperback edition: 2022.

<3

For you, you wonderful creature.

And for Annie Rich Thompson,
without whose creative encouragement this book and
forthcoming series + prequel would never have moved from my
brain to manuscript.

~ 1 ~

"Order up!"

The sharp voice cut through the myriad sounds of laughter and chatter, forks clinking against plates, and the hum from the jukebox in the diner's back corner. Bridgette Conner glanced out the large front window at the line forming, just as it did every Saturday and Sunday. Rain or shine, the Nashville, Tennessee, hole-in-the-wall meat-and-three was always full, especially on weekends.

The warm, tangy scent of fresh sausage patties mingled with that of bacon and eggs, along with the sweet odors of cinnamon and sugar wafting from the waffle iron.

Bridgette deftly slid a hand under each tray for her next table, and smoothly wove through the crowd to deliver her fare. She heard the front door jingle as she made her way to the tray return, and noticed a man about her age walk in and head straight to the bar seating. A server greeted him and handed him the set of Sunday menus: breakfast plates, lunch plates, the day's specials.

She couldn't put a finger on why, but the man immediately gave her a sense of uneasy curiosity. Something about him seemed … off.

"Hey, Jamie?" Bridgette turned to her manager, Jamie, who'd stepped next to her for a quick sip of coffee at the server station.

"What's up? You're killing it this morning, by the way — thanks for taking over table twenty-three!"

"Ha! Of course. That guy at the bar, the one who just sat down. Have you seen him before?"

Jamie looked over to where Bridgette inclined her head. "No, I don't think so. Why do you ask?"

Bridgette furrowed her brow. "I haven't either. But, I don't know. I've worked here just about every Sunday for three years. I know who our Sunday crowd regulars are. I don't recognize him, but he sauntered inside and sat down like he knew exactly where he was going. Like he'd been here plenty. And if he was a first-timer or tourist, he'd have waited to ask about sitting at the bar. It just seemed weird to me."

Jamie looked amused. "Girl, calm down. Maybe he's just confident!" she laughed. "I'll mention to Wade to keep an eye on him, but I'm sure it's fine."

This time as Bridgette went to check her tables, she had to walk across the diner, passing the stranger in her path. She made no move toward him, but had the oddest feeling he was watching her as she walked. The hair on the back of her neck stood up, and she tried not to let her wariness show as she refilled water glasses and coffee mugs.

Wade, who manned bar service on Sundays, was a large, burly man in his forties. Bridgette avoided the bar as best she could the rest of her shift, watching as Wade poured the man what seemed like endless cups of hot, black coffee. Bridgette turned two tables in the time it took for Wade to convince him to order something to eat.

She took that as further proof that the man didn't belong. Even tourists who came in usually knew what they wanted: a world-famous Wafflewich, nine times out of ten.

As the crowd began to thin and she was down to two tables, Bridgette walked back to the server station to start her closing sidework. Rolling silverware inside oversized paper napkins put her in the perfect vantage point to watch the man at the bar, who'd at this point been drinking coffee in the same spot for nearly four hours. He had good posture, wasn't hunched over depressed or hiding. But his eyes were downcast, almost as if he was focused on the bar, and any sensation came to him from sound or aura alone. His skin was light with olive undertones, and he wore a deep navy button-up, sleeves rolled to the crook of his elbows. His dark brown hair was wavy and covered by a trendy, slouchy knit beanie. He could have been a college student like herself, but his manner appeared almost a feigned aloofness. And those clothes — the style was on point, but the fabric quality looked too nice for a college student's budget, even from a slight distance. He was completely unfamiliar, yet his air reminded her of a celebrity doing its best to blend in with the public, and thus be out of the public eye.

Three o'clock hit and Jamie flipped the door sign to "closed." Bridgette, Wade, and their fellow front-of-house team began the ritual of closing shop, pausing to thank their remaining tables as they finalized their checks.

"Whoa — thanks man!" Wade's voice boomed across the nearly empty diner. The man was gone, and in his place was a fifty-dollar bill, crisp and fresh from the bank.

"He didn't even ask for a receipt!" Wade said incredulously as everyone gathered around. "I don't think he said a word to me at all except to order. Strange dude, but damn!"

Bridgette bristled. "He gave me a weird vibe."

Wade looked at her and his eyes widened. "Holy shit, Bridge! I didn't even realize it until just now. He had eyes like yours!"

She reached up instinctively for her face. As a youngster in the system, one of her foster mothers tried to convince Bridgette that she was destined to be a model and make them all rich: "Nobody has eyes like that! The cameras will love you!" she'd claimed. Bridgette's eyes were naturally opalescent, a light gray lilac flecked with white and gold, shifting between different shades of purple depending on how the light hit them.

"What do you mean?" she asked Wade.

"They did that shifty color thing!" Wade exclaimed. "But your eyes are purple and his are blue."

No wonder the guy kept looking down instead of making eye contact. Her whole life, but especially during her younger years, Bridgette was bullied for her most defining features. Her eyes. Her ears, with the slightest point instead of a curve at the top, that stuck out whenever she wore a ponytail or baseball cap. Her height — she was lithe and athletically built, fit and trim without even trying, and nearly six feet tall. Not uncommon, but having been well on her way to that height in fourth grade, boys and girls alike called her a giant and a freak monster.

Hearing that the man shared one of those features did not make her feel any better about him. It somehow seemed even stranger.

Bridgette and Jamie were the last to leave, locking the diner door behind them.

"Do you want me to drive you home?" Jamie asked. "I know it's close, but that guy really seemed to give you the creeps."

Bridgette gave her a half-smile. "Nah, I'm good. I don't want to overreact. He's probably just some guy."

"Well, if I see y'all on one of those serial killer documentaries —"

Bridgette threw her head back in laughter. She punched Jamie lightly in the shoulder and turned to walk to her apartment. It wasn't a far walk, but the short distance was a pretty one. There was a river greenway trail below the bridge that separated the downtown area from her university and its surrounding apartments, and the city kept plenty of green space lining the sidewalk and in the medians. Her building was just over the bridge, and even though it was less than a half-mile from the diner, Bridgette gave an involuntary sigh of relief when it came into view. She still couldn't figure out why the man made her so uncomfortable.

Bridgette fumbled in her pocket for her keys, then slipped inside and headed toward the elevator. Her apartment was on an upper floor, a corner one-bedroom unit with a view of the greenway and downtown. It was small and there weren't a lot of decorations, but that was fine. Brigette had no true family. She'd been left essentially orphaned, abandoned at the hospital. Her birth mother had come alone and given a false name, then checked herself out the moment Bridgette was stable. She'd left a note on the pillow of the hospital bed, giving her baby a name — Bridgette Eileen Conner — and wrote that she hoped one day, Bridgette would understand why it had to be this way.

Until about age thirteen, Bridgette spent no more than three years with any foster family. She was quiet and bookish, often picked on, and tried to keep to herself. Bridgette never knew what led any of the families to move on, just knew that her caseworker would come with little warning, and she had to pack up and leave.

Even now, at age twenty-two, Bridgette's most treasured possessions could fit inside a pillowcase. The last time she was placed, it was just before her thirteenth birthday. The older couple, Martha and "Doc" Joel Simmons, were probably the closest Bridgette ever came to having a real family. But after thirteen years of being whisked away at a moment's notice, Bridgette spent her first three years with the Simmonses petrified that they, too, would tire of her. When the three-year mark hit and subsequently passed, it felt like a weight came off her chest.

Doc and Martha noticed her change, but attributed it to Bridgette turning sixteen. They saw her become freer and lighter, and her lilac eyes seemed to glow brighter. Though she rarely went back to Georgia now, Bridgette made sure to talk to the Simmonses on the phone several times a week, and she kept a picture of the three of them on her nightstand.

That was the only photograph in the whole apartment. Bridgette still typically kept to herself, preferring solitary creative and athletic pursuits to joining clubs or team sports. Even as an adult, she never quite found her niche.

Bridgette sighed, feeling the stress of another Sunday ease. She strode to her bedroom, stripping off her diner uniform in favor of a pair of leggings and an oversized lightweight sweatshirt. She had every intention of taking her latest book purchase to the little park and duck pond by the greenway. Her building had a downstairs exit that backed up to a tree-lined gravel trail down to the river. It was her favorite spot to read, write, and paint. She grabbed a shoulder bag, tucked the novel inside, and slung a foldable chair over her other shoulder. She ducked her head in the fridge to grab a can of sparkling water, then headed out to find a sunny spot in the grass.

The area by the pond wasn't quiet, ever — ducks and geese honked and quacked, and kids loved to buy handfuls of feed pellets from a dispenser at the trailhead to toss their way. Their shrieks of both delight and terror filled the air as the birds, by now accustomed to being fed, scrambled up the banks to be closer to the tiny handfuls of treats.

Bridgette got lost in her book, her mind miles and years

away. It was late afternoon, and the air around her grew more golden and warm. Wholly absorbed between pages, she became immune to the cacophony of families and waterfowl.

Suddenly, Bridgette sat straight up, jerked out of her reverie by something she couldn't place. She glanced to the pond, where all seemed oblivious to any change in her surroundings.

Out of the corner of her eye, though, she saw him — the strange man from the diner. He seemed to be sunning himself, leaned against a thick tree trunk, his face turned up toward the sky. Sunlight flowed through the leaves to dapple his skin with early spring glow. The man wore sunglasses now, black-rimmed with indigo-hued polarized lenses, that complemented his navy shirt. His pants were dark-colored and fitted, and his shoes were navy Chucks.

Bridgette couldn't tell if he was close enough to hear her, nor did she know if he'd even seen her. She sat frozen, unsure if it was wise to try packing up and walking away. There was no way his presence was a coincidence. There was also no way she was letting him wait until she packed up, then stealthily follow her to her apartment.

There were enough people within earshot that if she screamed, someone would come to her aid. Or, well, so she hoped.

"What the fuck dude, are you following me?" she called out.

"Not exactly."

The man's gaze moved from the slowly setting sun to Bridgette, who was tucking her book and chair into their respective bags. He pushed himself away from the tree and began a purposeful walk toward her.

Holy shit, is this how it felt to be one of Ted Bundy's girls? Bridgette thought as she struggled deciding between walking back to her apartment with this guy following her, or pretending to go further down the path to the greenway.

"There's no need to be frightened or lash out."

Ted Bundy probably said that.

"As I live and breathe, I vow that I mean you no harm."

Oh good, a serial killer who sounds like he's quoting Shakespeare.

Bridgette made a split-second decision to haul ass back to her apartment, where she would lock the door and call the cops. She'd have done so already, except for poor cell service by the pond.

"Please. It is imperative we speak." He wasn't following, but she felt his eyes trail her as she sped up the gravel walk.

"Actually, it is imperative you stay the fuck far away from me, or I'll sic the entire Davidson County police force on you," Bridgette called back, not looking over her shoulder. She'd get her phone out the second she got to the trailhead and the trees cleared.

But that was impossible. The moment Bridgette reached the landscaped clearing behind her building, the man stepped into her path. She stopped dead.

How did he get here before me?

"I am not going to hurt you, Liluthuaé."

Lih-loo-thoo-what? she thought, then addressed him directly.

"Look, dude, I think you have me confused with someone else. You need to leave me alone, leave this park. Last warning." Bridgette reached for her phone. "See? Nine-one-one. You have five seconds to scatter or I'm having you arrested for stalking me."

Before she could process what was happening, the man's hand was firmly around her wrist, pulling it out of her bag.

"There is no need to involve the law. Come with me. We must speak. I will buy you tea."

Awesome. I'm fodder for a Lifetime movie.

"I don't. Like. Tea." Bridgette muttered through gritted teeth, trying to pry her hand free.

"Venti iced chai, with a pump of dark caramel, and just a bit of cinnamon on top."

She froze. Her regular order. How long had this creep been following her, close enough to hear and memorize her drink order, before she noticed him at the diner that morning? If he knew that, he already knew where she lived: the campus coffee shop was across the street.

"Come with me," he said again.

- 7 -

Bridgette glanced around. There was no one to hear her if she screamed. This far from the duck pond, her terror-stricken shouts would be faint, blending in with the noises from the kids and the birds. But surely on a Sunday before midterms, there would be plenty of people at the coffee shop. A room full of witnesses.

So she jerked her head in some semblance of a nod. He removed his hand from hers and beckoned ahead, inviting her to lead the way.

~ 2 ~

Bridgette stepped past him, casting a sidelong glance at her apartment. She thought again briefly about making a run for it ... but the man already proved his superhuman speed. By the time she so much as stepped to the right instead of straight ahead, he'd already be there to turn her back around. She was stuck. So across the street she led him, the sky turning a vibrant gradient of peach and tangerine. It would be dark soon and she felt queasy at the thought of the stranger walking with her once the sun set.

Wonderful, she thought. *He's going to take me on a date and then use the darkness to hide us as he kills me and stuffs me in a trunk.*

She reached the door at the coffee shop. His hand pushed it open before she stretched hers out to do so. They walked inside to find the place bustling, a line at the counter and slim pickings for seating.

"Wait here. May I borrow that to reserve a table?" He indicated the foldable chair, still slung over her shoulder. She shrugged it off and handed it over, watching as he moved between study groups to a two-top by the side window.

He returned to the line with her, where they waited in shared silence until they reached the counter.

"These will be together," the man told the barista, whose look indicated amusement that he still had on sunglasses, at night and inside. "I will have a large iced coffee, dark roast, with room for cream."

He looked at Bridgette, who begrudgingly repeated the order he somehow knew so well.

"Name for the order?" the barista asked.

"Collum."

A name. He has a name. And of course it sounds made up. Who names their kid "Column?" Maybe his parents were architects.

Collum led Bridgette to the table he'd saved. They again sat in silence, waiting for their drinks.

I'm not saying a damn word to this joker ... he drug me here and he better explain why, Bridgette thought.

He brought back their drinks, then disappeared momentarily to add his cream and sugar. When he returned, Bridgette forgot her vow not to speak first, and blurted out, "Why did your parents name you after a pillar?"

Collum, who'd been sliding his sunglasses to the top of his head, chuckled. "They did no such thing," he said. "Though it is a homonym, my name is C – O – L – L – U – M. Where I am from, it is a strong name that means I am blessed with vitality and maturity."

Is serial killer Collum trying to hit on me?

"Vitality and maturity," Bridgette repeated dryly. Her eyes met his, and for the first time, she saw what Wade mentioned earlier. Collum indeed had eyes like hers, and the way those deep blue and nearly obsidian shades played together, his eyes looked like Gulf tidal pools bathed in moonlight.

"Yes." He took a sip of coffee, still staring at her, as if patiently waiting for her to ask why he'd drug her here; why she followed him.

"Fine," she snapped, more to the Universe than to him. "Who are you? Why are you stalking me?" — she said that part a bit louder, in case someone overheard — "And how do you know my chai order?"

Collum leaned forward, putting his elbows on the table.

"Before I answer you, I must prepare you," he said, his voice notably lower than it had been moments before. "The responses you seek may not be easy to hear. You may also laugh and tell me what I say is unbelievable, that it cannot be, that I am lying. But I assure you that what I say is the truth. And I will tell you the truth, be wholly honest and complete with you, until you understand." He paused his soliloquy and waited for Bridgette to agree.

She gave a cautious nod, hiding her smile of disbelief. *This dude is cuckoo for Cocoa Puffs.*

"I am Collum Andoralain, and I am not of this world."

His face was stone-cold serious, but Bridgette threw her head back in laughter. She calmed herself, clutching at her chest in a fit of giggles.

This. Is. Not. Real. Life. I've been stalked and kidnapped by a serial killer who calls me Lithuania and is convinced he's an alien, she thought. *The Lifetime execs are going to die over this storyline.*

Every time Bridgette thought she'd gotten ahold of herself, she caught Collum's calm and focused eyes, and started snickering again.

"I am not a serial killer, nor an alien, and I very much assure you this is real life," he said, eyebrows raised as he lifted his coffee cup. His mouth was cocked in a bit of a half-smile.

Her laughter stopped abruptly. "I didn't say —"

"Not out loud, but you did in your mind."

Holy shit.

"I was born with an ability that humans call 'mind-reading,' but it is not quite like that. Each of us speaks to ourselves, and it is almost as if my ears are highly sensitized. I can hear unspoken words if I am close enough to an individual, and if an emotion is high enough, my hearing is able to pick it up from quite a distance," he said. "I'm afraid I may have to buy you dinner, as what you will learn tonight may take some time. What would you like?"

Bridgette blinked. His sudden change in demeanor and subject took a moment to process.

"What would you like?" Collum repeated.

Her eyes narrowed slightly and she smirked. *Two can play this game*, she thought. *I would like filet mignon and an old fashioned.*

"I don't believe the coffee shop has either of those items." Collum's eyes met hers, the silver highlights shimmering. He knew she was testing him, thinking instead of speaking aloud.

"Fine. I want one of the caprese sandwiches," she sighed. He really could hear her inner monologue. Which begged the question of how long he'd been listening, and what else he'd overheard.

"Nothing *too* incriminating." This time, Collum flashed her a smirk, and his eyes were bright with laughter as he pushed his chair back from the table.

Oh-ho, Ted Bundy's got jokes, does he!

At the counter, Collum casually reached one hand back as if to adjust his beanie, and pointedly used his middle finger to do so.

"Why are you convinced I am here to murder you?" he asked when he returned, two hot sandwiches in hand.

"Um, let's see. So far today, you came to my job, you followed me home, you prevented me from calling the cops —"

Collum laughed, a deep and musical laugh that reflected in his tidal pool eyes. "Well, when you put it that way ..."

Bridgette took a bite of the sandwich, the melty mozzarella and aromatic basil anchoring her in reality, assuring her this was somehow not a dream.

"Spill," she instructed. "What's this big, unbelievable story you have?"

Collum sat back in his chair and took a deep, centering breath.

"When I say I am not of this Earth, I mean it truly. Are you familiar with what was known to humans as the Salem Witch Trials?"

Bridgette nodded, feeling a bit as though she was in the midst of an out-of-body experience the longer she sat with Collum. She wasn't quite sure what made her stay, if she was being honest.

"Though most of the Trials were a sham, and many, many innocent humans were unjustly targeted and murdered, there were magical and spiritual folk that were affected," Collum said. "This was certainly not the first time those kind were persecuted for natural-born abilities or rare features, but it was in some sense a final straw. A witch named Artur Cromwell and his family were attacked one night and though there was no loss of life then, he felt something must change. He was a brilliant man and knew how to develop spells, and manipulate elements and Nature in ways few could, giving him great power. Artur Cromwell divined a new continent, born from Earth but not quite Earth, and sent it skyward. His creating this new continent meant he and those of his blood were infinitely connected to it, allowing him to open a portal to this new world. And so he did, taking his family with him.

"The Cromwells nurtured and cultivated their sky-land, but soon knew they had a greater purpose. Being witch or wizard, or any manner of magical or spiritual creature, does not preclude one from religious beliefs, and for his ways, Artur Cromwell felt called to follow a — for that time — somewhat progressive Christian faith," Collum continued. "They believed they had been spared death in the Salem Witch Trials in order to save others facing this persecution. Thus, periodically, Artur Cromwell would descend the portal and return to Earth, searching and spreading word. All manner of magical and spiritual beings joined him, and over many years, what was once a plot of land became a sprawling continent in the sky, hidden just over the cloud line, coated in old magick and reinforced with spell magic so as to be undetectable. This is where I am from. It is also, in part, where you are from."

Bridgette had barely moved as Collum spoke. His eyes seemed far away, remembering a history she'd never imagined possible, much less real.

"I think you just described the plot of 'Peter Pan,'" she finally said. "Second star to the right and straight on 'til morning."

"Not quite," Collum grinned, his eyes brightening again. "In 'Peter Pan,' I don't believe there were Elves or Elflings."

Bridgette raised an eyebrow. "Are you really trying to tell me —"

Collum removed his beanie, and two elegant, unmistakably pointed ears poked through his casually mussed hair.

"That's not — I mean — no, look, this — you're lying. You are making this up. Take the costume off," Bridgette stammered. She wasn't sure if she was panicking from feeling like she might be murdered most of the evening, or from the jarring revelation that made an awful lot of sense to something deep in her subconscious. Either way, she was done with Collum and his fairytales. She moved to get up, to escape, but damn it if Collum and his speed-demon swiftness was already next to her, stopping her.

"Please, Bridgette."

It was the first time he said her name that whole day. Of

course he knew her name if he knew her diner and her reading spot and her chai order. But hearing him say it, in that warm voice that barely hinted at the lilt of an Irish or perhaps Scottish accent, was sobering. She paused.

"Okay. Keep going. Start with the part about us being … Elves."

Collum sipped his coffee again, as if to fuel his task of telling this tale, proselytizing to a nonbeliever. He took another deep breath — and adjusted his hat back over his ears — before continuing.

"Well. We are not Elves."

"But you just said — "

He held up his hand in a gesture to quiet her. "*We* are not Elves. I am an Elf. You are an Elfling. A hybrid with one Elf parent. In this case, your mother was an Elf and your father was … not."

Bridgette resisted the urge to implore he go on about what her father was and wasn't.

"There is much history still to share with you, both of you personally and our world above the world. Artur Cromwell named it Heáhwolcen, an Old English word that quite literally means 'a cloud of heaven in the sky,'" Collum paused, considering. "But I feel this is enough for now. You have university tests during these next few days, yes?"

Bridgette nodded.

"Those should be your focus. I am staying in the hotel on your campus. Though I carry no cell phone, I will be there most of the day should you need to reach me. We will meet again when you have completed these examinations and this history is not a distraction. I trust you can walk home?"

Bridgette was again taken aback by his ability to delve deep into strange history one moment and be one-hundred percent rational the next.

"Yep," she managed to squeak out, still dumbfounded that any of what he said could be true. She watched as Collum stood and walked out the door, turning away from the cross street to her apartment building.

What the hell have I gotten myself into? she thought as she got up to throw her trash away and leave.

Once at home, Bridgette locked her door, shoved a desk chair in front of it just in case Collum *was* a serial killer with a strange imagination, and fell onto her soft mattress. Her sleep was fitful. She tossed and turned as dreams of death, magic, and plots of fantasy novels filled her brain. In some dreams, she died. In others, Collum saved her. Just before her alarm went off, one final nightmare plagued her: A cruel, bat-like creature plucked her up and flew her higher and higher on a never-ending pathway, screeching the whole way as she kicked and screamed to get free. The creature was an amalgamation of every bully Bridgette really had been tormented by, and each horrible movie villain that scared her younger self.

The next few days seemed a slow-motion blur. Bridgette saw figures and shadows in her peripheral vision, several times swearing she saw Collum in his knit beanie on a park bench or at the student center. But each time she took a second glance, she saw nothing out of the ordinary. Her midterms flew by and she was beyond ready for the nine days of work-free, school-free spring break that followed. Not that she had any particular plans or place to be, just having the bliss of no one needing anything from her was plan enough.

On Friday, when she practically waltzed out of the classroom, Collum Andoralain was the absolute last creature — human or Elf — she anticipated seeing. Yet there he was, those same sunglasses and knit beanie hiding his allegedly Elven ears and eyes. He was propped up against a light post, casually reading the university paper, trying to ignore the small gaggle of freshmen girls who seemed quite interested in his presence on campus. But Bridgette saw one corner of his mouth half-up in a smile, and whatever those girls were saying or thinking, it highly amused him. They gave Bridgette dirty looks as she walked up to him.

"What's up, Bundy?" she called out. "Still stalking me, I see."

Collum folded the paper and pretended not to hear her attempt at goading him.

"Your examinations are done. It is now time for history lesson number two."

"Oh, so you're *Professor* Bundy today!" she quipped.

He ignored her jibe. "Come. We're going to get milkshakes. Humans have more ice cream flavors than I ever imagined possible."

"You like ice cream?" Bridgette commented, incredulity in her voice.

Collum raised both brows in surprise. "Who doesn't?"

Bundy's thirty-one flavors of surprise.

"I heard that," Collum laughed. "Come on."

She followed him to The Creamery, one of several university-run eateries on campus. This one was managed by its business school, and fully supplied by area farmers.

"This little place has been one of my favorite discoveries," Collum said as he led her inside, turning his attention to the cashier. "I'll have a large milkshake with strawberries and cream, and whatever the lady would like."

"Hmm. I'll also have a milkshake. Pink lemon icebox pie, please."

The refurbished milkshake machines whirred to life, and Collum and Bridgette watched quietly as first milk, then scoops of rich, fluffy ice cream were added to the tall metal canisters. The resulting shakes were thick and decadent, each served with whipped cream, a slice of strawberry and lemon, and an oversized sipping straw.

"God, this is dreamy," Bridgette murmured. She couldn't remember the last time she'd had a milkshake, now that she thought about it. They moved to the patio, enjoying the early spring sunshine beaming down. She realized that she no longer felt uneasy and scared around Collum. Not ready to say she trusted him, but definitely felt almost friendly toward him. *I wonder when that happened*, she mused to herself, then asked aloud, "How long have you been here?"

"Long enough to know that getting chocolate milk mixed

with peppermint ice cream in a shake is the best flavor."

A non-answer.

Collum instead dove head-first into the history lesson. "When last we spoke, you learned how the world above the world was formed. For more than a century, it was a place of refuge. We formed governments and land boundaries, continuing to build on as more rose to join us. There is one country, though, called Palna, that is … different. It is an evil place, ripe with a magic of ill-intent called Craft Wizardry, or Craft magic, and led to a civil war in Heáhwolcen, until the other countries defeated those forces and effectively imprisoned them within their own boundaries. For the safety of magical beings and humans alike, and to keep Palna in check, the portal to Earth was largely closed. It remained that way until perhaps sixty years ago, when the Fairies, who are naturally goodwill ambassadors, learned of rifts between humans on Earth and desired to help. The portal again was fully open, but with stricter regulations and was heavily monitored. Primarily Fairies are the only ones who come and go."

"So how did you get through? And why?" Bridgette interrupted, momentarily ignoring his nonchalant mention of Fairies.

"I got through because I was sent here."

"So the Fairies sent you?"

Collum didn't seem to pick up on the skepticism in her tone. "Yes. As I was saying, the Fairies reopened the portal in more recent decades. Since that time, it became evident that there was a shift in some of the magic keeping Palna in check. But no one thought such a thing was possible, so no one realized it was happening. I cannot divulge specifics, not yet, but Palna was able to begin causing trouble. And in recent years, it has gotten worse. The Palnans were able to wall themselves off inside a second barrier, further isolating themselves and keeping others out. The remaining countries met to formulate a plan of attack, and it was revealed we may have one hope, one secret weapon, if you will, to conquer and defeat Craft Wizardry for good. I was sent to find and secure that hope."

"How does that explain why you've been keeping tabs on me, and buying me tea and milkshakes?" Bridgette was half-intrigued, half-playing along. Perhaps Collum was an author, testing how believable his plot was.

"In Elvish, we call this final hope the Bright Star. The Liluthuaé."

Her eyes narrowed. The name, that strange thing he called her in the clearing.

"You, Bridgette. You're the Bright Star."

~ 3 ~

Bridgette stared at Collum, unsure if she should nod or laugh. His eyes, hidden behind those sunglasses, were unreadable.

"Dude. What the fuck?" she finally said. "First you try to convince me I'm an Elf. Now you're going all, 'Obi-wan, you're my only hope' on me."

"Would I be more convincing if I sent you a hologram message and wore space buns?"

"You are the strangest Elf I've ever met."

"I believe I'm the only Elf you've ever met."

He had her there.

"What does it even mean to be an Elf?" she asked, tucking her wavy reddish-blonde hair behind one lightly pointed ear, momentarily pretending Collum hadn't just told her she was a magical heroine.

"Elves are tall and trim, natural-born warriors and athletes. Some have affinities or abilities, like my hearing. Elflings, though, like you, have the Elven physical characteristics, in part. They also have characteristics from their other parent."

Collum still hadn't told her what her father was.

"It is ... not safe to tell you that yet," he said quietly.

She already hated his sensitive hearing.

"So you found me," Bridgette said. "Assuming I believe you — and trust me, I don't — what do you want with me? How do I know you're not one of those evil palm tree wizards coming to collect me for your own devices?"

Collum laughed. "It's Palna, not palm. And no other being can impersonate these."

He took off his sunglasses, those tidal pool eyes looking especially blue and silvery in the sun.

"As for what's next, you have a choice. I was sent to find you, to show you who you are, but I cannot force you to do anything with that knowledge. If you wish, you may stay here. I will leave and you will never see me again. But in doing so, you may resign Earth and the rest of the world above the world to a miserable future. Or, you can come through the portal, and give us a fighting chance."

"Me? A fighting chance?" Bridgette laughed. "Look, Collum, the only thing I've ever fought was the foster sibling who tried to pull my hair when I was seven. And that fight did not go in my favor."

Collum leaned forward, taking a purposeful sip from his milkshake. "Come with me."

He wasn't pleading, exactly, but he sounded … shaky, perhaps. As if he had plenty more to tell and show her, but didn't want to be overheard. Bridgette felt a wave of anxiety rush over her, and suddenly, despite how unbelievable it sounded, wondered how real, how serious this threat was.

"Please," he implored again. "Spend your spring vacation with me. With us, above the world. We won't ask you to make your decision until the end."

He locked his eyes with hers, and Bridgette shivered slightly.

Do I believe him? Do I trust him? What if this whole week he's been biding his time, is really the serial killer I thought he was?

Her heartbeat quickened. So many what-ifs, and none of them particularly appealing.

"Nine days. I don't — I don't think I can do that. How do I even know this is real? Everything you've told me is something out of a fairytale. I don't know you. You really might be a murderer. How am I supposed to blindly just go with you, a total stranger with pretty eyes, and hope you'll magically grant me three wishes instead of suck my blood?"

Collum fought back a laugh, amused at her metaphor. He saw the uncertainty in her lilac irises, pupils widening with trepidation as her anxiety built. She started rambling, panic building for a reason she couldn't place.

Collum closed his eyes and put his hands on the table, palms up. He loosened his shoulders, breathed in through his nose and as he exhaled, barely spoke above a whisper.

Bridgette, moments away from heaving herself into The Creamery's bathroom to freak out in private, felt a light breeze settle over her, waft around her. She became hyper-aware of the scents of honeysuckle and soft vanilla, yet had no idea from where they emanated. She breathed them in, welcoming their comfort as her heartbeat slowed and temperature cooled.

"Are you better?"

Bridgette hadn't realized she'd closed her eyes, nor that she'd clenched her fists. "I think so. I'm so sorry, I don't usually … I don't usually get attacks like that anymore."

"There is no need to apologize," Collum said quietly. "It was not my intention to incite panic. I am the one who should have been more tactful."

Bridgette took another deep breath, but now the air smelled … normal. She wrinkled her nose slightly, searching for those sweet floral and spice tones.

"What did you smell?" Collum asked.

"For a minute, it smelled like honeysuckle and vanilla. That was weird."

As soon as the words left her mouth, she tilted her head, her brain processing an important realization. Collum asked what *did* she smell, not what *does* she smell. Almost as if he knew the air had changed.

She lifted her eyes. "Did you …"

"I may not be Ted Bundy, but I am guilty as charged on that account."

Bridgette balled up a napkin and threw it across the table. "You punk! How the hell'd you do that?"

Collum dodged the paper ball and let out an amused snort. "I happen to be quite adept at my meditation practice, thank you! But as my Elven ability allows me to gauge emotion and hear quiet thoughts, it also allows me, to a point, to influence a person or crowd's overall mood, and manifest certain energies. The spell I used is my chosen word to bring calm, and because my calmness relies on being surrounded by nature and certain scents, when I direct this energy, it brings comforting aromas and sometimes sound."

Bridgette took another deep breath of her own. She had no idea how it was remotely possible, but she believed him. Whether he spoke truly of a continent floating above the clouds, or whether it was all in his head, Collum fully believed what he told her was reality. She stood and tilted her head back, savoring the final swallow of her milkshake.

Their eyes met. "So. When do we leave?"

A broad, dazzling smile spread across Collum's face.

He told her to pack light, that she'd find everything she needed once they arrived. Bridgette met him at his hotel the next morning, dressed in jeans, ruddy cowboy boots, a T-shirt and her favorite oversized university logo hoodie. She carried a shoulder bag with her book, phone, wallet, and not much else tucked inside.

Collum was checking out as she walked in. "Perfect timing. I have a car waiting."

Indeed he did, a black SUV with complete separation between driver and passenger. Collum was antsy, nearly giddy with excitement, though in the spirit of professionalism did his best to hide those emotions. He instructed the driver to please deposit them at the airport, then settled into the backseat with Bridgette.

"What are you studying at the university?" he asked, though he already knew.

"Communications and marketing," she answered. "And minoring in violin. It's a music school. Everyone studies an instrument, songwriting or vocals."

Collum cocked his head, studying *her*. "How long have you played violin?"

"Since I was nine," Bridgette said. "One of the schools I went to in fourth grade had a violin program and I sort of fell in love with it. I've never been able to read music like you're supposed to, on the little chart. But I memorized the finger position of each note and, I don't know, translated the notes into letters that corresponded to those positions. Numbers and symbols have never been my strong suit. Letters make sense."

"What do you want to do in your future?"

Now Bridgette cocked her head, thinking. She hated that question. What will you do when you grow up, when you graduate? What does your future hold? The truth was, Bridgette had never known what her future held. Being swept off to a new home so often until she was thirteen never gave her much time to think of it, to dream.

"I have no idea," she finally told him. "Seriously."

Collum nodded thoughtfully, and the two sat in silence for a while. It wasn't a long way to the airport, but spring break traffic slowed the drive.

"Why are we going to the airport?" Bridgette asked. "If you're really an Elf, shouldn't you just be able to magic us away or something up this alleged portal?"

The warm, musical laughter echoed in the backseat. Collum was highly amused, and he didn't try to hide it now. The two had come a long way in a week, Bridgette realized, from her seeing him first as the brooding, unknown stranger at her diner, to now being someone she was curious about disappearing with for nine days.

Good grief, I hope he's laughing too hard to hear that, Bridgette thought.

The silver in Collum's eyes told her he most definitely heard her, and she stared straight ahead, trying to make her mind go blank.

"We are going to, as you say, 'magic up' the portal. But we must get there first."

Bridgette gave him a curious look. "Get where?"

"The portal. It's a specific place and highly guarded. Travel is monitored, as I mentioned yesterday, especially given the recent events in Palna," he said, casually dropping the name of this likely made-up country. "We can't simply go above the United States anywhere, look to the left and suddenly Heáhwolcen appears. It doesn't work that way. Artur Cromwell created the portal so no human or being with ill-intent could find it and 'magic up.'"

Bridgette considered this. *Cool. Even more proof this is one-hundred percent made up and I signed myself up for trouble.*

The SUV pulled up to the departure gates then, and its driver hopped out to open the doors for his passengers.

"Okay, so, where are we going? Where is this magic portal?" Bridgette asked as she climbed out of the car. That silver twinkle came into Collum's blue eyes again.

"In Salem, of course."

~ 4 ~

Bridgette had been completely unprepared to walk from the security checkpoint to a terminal she had no clue existed.

"This is a terminal reserved for diplomatic and government flights," Collum said, sensing her confusion.

The shimmering aircraft in front of them glittered silver, mint, and seafoam. It looked like an airplane, but just as Collum looked like a man … was somehow not quite like any other aircraft she'd ever seen. Its engines hummed more than roared as it idled on the tarmac, and the stewardess who greeted them had skin so perfect it looked airbrushed on. Her hair was so platinum blonde it was practically white, save for a dyed streak of lime green that complemented the mint uniform she wore.

"Welcome, Fyrdwisa Andoralain!" she said, her voice alarmingly chipper.

The hell is a fuh-yord-weesa? Bridgette thought, the syllables sounding both powerful and foreign. Collum caught her eye, and she took that to mean he'd fill her in on the flight.

"And welcome, Sigewíf!" This time, the chipper voice was directed at Bridgette, who inclined her head in a sign of acknowledgement. "Please sit anywhere you'd like. I am Zurina, and it is my honor to accompany you today! We do not anticipate any diversions or poor weather! Refreshments will be available after we alight the skies! Should you require any services whilst we travel, simply press the bell button above your seat!"

Bridgette gave Collum a wide-eyed look and intentionally sent a thought his way: *Is it just me, or did all of her sentences end in exclamation marks?*

Collum quickly turned his laugh into a cough and lightly shoved Bridgette's shoulder. They walked to a set of four seats that faced each other, Bridgette on one side and her companion across. There were no seatbelts, but as the engine's hum grew louder, Bridgette shifted and realized she'd been pinned to her seat by an invisible force.

"What — how? Collum, I'm stuck!" She wriggled to free

herself, but suddenly those misty scents of vanilla and honeysuckle were there. Collum was seated straight-backed and stiff, as if he, too, was held against his chair.

"Magic, Bridgette." His voice was matter-of-fact.

"How? Collum, don't lie to me. Magic isn't real. This is bullshit."

"Magic is very real, Bridgette. This is a protective binding spell, to keep us seated until it is safe for us to walk the cabin once we're in the air."

Bridgette closed her eyes and rubbed them. *This has to be a dream.*

"You're not dreaming. Just breathe, okay?" Collum wished fervently that he had sat next to instead of across from Bridgette. He had no idea how badly she'd reject the idea of magic existing. Even now, after millennia, humans still did a good job of tamping it out. "Fairytales," that's what Bridgette kept calling his history. She knew magic and myth were possible, but never experienced them to know they existed. Which also meant — he shook his head as if to clear it.

No, he thought. *The intelligence is solid.*

Turning away from his concerns to face Bridgette, he asked, "What can I teach you? Your mind is practically exploding with questions."

"Why did Zurina call us those names?"

"Sigewíf, what she greeted you as, is a traditional title for a female of great standing or reverence. It means 'victorious woman' or 'wise woman' in modern English," Collum said. "As for being Fyrdwisa Andoralain, well, that's my title."

Bridgette felt the air go from her lungs and a drop in her stomach. She thought at first it was shock, but then realized the plane had taken off.

"You have a title?"

"I do. Fyrdwisans are leaders of expeditions. We are treasure hunters and intelligence gatherers, advisors to the military and leaders of Heáhwolcen."

"How long were you stalking me as part of this intelligence gathering?"

"Once we were certain you were you, a few months."

Bridgette narrowed her eyes. "We?"

"Yes, 'we.' The leaders and top advisors, representing each country and group of interest in the world above the world."

A map appeared on the table between them. Bridgette blinked.

"The portal will take us to Fairevella," Collum pointed to a spot on the map. "In front of it lies Endorsa, the oldest country in Heáhwolcen. Here, connecting on one end to Endorsa and one end to Fairevella, is Eckenbourne. In the very center is Palna, and totally surrounding it is the borderland Bondrie. There is also the in-between, Ifrinnevatt, a spirit place where the dead may choose to spend their eternity."

"Is that like, Heaven and Hell?" Bridgette asked, both curious and horrified.

"Yes and no," Collum said, sensing another wave of panic. He breathed out his calming word and directed the energy toward her. "Do you remember when I told you that magic does not preclude one from religion? Every sentient being has a choice of faith or no faith, and thus their spirit a choice to follow a life path resulting in a positive or negative afterlife experience. The existence of Ifrinnevatt doesn't mean there is no Heaven or Hell. It is simply a place for the soul to belong, though typically it is inhabited by souls whose worldly bodies did not follow a major faith structure."

Collum's religious teaching was interrupted by Zurina reappearing, followed immediately by the force around their bodies evaporating.

"We have reached cruising altitude, and it is safe to move about! The lavatory is just ahead of me to the left. I am now happy to bring you refreshments! From our Earth allies, we are pleased to offer the in-flight favorite of Coca-Cola and peanuts or chocolate chip cookies! From the world above the world, today's selection is a variety of local teas and coffees, as well as Eagerstream sparkling! For additional snacks, we made sure to have your favorite, Fyrdwisa! What would you like?"

Bridgette answered first, glad for the unexpected comfort of

Coke in this strange situation she still wasn't sure was real.

"And how could I resist the offer of venison jerky brimlad? I would also like hot tea. Something with cinnamon."

Zurina nodded exuberantly and sped off to the back of the plane, where Bridgette imagined the kitchen was.

"Collum, did you drug me?"

He shot her a quizzical look. "No, of course not."

"Then how is this real? How?" Bridgette trailed off.

"Magic has always been real. Think of the Earth history you know to be true. When electricity, telephone communication, all of these technologies came to be, what did critics dismiss them as? Magic. All magic is, Bridgette, is manipulation and direction of the energies and elements around us," Collum explained. "Sometimes the magic requires a tool: a wand for spell magic, a wired pole to direct invisible signals so your foster parents get a cell phone call from you. Other magic, old magick, typically requires no tool, but a heightened awareness, understanding and partnership with those elements and energies. The difference lies between human being and magical being in the form of ability. Humans are not naturally gifted with the ability to commune with energy and element, but they can control them through more mechanical than ethereal means."

He paused when Zurina reappeared, to accept a steaming ceramic mug of tea and a container of what looked like trail mix. Bridgette inclined her head toward it as she popped the tab on the coldest can of soda she'd ever touched.

"What are you eating?"

Collum offered the container to her. "Venison jerky brimlad. It is very much like trail mix. Cubes or strips of dried venison, tart cherries, spiced almonds, and clusters of dark chocolate with either oats or granola."

It smelled amazing. Bridgette reached for a bite and her eyes widened at how perfectly balanced the flavors and textures were. She'd never tasted anything like it.

"I can see why that's your favorite," she said.

As if by magic — it probably *was* magic, Bridgette realized with a start — Zurina appeared with a second container of brimlad. She placed it in front of Bridgette, who resisted the urge to gobble the whole thing immediately.

"I think you're going to enjoy Heáhwolcen," Collum teased. "Or the food and drink, at least."

"I can assure you, I've never had a stranger start to a spring break trip," Bridgette said. "I still can't believe this is real. I mean, obviously we are in an airplane with magic seatbelts and you can hear my thoughts and talk me out of anxiety attacks like an emotional support Elf. But after twenty-two years of being told it's not real? This is crazy."

She glanced out the window next to her and realized how fast they were going.

"What can I say?," Collum said quietly. "Our aircraft are magic."

She heard the taunt in his voice. "Okay Bundy. Tell me more about this continent of yours. How did Artur Cromwell come to create a floating world?"

"Old magick," Collum replied. "Very, very old magick. Artur Cromwell was, and remains, the most powerful wizard to have ever been born. He and his wife Felicity escaped detection in England and made their way to the colonies with a group being ostracized for its religion. They thought this New World would be better, more free and wild, perhaps more accepting of magick. No such luck, alas. But Artur Cromwell was so skilled, so in tune to his abilities, and so learned from other beings and books, that he could perform incredible magick.

"He began to dream of a place where any and all magical beings could live freely and not be unjustly treated because of it. He began to experiment with molding rich soil and essential elements, working by candlelight in his little farmhouse by the water in Salemport. He was, without realizing, producing so much magical energy that others could feel it and were drawn to it. One of those was a Fairy by the name of Galdúr," Collum said. "Galdúr knew powerful magick himself, and as Artur figured out how to conjure a new land, Galdúr knew how to position it skyward, and how to create the portal. Artur Cromwell lived as a Puritan white man. Galdúr and others from his native village had been kidnapped and sold as Black slaves. The king who did this was a wizard, and bound Galdúr's magick and wings. But when the king died, the binding lifted, and Galdúr was able to escape his plantation and fly away. Together, these two created Heáhwolcen, and Artur Cromwell's dream was realized."

Bridgette found she wanted to know more. "That explains the witches and the Fairies. What about Elves?"

"Ah." Collum took a sip of cinnamon tea. "The first Elf to be drawn to the portal was a female named Aelys Frost. Elves typically live together in large groups, and have been traditionally found in wooded areas where they can live without detection. Aelys brought her dúnaelfen, her group, with her once she realized what the portal was."

"So, all of these beings already existed?" It seemed so odd to consider that, all this time, there'd been magic and magical folk all around her, with her having no idea it existed beyond the pages of her books.

"Of course they existed!" Collum didn't mean to sound incredulous, didn't mean to judge her ignorance, but her complete disregard for magic was unnerving. "Magical abilities and affinities are like any other trait. It's all genetic."

"What do you mean?" Bridgette asked.

"Didn't they teach you genetics? Punnett squares? Gregor Mendel?" Collum was beyond perplexed. *What do they teach at schools on Earth nowadays?* he wondered.

Bridgette put her face in her hands, exasperated at having exasperated Collum, and realized the binding spell was back. They must be getting ready to land.

"Why are you getting pissy with me?' she asked snappily. "I'm not the one who shows up and tries to convince someone that magic, after twenty-two years of being told is made up, is not only real, but passed down through genetics!"

Collum sighed. He hadn't meant to get upset. He also couldn't quite tell her *why* her resistance was so upsetting. Not until they were safely in Heáhwolcen, anyway. There was no telling who Zurina or the pilot reported to or sympathized with. Per the flight plan, he'd had to report his mission was to find and secure an Elfling who wanted to learn more about her true self. Which … was not a lie. Collum had simply neglected to mention why *this* Elfling was so important, in case the wrong beings viewed his paperwork.

"When we arrive at the world above the world, I'll take you to the University there. We have a phenomenal team of geneticists who study innate and magical abilities."

Bridgette's stomach swooped as the plane circled lower.

"If abilities are genetic, then what can I do? I've never done magic or had anything weird happen to me that I couldn't explain. Maybe I'm not magical at all, just look like I might be."

Though she'd spoken aloud, Collum knew it wasn't a question for him to answer. Bridgette was merely voicing her thoughts — thoughts that didn't sit well on his stomach.

The intelligence is solid, he reminded himself.

Zurina reappeared moments after the plane landed, informing them they were safely arrived in Beverly and their transportation was parked outside.

"Beverly? I thought we were going to Salem," Bridgette

remarked, following Collum to a waiting silver SUV.

He chuckled, and for a moment Bridgette breathed, glad the tense frustration in the air a few minutes before was gone.

"Technically we are going to Danvers, which was Salem Village in Artur Cromwell's day," Collum said. "Beverly is the closest private airport. This saves us from getting stuck in awful city traffic in Boston."

That made sense enough. He gave an address to the driver, and the vehicle sped off. Bridgette watched the New England countryside as it flew past the window. She'd never been to this part of the States before. The scenery was pristine and lovely, the idyllic views similar to what she'd imagined they might be. The SUV snaked through commercial and residential districts, then by farms and lush green pasture that contrasted with the clear blue sky. The whole thing could have been the scene of a jigsaw puzzle.

Collum watched her gaze, trying not to listen to her thoughts. He was partly lost in his own. He wondered how his charge would take to Heáhwolcen, to the Samnung, to who she was and what they must ask of her. And what would the Samnung members think of this lilac-eyed, spicy dreamer he brought them? Despite the treasure trove of theory that University researchers dredged up about the legendary Bright Star, none of them knew what the Liluthuaé would look or act like. They simply knew that this being would be vital to their survival as a species and a continent.

Bridgette certainly wasn't what he'd expected. He assumed the Bright Star would be sweet and willowy and, well, magical. Bridgette Conner was none of those things.

She was sharp in wit and mind, and didn't seem to trust a soul. Her build was much more athlete than waif, and every move she made professed both a physical and mental strength she did not have. This woman did not want anyone pitying her or thinking she was weak, nor did she want to acknowledge her demons. Feigning aloofness and attitude were defense mechanisms. But the magic …

Their earlier discussion had been cut short due to the plane landing. It *did* worry Collum that Bridgette claimed she had no abilities. Not that anyone on Earth would have recognized them if she displayed any, of course, but most halflings would have shown magic long before their early twenties. Especially knowing who her father was, the magic Bridgette should be capable of — Liluthuaé or not — would be mind-blowing.

"Where are we going?" Bridgette had turned away from observing pastoral scenes in the window, and realized Collum was lost in thought.

"What?" he started. "Oh. I wanted to show you a few things today. More history lessons."

As if on cue, the SUV slowed to a crawl and put on its hazard lights. Outside, Bridgette saw a massive stone structure several feet back from the main road. She and Collum stepped onto the sidewalk and waved to the driver, who pulled away, leaving them to their afternoon of adventuring. The closer they got to the structure, the clearer its meaning became. At the back was a multi-paneled partition, and in front of it, a giant Bible and set of metal shackles were positioned on top of a rectangular box.

"This is the Witchcraft Victim's Memorial," Collum said quietly. He stood a few feet away from Bridgette, letting her experience the sight for herself.

The memorial was larger than life. At nearly six feet tall, Bridgette was no petite female, but even she felt dwarfed by the height of the monument.

Bridgette studied the pink stone-carved Bible box, lightly tracing the words with a forefinger. The air around them was silent; reverent, perhaps, as if the birds and squirrels that frequented the trees knew this was a sacred place.

"Who were these people?" Bridgette asked. "Why did people think they were witches? Why did people think witches and magic were like, collectively bad?"

"So many questions!" Collum quipped. But he understood — most Earth schools taught a history that didn't delve into details of the Salem Witch Trials. The curricula barely scratched the surface. Even television shows and movies were confined to time slots and could only share so much.

"The names memorialized here are the deceased victims; the accused who were hanged or died in jail awaiting sentencing," Collum said. "As for why people thought they were witches? In short, a group of young girls started having fits and spells that at the time, couldn't be explained by rudimentary medical science. The girls began to accuse others of witchcraft and Satanic worship, claiming these individuals either cursed them personally or they'd been observed performing rituals."

Bridgette stepped back from the platform to read the twenty-four names inscribed on the stone: Sarah Osburn, Bridget Bishop, Roger Toothaker, an unnamed infant daughter, Sarah Good, Elizabeth How, Susannah Martin, Rebecca Nurse, Sarah Wilds, George Burroughs, Martha Carrier, George Jacobs, John Proctor, John Willard, Giles Cory — who'd been tortured, not hanged — Martha Cory, Mary Esty, Alice Parker, Mary Parker, Ann Pudeator, Wilmot Redd, Margaret Scott, Samuel Wardwell, Ann Foster, Lydia Dastin. Some of the names she vaguely recognized from long-ago grade school lessons.

"There were others," she mused quietly.

"Yes." His voice caught slightly. "There were many others who were victims, victims who didn't die but whose lives were forever ruined and changed because of the accusations."

"Were any of them really witches?"

"Just one. An enslaved woman named Tituba," Collum answered.

Bridgette frowned. Tituba's name wasn't on the memorial. Tituba's name was also one she recognized from school, though she was fairly certain that lesson glossed over any actual witchcraft the woman was able to perform.

"There are a thousand myths and misconceptions about Tituba, to the point that today no one really knows much about her. What is known is that she was a Black woman, and though she was indeed a witch, the testimony she gave at trial was forced upon her by her white master, whose daughters were some of the early accusers. He threatened her and her child if she didn't tell this elaborate story that was so unbelievable it must be the Satanic gospel of truth," Collum continued, his voice turning bitter. "Actual witches, wizards, and magical beings were well-hidden, including Tituba. She was descended from the Ciguapas of the Dominican Republic, and was highly skilled at reading and manipulating people to do her bidding. Her magick was old and eclectic, as slaves who were magical beings each brought traditions, ritual, and spirituality from their home countries to the colonies. When we teach about her story at our University, it is thought that she was a type of witch known as obeah. She used more ritual to spell-cast than is common today, and her spellwork was 'big picture' as opposed to a specific task."

Bridgette shot him a questioning glance from where she stood, taking in the pair of broken shackles.

"Ah. Think of my spell for calming, and how it is specific to each person. That's different from a ritual spell, which would, say, bring together energies from multiple beings, as well as various artifacts, to produce a protective spell for a village," Collum explained. "The latter is more of the work Tituba was known for. But it was not what she confessed to being. We do not know why she was unable to withstand the force of her master — perhaps she didn't have enough time to perform a ritual, or perhaps her magick could not protect her physically. Whatever it was, the torture took its toll. She told the entirety of Salem Village that there were magical beings out to get the Puritan villagers. Which … well, that was and was not true. There were those who wanted humans dead for the millennia of awful injustices done to them. But Tituba was not one of those, though truth be told I have no doubt she would have liked to take the life of every slave owner in Massachusetts if she'd been given the opportunity. In fact, no witch or wizard, or Elf or Fairy, or any matter of magical creature with that level of hatred and intent against humans, even lived in the colonial United States."

He looked at Bridgette, who still stood next to those broken shackles. She tucked a strand of hair that had blown loose from her braid back behind one of those lightly pointed ears, her face set in an expression of stony processing. When she returned his gaze, her lilac eyes were strained.

"Why do people hate witchcraft so much?"

Collum shrugged. "Why do people hate anything different from themselves?"

"Fear," she answered quietly, the thought coming to her clear as day. "They're afraid of what they don't know."

"That is part of it," Collum said, taking a step toward her. He had an overwhelming urge to put his arm around her — that pained look on her face was difficult to see — but thought better about it. "The other part is religion. The idea, and yes, it *is* partly rooted in fear as well, that deep, dark forces exist that seek to destroy all that is good and pure in the world and damn us all to Hell, is a powerful thing Puritans and many of today's Christians abhor. Are you familiar with the Bible?"

Bridgette tilted her head from side to side. "Kind of? Some of my foster families did the whole church thing, but I never took to it."

"The book of Exodus has a particularly influential verse in it that says, 'Thou shalt not suffer a witch to live,'" Collum said. "For those who take the Bible as truth at face value, and leave no room for interpretation or context? Witches had to die."

He watched her swallow long and hard.

"What about other magical beings?" Bridgette asked.

"There wasn't a common nomenclature for every being," Collum replied. "Different ones of us originated in different parts of the world, and very few of us were native to what is now the United States. Magic exists worldwide, but magical beings aside from what got collectively categorized as witches and wizards were much more common in Eurasia and Africa, and Central to South America. The first Elves came to be in what is now the Scandinavian region, for example, and our University traced Fairy ancestry to two distinct bloodlines — the Celtic Fae and African Aziza."

Some bit of knowledge stirred in Bridgette's recent memory. "African Aziza. So the slave guy who helped found Hey — your country — was one of those?"

Collum flashed her a pleased grin. "Yes. Galdúr was indeed Aziza. There were no photographs available in the 1600s and 1700s, of course, but there are many portraits of him and his family in Heáhwolcen. The capital city of Endorsa, the first country Artur Cromwell created, bears the name Galdúr in his honor. He had skin so dark it was nearly the color of pitch, and Aziza differ from Celtic Fae in that their wings resemble those of bugs and insects rather than bats and, well, glittering shapes. Galdúr's wings were those of a beetle that shifted in color from ebony to turquoise to radiant orchid."

Bridgette closed her eyes, imagining the scene — a tall, muscled Black man escaping the confines of his master, breaking the chains that held back his magic, finally able to unleash his powerful set of iridescent wings. She visualized them flared out behind him as he flew to safety, flew to this mysterious world that Collum was taking her to. She felt as if she was inside the plot of books she read in high school, the ones where magic abounded and was revered rather than feared.

"I still don't understand how this is real," she told Collum. It was possibly the eight thousandth time she'd said those words in the week she'd known him, even though by this point she'd seen *him* do magic and been bound by a spell on the plane earlier. "Are you sure I'm this secret special person you claim I am?"

Collum tilted his head to one side, looking at the Elfling he'd been charged with procuring. "Of course I'm sure."

She glanced back at the memorial, feeling an odd sort of draw to the hewn pink structure. "Should we … should we say something? Before we go?"

"What?"

"You know. Like, a eulogy? Something to honor them. To honor these humans who were murdered for magic."

"If you wish, then of course." He looked at her patiently.

Bridgette turned fully to face the memorial, and walked back to put her hands on those metal shackles. She bowed her head and whispered a prayer of sorts. She hardly knew what she was saying, but felt as though she needed to say something. Needed to acknowledge for herself that magic existed, and like so many people, those who were thought to possess it were persecuted for their natural-born abilities.

"I do not know you, but I feel your spirits. You did not

deserve to die for … for false accusations," she whispered. "Even if you were witches and wizards, y'all did not deserve to die for being something else. I hope wherever your spirits are, that you found peace. I hope your sacrifices will be honored, because your deaths protected the lives of others."

She wasn't sure why she was blinking back tears, but her next words were to a specific spirit. "Miss Tituba, I am sorry for what you endured during your time on Earth. That you were forced into slavery, forced into a false confession, and forced to hide your magick from the world. I want to learn your story and share it, because in death you have been done a disservice. They teach about you in school, but not the way you should be remembered. May your spirit find rest."

A cool breeze ruffled her hair, shocking her into standing straight up. She whirled to look at Collum, who'd been watching and — though trying not to — listening as she spoke her tribute.

"Did you do that?" Bridgette gasped. The puzzled look Collum returned her was answer enough. "Shit. I think … did you see that? That wind?"

"It's not windy." Collum gestured to the still air under the sunny sky.

"Fuck. I think I just talked to a ghost."

"You probably did." He chuckled at her wide eyes and reached his hand for her. "Come with me. We've got somewhere else I want you to see today."

~ 6 ~

Collum linked his arm through Bridgette's and led her down the path to the main road. They passed a historic cemetery, fenced in by age-old boulders, and beautiful Craftsman-style homes. Each had a perfectly manicured lawn and well-kept foliage. A few had white picket fences lining the road, with gates at the sidewalk. "Quaint" was the first word that came to Bridgette's mind as they walked. Just a few blocks later they passed a bit of a commercial district, where most everything looked locally owned. Their walk ended at a rather nondescript paved driveway, marked with a red sign that proclaimed it to be the Rebecca Nurse homestead.

"She was one of the accused," Bridgette said, studying the sign.

"She was."

They walked up the driveway to see an aging three-story red farmhouse looming in front of them. The historic site appeared closed; no tour guides scurried around; no tourists posed for photos.

"Technically the site doesn't open to the public until May," Collum said, grinning at Bridgette. "Thankfully I have connections that let me walk up unscathed."

She gave him a sly half-smile. "Tell me about her."

Collum stood straighter and made a show of straightening the collar of his shirt, then waved his left arm in a wide gesture. "Rebecca Nurse is a fascinating historical figure. I won't bore you with the history of the homestead itself, especially since we can't *actually* walk around or I'll get my connection in trouble, but I do think it's vital you know her story. She was accused essentially on her deathbed, found innocent at trial. But the girls who accused her did not react well to the 'not guilty' verdict, and the verdict was reversed. She was hanged."

Bridgette gaped. "Seriously? They reversed the verdict because these girls faked some Satanic disease?"

"Well, actually, not that you would hear this in Earth history, but the girls *did*, in fact, observe some witchcraft occurring in

Salem Village. But they misinterpreted what they saw, and *who* they saw, which led to Rebecca Nurse's charges. A few of the accusers saw a gathering of spirits and magical beings in a nearby pasture, and they truly were haunted by it. But when it came time to identify who they saw, they had no idea, and were easily pressured by family members into naming men and women with whom they had quarreled."

"Why did you want me to see this place?" Bridgette asked.

"To see what happens when people don't understand magic."

"What? Collum, I'm not going to go around hanging people who wave wands, okay? That's horrifying and I'm offended you think —"

He interrupted her, his tone harsh. "I don't for one moment think you'd do harm to anyone, witch or no. Okay?"

Bridgette narrowed her eyes, but nodded.

"You need to see this, to understand at least in a brief sense, what happens when humans get the wrong idea about magic. The key with magic is its intent. Energy is neither inherently good nor bad, it just *is*. It's how that energy and why that energy is manipulated that offer morality or immorality to it," Collum said. "Some beings are gifted with the ability to channel energy, 'perform magic,' if you will, with their hands and minds. Others must use an implement. Humans, as I said earlier, use practical and physical means.

"Few humans understand the nuances between 'good' and 'dark' magic, especially humans of old and particularly humans of certain religious persuasions. Truth be told, most witches and wizards are … witches and wizards. There aren't many 'dark' ones. But there are some branches of magick that were designed to be used specifically with ill intent. Craft Wizardry is one of those. It is exclusively practiced, for what we know, in Palna. I do not wish to stereotype, but in large part the witches and wizards of Palna were driven by that ill intent," he continued. "It is why Palna is now imprisoned in its own walls, the magic honed and maintained by the rest of Heáhwolcen's leadership. We do not want this magic in the world above the world or on Earth.

Especially not on Earth. There are still, of course, practicing witches and wizards on the planet, not to mention the gifted humans who alternate Pagan and Wiccan practices, and they do not need to be marred by Craft Wizardry. That type of magic seeks to destroy, and should it become known, I fear there would be a second coming of these Salem Witch Trials across the globe. Anyone with a potential to be associated with magic could be tried in an Earthly court for 'dark' magic, and humans do not have the ability to differentiate between Craft Wizardry and Hoodoo."

He looked sickened at the thought of a twelve-member human jury taking one look at a Pagan priestess and sentencing her to prison time for magic she didn't commit.

Bridgette had an overwhelming urge to comfort him, but stopped herself. He baffled her, this not-so-deadly historian and spy she'd fallen into company with. At times, her lack of understanding and magic seemed to frustrate him. But then at times like this, he reveled in storytelling and teaching, eager for her to learn about his world.

Our world, she thought. Collum's ears twitched slightly, and she knew he'd heard her. The first time she admitted she felt a … connection to the place they'd be going.

"When are we going there?" Bridgette asked him. "To … Hey-uh-walsh-en?"

The name was foreign on her tongue, her mouth struggling to slowly form the strange syllables of a language much older than any she'd ever known.

"Tomorrow," he answered. "Tonight, I'm wining and dining you and letting you ask whatever questions you'd like."

"Wining and dining? First you stalk me, then you convince me to go on spring break with you, and now you're taking me on a date?"

Collum gave her a dry look and shook his head in exasperation. She winked and followed him back down the driveway, where the silver SUV waited. Bridgette wondered briefly how magical beings could communicate without the use of cell phones, but gave her companion a sour look when he replied, "I told the driver what time to pick us up."

She resisted the urge to punch his shoulder.

The SUV drove them to what had to be a historic restaurant: it looked just like an old tavern she'd seen in movies. Her stomach growled as they got out of the vehicle and the smells of fresh bread and brick oven cooking wafted toward her. Aside from snacks on the flight, she realized she hadn't eaten since a quick breakfast back at her apartment.

"Order whatever you'd like," Collum said, pulling a chair out for her once they'd been led to a table. "I am partial to the brick oven pizza, but I haven't had anything here I haven't liked."

"It all looks scrumptious!" Bridgette exclaimed, her stomach practically ready to eat itself now that the menu was in front of her. "How did you find this place?"

"Not to age myself, but I have been coming here since the original building was standing."

Her grin faltered. "Excuse me? That was —" she flipped to the back of the menu — "1748."

Collum flashed a lupine smile. "It was taken down in 1838, actually. I'm not quite two-hundred-seventy years old."

"Damn, I didn't peg you for a day over two-fifty," Bridgette said, stone-faced. But her eyes glittered. "Split a pizza? And an appetizer. The carpaccio sounds amazing."

"Yes. I approve of that choice. May I suggest the Endicott Park pizza, the one with prosciutto and soppressata, or the house pizza with caramelized onions and eggplant?"

Bridgette hadn't gotten past the appetizer section and her mouth was already watering. "Yes please. I mean, both sound great. You pick, since I chose the appetizer. And since you're paying."

He chuckled. "Technically it is the Samnung that is paying."

"The what?"

Collum was spared answering by the arrival of their server, a petite brunette woman who offered the evening's specials, craft beverages and feature cocktails before turning to the Elf and complimenting how well his shirt matched his eyes. Bridgette's own eyes narrowed, annoyed.

"I'll have the local lager on draft and we'll split the carpaccio," she said, drawing the server's attention away from her companion, who was trying not to laugh at her expression.

"And I'll have an old fashioned, please," he said, gathering their menus to hand back. "We'll also split an Endicott Park pizza."

The server looked miffed, but smiled sweetly and walked away. Collum faced Bridgette, who was glowering at the little woman, his own eyes shining.

"Fess up, Bright Star. What's gotten under your skin?"

"Calm down, Bundy. Don't think too highly of yourself. She interrupted me, that's all. What's a Samnung?"

Well, she's certainly smooth at changing the subject, he thought.

"The Samnung is our leadership. It consists of the ruling king or queen of Endorsa — sometimes both, depending on marriage — and that ruler's advisor; the Fairy of All Fairies; the leader of Eckenbourne; representatives of other magical species who are not necessarily associated with a specific country; and the master swordsman or swordswoman of Bondrie," Collum explained.

"And you?"

"And me. And occasionally military leaders, depending on the agenda of a particular meeting."

"You said I could ask you whatever questions tonight, right?" Bridgette asked. He nodded in response. "Tell me about the University. Did you study there?"

"I did," Collum said. "The University is in Endorsa. It's not that different from a human college on Earth, except that there are magical components to each field of study. And since the Earth portal was fully reopened in the 1960s, it became possible again for collegiate-age beings to attend college on Earth if they wished. We have set partnerships with several in North America and Europe, and of course young Fairies can choose to attend college in their assigned country."

"What do you mean, assigned country?"

Collum's eyes shined with excitement — she had no idea the

world she was going to see for the next few days. "Fairies have long been our ambassadors. In the time before Heáhwolcen, they were ambassadors of magic on Earth. It seemed an appropriate appointment, given they have wings for transport. During an early time period after our founding, a number of Fairies consulted with the Samnung about returning in a diplomatic capacity. Now, every country has at least one Fairy ambassador or ambassadora assigned to it.

"To become such a diplomat is both a rigorous career decision and an honor to be selected," he continued. "Ambassadors are chosen as early as age eighteen and serve in their role a full century, unless a tragedy befalls them. They spend the following century as an emeritus, helping guide the next Fairy assigned to their territory, and the remainder of their life is usually spent working with scholars to archive their observed history."

"That's fascinating," Bridgette breathed. "How do they select who becomes one? And who goes where?"

"Well, the 'who goes where' part depends on who is retiring each year, and which territories need either a second ambassador or an apprentice. The selection itself begins when a Fairy is age ten, and has completed all of their basic education in language, mathematics, reading, and history. Fairies who are gifted with strong magic, a penchant for networking and communicating, and who are born leaders with a servant's heart, are offered the opportunity to pursue a curriculum geared toward diplomacy and international relations. For six years they study this advanced curriculum. Then, when they turn sixteen, they spend two years shadowing existing ambassadors and ambassadoras. If they have a desire to work with a specific territory, they can request it — either as a primary appointment if the existing ambassador is about to retire, a secondary appointment if it is determined one is needed, or an apprenticeship if the ambassador has a number of years left before retirement." Collum paused for a sip of water.

"When they turn eighteen, students must turn in letters of recommendation or critique from each ambassador they worked with for the past two years," he said. "They must also undergo a diplomatic simulation led by the Fairy of All Fairies, in front of an audience of judges, and complete an interview portion with questions submitted by Earth leaders."

"Holy shit. That sounds like a beauty pageant, but for like, nerds."

Collum nearly spit out the water he'd taken a sip of. "You have a gift for flowery language. But yes, it is an apt comparison."

Their waitress returned with a heady beer and a squat cocktail. She gave Bridgette a dirty look, and the moment she'd turned the corner, both Bridgette and Collum burst out laughing.

"And you have a strange gift for charming waitresses," the Elfling said quietly, bringing her beer to her lips.

"Don't worry, you're the only one I'm taking on spring break to see a magic show."

This time, it was Bridgette who almost spewed a drink across the table. "I like you, Bundy. I've decided. Even if you did stalk me and memorize my chai order like some creep."

Collum raised his old fashioned in a mock toast. "What else can I tell you?"

"Why do you keep hinting at something about my birth father, but won't actually tell me anything?"

His grin didn't falter, but he didn't joke, either. "That I cannot tell you, not yet. When we get to Heáhwolcen, we can talk about your birth father. Your mother, too, for that matter."

"Why was I the one you were searching for?"

"New rule, Bridgette. I can't answer anything about your heritage or your task. Not here. Not for lack of avoiding answering, either, but I am sworn to certain duties. Keeping our secrets is one of them."

"Oh." Bridgette took another sip of her crisp lager, the smooth head leaving a bit of a mustache on her upper lip. She licked it off absentmindedly, considering what she wanted to ask next.

"So I can still ask you anything, as long as it isn't about me?"

"Correct."

"Fine, then. How old *are* you?"

~ 7 ~

He would turn two-hundred the following year. But he looked no older than his late twenties, perhaps early thirties. *Immortality is wild*, Bridgette thought.

The waitress returned with their carpaccio, the bright red beef contrasting sharply against the white platter on which it was served. "Anything else right now?" she pointedly asked Collum, wholly ignoring the Elfling.

"No thank you. Except — what is your name?" She wasn't wearing a nametag.

"Brittany!" the server answered brightly. Flattered.

"Thank you, Brittany. This looks delicious."

She flashed him another winning smile, and Bridgette shot him a look.

Jerk. Taunting me, flirting with some stranger when you've already got a perfectly fine spring break companion at your table. She hadn't directly sent him the thought, but didn't mind if he listened to it.

Collum wished he had the ability to speak to her mind-to-mind — partially to shock her when his voice echoed between her ears. Instead, he raised an eyebrow and his cocktail.

"Friendly banter is acceptable, but I draw the line at that with my colleagues." A part of him immediately regretted saying that, though it was true. The Samnung would have his head if he so much as thought inappropriately about his charge. What they would ask of her, what she was forebode to do, must be her choice and hers alone. He could not sway her in any capacity one way or another.

Bridgette frowned, spearing a piece of the thinly sliced tenderloin on her fork. "You think of me as a colleague?"

"I must. I was assigned to find you, to tell you who you are, and to introduce you to Heáhwolcen, where if you choose to, we will work together in some capacity. So, yes."

She sat back in her chair, letting her mind wander for a moment. She knew very little of the Elf across the table from her, though she had an unexplainably high level of trust in him. She'd never had friends, not really. Classmates and foster siblings, and people she worked with, but not really a friend and confidante. Bridgette got the sense that Collum Andoralain would be both of those things, if she let him.

The Elfling had a tendency to become easily attached, something a therapist once told her was related to the trauma of feeling like she never quite belonged, never was quite good enough, with peer groups and foster family situations. Bridgette felt perhaps this early trust in Collum was dangerous. She didn't like it, that quality about herself. She especially didn't like that she had those twinges of jealously when a complete stranger made googly eyes at the companion who was an almost-complete stranger.

He's only here because he has to be. Stop fucking with yourself and just figure out what he wants from you, what these Samnung people want from you, she chided herself. *Go do it and move on.*

They spent the rest of their dinner in near silence, Bridgette barely touching her pizza when it arrived, though it smelled smoky and rich. Collum gobbled two slices before he took note of the morose expression she tried to keep hidden from her face, and could have kicked himself for sending her into that mood. He hadn't listened to her thoughts, though; hadn't realized she was mostly upset with herself, not with him.

The SUV was again waiting out front after they finished eating. Bridgette slipped in without a word. She sat in sullen silence, brooding, until they pulled up outside a little cottage. Their home for the night. Bridgette tried her damndest not to show her pleasure at the precious dwelling. It looked like it belonged on a postage stamp, some relic of bed and breakfasts past, inviting people to weekend in New England.

"Do you like it?" Collum asked. He fiddled with the key box until it opened, dropping a fob into his palm that he used to unlock the door.

"It's adorable." She tried to stay plain-faced, but the corners of Collum's mouth turned up slightly as he noted wonderment in her voice.

"There are two bedrooms. You're welcome to have first pick."

Bridgette walked herself around the house, its miniscule kitchen barely big enough for appliances and a two-top kitchen table. A wood stove was just inside the front door in what must be the living room, and the coziest leather couch she'd ever seen sat across from it. There was no television, but there was a floor-to-ceiling bookshelf full of novels and nonfiction. The bedrooms and bathroom were upstairs, each of the former holding a full-size bed, small dresser, and nightstands. The decorations were simple: shades of cream, periwinkle, and gray. She loved it instantly.

"This belongs to Heáhwolcen," Collum said. Bridgette jumped; she hadn't realized he was behind her. "I think the colors need to be updated, but it'll do."

"I'll take this bedroom." She still refused to show any emotion, reverting back to the stand-offish, cautious woman in the woods from the first day they'd met.

Collum noted her tone and said, "There should be clothes for you in the dresser. I'll see you in the morning."

He walked to the room across from her and closed the door. *Fuck. Now I've gone and done it. The Samnung are going to get a very aloof impression of her and it's my fault. Months of searching down the drain. Nehemi is going to lose her mind.*

The Elf summoned a bottle of whiskey from the kitchen and poured himself a double. He was so nervous about introducing Bridgette to the Samnung. He assumed they'd have impressions or assumptions of who and what she would be, as he had. And though he'd been reckoning with his personal presumptiveness for a few weeks now, especially in the last few days of spending time with Bridgette instead of observing from afar, he continued to worry she wouldn't be up to snuff. Especially for Nehemi, the cunning, calculating queen of Endorsa. The unspoken dominatrix of the war room, despite the fact that most Samnung members looked to the ancient Fairy of All Fairies for decisions and feedback. Nehemi had been the one to balk at the revelation that a Bright Star had not only been forebode, but born. She'd been the one to dare rather than instruct Collum to fetch the Elfling. She made it clear she didn't believe a word of truth regarding the Liluthuaé legends.

Collum took a long, hard sip of the whiskey, now chilled by the cold thoughts running through his head and into his veins. This plan had to work. It had to. There was no other way.

His musings were interrupted by the sounds of Bridgette brushing her teeth in the bathroom between their two bedrooms. The Elf talked himself into blocking her out; not listening to a single thought tonight, no matter how curious he was to know what was on her mind.

Had he tuned in, he'd find that on her mind was an inner monologue berating herself for coming to Massachusetts and this magical world Collum invited her to.

You're so stupid, Bridgette fumed at herself in the bathroom mirror, brushing her teeth so hard her gums began to bleed. *You let yourself get talked into situations and you just go do it. You may be an Elfling, but you're heavy on the 'ling' part. You can't do magic. You've never fought, not for real. You're useless. There is no way you are going to be this whole world savior.*

Tears were running down her cheeks now, leaving cold, salty trails in their wake.

He doesn't even believe you're good enough. You saw it in his eyes. Every time you ask what magic you should have, it shuts him up because he knows you should have some abilities and yet you have nothing. Squat. Zip. Zero. That's why you default to flirting. You know you have nothing to offer so you deflect attention away into something you can control. I hate you, you know that? You, with the … with the …

Bridgette fought back the sob that threatened to release from her chest. She didn't want Collum to hear, not audibly anyway, what she was thinking. Didn't want him to know how much she doubted and hated herself; to admit that for one brief moment she felt she could have a fulfilled life doing something important for someone. Her whole existence thus far had revolved around pleasing others: fearing being abandoned by yet another foster family weighed particularly hard on her soul. She felt most alive when she was doing something good, productive, and vital. She didn't want gifts or even compliments necessarily, just wanted to feel appreciated. To know that she was contributing somehow to making the world a better place. Yet this … it seemed a contribution she wouldn't be able to make.

Bridgette sat on the cold bathroom floor and wrapped her knees to her chest. She cried quietly into her arms, angry at this feeling of never belonging. Angry for how much she loathed herself, for this shell of a being she was. She was terrified of this unknown task Collum kept implying she'd be asked to do. What if it was something she couldn't do? Would she be okay letting him down? Letting his people — *their* people — down? The thought of a failure that deep, and that public too, made her stomach churn.

The sob escaped, more a choked shriek of anguish than anything.

Collum heard, and he set his whiskey glass down. He walked to the bathroom and knocked politely. "Are you alright?"

"I'm fine." Her terse words sounded anything but, yet Collum learned a long time ago that it wasn't his place to interfere in others' emotions if they preferred to shut him out. He turned back to his room, finished the whiskey, and snapped his fingers to switch the light off.

When Bridgette finally took herself to bed, anxiety waning a bit after letting it all out on that cold bathroom floor, she was mentally exhausted. She slept fitfully, dreaming of fire devouring everything beautiful, with her powerless body being unharmed … but unable to stop the burning.

She woke to the sounds and smells of coffee brewing and bacon frying. The pajamas she'd found the night before in the dresser seemed standard Heáhwolcen issue in color, the pattern of the pants and top in swirls of seafoam green and mint. Her reddish-blonde hair was a tangled mess from tossing and turning, but she didn't care if Collum saw. He made it clear there was no impressing that would be done.

Collum was at the stove when she made it downstairs, clad in drawstring pajama pants identical to hers, and a fitted white sleep shirt. An elaborate "H" was embroidered in seafoam green on the left front chest. He heard her soft footsteps and gave her a hesitant smile of greeting.

"Good morning, Liluthuaé."

"Merghh," she mumbled, and he chuckled.

"Coffee's on the counter. I did not know if you preferred creamer or milk and sugar, but the first two are in the refrigerator and the second is next to the coffee pot. Would you prefer scrambled or fried eggs this morning?"

Bridgette stretched her arms over her head and rubbed her sleepy lilac eyes. "Fried, I think."

"So it shall be. You're welcome to take your coffee on the porch if you'd prefer some time to yourself. The driveway's long and the property has many trees, so you won't be seen by neighbors."

She welcomed that invitation, and strode to pour steaming hot liquid in the handmade mug that sat by the coffee pot.

"Did you sleep well?" Collum asked.

"No."

He suspected as much. "I'm sorry to hear that. Go rest."

Bridgette took the creamer container from inside the fridge and added a generous bit to her mug. She slipped to the front porch and took in the beauty of the little yard and driveway. When they drove up the previous night, it had been too dark for her to see much of anything except the house itself. Now, seeing it in the ice cream sherbet hues of sunrise, she saw beech, oak, and pine trees surrounding her. At least four different species of birds chirped, welcoming the sunshine, and squirrels scurried up and down the trees, chasing each other. The air was chill and still, and Bridgette was grateful her pajama top had long sleeves. The mug of coffee warmed her hands — and her spirit — as she took in the quiet, pastoral atmosphere of the New England morning.

A few minutes later, Collum poked his head outside to ask if he could join her, or if she'd prefer to eat alone. He was pleasantly surprised when she patted the spot next to her on the front steps.

"Thank you," Bridgette said, accepting the plate of warm bacon and fried eggs a moment later. "I can't tell you the last time I had a home-cooked breakfast that wasn't at the diner."

"It's no waffle sandwich, but I do my best."

She shot him a glance. *Friendly banter it is, then.*

"What are we doing today?" she asked, slicing open her egg so the golden yolk ran over the plate.

"After breakfast, I suggest you shower and get dressed while I clean up the breakfast dishes. Once we're both ready, we're going to the portal. I want you to see where it is and meet a few people, and then up we'll go to Heáhwolcen."

The outfit remaining in her dresser was a pair of high-waisted, supple aubergine leather leggings and a flowing lavender tunic, its hem higher in the front than in the back. She put it on and wondered if Collum, or whoever picked it out, did so because it accented her eyes. Bridgette tamed her hair into soft waves instead of the tangles she woke up with, and went downstairs to wait on her companion.

His own leggings were a deep chocolate brown, and he wore a long-sleeved cream top belted at the hips. The knit cap was gone, and he let his own curls go free. Those tidal pool eyes were gleaming as he took Bridgette in, from her flowing reddish hair to the dingy cowboy boots she still wore. The shades of purple did indeed bring out the violet of her eyes.

"You look like an Elf," Collum commented.

Despite herself, Bridgette grinned. "So do you," she said.

She linked arms with him, and together they walked down the drive to meet the awaiting vehicle.

~ 8 ~

Their drive was short. It took them back past the witchcraft memorial, then up a path to Endicott Park, the name of last night's pizza suddenly making sense. Bridgette gave Collum a confused look.

"We're going to a park?"

"We are going to Heáhwolcen, by way of a park."

She furrowed her brow, but didn't inquire further. The driver let them out, and the first thing Collum did was turn around and walk back toward the main road they'd just come off.

"Where are we going?"

"You'll see!" he called back to her, an air of mystery in his voice.

Bridgette rolled her eyes and followed. He led her to a small trail across the street, and together they hiked up a shallow incline toward a clearing surrounded by leafy green trees.

"This, Bridgette, is Whipple Hill."

Her responding look told him she had no idea what was significant about the ground on which they stood. Collum sighed. *I suppose they don't teach this part in Earth history classes.*

"Remember yesterday, when I told you that Rebecca Nurse was accused after the girls saw witchcraft take place?"

Bridgette nodded.

"This is where they were looking," the Elf explained. "Whipple Hill is our sacred ground. Surrounded by trees, it was largely hidden from view of nosy neighbors and passersby. The land was owned at the time by a villager who Felicity Cromwell, Artur's wife, helped heal after a horrible, horrible accident shortly after the Cromwells arrived in Salem Village. The landowner would have died had Felicity not used magick on him, and he knew it, too. Though they never spoke of it, not directly, the landowner told Felicity she and her family would always be protected on his lands. That protection created a shield of sorts when the Cromwells and other magical beings communed on Whipple Hill, hence why the girls didn't see who was communing with the spirits. They saw figures and people, but the images were foggy, making them seem all the more spectral."

"What kind of magic were they doing here?" Bridgette turned in place, imagining a circle of witches gathered on the lush green hillside.

"Ritual, mostly. Holiday celebrations. Artur came here to meditate and write frequently, and this is where they snuck their children in the night to teach them how to hone their magick. It was on Whipple Hill that the original portal was placed."

Bridgette whipped her head, as if looking for some magical, glimmering straw that would suck the two of them up into the sky. "Where is it?"

"Now? Across the street. We couldn't rightly have a full Fairy travel station in this clearing. But the magick of it was strong here, so we needed it to be reconstructed nearby. Somewhere that it could be watched by magical beings, but not so as to be suspicious to humans."

"Did you ever use the original portal?"

Collum cocked his head to one side, remembering. "Yes, but only twice. Once to come to Earth, once to go back. That was before I was fyrdwisa, and the portal was closed shortly after."

"Why?"

The Elf leaned up against a tall pine tree that surrounded the clearing. They'd discussed some of this already, but he did not mind indulging with more detail. "When Artur founded Heáhwolcen, it wasn't split into different countries originally. But as more and more beings sought refuge there, many expressed desire for a magical government. Different beings have different needs. It didn't make sense for a wizard to lead everyone and make decisions for Elves and Fairies unless Elves and Fairies consulted with him. So, Artur and his second, Galdúr, met with the then-Fairy of All Fairies, with Aelys Frost of the Elves, with representatives of various beings and creatures, and borders were drawn. This was the day the Samnung was born. There were just the three countries then; Endorsa, Eckenbourne, and Fairevella. For decades, this thrived. Then one day a bright, spectacular young wizard came through the portal. His name was Baize

Sammael.

"Baize Sammael had a vision," Collum went on. "He wanted to secure a place for his type of magick — something no being in Heáhwolcen had ever seen before. It was power they had never known, an innate ability not to harness the elements and energies, but to control them. To become them. The Samnung agreed to give Baize his own lands, in the center of Heáhwolcen, so scholars of all kinds could easily travel to and observe this magick. He named the country Palna, a word that translates roughly to 'flourish,' born of his goal to let this magick rule the worlds. He was a master manipulator, very cunning and charming, but his heart was pure death. His spirit was the stuff of nightmares, Bridgette. He worked with the Palnan ambassador and a few of the Earth ambassadors from Fairevella to spread his vision across the worlds. He desired to teach and transmit his magick so all could come to appreciate it."

Collum shifted his weight against the tree, taking a deep breath before continuing. "Heáhwolcen is large enough to where unless you are intimately aware of what's happening in another country, you probably wouldn't know anything was amiss. Baize Sammael was quite talented at keeping secrets, at smoothing over suspicions. The Samnung had no idea what he was really up to in Palna. His vision, that plan to educate, was a mistruth. He wanted to educate with the intent of eradicating. Baize Sammael was not just a powerful wizard. He was a very rare immortal warlock, who could only die of poison, disease, or irreversible injury. He was an ancient being even to our ancient beings at the time, and it was rumored later that perhaps he was born of Hades himself. His years had seen every atrocity humans committed against witchcraft. He wanted them dead, to create a world where magic ruled without having to form its own secret continent above the clouds. He resented having to be scuttled away; resented having to work with the Fairies for frequent trips to and from Earth.

"Baize established a network of contacts across the globe during these trips," Collum said. Bridgette was deadly still, her eyes wide as she listened. "He wanted to know what was going on, where he could insert himself and his magick. He was adept at those mistruths and placed just enough in the right places to spark wars. He pit human against human, with the desire to sow discord and anarchy, so they would attack and kill one another, leaving a new world in which magick could take hold. I was but a boy when the Samnung was tipped off to his Earthly dealings. The Fairies finally sealed the portal several decades later, as the United States erupted into its Civil War, but it was too late to make a difference. Heáhwolcen, too. We lost many a great magical being in that time, fighting Palna and Craft Wizardry. But the war was won, and Baize Sammael was killed. The wall was put up, Bondrie was created, and as they say, the rest is history."

Collum moved from the tree, stretched a moment, then extended his arm for Bridgette to grab, giving her no time to process what he'd said. "Come now. We've seen enough here."

Bridgette wanted to ask more about this evil wizard, but the look on her companion's face suggested that would be a poor choice.

They walked across the street, through what looked to be a historic farm, and to the visitor center for Endicott Park. A park ranger opened the door for them.

"Welcome to Endicott Park!" he said jovially. "How can I help you today?"

"We are here to tour the archives," Collum said.

Bridgette realized that must have been a code of some sort, because the park ranger followed them inside and used a key card to open a second door to their left, marked "Do Not Enter" in bold letters. "Enjoy your visit," he told them.

Collum led Bridgette through the door and into the busiest room she'd ever laid eyes on. There were cubicles and desks mounted up the walls, and at each sat a Fairy. A real, live Fairy: wings glittering and fluttering in the sunlight that poured in from a floor-to-ceiling window at the back of the area. Lines of creatures and people were organized at specific locations, radiating out from a central zone in front of that window that seemed to glow and ooze pure rainbow and starlight. Winged beings led groups of children — with what looked to be watchful parent chaperones — around the room, and Bridgette caught snippets of what must be a guided tour. She spun slowly, awed, taking it in. The walls, desks, furniture, everything was the most sparkling, pure white. She was surrounded by the sheer cacophony of sound from the tour guides, the faint fluttering of wings producing endless breezes, chattering from each of the cubicles where Fairies wore headsets and monitored the magical equivalent of computer screens.

"I cannot believe this." She was breathless. It was so much to take in at once. When she finally turned back to Collum, she'd never seen anyone smile so widely, so genuine. "This is beyond words."

His tidal blue eyes softened, and Bridgette realized he'd been waiting for this moment. To see what she thought of being surrounded by magic and magical beings, her first real impression of what Heáhwolcen had to offer.

"Collum, I don't know what to say. 'Beautiful' doesn't quite cut it, and 'magical' seems too much of a pun," she whispered.

Even the air seemed different here, soft, clean, and gently fragrant. She could scarcely believe that it was real.

"Do you want me to pinch you?" Collum whispered to her.

"No, jerk, don't you dare!" she hissed in response, but she smiled. *And we're back at friend-level.*

In front of them was a check-in desk, monitored by a Fairy named Akiko, according to the name badge pinned to her dress. She had creamy skin and hooded eyes of deep brown, and her dress looked more like a ballerina tutu than professional attire. It was neon lime with a layer of pale turquoise tulle underneath. Her bright blue hair was in two buns, one on either side of her head, and wrapped in a lime green headband. She glanced up and, realizing who stood in front of her, jumped from her stool and squealed.

"Fyrdwisa! You found her!" The Fairy, whose wings were practically shaking with excitement, bowed deeply and quickly at Collum and Bridgette. "We were unsure of your preferred departure time, so I reserved you spots at eleven and at two-fifteen just in case."

Collum bowed back. "Thank you, Geongre Akiko. It is a pleasure to see you after so many months. I trust there has been no news?"

Akiko inclined her head. "We have a few minutes. Let me bring an associate travel deputy to the desk and we shall talk."

She scurried off, wings lifting her into the air above her desk, to find a replacement. Bridgette's eyes widened, watching her fly. She realized Akiko had an intricate tattoo down the back of her calf that looked vaguely Japanese, intertwined with what were assuredly Celtic knots.

"Who is she?" Bridgette asked, still gazing upward.

"Geongre Akiko is the lead travel deputy, the only titled one, for the portal. In Fairevellan leadership, she's somewhat of an international minister. The Fairy of All Fairies is their supreme leader, a member of the Samnung, but she has a wealth of advisors in her council. Akiko is one of those," Collum explained. "Her staff here monitors weather and travel patterns, climate and conditions worldwide. They maintain our travel logs for both arrivals and departures, and a few even help plan vacations to Earth destinations. There is also a group that works with our collegiate students studying at Earth universities, ensuring they will have adequate flights to and from their schools for holidays and start of term. Some days Akiko is on Earth, some days she is at the twin to this building in Fairevella. It is fortunate that she is here, as there will be far less explaining to do as to why I am showing up slightly unannounced, with someone who has no arrival record."

She hadn't considered that.

When Akiko returned, a male Fairy followed to take her place at the desk. She motioned for Collum and Bridgette to come with her down a hallway to the right of the bustling room, then inside a small office. The quietness was jarring after having been in the travel terminal.

"Sit," the Fairy beckoned, motioning to two stools inside the little office. Before she sat, she turned to Bridgette, and leaned forward in a full bow. "Liluthuaé," she murmured reverently. "It is an honor."

Bridgette wasn't sure how to react; she'd never been bowed to before. But she had the sense to tilt her head forward in acknowledgement. When Akiko stood, Bridgette saw — really saw — her eyes for the first time. They weren't just brown; they were swirls of chocolate and deep earth. The swirls moved in an almost hypnotic spiral, and had Akiko not blinked, Bridgette probably would have continued staring.

"I'm so sorry," she stuttered. "I've just ... I've never seen a real Fairy before. I didn't know your eyes could do that."

Akiko smiled widely. "It is one of our most-studied traits at the University. Like Elves, all Fairies and some Faeling are marked by their eyes."

Collum interrupted their chatter. "Geongre Akiko, I beg pardon for the urgency. What news do you have? I have not been alerted of anything." He motioned toward his left wrist, where for the first time, Bridgette noticed a stack of braids, cords, and leather bands wrapped up his forearm. They'd been hidden before by shirtsleeves pulled down, but he'd rolled the sweater sleeves to his elbows inside the travel chamber.

She shot him a glance: *What's with all the jewelry?* His sideways look was enough for her to know he'd, as usual, fill her in later.

"There has not been much, Fyrdwisa," Akiko admitted. The Samnung wished to be alerted to your arrival, so I had an assistant dispatch a notice just now. I assume they will commune immediately when you portal up, but they did not respond. Aristoces has, to my knowledge, only attended the regular meetings. There has been nothing called out of the ordinary."

The Elf furrowed his brow. *Odd,* he thought to himself. *So odd, that nothing happens for months, after the urgency to send me to find her.*

He collected himself quickly, and gave a nod of thanks to Akiko. "I apologize for my rudeness, Geongre. Allow me to properly introduce you to Bridgette Conner. This, as I'm sure you've guessed, is her first real introduction to Heáhwolcen." He flashed his companion a quick half-grin.

"And what do you think, Liluthuaé?" the Fairy asked with unveiled interest, her swirling chocolate eyes tilting up at the corners.

"It's …" Bridgette struggled to find the words. "Not at all what I expected. It's so, clean?"

Collum's laugh quickly turned into a cough. "Clean?!" he repeated. "Please elaborate."

"Every book I've ever read about magic takes place in the woods and olden days. This is so different. All the bright white, the technology, the — branding even — it just seems so pristine. So modern and normal. Except you know, for the whole eyes thing. And the wings," Bridgette stammered.

That was hugely embarrassing. She sent the thought directly to Collum, hoping it was coated in the venom she'd used had she been able to speak it aloud.

But Akiko smiled. "I understand," she said. "It can be overwhelming, at first, and this is but a taste. Heáhwolcen, you'll come to find, isn't stuck in a time warp. Though other magical worlds may prefer a more, rustic aesthetic, shall we say? Our world above the world celebrates 2018 just as everyone else does on Earth."

Her words hit Bridgette like a brick. "Other magical worlds?"

"Of course! Heáhwolcen is but one of, assumedly, many. We keep to ourselves, but it is known there are others out there," Akiko said, her voice matter-of-fact.

"Geongre Akiko —"

But whatever Collum was about to ask would have to wait. The sweet sounds of a windchime flowed over their heads, and a peppy voice filled the little office. It announced the line-up time for the eleven o'clock departure to Heáhwolcen.

Akiko rose from her stool and escorted Collum and Bridgette back to the terminal, where they were guided to one of the lines radiating out from that shifting, shimmering pillar of light.

"It was a pleasure to meet you, Liluthuaé," she said quietly, so no one would hear. "May the deities be by your side in all that is to come."

"The hell does that mean?" Bridgette whispered to Collum, watching as the Fairy flitted away.

He put a comforting hand on her shoulder. "You have nothing to worry about, Bridgette. You will not be asked to do anything without consent."

She opened her mouth to fire back a snappy retort about just what life-threatening things she had zero desire to consent to, but stopped short at Collum squeezing her shoulder. Hard. The line was moving, and he clearly didn't want to be overheard.

As they neared the source of the light — the portal, Bridgette realized — she could see the creatures in front of her step forward in turn, present what she assumed were passports or travel documents, and then walk straight through a gateway into blinding, opalescent light.

When the first group she saw sparkled, then vanished, her heart skipped a beat. "Where did they go?"

Collum glanced at her, laughter in his eyes and dry sarcasm filling his voice. "Bridgette. It's a *portal*. It, as you so eloquently said, 'magicked them away.'"

She elbowed him in the ribs, and he really did laugh then. "You're such a punk, Collum." But she smirked despite herself, and pointedly rolled her eyes at him. He squeezed her shoulder again, gentler this time, and led her forward.

"Passport?" the wizened Fairy at the gateway asked. He reached out a withered, green-tinged hand, barely glancing at them.

Collum flicked his wrist, and a folder appeared out of thin air. "You'll find the necessary documentation for my companion and I in here, sir."

The Fairy looked now. His eyes widened with awe, and he, too, bent into a full bow. "Fyrdwisa. It is an honor."

Whatever Akiko had done to their documents, the Fairy had no questions as to who Bridgette was or why she accompanied this spy and leader to the portal. He beckoned them forward, and the gate opened in front.

Bridgette had a momentary panic: *What if I don't come back together again?*

"What does it feel like? To … to portal up?" she asked.

Collum noted the terror in her voice, and surrounded her with those comforting scents of honeysuckle and vanilla. He looked her straight in the eyes, a hand on either wrist. "Like the wind is sucked from you. Like pure exhilaration. It's the feeling you get when an elevator drops quickly, or a rollercoaster goes down the hill. You are safe, Bridgette. I promise."

She gulped and tried to breathe in those smells, imagining herself anywhere other than shattering into a million glittering shards of dust as the portal realized she was just human and didn't deserve to be transported up. Collum's grip on her wrists became tighter, and she realized he heard what she'd imagined.

"You are safe." His blue eyes swam with concern as they held her frightened gaze. "The chimes are going to ring, and we are going to be whisked up. Okay?"

Bridgette nodded. The sound of the windchime filled her ears again, and the world around her became hazy and shimmering, like the sight of steam rising off hot asphalt after a summer storm. She'd barely registered the sight when indeed, she felt her whole body hoisted upward, as if a platform underneath their feet was pushing them higher than she could possibly see. Her stomach and heart were in her mouth, and she did not quite understand Collum's description of this being "exhilarating."

The Elfling didn't know how long they'd been in the portal. It could have been seconds; it could have been a lifetime. But she realized the feeling of zooming was gone, though the hazy light still surrounded her.

"Bridgette?"

She also realized she'd buried her face in Collum's neck and was clinging tightly to his cream-colored tunic. She stepped back, embarrassed, then stopped dead — what if there wasn't anywhere solid to step on? Just to be sure, she tentatively tapped her toes in a circle, testing whether it was ground or air underneath her.

The haze faded, and they were in another bright white travel chamber as Collum led her through the exit gate. He procured that same folder of travel documents, and Bridgette was barely aware of what was happening as she slowly turned in place again. This terminal was just as bustling as the one they departed from, but where the one in Massachusetts towered upward alongside the portal, this one seemed a more standard three-story building. Which made sense, as they were at the top of the portal now. No need to go higher.

Bridgette took a deep, stabilizing breath. "Where to now?" she asked, trying to keep her voice steady.

"First, we're going to Endorsa, to meet with the Samnung. I assume they will have a luncheon prepared, but after that introduction, we're going exploring. I only have —" he thought for a moment, "seven and a half days to show you everything. I'm going to do my best to not leave anything out."

"Seven days to charm me, torture me, and murder me, and a half-day to bury my body somewhere in a magical wood?" The light danced in her lilac eyes, and Collum gave her a wry stare.

"Keep the Ted Bundy jokes to a minimum around the Samnung, will you? I don't fancy having to explain to the leaders of the world above the world why their beloved Liluthuaé thinks I'm a serial killer."

Bridgette stuck her tongue out at Collum. "Fine. Lead the way, oh lord Fyrdwisa."

He laughed at her exaggerated bow, then grabbed her gently by the wrist. "As you command, Sigewíf Liluthuaé."

But instead of going outside, Collum only took her a few feet ahead, into the terminal lobby. Bridgette looked confused, then said "Oh fuck" just before the air whorled around them, fading quickly into coils of navy and ice blue. Just as quickly as the coils formed, they dissipated, and Bridgette found herself with one hand at her throat, gasping for breath, Collum's arm around her shoulders. They were no longer in the terminal lobby, but instead in a warm, open foyer surrounded by glass walls that let in brilliant, soft sunlight. Plants of all manner — succulents, florals, and topiaries — were spaced strategically throughout, offering a fresh, vital scent to the air in the room. A barely perceptible melody of windchimes rang in the distance, as the outside breezes hit sweet metal and wooden rods against each other. She didn't know if it was the plants or the magic, but the whole room felt alive.

"Welcome to Cyneham Breonna, the noble residence of Endorsa," Collum said quietly. "This is where official and political Endorsan business is conducted. The royal family maintains their personal quarters in Deu Medgar, which is attached through a skywalk to this building."

"So the Samnung meets here?" Bridgette asked quietly. She wasn't sure why, but she felt as if she were to speak any louder, it would disturb the tranquility of the room. She also wondered if the plants were listening to their every word; mute spies somehow able to report back to their queen.

"It does indeed," Collum answered, tilting his head toward where a tasteful mahogany desk sat, partially blocking a winding grand staircase up to the next floor.

Bridgette followed him to the desk, where a young woman materialized out of thin air to fill the seat behind it. The Elfling jumped back, startled, and Collum fought back a chuckle.

"Welcome home, Fyrdwisa," the receptionist murmured. She barely looked at him, but waved a hand to her left and a thick folder flew from the shelf next to her. "Your reports and paperwork from your absence."

Collum gave her a dry stare. "Really? Trystane can reach me at any time, and yet they save me enough paperwork to occupy me for the next decade?"

The woman shrugged. "Not my place, Fyrdwisa. For archival purposes, your full journey report will be due in ten days' time."

She was ignoring Bridgette, who immediately wondered if she'd be subjected to sharing whatever a journey report was as well.

"Lucilla, look — "

The plea in Collum's voice made Bridgette raise her brows and cock her head. *Oh, somebody made the little witch mad before he disappeared to Earth without a word, didn't he?*

The Elf shot her a look of such annoyance, she knew she'd hit a nerve.

"Fyrdwisa, you and your — " she finally deigned to give Bridgette a once-over, then scoffed, "— companion may ascend the stairs. The Samnung will be waiting. Do not delay on that report." With that, the receptionist pointed a finger at the staircase, and a protective veil Bridgette hadn't realized was there simply wilted away, providing entry for the two of them.

"Keep your thoughts to yourself," Collum muttered coldly, but Bridgette gave him a wicked grin.

Oooh, Bundy's mad one of his girls got away?

"I should warn you that the Samnung chamber is protected with spells and wards to prevent magic from occurring within. I am not able to utilize my gifts or powers inside those walls, so whatever you think, I will not be able to hear. If you have questions, or, when you have questions, I should say, keep them in your mind and I'll debrief you as soon as I can."

"Debrief me?" Bridgette said. "You went from real friendly to real official in about three seconds there, *Fyrdwisa.*" She said that last word in a near-scathing tone.

He stopped and faced her. "May I remind you: It was my *job* to track you down, find you, tell you who you are, and bring you here, if you chose to come. This is my work. So yes, Bridgette, I am going to be 'real official' for the next bit, because I have to be. And so should you."

With that, he turned again and led her up the ever-higher winding spiral of steps to the enchanted chamber at the top. When they arrived, he squared his shoulders and Bridgette was momentarily startled to see an air of self-assurance and confidence fall over his body. He reached for the door that opened at his touch, and the two walked into the room.

The Samnung chamber held an oblong table surrounded by stools, on which sat a small, but diverse group of folk. There was no head of the table; just equals arranged in such a way that no one had an upper hand. The first to greet them was a tall, waif-like woman with sharp, angular features, deep golden skin, and flaming auburn hair. Those red-gold locks were complemented by both her hefty bronze crown and the regal dress she wore. Its sheer blue neckline came almost to her chin, yet dipped into a deep V-neck that met between her breasts, where the sheer blue ended and peacock green velvet began. It was fitted at the chest and torso, then flowed out with layers of that same sheer blue fabric visible underneath. Long sleeves were trimmed with intricate blue and metal beading at the wrist cuffs, and upon further inspection, the woman's crown was designed to look like delicate peacock feathers, lined with brilliant sapphires and emeralds.

What struck Bridgette most, though, was the woman's eyes. They were normal. Hazel, and dull, compared to hers, Collum's, and the Fairy Akiko's. Which meant —

"We are glad you chose to make the journey, Liluthuaé. I am Nehemi, queen of Endorsa. Welcome to our circle; welcome to our world."

Her accent was somewhere between British and Australian, her voice as sharp as her cheekbones and jawline. Those eyes may be dull compared to Fairies and Elves, but Bridgette had no doubt they didn't miss a beat. She seemed shrewd, and though there was no head of the table, Bridgette got the feeling Nehemi felt she was the unofficial leader of the Samnung.

"Um, thank you," Bridgette said, unsure if that was even the right thing to say in such a situation. She bowed her head slightly and took in the rest of the room. Collum noticed her looking and made quick introductions.

To Nehemi's right was a bent-over old wizard, his face weathered and worn with the spells and wars of a hundred years or more. He wore velvet robes the same blue as the sheer fabric of Nehemi's dress, and an intricate bronze symbol was embroidered on the chest. The robes tied at the waist with a belt braided in bronze and deep navy blue. This was Kharis, Nehemi's right-hand and trusted advisor. Next to him, looking completely bored, was an individual named Verivol who was so pale-skinned that Bridgette was reminded of horror movies she'd watched in her youth. He — or she, Bridgette couldn't quite tell, and wasn't sure that she was supposed to — smiled vaguely at her, and she noticed two pearly white fangs instead of canines.

"Hello, Bright Star," the being purred, shifting its legs. Bridgette realized Verivol wore a ruby red ballgown skirt and skin-tight white blouse, unbuttoned halfway down to reveal a firm, masculine chest. She made a mental note to ask Collum just what Verivol was, and how she should address him … or her. Or neither.

On the other side of Verivol sat a male figure with curly blonde hair, skin of actual golden hue, and delicate horns growing from either side of his head. His eyes were as blue as Collum's, but maintained a distinctly human look. Bridgette was introduced to him as Bryten, and she wondered exactly what type of being he was. Bryten wore a loose-fitting, cream-colored tunic, brown leggings that accentuated well-muscled legs, and soft shoes that looked like moccasins. A fierce woman sat next to him, her skin a deep mahogany and eyes so dark brown Bridgette could have sworn they were black. Her stare was fixed and intense, and her attire was head-to-toe gray leather, topped with a set of armored chrome shoulder pads, breastplate, shin guards, and boots. Her breastplate was stamped with an ornate letter "B," and Bridgette couldn't help but notice the coordinating chrome helmet and sheathed sword tucked in the corner of the room behind her.

Collum introduced her as Corria Deathhunter, first of her name and master swordswoman of Bondrie. Bridgette wasn't sure if this woman with pitch-colored, gleaming braids was someone she should fear or welcome as friend.

Continuing around the table was Trystane Eiríkr, leader of Eckenbourne. His pointed ears and gleaming eyes of moss green and gold marked him as definitively Elf. Like Collum, he was tall and trim, and similarly dressed in a tunic, leggings, and boots. Trystane's ice-blonde hair was fashioned into a braided faux hawk of sorts, and his ears were pierced with gold-rimmed wooden gauges. He seemed stately and calm, and Bridgette instantly warmed to him. But it was the woman next to Trystane whom Bridgette had been most excited to meet: the esteemed Fairy of All Fairies, the true leader of this Samnung, no matter what Nehemi thought of herself.

Aristoces had skin so dark and smooth it brought to mind rich earth after a spring rain. She wore a floor-length dress of seafoam green that rivaled Nehemi's in its regality, though Aristoces' attire was far simpler. It tied at the top of her strong shoulders, revealing a flowing white cape that draped between her flittering butterfly wings. The wings were regal too, melding from turquoise to crimson to fire orange. The whirls of color in her eyes made them look like storm clouds, tendrils of gray and charcoal pulsating within her irises. Her black hair was styled in a glorious afro, pulled back slightly from her face with a delicate silver circlet. Aristoces had finely pointed ears not dissimilar from Bridgette's own, and the tips of each were adorned with coordinating silver cuffs from which dangled a droplet of jade and diamond.

She stood to face Bridgette, so tall and with such an aura of wisdom and power around her, that the Elfling sank into a bow without thinking. Nehemi looked peeved that Bridgette bowed for the Fairy and not for her, a queen, but she let the glimmer of dissatisfaction slide off her face too quickly for anyone else to notice.

"Rise, Liluthuaé," Aristoces commanded, her voice rich and

warm and compelling. "You have much to learn, and we have much to share. Our home is your home. Our world is your world. Nothing is off limits to you, Bright Star."

Bridgette felt overwhelmed. There was so much — so much! — she wanted to know. Who were they? What were their histories? Was Aristoces an Aziza, like Galdúr? Was Nehemi descended from Artur Cromwell? How did they do magic?

Collum sensed the questions about to spill out of her and put a hand lightly on her shoulder. He had one last introduction to make, the one he was least excited about. On Nehemi's other side was Princess Cloa of Endorsa. A simpleton, truly; he did not know why she was constantly with the Samnung other than tradition. Not that he was about to share in this group his personal feelings towards the girl, but Bridgette should know who she was.

The girl had fair skin with a golden hue, perhaps olive, like her mother's, but that was about where the similarity ended. Her hair was a plain dark brown; her eyes clouded and some days green, some days hazel. Cloa almost always had a far-off look to those eyes. She never seemed quite *here* with the rest of the world, and only occasionally offered some snippet of conversation. But Nehemi made sure she was regally dressed like herself, in a tasteful, high-necked gown. Hers was the bronze that accented Nehemi's crown and the Endorsan crest, and it was all velvet. No adornments; no sheer panel in the v of her chest. Cloa was barely sixteen; hardly an age where her mother felt she should be promoting any kind of physical assets.

Bridgette took in the girl, several years her junior, and was hard-pressed not to wonder why such a child was part of the elite group, other than perhaps tradition. Cloa looked up at her and smiled sweetly, not wholly present in the room. Her fingers stroked the long coat of a tabby in her lab, and where Cloa's eyes struggled to focus, the feline's did not.

Like Collum, like the airplane, the cat wasn't … right. There was something off about the well-groomed, one-eyed creature, whose working golden iris widened, then narrowed, as it met Bridgette's own lilac eyes.

She paused in front of the princess, startled. "What ... is it?" she asked.

Cloa's laugh was high-pitched and somewhat annoying.

"This is Arctura, her cat," Nehemi answered for the princess, a sneer twisting her lips.

"Just ... a cat?"

Cloa laughed again, and the queen reiterated: "Just a cat."

~ 10 ~

"Be seated, Fyrdwisa. You too, Bridgette." Aristoces lifted a graceful hand and motioned to the two stools between herself and Cloa.

Stools, Bridgette realized, to intentionally account for wing-bearing Fairies that may need to be seated at the table. *That's kind*, she thought. *Though Aristoces is clearly the only Fairy here, there wasn't a set spot for her at the table.*

Collum froze. He looked at Kharis and asked, "Is the chamber properly sealed and warded?"

The old wizard nodded, and Collum glanced down at his hands, fingers laced together on the table in front of him. He could have sworn he just heard Bridgette, and that was supposed to be impossible. He shouldn't have been able to hear anyone in this room, not if it was adequately protected. Perhaps he was imagining things.

Nehemi revealed a wand of white birch and waved it in a specific manner. Bridgette couldn't hear the words that came from her mouth, but whatever she said, it made food appear on the table, along with glasses of ice-cold sparkling spring water.

Holy hellfire, the Elfling thought. She'd never seen such a spread in her life. It made sense, she supposed, given that whatever Verivol was probably required significantly different dietary needs than Bryten, an Elf, or a Fairy. In fact, she noticed, a specific platter appeared in front of her fang-toothed new friend, featuring meat barely singed with heat and seasoning.

The rest of the table was piled with crisp salad greens and wobbly, misshapen tomatoes; bowls of ruby red strawberries macerated with sugar; a roast duck with steam rising from its bourbon-laced glaze; and roasted parsnips seasoned so aromatically Bridgette wondered if the scent could be bottled and sold as culinary essential oil.

"I believe it is my turn, your majesties," Corria Deathhunter said, rising from her stool. With a snap of her fingers, a sharp knife and giant fork appeared for her to carve the duck with. As she worked, the rest of the Samnung began passing bowls and platters around, filling their plates. The master swordswoman would follow shortly, going around the table to serve her comrades their slice of duck, should they choose to partake.

Bridgette wondered how long it had been since she and Collum ate those eggs on the front porch of the little cottage. Probably only a few hours, but it seemed millennia. Earth, and the normal life she had until just a week ago, was already so far.

The Elfling chose to keep quiet during the meal, unsure how to engage the Samnung. Especially unsure how to address the noble Fairy next to her. *If I have any sort of abilities, I hope they make me as regal and stoic as Aristoces,* Bridgette thought to herself.

Collum dropped his fork. Definitely. He definitely heard her that time. *What in the deity-forsaken seven hells?* He didn't know if it was appropriate to bring up the faltering spellwork. Wondered if it even *was* faulty spells that caused this phenomenon.

"Trystane?" he called out down the table. "A word, if you don't mind?"

The Elven leader rose, and together the two males walked into the main hall, shutting the chamber door behind them.

"What is it?" Trystane's brow furrowed. It was most unusual for the fyrdwisa to request a private audience while amongst the full Samnung.

"I think there's something wrong with the magic in the chamber," Collum whispered, his eyes wide. "I can hear her. I can hear Bridgette. And I most certainly should not be able to hear anyone if those wards are up and strong."

The furrow deepened in Trystane's forehead. "Deity save us," he muttered. "You've never heard anyone in the chamber before?"

"Not with its magic at full force, no. And I can't hear anyone else, just her. At least, not that I'm aware of."

"Keep an eye on it. I do not think there is cause for concern, not yet. Bridgette *is* the Liluthuaé, after all. Perchance it's an ability no one knew existed," Trystane said quietly.

Collum hadn't considered that. It was, truth be told, the first time she'd likely emitted anything remotely like a magical characteristic or gift. Being able to commune with him despite the spells? Maybe that meant she would be able to break something deeper and stronger. Like the inner border of Palna.

Trystane seemed to have simultaneously come to the same conclusion. Their eyes met, wide and frenzied.

"Later. Bring her to me later, and we will discuss further," Trystane said. "I have much to tell you, much we could not send word of, but not here. Not yet."

That sounds foreboding, Collum thought as they returned to the chamber. He found his roast duck still steaming and the perfect temperature and texture as he slid his knife through a slice. At least his day was shaping up to be productive. First, whatever the rest of this meeting held, then they would go to Eckenbourne with Trystane and set Bridgette up with her lodgings and clothes for the week. And then, he supposed, he would meet with the leader in private to discuss whatever couldn't be shared in the hallway.

Lost in his thoughts, Collum barely registered that Aristoces had begun speaking to Bridgette.

"Tell us, Bridgette Conner, of your life on Earth. We understand your backstory, but it is important for us to learn from your experience in the world," the Fairy murmured.

Bridgette gulped down a glass of the sparkling water. "Well. When you're orphaned or abandoned without any living relatives, like I was, you usually wind up in the system," she said. "The foster care system. Where you're passed off from family to family every few years until you're either adopted by one of them, or you age out and can live on your own."

She went on to explain briefly about those years, most of her life until now, where she was given to family after family, none for more than three years, until finally at age thirteen she was handed off to an older couple who, though they never adopted her, became the closest thing she had to real parents. Corria Deathhunter's brows rose as Bridgette shared about living with possessions that were rarely more than what would fit into a pillowcase. Verivol actually growled with distaste when she answered a question about how she addressed her physical characteristics, and explained about being bullied because of them. Bridgette spoke of her university, and Bryten was fascinated with the idea that a whole college could exist just for music. He played the harp, apparently, as was custom with those of his kind.

"Coll — the fyrdwisa, I mean — explained to me that it was possible for magical beings to study on Earth? Maybe beings like you could focus on music at a college like mine," Bridgette offered.

The horned creature laughed. "Would that they could, Bright Star. However, our magic is not that of spells and glamour. It would be quite an undertaking to have anything less than human-looking portal down for four years of study."

"Then maybe your university here could start a music program."

Nehemi pursed her lips. "What a thought. Our university does not dabble in such feeble-minded professions. Those do not require higher learning. They are but hobbies," the queen said.

Bridgette stiffened noticeably, and Collum put a hand on her knee under the table. *Shut up; shut up ...* he thought fervently. *This is going to end very poorly for your first introduction ...*

But Bridgette, not gifted as Collum was with the ability to hear thoughts, put her fork and knife on her plate, and turned her now-intensely purple eyes to meet those of Nehemi.

"There is nothing 'feeble-minded' about creating," she said coldly. "At least studying to better myself and my culture can provide meaning in life and enjoyment to others. What, exactly, sort of degree does it take to become a queen? The MRS instead of a Ph.D.?"

Fucking hell, Bridgette ... Collum sincerely hoped his face was a mask of mere interest instead of the horror churning in his stomach. She was about to get them both kicked out of the chamber for being that feisty and headstrong, although Nehemi wasn't innocent in the rising tension.

"I became queen when my parents were killed in a vehicle accident, girl," Nehemi spat bitterly. "I suggest you watch yourself while you're here. Such insolence will not be so quick to get brushed under the rug elsewhere in Heáhwolcen, no matter what the Elves call you."

Bridgette wasn't much for arguing, but she did not like to not have the last word, especially in something that shouldn't have been an argument to begin with.

"Why *do* the Elves call me the Bright Star?" she asked innocently, smiling sweetly at Nehemi.

Collum stifled a groan. *Deity damn us all, Bridgette.* He glanced down the table at the rest of the Samnung. Verivol's eyes glimmered, and Bryten was practically leaning his whole weight on the table, smiling wickedly at the pair. Aristoces watched sharply, her eyes narrowed. Trystane and Corria, meanwhile, continued eating, trying to ignore the conversation at the other side of the circle.

"A wonderful question I've been trying to answer ever since the fyrdwisa insisted he waste months of our time and our salary searching for you on Earth, despite the fact that you have arrived here with practically no understanding of who you are and what this world is, and even less of an ability to perform any of the rare and powerful magic the Bright Star allegedly should be able to," Nehemi snarled. "Collum, why don't you explain?"

But Aristoces raised her hand.

"Tensions are high, and this is not the introduction the Liluthuaé should have to our governing body, Your Majesty," she said. "I move that we dismiss for this afternoon and reconvene in the mid-morning. I am sure the Liluthuaé would like to see Heáhwolcen and get her bearings before we delve too far into the realm of responsibilities and history."

Collum shot the Fairy a grateful glance. "I second that motion," the fyrdwisa said quickly. "Ceannairí, it has been a pleasure."

He rose and reached his hand for Bridgette's. She grabbed it and flashed an angry glare aimed at Queen Nehemi. The two had barely stepped out of the chamber when again, they were surrounded by those shades of blue whorls, and Bridgette registered the feeling of spinning, jumping, swooping, flying, and falling all in about a single heartbeat's time.

When she came to, gasping for breath again, she realized

they were in an apartment. Collum's apartment.

"Home sweet home," the Elf said, gesturing an arm out for her to step away from him and into his dwelling.

The apartment was spacious. They'd appeared directly in his living room, where a cushy, toffee-colored leather sofa and matching armchair were arranged around a table stacked high with books and papers. A kitchen was off to one side, and next to it, a hallway that Bridgette assumed led to his bedroom.

"My bedroom and home office are through that door. Down the hallway you'll find your bedroom," the Elf clarified, indicating a door next to the sofa. He was grateful that he could now not only hear her, but reply without raising suspicion.

"My bedroom?"

"Of course. We weren't going to make you sleep on my couch or on the street, now, were we?" Collum grinned and led her toward his second bedroom.

It was tastefully decorated in shades of gray and blue, with a full-size bed draped in a warm, slate-colored fluffy throw. Simple wood furniture made up the bedroom suite that included a nightstand, dresser, and armoire, and the dark gray accent wall across from the headboard was speckled with silver, gold, chrome, and bronze. The metals, she now knew, represented the four countries of the Samnung: silver for Fairevella, gold for Eckenbourne, bronze for Endorsa, chrome for Bondrie.

"What do you think?" Collum asked. "Are these sufficient accommodations for a few nights?"

"Of course. Thank you. And thank you for getting me out of there," Bridgette said, somewhat sheepishly. "I was probably about to say something really stupid and make a fool out of myself."

"Yes, you were." He shot her a wry glance, and she stuck her tongue out in return.

"Ugh, you're *such* a punk, Bundy."

~ 11 ~

The dresser and armoire, Bridgette discovered, were stocked with an array of leggings, tops, dresses, and shoes that were suited for an Elf of Heáhwolcen. The fabrics were beautiful and finely made, and she had no doubt they'd fit perfectly.

"Collum, why is Nehemi such a bitch?" she called as she walked back into the hall.

The Elf, who'd been pouring them both tea in the kitchen, practically spat his out on the counter. "Well, that was fast."

"I'm serious!" Bridgette whined, reaching for the second mug in his hand. "What's up with her being so against being creative and studying creativity?"

"That I'm honestly not sure about," Collum replied. "As to why she was being so ... bitchy? Nehemi has made it no secret she does not, as she puts it, 'buy into the Bright Star myth.'"

"And me having absolutely no magic probably didn't help that, did it."

"No. I cannot say that it did," he answered honestly. Collum fingered one of the stacked bracelets and cuffs on his left wrist. Navy blue, with a small gold and wooden hoop charm in the middle that looked like one of Trystane's ear gauges.

"What are all those?" Bridgette asked, cocking her head to one side. She reached out to touch them.

"Covenants. They are ways to communicate with those I need to," Collum said. "This one is for Trystane, who had a few very interesting words with me during the Samnung meeting. I know we've thrown quite a lot at you in a such a brief time, but I believe it's time the three of us sat down together."

He slipped two fingers underneath and around the navy blue bracelet. He closed his eyes, whispered something wholly unintelligible, and Bridgette watched with awe as the gold and wood began to glow.

"It's a summons," the Elf explained. "When you enter a covenant with another magical being, or human I suppose; I don't know that's ever been done; each of you has a marker of the commitment you've made to one another. Most Elves choose to use wrist adornments, although in witch custom tattoos or charmed coins are popular. Honestly it depends on what your preference is. Nobody's going to force someone to wear a bracelet, get a tattoo, or carry a bronze key around. It just needs to be something easily accessible. But whatever it is, the covenant is a way to reach, summon, or share information with one another."

"You have more than a dozen," Bridgette observed, still touching each band in turn.

"Some are no longer active covenants, but I keep them as a reminder."

"Of what?"

But their conversation was interrupted by a rapt knock at the front door. Collum snapped his fingers, and the door swung open without a word as Trystane Eiríkr strode inside.

"That was quite a show you gave today, Liluthuaé," he said, not hiding the amusement in his voice. "Most enjoyable Samnung meeting I've attended in years."

Bridgette blushed. "I'm sorry about that. I don't mean to reflect badly on the Elves by saying what I said. But really, she was out of her damn mind, going on about creating 'not being worthy' and all that."

"I agree," the Elven leader said, an eyebrow raised. "Nehemi's a bitch."

Collum nearly choked on his tea laughing so hard. "Shit, Trystane. I was attempting to keep some modicum of decorum going here, dammit."

"What? She is. Endorsa's gotten some hellacious tides turned its way these past couple decades. First all the nonsense with Hermann and Lalora struggling to conceive, now we end up with a queen who was locked inside a castle for eighteen years with zero human contact to rule its people. And her daughter … Cloa's a whole 'nother can of worms," Trystane said.

"What's wrong with her?" Bridgette asked.

Trystane shrugged. "Nobody knows. For as long as she's been old enough to attend the Samnung meetings, which in Endorsan custom is age thirteen for the upcoming ruler in line, she's been that way. Totally quiet. The fact she responded to you, laughed, today when you asked about the stupid cat was a small miracle."

"Who's her father? Is there a king of Endorsa?"

"Not now. Nehemi's lover, Cloa's father, was killed in the same accident that took the lives of Nehemi's parents, the late King Hermann and Queen Lalora," Collum explained. "Cloa never knew her father. She was only a couple months old when the accident happened."

Bridgette quieted, thinking of the poor princess. She knew what it felt like to grow up without much family, though she couldn't fathom why Cloa was allowed to attend the meetings when her head was clearly not in the game.

Collum broke the silence and turned to his leader. "What didn't you want to tell me in the hallway?"

Trystane flicked his wrist and murmured a command, and a tall glass of reddish liquid appeared in his opposite hand. "I can attest to Nehemi being a bitch because she's been that way the whole time you've been gone. She's been against the idea of searching for the Bright Star ever since it came about that you existed, Bridgette. I don't know why; I can't figure it out. But when Collum left to portal to Earth, the dynamics in that chamber changed completely. Nehemi became irritable. She didn't want there to be communication, which is why it was few and far-between during your visits, and nonexistent in the last few months. I think, I truly believe, she thought we'd been bewitched into going ahead with this plan."

"Bewitched? By whom?" Bridgette asked.

"By the Craft wizards of Palna," Trystane answered glumly. "She doesn't believe there's any hope besides practical magic in fighting them and containing them."

Bridgette furrowed her brow. "I thought they *were* contained. By a wall of magic and then their own wall inside that. Collum told me."

Collum, who'd been leaning against the kitchen wall, shifted his weight. "That's true. The inner wall is illegal Palnan magic only. The outer wall, the wall the Samnung formed after our own unrest, is maintained by constantly sacrificed magic by each of our leaders. Trystane, Aristoces, Corria Deathhunter, and Nehemi all wield their own wards together to form this wall. Any other beings are welcome to offer support, which is why Verivol, Bryten, myself, and a few others are so invested in what happens to Palna."

The Elfling considered that. "So why do people get so up in arms about Palna, anyways?"

Trystane settled into the toffee-colored leather armchair and took a sip of whatever spirit was in his hand. "Let's have a little story time, shall we?"

Collum and Bridgette settled catty-corner to him, sharing the couch.

"You've heard us mention, Bridgette, several times now that Nehemi's parents were killed in a carriage accident," the Elven leader said. When Bridgette nodded, he continued. "At least one of the ruling couple of Endorsa is directly descended from Artur Cromwell. I assume you're aware of his family and the role they played in creating Heáhwolcen?"

Bridgette nodded again.

"Good. King Hermann, Nehemi's late father, was descended from the Cromwells. He and his wife, Queen Lalora, longed desperately for a child. Partly so that Endorsa could continue to be led by a direct descendant of Artur Cromwell, but also because Lalora hadn't necessarily wanted to be any sort of leader … but she had always wanted to be a mother. When she was found to be with child, the entire world above the world rejoiced for her. It was divined by a birth healer that this child would be born a boy. But a great illness befell Lalora late during her pregnancy, and she miscarried." Trystane paused, remembering. "It was … it was horrible. She mourned; the king mourned; all of us mourned, really. For many, many years after that, the queen became a recluse. She would attend various state functions, and the occasional Samnung meeting, but was rarely seen outside of her residences.

"At some point during this time period, rumors began circulating that a Craft curse had been cast on her womb, which prevented her from carrying a successful pregnancy and thus affecting Endorsa's ability to have stable leadership," he continued. "The theory makes sense, of course, but there was the issue where no one could leave Palna or go inside Palna without strict permission and monitoring. It'd been that way for decades. We had no idea where the rumors started; we had no idea how — if they were true! — any witch or wizard in Palna would have been able to cast a spell that got past magical barriers. So, the Samnung, particularly at this point pushed by King Hermann, found a way in, and a way to learn what we needed to learn."

Collum interjected. "At this point I was set to take the post of fyrdwisa, studying under my predecessor who planned to leave his post in a few years. I was attending Samnung meetings regularly as his aide, and Master Swordsman Druan Heart of Stones suggested offering a bribe to Palnan citizens. Encourage good behavior by sending in rewards and companionship from the outside world. The previous Fairy ambassador to Palna was the only being able to easily access the country then, and he brought the proposal up to its leaders, Ydessa Tinuviel and her partner Eryth. The ambassador was under strict spell and instruction not to let it be known any of the rumors about a Palnan curse on Queen Lalora. It took some time, but eventually Ydessa and Eryth agreed to the terms suggested. From then on, if the Palnans performed no errant magick and maintained decorum inside their borders — and so long as no one tried to escape and infiltrate Heáhwolcen with Craft magic — a group of specially selected companions, as well as trade goods, would be sent in periodically."

"We learned much from these spies," Trystane said, shooting Collum a warning glance. "We learned that indeed, there was resentment toward Endorsa and Bondrie, particularly from those in the working class. We learned about the ways of life in Palna, about how Ydessa and Eryth ruled, and about the legends told of their beloved founder, Baize Sammael. But we found no trace that there was Craft magic actively being practiced. Still, we kept our eyes and ears open by way of this dedicated group of beings. Elves, witches, wizards, even the occasional Sanguisuge or nymph. All carefully vetted and many with covenants to report back on a regular basis, either to myself, to their specific leader, and a few directly to the acting fyrdwisa and to Collum.

"On the day of the carriage accident, Hermann and Lalora, along with a few members of their staff and court, were off to Fairevella for some official business," Trystane continued. "It was to be one of the first times in over a year Lalora had been in public. No one knows precisely what happened, but there was a horrible explosion as they came near the border of Bondrie and Palna. Some say it was errant magick that we'd thought had been squashed. Others say it was a hidden defense system gone awry; that the border was spelled to erupt should someone get too close to invade Palna or escape the other side. Either way, the results were disastrous. Everyone on that carriage was killed instantly. Word spread quickly, and the Samnung was summoned that very evening."

"That was a night I will never, ever forget," Collum said quietly, looking down at his tea. "It was the night I officially became fyrdwisa, because my predecessor was on that carriage."

Bridgette reached out and put a comforting hand on his knee. "I'm so, so sorry," she whispered, then turned back to Trystane as he continued the tale.

"Kharis, who has served as the main advisor to Endorsan leadership for nearly a century, gave us the shock of a lifetime at that gathering. He brought Nehemi, who carried a two-month-old baby girl in her arms, into the room, and introduced all of us to the hidden child of Endorsa. She was newly eighteen, old enough to rule immediately, with her infant daughter as future successor," Trystane said. "None of us knew what to think. The whole day was both a blur and an unending tragedy — punch after punch of disaster and new normal thrown our way. Losing our king and queen; thinking we *had no* king and queen; losing our fyrdwisa; inducting a new fyrdwisa on the spot; suddenly learning we not only had a queen but a princess too ... I don't think I've ever, in my whole existence, had so much emotional range spent in one day."

The trio sat quietly for a moment, allowing Bridgette time to process all she'd learned.

"So …" she began, "people dislike Palna because they practice some evil spells, and probably killed Endorsa's last king and queen? And the old fyrdwisa?"

Trystane chuckled. "That's about it in a nutshell, actually."

"But why, then, does Nehemi seem to have it in for me? And for y'all, for bringing me here?" Bridgette asked curiously. She still wasn't quite sure why her presence was so offensive to the queen.

"As I said, Nehemi is under the impression that only practical magic can control Palna and any potential threat," Trystane answered. "It is my opinion that she has always felt some level of inadequacy when compared to other leaders. Whether that stems from her youth — she's only thirty-four — or her magic not being as powerful, or something else entirely, who knows. But I do think it led to an internalized idea that the rest of the Samnung choosing to bring in 'an outsider' to help quell the problems meant we were critical of her abilities to lead and cast spellwork."

Bridgette was tired of these vague mentions of whatever it was the Samnung wanted her to do, and the fact that it caused a rift between leaders made her wholly uncomfortable.

"If it's such an issue, why bring me here to begin with?" she asked. "What is it I'm supposed to do?"

~ 12 ~

"We'll tell you in due time," Trystane answered quickly, seeing that Collum had opened his mouth and was liable to tell her everything. Bridgette's touch of his knee earlier hadn't escaped the Elven Ard Rialóir, and he wondered just what level of sway the Bright Star might hold on his fyrdwisa. "That is not the purpose of this visit, though I don't apologize for the distraction to give you some historical context as to our current situation. Which is that there has been continued unrest, and Aristoces and I begin to worry that the inner border is weakening the primary wall."

Collum's eyebrows rose. "What?"

"When it became clear that there was tension between Nehemi, Kharis and, well, everyone else whose head is on straight regarding your mission, I began meeting secretly and separately with Aristoces and Corria Deathhunter. The Fairy Ambassador to Palna has … disappeared, for starters, following a deployment into the country. He was supposed to report back to Aristoces weekly. When he missed a week, she didn't think too much of it, but after a second week with no word, she attempted to Summon him back to Fairevella, only to find her covenant with him was dissolved," Trystane said.

"What?!" Collum nearly shouted. "That is impossible!"

"No. It's not. Not when someone is illegally practicing Craft magic again," the Elven leader said quietly. "So Ulerion disappeared. In addition, the Bondrie Guard found what appeared to be a handful of weak spots, small and evenly spaced, around the edge of the outer wall. They're spread thin to keep watch, more so than ever before."

"What does the Bondrie Guard do?" Bridgette inquired. She'd seen Corria perform a bit of magic during the luncheon, when she brought the cutting utensils out of thin air, but mostly she looked like a modern-day take on a medieval knight.

"The Bondrie Guard are Heáhwolcen's most well-trained warriors," Collum said. "Most are of human descent with the ability to do some magic, but not all."

"So if they can't do much magic, how are they supposed to fight off these evil Palnan people and their magick that you said is the most powerful ever known?" the Elfling asked.

Trystane raised a brow, and his second glass of spirits. "A fair question, Liluthuaé. The idea is that because of the wall, Palnans weren't supposed to be able to practice magic at all, much less Craft Wizardry, meaning they'd be susceptible to physical damage pretty easily."

"And the weak spots?" Collum urged Trystane to continue.

"Yes. There are six that the Bondrie Guard found. They don't think they're much to worry about, but even after reinforcing our spellwork they barely began to close. We think it's because the magic of the inner wall, the Palnan wall, is somehow counteracting ours. Like two same-poled magnets trying to be forced together. In doing so, they only force each other apart," Trystane explained. "Nehemi and Kharis believe there are rituals of the old magick that can be merged with our collective spells to fix the problem, but they have to track down and find said rituals. Kharis has a strong suspicion that they're Druidic, which means we have exactly no living record of them in Heáhwolcen."

He turned to Bridgette to clarify. "Artur Cromwell, and thus every leader of Endorsa after, has Druid ancestors. But we have no known Druids *here*, and Druids historically did not use a written language for much of their work. We do know some rituals and healing conjurations, because of what Artur knew and recorded for future generations when he and his family immigrated to the New World. However. Much of what he knew wasn't direct ritual, potion or spellwork. Rather, it was magical theory, history, and properties of elements and natural ingredients, and how they might perhaps be used together."

"Can't you just send someone down to Earth then, to talk to the Druids?" Bridgette asked. "There *are* still Druids, right? Like it's not just crazy people who gather at Stonehenge a few times a year to wear cloaks; they are magic?"

Collum was impressed with Bridgette's insistence on rational solutions. Sending someone to Earth seemed such an obvious thing.

"Did the Samnung consider that? Sending an ambassador to the Druids?" he asked.

Trystane shook his head. "Actually, no, but that would seem to be an excellent suggestion. Nehemi and Kharis amassed a group of students at the University to do as much research as they could, and there has been talk of reaching out to the spirits of Ifrinnevatt for assistance. Though communing with the spirits is not an easy task, at least, not for us."

"Why not?" Bridgette asked.

"Summoning spirits is very precise work, firstly, and only a witch or wizard educated in that specific type of ritual is able to do so effectively. For example, we would want to speak to spirits whose worldly bodies were Druidic or knew intimate knowledge of Druidic customs and history. That's quite a different spell and ask than issuing a summons for, say, your grandmother," Trystane explained. "To further difficult matters, we have the issue where Ifrinnevatt is but one spirit realm. There is the positive afterlife, which many Earthly religions call 'Heaven,' and then there is the dark river that leads to Hades. And for communing with those spirits down below, it's much easier for us to go to them. Deity forbid we accidentally open some portal from Hell."

"Let me get this straight," Bridgette announced. She hoisted herself from the couch and started pacing the living room, glancing at Collum and Trystane in turn. "Palnans aren't supposed to do magic at all, much less Craft magic. But they somehow can, and it's threatening to tear apart the barrier everyone else put on them to keep them imprisoned. Which means Craft magic could come back into the rest of the world. And that would be a very bad thing. They also kidnapped a Fairy. Not a good move, dudes.

"We don't know what they're doing or exactly why they're doing it, but it's fucking everything else up," she mused. "There are three solutions, right? Option one. Teach the Bondrie Guard to use magic as well as swordplay — or teach witches and wizards to fight and send in reinforcements — to expand the number of bodies able to keep watch on the border. Option two. This group of students at the University finds some old ritual from the Druids that can strengthen the barrier, thus keeping Palna in check. Finally, option three, which is tear down both walls and get rid of the viruses causing this disease that is evil magic, and Palna can become a regular country again."

The Elves stared at her.

"What?" she asked, befuddled.

"Those aren't options," Trystane breathed. "Those are steps forward. That's a damn plan, Liluthuaé."

"What …?" Bridgette asked again. "That's not a plan. It's just … things that make sense, right? Like, you have a goal of eradicating Craft magic. How do we do that? I don't know who those names are, the people you said rule it now, but if there's one thing I know about corrupt or inept governments, it's that they're typically not so much the disease as they are a symptom. Treat the symptom, and the disease gets gone."

She sounded so matter-of-fact, so sure of herself … so far from the Elfling he *knew* had not been one-hundred percent emotionally secure less than twenty-four hours ago. Collum was blown away by the change in demeanor. He cocked his head to one side thoughtfully.

"Why are you both staring at me like I've gone mad?" Bridgette asked, bringing Collum out of his reverie.

"I'm not," he said. "I'm just … surprised, that's all. You seem to have quite a head for strategy. I wasn't expecting it."

"What, like women can't problem-solve?" she retorted.

"No, that's not at all what I'm saying," Collum answered quietly. "Strategy is usually the fyrdwisa's job. I'm impressed you came up with such recommendations and plans without much context at all into what we are facing. I am also disappointed in myself for not thinking similarly to begin with. But Bridgette" — he paused and raised his eyes to hers — "you've forgotten the other part of our strategy. We have an extra benefit that Palna doesn't even know exists."

"And what, pray tell, is that, Bundy?" Bridgette drawled, forgetting for a moment her promise not to mention the nickname in front of Samnung members.

"We have you, Bright Star."

~ 13 ~

Out of nowhere, Bridgette was suddenly furious. She was tired, she was pissed off and she didn't care that it wasn't perhaps the most professional thing to start yelling at someone who was technically her superior.

The Elfling gave him a look that could melt ice.

Shit, Collum thought.

"For fuck's sake, I am going to need you — one of you — to tell me what the hell that means. You've been dragging it out for a week now, ever since you followed me to my secret reading spot —"

"It wasn't much a secret if anyone could find it, Bridgette —"

"— That doesn't matter, Collum! What the hell is a Bright Star? What is this illicit task you keep alluding to that no one wants to tell me? And while we're at it, am I allowed to know who my father is yet? Or are you going to keep that hanging over my head like it's a sugar cube to a horse you're leading to some miserable magical, sacrificial slaughter?"

And don't you try your stupid smell thing on me right now, either. She sent that thought straight to the fyrdwisa, who wasn't sure whether to remain in stunned silence or rise to her challenge of a shouting match.

"Bridgette, I —"

But Trystane held up a hand and rose to his feet. "Let us go to Fairevella, Liluthuaé. It is best for Aristoces to share in this story, and it is a story best told somewhere more … protected."

Collum began to protest; his apartment was plenty warded; but his leader had spoken. Now was not the time to argue.

If Bridgette gets too antsy or afraid, or thinks we're lying to her, she's not going to do us any good, Trystane thought to him. *The Liluthuaé has every right to have all of those questions answered, but Aristoces and you need to do the answering. I am but a host to her.*

Collum shot the Elven leader an understanding look.

"Okay. Let us go." Collum held a hand to Bridgette, who

still looked angry.

"Are we going to do that vanishing thing again …?"

The Elf laughed. "Yes. It's called evanescing, and it does take some getting used to. Just hold on."

I don't think I'll ever get used to this, Collum, she thought to him. The feeling of having the wind knocked out of her wasn't one she relished, even if it was a quicker means of traveling than anything on Earth.

Moments later, the trio appeared on a bustling city street in the heart of Fairevella, and Bridgette was again struck with amazement at the beauty, balance, sheer radiance, and splendor of the Fairy aesthetic. The buildings were all shades of glistening pastel or neutral tone with coordinating, contrast-color shutters and doors, and deep slate rooftops. Storefronts had bay windows decorated with all sorts of wares and foodstuffs, and the Elfling was struck to see equal amounts of beings flying and walking, some winged and some not. She watched as a group of women hung glittering streamers from the awnings of each building: different hues of pink, violet, gold, and lemongrass.

"What's all that for?" Bridgette asked her companions.

Collum gave her one of those soft smiles again, his blue eyes glittering nearly as bright as the decorations. "Your spring break coincided with one of our most beloved holidays. Ostara, the celebration of the spring equinox, will be the second-to-final night of your visit."

The Efling grinned. "Do we get to celebrate?"

"Of course." He offered her an arm, and the two followed Trystane down the busy street. Beings of all sorts greeted the Elven leader and fyrdwisa, some with waves, others with quick bows.

Fairevella was, aside from the Fairy-influenced portal terminal on Earth, the most magical and beautiful place Bridgette had ever laid eyes on. Even the air had an ethereal feel to it: she could have sworn again she heard tinkling wind chimes and musical bird chirps. The Fairies of Fairevella flitted in and out of sunlight and shadow, adding color and iridescence to the scene in front of her. Bridgette squeezed Collum's arm slightly against her own, and, not wanting Trystane to hear, thought directly to the Elf at her side:

I'm sorry I got angry. I don't like getting upset with people, Collum. Just sometimes things … explode and I don't know how to stop it. I am upset that I know nothing, really, about why you brought me here, and I'm upset I don't know magic or anything to be any use to y'all. But this … this place! Even if I don't have magic, I could stay here forever and never stop finding something to be awed by.

Collum squeezed her arm back, keeping his expression vague. *This girl is so worried about not being enough that she's convinced herself she isn't,* he thought sadly to himself.

Trystane looked backward then, seeing them arm-in-arm, and noticed Collum's responding glance that dared him to say something about it. The Elven leader rolled his eyes at his fyrdwisa. "You're quiet back there, you two. Having conversations between your minds?"

"We can't do that," Bridgette said quickly. "I mean, I can't do that."

"She can whisper taunts straight to my frontal cortex, but sadly is unable to hear my admittedly witty and sharp responses," Collum said, a slight smile tugging at one corner of his lips.

Punk.

Bridgette wondered, then, what it would be like if the two *were* able to communicate together like that. As far as she knew, no one could hear Collum the way he could hear everyone else, assuming there weren't secret spells or magic in place to keep his ears out of their heads. It was such a conundrum, and still somewhat unbelievable, that the potential for such magic existed; that she was in this place where it did. Heáhwolcen felt equally foreign and familiar. She knew she'd never been here before, but she wasn't lying when she'd sent that thought to Collum, telling him she'd happily make a home here. It just felt, right? Was that the word?

The Elfling had grown up in so many houses, so many existing families while in foster care, that she'd forever desired nothing more than a place to finally feel like home. Bridgette felt far more "at home" at the diner and secluded away in her secret little places, part of the aura of the university and its music, than she ever did in the world of academia itself, or even with the Simmonses. But here … she'd not even been here twelve hours and felt stirrings in her soul that she'd never deigned to imagine.

Her spat with Nehemi aside, Bridgette felt she could *belong* in Heáhwolcen. She'd seen two rooms inside a palace, Collum's spacious apartment, and one city street in Fairevella, and she was sold. The people — *beings*, she corrected herself — in this world looked like her. Some truly were human, but many others had ears and eyes like her. Moved like her and were tall like her. And she had *friends* here. Or, a friend at least, whenever Collum was being Collum and not acting as fyrdwisa. That was more than she could say for the previous twenty-two years of her life.

"What's on your mind, Bright Star?" Collum asked her. His lips barely moved, and Bridgette wondered if he was intentionally trying not to draw attention to them having a conversation.

None of your beeswax, Bundy.

The Elf couldn't help but grin. "I should answer your question better, about Ostara. We can go into the origins later — you *really* have much to learn — but the celebrations that take place in Heáhwolcen are particularly enjoyed in Fairevella and Endorsa. Elves have our own traditions and holidays we celebrate, but many of us do traverse to one country or the other to join in the festivities for traditionally 'witchy' things. Ostara is a celebration of spring and the awakening and rebirth of the lands. It's also, by default, an occasion to honor fertility of womb and soil."

"What are the celebrations?" Bridgette asked, glancing up at him as they walked past yet another group of Fairies hanging streamers.

"The whole of each city or town will gather together for a communal feast, and every family brings something to the table," he answered. "Some beings will travel to their capital city, which is Galdúr in Endorsa and Çeofilye in Fairevella — where we are now, by the way — for grand celebrations that include speeches and ceremonies led by their country's leaders. In Endorsa specifically, there are rituals of old magick and blessings for the coming year. Young beings typically receive small gifts. In Fairevella, the old legend of the Goddess Eostre is performed with theatrics in several cities, where a Fairy is glamoured to be a March hare and parade through the streets with eggs and treats.

"Once," Collum said, smiling, "a Fairy ambassadora observed an unusual custom at a restaurant on Earth, where customers would receive a folded piece of dough that had been baked with paper wrapped inside. She was so intrigued by this idea of eating an after-dinner bite to learn one's future that she encouraged the custom here for Ostara. What better time to offer well-wishes and promises for abundance than the spring equinox?"

Bridgette looked him dead in the eye and held back a laugh. "Are you seriously telling me that Fairies are into *fortune cookies*?"

"Why, yes," Collum's eyes twinkled. "I suppose I am. Though I was unaware that was their true name. We call them 'frihtri,' which comes from an old word about divining the future."

"That is both the most astounding and amusing thing I've heard all day," Bridgette said, shaking her head. "Who would've thought. Are we going to go to the Fairevellan or the Endorsan parties?"

"Likely Fairevella. Endorsans, deity love them, are many things, but revelry-workers they are not," the Elf said back. His blue eyes still sparkled with laughter at the wonder and questions of his Elfling companion. It was hard, he'd discovered, not to look back and listen to every word she hid behind her own majestic irises.

"In hindsight, I probably should have warned Aristoces we were coming," Trystane said, slowing his walk to be next to Bridgette and Collum. "I don't feel it's appropriate to summon her, so if she's not at the Seledréam, we'll leave word and continue exploring the city."

The Elfling nodded, delighted with the idea of continued exploration. Collum hadn't been specific, aside from talking about Ostara and Samnung meetings, as to what she'd see and experience while in Heáhwolcen. She didn't want to seem too young and excited, not when she was allegedly supposed to be some world savior, but inwardly, she couldn't wait to celebrate the spring equinox. Bridgette did not have much in the way of positive childhood memories when it came to holidays.

Çeofilye, Bridgette noticed, seemed to be arranged with four main avenues that intersected at the city center, where shops, restaurants and most of the Ostara decorating were concentrated. Where they'd landed upon evanescing was a number of blocks away from a glistening building she could see in the distance ahead. As they neared, she struggled to tell whether it was a home, a corporate building of some type, or a palace. The closer they got, the more expansive it seemed, stretching for hundreds of yards on either side of a central entrance, marked by a gleaming silver gate. Like everything in Fairevella, its twinkle was subtle, yet unmistakably Fae. Behind the gate were what seemed acres and acres of greenery and gardens lining various stone paths to parts of the building, which itself looked to be made of a pale periwinkle-colored stone that complemented its slate gray and bright white roof, shutters, and doors.

"What *is* this place?" Bridgette whispered to Collum as they approached that silver gate, feeling as though to speak much louder would disturb the magic she felt emanating from it.

He beamed, gripping her arm tighter in his. "This, sweet Liluthuaé, is the Seledréam — the Noble House of Fae."

~ 14 ~

The Seledréam. Bridgette rolled the name around in her mind, feeling each syllable in silent movement on her tongue. It had power and might, humility and beauty and death all at once. She shivered at the thought of crossing that silver gate they'd now reached. She stopped and looked at Collum, whose eyes narrowed at the fright he sensed in her expression.

Collum, I don't think I'm supposed to go through that, she thought to him. *It feels ... it feels wrong.*

"You're fine, Bridgette. You're safe. Nothing can touch you here, and there is nothing to fear before or behind the Seolformúr," Collum whispered. "Come on."

The Elfling couldn't shake that feeling though, that by crossing through the gate she might be sick to her stomach. The fear was completely irrational, she told herself, furrowing her brow. There was no need to be so anxious. It was just a gate, after all. And she was just an Elfling of little consequence and less magic, no matter what the Samnung might believe of her.

A quadrant of winged guards flew to the gate and bowed deeply at the Elven trio.

"Fyrdwisa, and Ard Rialóir — deity dhaoibh!" one greeted them. "Sigewíf, fáilte."

Trystane and Collum bowed in return, and Bridgette, arm still wrapped in Collum's, did as well. The Elven leader greeted the four guards with equally unknown words: "Nonóir es linne, Caomhnóir Feeric."

Formal salutations seemingly done with, the Fairy who spoke addressed the trio. "Ceannairí, what brings you to the Seledréam this afternoon? I presume you are here to see our Aristoces, Fairy of All Fairies?"

"We are, Hafiz. Is Aristoces present?" Trystane asked.

"She is, Ard Rialóir. Come; we'll take you inside."

The guard — Hafiz, his name seemed to be — swept one arm out and the gate opened before them. Bridgette felt bile rising in her throat and fought back the urge to run. She gripped Collum's arm with both her hands as he led her forward, and began shaking slightly.

This isn't right, Collum. I think I'm going to be sick.

As they passed through the silver gate, a wave of nausea hit Bridgette without warning and she broke from Collum's grasp, the force surprising both of them, and backpedaled into the street. He and Trystane turned together, staring at her face, white with shock. She looked as though she'd seen a ghost.

"I'm so sorry — I ... I can't. I think something made me sick. Maybe that duck from lunch; I don't know that I've ever eaten duck before," she said quietly, turning her head from side to side, desperate for something to grab hold of to stabilize her. *What the fuck is wrong with me? Why can't I go through the gate?*

The fyrdwisa turned to Trystane, his blue eyes fierce with concern. "I'll take Bridgette back into the city. Tell me where to meet you and Aristoces, and summon us when it is safe to evanesce."

Trystane nodded. "You know what to do," he said quietly, and turned to walk into the grand, noble house of Fae.

"Our apologies, Hafiz. It seems our guest is unwell. Your hospitality and graciousness are appreciated," Collum said to the Fairy guard, whose silvery-green eyes whorled with apparent unease.

Hafiz lowered his head in acknowledgement. "It is most unusual, Fyrdwisa, for an Elven-born being to be unable to pass through the Seolformúr."

"It is, indeed," Collum agreed.

He turned to walk to Bridgette, whose skin had gone from the golden tan of summertime to a sickly pale pallor. The Elf extended his arm to her again, and in the blink of an eye, the two were gone. They reappeared in his living room, where Bridgette promptly fell to her knees and vomited on his hardwood floor.

"Fuck — Collum I'm so sorry —"

"It's fine," he said, snapping his fingers and uttering a quick word. The mess was gone instantly, and in its place was a sparkling clean floor that smelled faintly of cedar. "I knew that would probably happen if we evanesced, but I couldn't risk you being out and about in this condition. What happened? Are you alright?"

He knelt down next to her on the floor on the floor.

"No? Maybe? I don't know, honestly. I've never felt like that before."

Collum led her to the couch. "Cuddle up. I'm going to get you something."

"Do Elves have ginger ale? That's like, the penultimate Earth cure for suddenly ill stomachs," Bridgette moaned, curling into a ball against the soft leather.

She got a wink in response. "Trust me, Starshine, this is better."

"Starshine?!" she called after Collum as he turned his back to walk into the kitchen. "Since when do I have a nickname?"

"Since you bristle every time we call you what you are. You can call me Bundy, I get to call you this," the Elf said back.

"Fine," Bridgette muttered, too mentally spent to argue. She closed her eyes and wished that instantaneous sleep was a magical power one could have. *Why couldn't I get through the gate?* she wondered again. *Why did it make me so sick? Just more proof I'm not going to be of any use to these people — I mean, beings — to do whatever bullshit task they want me to do.*

Collum returned a few minutes later with a glass of sparkling liquid that was bubblier, spicier, and more soothing than any ginger ale Bridgette ever had on Earth. "Told you so," he murmured.

She stuck her tongue out at him. "What is it?"

"It's gingewinde. Think of it as the magical form of ginger ale," Collum answered. He took a sip from his own cup, which seemed to be his preferred type of non-healing beverage. "Tell me exactly what happened to you back there, because that should not have happened."

"I felt …" Bridgette took a moment to find the right words. "It wasn't quite fear, but it just felt *wrong*. Like my brain told me it was fine, but my spirit or something knew that if I crossed that gate and went too far in, something really, really bad was going to happen, and my body reacted to make me stop moving. To walk through the gate was like trudging through a river of molasses. And when we got to the edge of where the gate ended and the walkway began, I felt so sick, like feverish and nauseous and I had this immediate sense of needing to get out of there."

Collum considered this. "The Seolformúr is a magical barrier older and more powerful than even Heáhwolcen. When Aristoces chose to move the home of the Earthly Fae to the world above the world, the ancient gate was transported from its then-location in the Torridon Wood. Only those who wish well upon the Fairies may pass through."

Bridgette looked confused. "But of course I 'wish well' about them!" she exclaimed. "Why would the gate assume I didn't? Is it because I'm too human?"

"No," Collum said sharply. "Firstly, you are *not* human. You are the Liluthuaé, and if anyone should be able to get through that gate without difficulty, it's *you*. Just because you aren't learned in the ways of magic doesn't mean you're human, Bridgette."

"How so?" she asked sullenly, sipping the gingewinde.

Collum breathed out. "Trystane is going to have my head on a silver platter if he finds out I told you this, so make sure he doesn't, please?"

She nodded.

"You can't be human because neither one of your parents is human. I can't say anything else because I'm under strict secrecy orders — "

"So what, is my dad a vampire?" Bridgette asked, interest piqued.

"No."

"A horned dude like Bryten?"

"No —"

"Also an Elf, like my mom?"

"Bridgette — "

"Oh shit, was he a Fairy?!"

"Please stop —"

"No, this is fun," Bridgette teased, suddenly feeling much improved. "Was he a wizard?" She leaned forward on her knees, eyes glinting teasingly.

"No, it's really not." Collum retorted dryly, leaning forward himself.

"Okay, fine. So he's not one of the *beings* I've met, and he's not human. What the hell was he, one of those evil Palnan Craft wizards?" she laughed.

And then she stopped.

Collum's eyes had gone very, very wide and very, very icy blue.

"Fuck me," the Elfling whispered. "You're joking."

The fyrdwisa shook his head slowly. "I'm not saying anything else about this, Bridgette."

Something clicked together in Bridgette's brain, like the final two pieces of a jigsaw puzzle. She widened her own eyes and grasped Collum's wrists, letting her gingewinde glass fall to the floor and shatter at her feet.

"Collum, holy shit. That's why I couldn't go through the gate," she gasped. "That's why it makes me sick. Not because I want to kill the Fairies, but because there's something wrong *in* me and that gate is powerful enough to detect it and protect against it."

Collum nodded. "Perhaps."

"No, not perhaps," Bridgette snapped, letting go of his hands. She stood up to pace again, the fyrdwisa's eyes following her every move. "That gate isn't supposed to let anything through that could harm the Fairies. And, well, from what little I know of this Craft magic shit, that's basically its whole deal, right? Get rid of the humans and any magical beings that 'sympathize' with humans, then take over the universe."

"A bit trite, that description, but yes."

"Okay. So … so say when Craft wizards and witches have kids, there's like, a nugget of that ability in them. You said magic is genetic, right?"

Collum was spared the pain of answering as his covenant band with Trystane glowed gold. "Bridgette, if you're feeling better, we need to go now. Trystane and Aristoces request our presence."

"Do I have to go back to the gate?" Bridgette whispered,

suddenly feeling cold.

"No — we're going to a safe space here, in Eckenbourne."

"Alright then." She held a hand out to him, and they vanished in deep tendrils of navy darkness.

The duo evanesced to the middle of a grassy clearing surrounded by trees in the dusky beginnings of twilight. After her time in the bustling streets of Fairevella, Bridgette was struck by how silent it was. Trystane and Aristoces were already there, on the other side of the knoll.

"Where are we?" she asked.

"This is Maluridae Wood," Collum answered. "It is sacred Elven ground, this place. The only way in or out is to evanesce, and the only way to learn it even exists is to be brought here by one who knows of it."

The two began walking toward the Elven and Fairy leaders. Something must have shown in Bridgette's face, because the first thing Trystane did when they were close enough to see was exclaim a few choice curse words in exasperation.

"He didn't tell me!" Bridgette said quickly. "I … kind of figured it out on accident.".

"She didn't figure it *all* out," Collum said pointedly. "Just managed to narrow down specifically what type of being the male was."

Trystane calmed slightly, but his fierce green eyes flicked sharply to the Elfling. "Tell us what you have inferred, then."

"Just that … just that he was one of those Craft wizards in Palna everyone freaks out about," she whispered, unable to meet his gaze.

"Tell them the other part. About the gate," Collum urged quietly. He put a hand on her shoulder and sent an almost imperceptible scent of honeysuckle wafting to her.

Bridgette took a deep breath, and in the silence and omniscient, ancient magic of the wood, Collum both felt and saw her change. It was slight; he doubted Aristoces and Trystane would have noticed. But Collum had spent so much time watching his charge these past months, and so closely for a few weeks, that he realized it immediately. He wondered how he'd missed it before, in particular those two times when she began pacing around his living room. It was undeniable now. As she breathed in, readying herself to relay this story and knowledge, Bridgette's shoulders straightened and the opalescent flecks in her eyes gleamed. They didn't just gleam … they *shifted*. Her eyes glowed brighter because they became true lilac opals.

"If my father is a Craft wizard, and magical ability is passed down through genetics, it is more than likely I contain some of whatever it is that allows someone to practice Craft magic. That gate in front of the Seledréam, Collum said it's protected against anyone with ill will toward the Fairies. *I* certainly don't mean them harm. But if Craft Wizardry is intended as the magic of anti-magic, it's entirely feasible to assume the gate detected some of that inside me. The gate physically would not let me pass, not fully, because there's something in my very veins that sends up a red flag," Bridgette said. "But I could get close. I could go almost all the way through because it senses enough *other*, enough non-Craft inside me, that it confused it momentarily. I think it would have given me the choice. The curse wouldn't have affected me if I continued through, but I would have been sick to my stomach if I made it. When I decided to go back, it acknowledged that choice and didn't attack."

Aristoces showed no emotion. "Liluthuaé, you say you have no magical abilities. How can this be, when the Seolformúr can only bar or protect against ill magics?"

"Because she *does* have magical abilities," Collum said, causing Bridgette to turn around in surprise. "They're just not quite like anything I've ever seen in person."

~ 15 ~

The fyrdwisa moved his arm in a circle. Four stools materialized out of thin air, and he bade them all sit.

"Bridgette is a sierwan. I never believed they existed. I thought the sierwen were as much myth as the Liluthuaé, but deity damn me if you're not both," he said. "A sierwan is not quite a diviner, but its abilities are similar. Whereas diviners can infer or observe future events, they must have a subject in mind to divine or forbode of. Sierwen are able to connect dots, to plan, to infer knowledge based on what they inherently know to be true of the future. They cannot explain how they know these things. They cannot offer a reasoning or context as to *why* their plan will work or *how* the knowledge makes sense. It simply *is*.

"The legends that tell of the sierwen show them to be advisors, hands of kings and queens, wartime leaders," the Elf went on. "Seeing Bridgette morph when she is faced with the need for a plan to exist or for something unknown to need to make sense, she fits all the markers of what these legends allude to. Her ability is innate. Like all magic when it's first discovered, she has no idea it's even happening — none of us did. The other marker is her eyes changing when these abilities come forward. They become true opals."

The Elfling self-consciously fingered the tip of one pointed ear. The only thing she'd ever heard about opals was that unless one was born in October, one couldn't wear opal jewelry or it would turn their earlobes green.

"What do you mean by true opals?" she asked, not sure now if she wanted to make eye contact with Collum.

"Elven eyes, as I'm sure you've noticed, are the most vivid colors known. Your eyes have those little opalescent flecks in them. When you begin to feel your sierwan abilities come forward for use — and eventually when you've learned how to summon and manage them — those flecks shift to fully surround your pupil. They cause your irises to glow and become ethereally iridescent," he answered.

Bridgette tried not to shudder or blush. Hearing Collum

describe her eyes in such extreme detail was a feeling she wasn't quite ready to think about.

"I assume you know naught of crystal lore. Opals enhance the consciousness above and around the Earthly plane, and are known to induce visions and creativity, as well as independence and intense emotions," the fyrdwisa continued. "The eyes of the sierwen, in the legends, are opals as a mark of this gift. To have such vision and the fierce independence to simply *know* without abandon can only come to those born with eyes like this."

Aristoces put a hand to her chest. "I think it is time, Liluthuaé, that we told you of your legend. I hesitate to make this choice, both without the remainder of the Samnung knowing it is being made, and because I do not know that you are ready to hear it. However, if one waits for what is a perfect time, or waits until one feels ready, perhaps one never will be. And so, this seems as opportune a moment as any."

"Are you sure?" Trystane asked her, cocking an eyebrow.

She nodded. "I believe it is best the two of you do the telling. The Bright Star is Elven, and I come at this revelation from an outside perspective."

"Alright then," Trystane said, taking up the task he'd meant to give Aristoces. As he had done only a few hours earlier, he summoned a glass of reddish-hued spirits, and took a sip before beginning to speak.

"The legend of the Liluthuaé is one of the most ancient Elven stories," he started. "It goes back to the time the world that was not became the world that is. The Demiurge. Though various religions and peoples believe different things about how that happened, the general consensus is a deity or power of some sort took the nothing and from it, made a something that flourished and grew into Earth and beings. The original magical being, called Ceannairí Álfar, was born millennia ago and worshipped by the humans in parts of what is now Europe. Álfar was both male and female, able to shape-shift, and like the Elves of today, very powerful in the abilities to work alongside its natural surroundings. It is said Álfar could commune with the deities of old, through its work with Nature, and was — one night a year! — able to perform a ritual to split into two beings. One was male, one female. This ritual let the *male* properties of Álfar reproduce with its *female* properties. The first Elves, known collectively as the Fyrst, were thus borne, with all the physical characteristics of their mother/father and the blessings of magickal abilities gifted by the deities that participated in Álfar's ritual. We commemorate this ritual now as part of the Beltane celebrations.

"One of the Fyrst was born with an unusual gift to manipulate and give life to things made of pure natural spirit," Trystane said. "This was Ylda, who would craft newborn beings from soil, sky, and sea, and through the rituals taught by Álfar, breathe existence into them under the Beltane moon. Because of her gifts and her own creation, borne directly from the womb of Álfar and containing genes of deities, Ylda's beings were those of magic. She created winged Fairies and human-like beings, horned creatures and scaled merfolk. Blessed by the powers of Mother Nature and the deities of the world, Ylda became the foremost birthmother of the magical lineage we are all part of today. She traveled the world to spawn magic in each corner and crevice of Gaia, and occasionally when she was bored with creating human-like things, she'd make something wholly new and unknown to play in the animal kingdom."

Bridgette tilted her head — and oddly, she *felt* her eyes begin to do the colorshift, now that she knew she could do it. "Sorry for interrupting but … that's the ritual that Artur Cromwell used to create Heáhwolcen, isn't it? To create life out of nothing?"

Trystane blinked. He'd been lost in his recitation, and briefly forgot the reason he was reciting it to begin with. "Well. Yes, actually."

The Elfling nodded, feeling her eyes return to normal. She flicked a hand outward, a sign to let Trystane know to continue now that her question was answered.

"One Beltane moon, near the end of Ylda's life when she would choose to walk amongst the spirits and give her soul and body back to soil, sky, and sea, she created a most precious being," he went on. "It was rare she named her creations, choosing instead to send them outward to families and creatures to do the dedication. This one, though, she called Liluthuaé. It was her magnum opus; the being that took her the longest to make. But as she began the ritual to give Liluthuaé life, a deity spoke to Ylda and bade her give this being to the stars. There would come a time in the far, far future when the Elves would need Liluthuaé, and to birth it now would perhaps cause irreversible damage should it not live to see that time. By offering it to the stars, the spirits and deities would know when Liluthuaé should enter the Earthly plane and continue the work Ylda created it for. So she agreed, and for centuries since, the Elves celebrated the legend of this Bright Star at Yule during the winter solstice, the longest night of the year, believing Liluthuaé to be amongst the stars and most visible in that deepest of darks."

He paused. Collum, as an Elf, was quite familiar with the Liluthuaé legend, and Aristoces had heard it before when it was first brought to the Samnung. But Bridgette seemed to be processing all Trystane said.

The sky was darkening, they realized, and within seconds, a circle of floating lit candles surrounded the four of them. That brought Bridgette back to life, though she wasn't sure what to say.

Collum filled the silence. "It was forebode during my time as the fyrdestre, the understudy to the acting fyrdwisa, that Liluthuaé would be born among us. Of course, knowing the legend —Liluthuaé would only come when the Elves were in great need — the Samnung agreed it would be best not to spread word of its coming. To our knowledge, nobody was in danger, and we did not want to cause panic. Elves are long-lived, most immortal save death by irreversible wound or disease, so in theory … it might be hundreds of years before this risk or need of rescue came to light. But not long after it was believed the Liluthuaé had been born, King Hermann, Queen Lalora, and the fyrdwisa were attacked and killed. The interior wall of Palna had already been established. We were unsure precisely *what* the danger was, but we had a pretty vague idea that it had something to do with Craft Wizardry rearing its wicked head again."

"And then, many years after, it was revealed what, or who, rather, we should go looking for," Aristoces said quietly, her wise voice resonating in the wood. "That is a tale for later, as is the exact responsibilities of your task, should you choose to accept it. Bridgette, it is important that you understand what we will ask of you is a *choice* to assist in these circumstances. You are the Liluthuaé, but you are under no obligation to the Samnung, to Heáhwolcen, to the deities of old and new."

"What if, when y'all tell me what it is, I decide not to do it?" Bridgette said. She couldn't look them in the eye at all, fearing they would see the terror and trepidation her gaze now harbored. *All that risk and burden, and the only magic I can do is put two and two together because my eyes are opalescent? We're all doomed if they want something big and important from me.*

"Then that is your choice, and we will trust it is the right one," Aristoces said simply.

"But … but will everyone die? If I say no?" Bridgette pressed.

"Perhaps. Perhaps not. None of us here are diviners," the Fairy answered.

Bridgette sighed. "But you *will* tell me what I have to do, right? Specifically?"

"Yes." This time, Trystane answered. "We would never ask you to blindly accept to help us without knowing what you're getting into. Though, truth be told, we do not fully know ourselves, but you will not be left in the dark, Bright Star."

She nodded. "Okay then."

Collum stood, and the other three followed. "I'm going to take Bridgette back to Eckenbourne for the night. What was discussed here is now sealed."

A glimmering shield wafted from the center of their circle outward to the edge of the clearing, and before she realized what he was doing, Collum grasped Bridgette around the waist and evanesced her back to his living room. She choked on her breath and fell into an immediate coughing fit.

"A warning would have been nice," she gasped out, doubling over to catch some air. "You have *got* to stop doing that."

"But why, Starshine? It's fun to drive you crazy after you do things like figure out what I'm not supposed to tell you," Collum said wickedly. "Here."

He materialized a glass of ice water and handed it over to drink.

She gratefully took a long swallow. "Not my fault I'm a seer-thing, Bundy."

"*Sierwan*," he corrected. "Nehemi's going to lose her mind when she finds out."

Bridgette smiled at that. She may not harbor ill will towards any Fairies, but Nehemi … she barely knew the witch queen, and already knew that would not be any sort of lasting friendship.

"What are we doing tonight? And the rest of the week?" she asked, taking another sip of water.

"You have quite the packed schedule," Collum answered. "Tomorrow I'm taking you to all my favorite places in Eckenbourne, least of all my office. Tuesday we're spending in Fairevella, where Aristoces has planned an extravagant welcome for you. I have a Samnung meeting Wednesday, and against my better judgement I'm sending you into Endorsa to do whatever you please. The next day tour the University, which I hope you're just as excited to see as I am to show you. Friday is Ostara, Saturday we both get the joy of sitting with the Samnung again, and Sunday it's time to take you home."

Home. The thought seemed foreign to Bridgette. It was odd to remember that she'd been here not even a full day; that it wasn't *home* in Heáhwolcen, no matter how she felt about it. *Fuck that stupid therapist and all the stuff about getting attached too easily.*

"What therapist?" Collum asked. The look Bridgette shot him made him realize he'd unintentionally listened to her thoughts.

"It's nothing," Bridgette answered, too quickly. Collum raised an eyebrow, but she didn't elaborate. She'd tell him eventually. Maybe. "Anyway. That's a whole lot for a week, I guess. So much for taking a break during spring break, huh?"

The Elf chuckled. "I suppose. As for this evening, you have

options. We can stay here, and I'll cook you dinner, or we can go to a little café I know, and spoil one of the places I'd intended to take you tomorrow."

"I'll let you cook for me, Bundy," Bridgette said sweetly, feigning innocence. "Meanwhile, I'm going to indulge in this glorious bathtub that I seem to have been allotted as part of my temporary stay here."

Collum grinned. "As it is, so mote it be. You'll find towels under the cabinet and an assortment of beauty products at your disposal."

She wandered back to the guest room, the adjoining bathroom now beckoning to her. Like the rest of Collum's apartment, it was decorated simply, but tastefully, in masculine neutrals accented with metallics representing the four countries. Bridgette wondered if all the apartments in this building were decorated similarly, or if Collum designed this one himself. The fixtures of the large claw-footed bath, big enough to fit two people and deep enough for the Elfling to soak up to her shoulders if she wished, were the shining chrome of Bondrie, and the tub itself was made of slate-colored porcelain. As Collum advised, a stack of fluffy, light gray towels was harbored under the white cabinet, over which a giant mirror reflected the whole of the room, making it seem even bigger than it was.

I don't think I've ever been in a bathroom quite this nice, she thought. *If this is the guest bath, I wonder what his bathroom looks like.*

Then Bridgette blushed, realizing that was probably not a good thought to have, given Collum's constant swapping between toeing lines of flirtation, friendship, and work-only relationship. *I seriously hope he's not listening. Or maybe he* should *be listening.*

She removed her clothes and wrapped herself in one of the towels to turn the water on in the tub. Lost in thought as the bath filled with steaming hot liquid, Bridgette came out of her reverie suddenly when there was a knock at the door.

Fuck. Do I … go to the door in a towel or …

She cracked the door open just barely, and Collum stood there. "What?"

"I don't mean to disturb your relaxing evening, but I realized I forgot to put these in here for you," the Elf muttered awkwardly. "It's scented oils for the bath. I know it's been a long day, so I thought perhaps you could use some added soothing."

He closed his eyes and jammed a hand through the door opening to gift Bridgette a small basket of essential oil bottles. "The lavender is good for relaxation, and the rose petals … just read the labels, will you? Bath magic can be healing, and I think you need that today."

Bridgette stifled a laugh and accepted the basket. "Thanks, I think. Bath magic?"

"*Read the labels, please*," he emphasized, eyes still shut. "I have to go finish cooking dinner. I'll knock to let you know when it's ready. Do I need to bring you sleeping clothes?"

"No, Bundy, I have pajamas in here. Heaven forbid your houseguest wander around in a towel like some heathen Elf," Bridgette quipped.

He rolled his eyes — not that she could see; they were still closed — and shut the door. *What a mess this is going to be*, he thought.

Though Collum's magical abilities included spellwork, ritual meditation, and that somewhat annoying gift of thought-hearing, he had non-magical talents as well. Such as cooking, Bridgette found out an hour later. She emerged from the bath, surprisingly refreshed after following the instructions for "bath magic" on the bottle of lavender oil, and found the Elf searing a pork loin in a cast-iron pan.

"This smells ridiculous," she commented, helping herself to a seat at his wooden table. The long sides each had a bench for seating, with a chair at either end. "What are you making?"

"Pork loin with roasted potatoes, asparagus, and a lemon-dill butter sauce," Collum answered. He didn't look up from his work, meticulously eyeing the meat to ensure it reached the proper level of sear before popping it in the oven to finish. "I watched you enough to know that you don't have any food allergies or spiritual aversions to anything."

"That's fucking creepy, Bundy."

He turned around and flashed her a quick grin before returning to the cast iron. "Drinks are in the refrigerator. Help yourself."

She rose from the table and opened the door of the sleek fridge to find a plethora of sparkling waters, spirits, and other liquids with artfully designed labels of brands she did not recognize. "Um. Collum? I don't know what any of this is."

Collum laughed. He put the cast-iron in the oven, set an hourglass timer and walked to where she knelt. "Sparkling water, of course; you should know what that is. Those bottles are gingewinde. This is Fairy wine, which is delicious, but I don't know that either of us should drink anything spirit-like this week. And these bottles are just juices."

Bridgette glanced at him skeptically. "I'm not naïve enough to assume anything in this place is 'just' a juice, Collum."

"Rightly so, Starshine," he laughed. "They're spelled, of course. If you'd like juice, the watermelon-basil is best to pair with what we have tonight."

"What's that one spelled to be?" Bridgette asked.

"Try it and find out."

Bridgette stuck her tongue out at him, but grabbed a glass bottle anyway. Returning to the table, she opened the cap and sipped ... and started to feel lighter. *That's weird,* she thought, closing her eyes and drinking more. She liked this feeling.

Her knees hit the bottom of the kitchen table with a loud crack, and Bridgette gasped audibly as she fell hard onto the bench again.

"What the *hell* did you give me?!" she screeched, holding both hands to the bench's edge. "I was ... I was *floating!*"

Collum, who'd been at the stove, turned to face her. He was doubled over in laughter. "No you weren't, silly. That elixir just alleviates tension and brings peaceful energy."

"Collum, I'm not joking. Watch," Bridgette commanded, taking another sip. But this time, nothing happened. She remained seated on the bench, as if she'd imagined the whole thing.

"See? No levitating," the Elf said, still chuckling. "But do you feel better? Between that and the bath magic, I'd assume you're much more relaxed than you have been all day."

"I mean, I am, but ... I swear I floated off this bench." Bridgette glanced skeptically at the bottle. *What on Earth. I did not imagine my knees slamming into the table. That hurt.*

The rest of their dinner together was wholly uneventful — she barely spoke a word as she shoveled the meal in her mouth. Collum had a gift for making complex flavors emerge from each bite, and she could scarcely believe he was a spy instead of a chef. He rolled his eyes when she mentioned that, and told her to keep eating.

"I didn't make a dessert, but I can if you'd like," he said.

"This is ... I don't think the English language has words for how good all of this is. I'm so full, but I also can't stop eating it," she replied.

Collum smiled softly. "Thank you," he said. "I'm going to clean up and go to bed — you should get some rest, too. We've got a bit of a day tomorrow. I'll knock to wake you."

She nodded and scooped up the last forkful. "May I take another one of those juices, or maybe a water, to bed? Or do you have a thing against drinking between the sheets?"

He shrugged. "Whatever you'd like."

She disappeared down the hall, another one of the watermelon-basil juices in her hand. Bridgette wasn't tired at all, but she was determined to figure out what happened earlier. She hadn't imagined having floated, but when she tried to make it happen again, she didn't budge. She closed the door to her room and sat on the bed, staring at the fresh bottle.

Why did I move the first time, but not the second? Bridgette thought, trying to recall the sensation and the moment she felt so light.

Suddenly she felt her eyes do what she'd begun to think of as "the weird shifty thing."

"Holy shit." And she knew exactly what happened.

Bridgette reached for the bottle, took off the cap and drank, eyes closed, recalling that feeling of weightlessness and lightness of spirit. This time, she knew what was coming, and she welcomed the feeling as her body began to rise off the bed. It had nothing to do with the juice —the elixir simply wakened her to her ability to feel this sensation. All she had to do was call it forth.

Collum? she thought to him, wondering if he could hear her through the walls. She didn't even know where he was in the apartment. *If you can hear me, come here please.*

He was at the door almost instantaneously and knocked. "What's wrong?"

Come inside.

"Bridgette …" he started to protest, unsure why she was calling to him like this.

Come. Inside.

He did. And let out a yelp.

"You can *fly*," he breathed, clutching a hand to his heart. "What in the deity-forsaken seven hells … How …"

Bridgette shrugged from her perch, six feet above her comforter, where she sat cross-legged in the air. "I guess so. Bring me more of those juices. I want to see what other magic I suddenly have."

"This is insane," Collum said. He still hadn't moved from the doorway, hardly believing what was in front of him. "Magic doesn't ... this isn't *possible*."

"HA!" Bridgette laughed and almost lost her balance, but wiggled back into place. "Nothing's impossible here. Is this not like, a thing?"

"It is not 'a thing,'" Collum replied. "Flight for non-winged beings is ... rarer than rare. Some witches have the ability to spell themselves upwards, but this is not the same thing at all. How are you doing this?"

"I just ... I mean, I'm not really flying; it's more like I'm floating ..." her voice trailed off. "It was that sierwan thingy. I knew I could do it, so I did."

"Try flying then. Fly to me."

"What is this, 'Peter Pan' again?" Bridgette said, raising an eyebrow.

"I want you to try," Collum commanded.

Bridgette twisted her head to one side. She knew how to get *up*, but going elsewhere while already in the air seemed ... questionable. *Do I flap my arms like wings or something?*

Just like the knowledge came before, it came again now. She could flap her arms as an easier way to alight in the sky, to provide more push upwards, but moving in a direction was more of a breaststroke. So she did, much to both of their surprise, and almost fell straight back to the ground.

She levitated a few inches off the floor, her eyes level now with Collum's. "That was ... unexpected," she gasped. "I can *fly*."

The Elf became serious. "We are keeping this knowledge between us. The Samnung can know you're a sierwan; that's helpful to your task. But ... I don't know that *this* is good for all to know."

"That's fine. It can be our little secret," Bridgette said, and without knowing exactly how she managed it, grabbed his hand and pulled him into the air with her. "You're not nearly as heavy as I thought you'd be."

Collum was frozen in midair, not sure he'd fall if he moved. "You lifted me into the air."

"I did!" She was delighted with herself. "I'm weightless, and now so are you. But if I let go —" she moved her hand away, then picked him back up before he fell fully "— then you go back to the ground."

"It takes much to astonish me, and I think you have reached that level."

"Are you scared?" Bridgette asked.

"Scared? Not quite. Floating here in disbelief? Absolutely. You are the most astonishing being I've ever met, Starshine."

Bridgette beamed. "I think this is the first time I've ever astonished anyone. I'm going to put you down now."

She tilted her body forward a bit to make them both descend, until his feet touched the ground. Then she pushed both arms down to her side to propel herself upward again, where she resumed her cross-legged position. Collum felt unsteady, as if he'd been on a boat for hours and obtained sea-legs.

"I want to fly outside now," Bridgette said, feeling oddly sure of herself and this newfound ability she'd had for perhaps two hours. "Please?"

"Not tonight, Bridgette." The business tone had returned to his voice. "I don't think that's a good idea yet."

"Pleeeease?"

"No."

"But —"

"No."

"Fine. You can go now, lame sauce."

"'Lame sauce?' Bridgette, you're going to find a way out of this apartment the moment I go to bed, aren't you?"

" … No."

"Liar," Collum laughed, giving in despite himself. "Lying is *not* one of your abilities. Fine. But you're not flying out of here; you can fly when we get somewhere safe. I'm taking you back to Maluridae Wood to do this. No one else will be there, and we can seal what we do inside the circle."

"Yay!" Bridgette squealed. She instinctively reached her arms above her head, and connected her palms together, which slowly twisted her downward until she reached the bed. "I should probably put on real clothes, shouldn't I?"

"I should have someone make you a feathered cape just for kicks," Collum said. "But yes, that would be ideal. It's chilly out. Come to the living room when you're ready to depart."

A few minutes later, clad in leggings and a light sweater — which seemed to be the Elven fashion; leggings and long tops of various fabrics with boots or sandals — Bridgette appeared, giddy with excitement. Collum looked at the Elfling, her lilac eyes shimmering with anticipation, and shook his head in exasperation. She was an enigma to him: so dedicated and strong with her sierwan gift, but yet equally unsure of herself and childlike in many ways. Her excitement at the thought of flying, at the thought of this being their little secret, made him laugh … and made him feel some smattering of joy, too.

He evanesced her to the clearing where they'd been earlier and summoned forth floating candles to light the wood. "Show me how you ascend."

Bridgette called upon that feeling of lightness and felt herself begin to rise. She raised her arms out to either side of her, then pushed them in toward her torso, propelling her upward. "Like this. And I think — I can power myself more to go higher and faster based on the force I use with my arms, or if I have a running start and jump into the air while doing so."

"And you said changing directions was more like a breaststroke motion?"

"Yep," Bridgette said. In answer, she turned her body in midair, leaned her chest forward and pulled her arms out in front and around her, which pushed her into that direction. "Although it feels … unnatural to do that this way. Inefficient."

"I surmise that with practice, you'll be able to control this ability and it won't require the same physical exertion as it does now," Collum suggested.

Bridgette nodded from her perch, several feet above his head. "That makes sense."

"I want you to come down, and just tonight, let's practice ascending and descending," Collum instructed. "Try what you said before, about the different ways you can change your speed and power."

So she did. For the next two hours, Bridgette exhausted herself and fascinated him with varying speeds and methods of rising into and lowering from the sky. Sometimes she brought Collum with her; other times, she used her own bodyweight.

"Collum," she gasped finally, hitting the ground so hard it shook, following a particularly fast descent, "I want to learn how to fight. I mean, you know, if I decide to stay and help."

"Fight, Starshine?"

"Well, yeah. I know you don't want anyone knowing I can fly, but wouldn't it be good to have someone who can fly and shoot arrows or something?" As the words left her mouth, Bridgette cringed. *That sounds horribly dramatic and stupid, like something a kid would say.*

"That's what the Fairy Mileta is for," Collum replied. "You'd be better suited using this gift in a different manner, I feel."

"What's the point of having all of these gifts if I can't use them?" she countered. *Guess it wasn't a stupid suggestion after all.*

"Bridgette, have you ever *seen* a battle of any kind?"

"Yeah, of course. In movies and on TV."

"Then you are aware that it's generally not a free-for-all, and there are ranks and orders and front lines, correct?" Collum said gently.

"… Oh. That's true."

He put a hand on her shoulder and looked her in the eye. "I have no doubt that you'd be a fine archer-mage of the skies, Starshine. However, it is one thing to have those skills, and another to have those skills and be trained to use them in a battle formation, should such be required of you. Unfortunately I do not believe such time will exist in the immediate future, not for what we will ask of you."

She bit the inside of her cheek, thinking hard.

"But," the Elf continued, "I promise that if you choose to

stay, you will learn to fight. Swords, hand-to-hand, and I anticipate you'll rather enjoy the art of Cath Draíochta."

"What's that?"

Collum grinned. "A battle of witchcraft, of course."

~ 17 ~

Bridgette sighed. "I'm sure I would, if I was able to *be* a witch."

"You've been here for less than a day and already had two magical abilities become known. You're a sierwan, and you can fly. I'm sure the ability to cast spells will appear soon," Collum said lightly. "Come now. It's quite late. We should both get rest. You'll probably be sore tomorrow; I have a salve that can help."

He waved a hand to seal their secret inside the clearing and evanesced them back to the apartment.

The Elf's promised knock woke her earlier than she hoped it would, just a few hours later. But upon opening her eyes, Bridgette's senses adjusted themselves and she found herself smelling bacon and eggs cooking. She also found that it ached to move a muscle. Her whole body was indeed sore from two solid hours of alighting and landing.

Bring me some of that salve. Please? she sent the thought to Collum. Even her jaw was tender; she must have clenched it while concentrating on staying in the sky last night. *Everything hurts.*

He arrived a few moments later, knocking again. "Come in," she said.

"I do hope you're clothed properly," he said, only halfway joking. She knew better than to push the boundaries he'd set, or so he hoped.

"Duh, Bundy. Don't be a punk," Bridgette said, slightly annoyed. "Just give me that stuff, please."

She tried to reach out a hand toward him, but grimaced as a dull ache went up her arm. Collum chuckled and came to sit on the edge of the bed. "Allow me, Starshine."

He unscrewed the container and a mild, almost coconutty scent entered the air. "Belladonna," he answered Bridgette's unasked question. "Mixed with a few other things, but it'll help."

Starting at her fingertips, Collum began massaging the salve into her skin and muscles. Bridgette groaned in a combination of relief and pain as she felt it work its — actual — magic. She felt ease and warmth begin to spread from every millimeter Collum touched.

"Fuuuuck, that feels amazing," she moaned. "Please don't stop."

"I'm only doing your hands and your arms so you can do everywhere else yourself, but nice try," he murmured.

"I can't reach my back?" Bridgette pointed out innocently.

Collum rolled his eyes. "Fine. Your hands, your arms, and your back. The rest, you're on your own while I make sure your breakfast doesn't burn."

She rolled over in answer, and he slid his hands under her soft sleepshirt to apply generous amounts of the salve on her shoulders and down her spine.

"When you were holding yourself up, you must have tensed your core. This entire area is taut," Collum observed.

Bridgette nodded. "And I clenched my jaw, too. Talking hurts, even."

"Poor, poor little Liluthuaé," the Elf crooned teasingly.

Talking hurt, but she still managed to turn her head to the side and stick her tongue out at him as he worked. "Punk."

He gave Bridgette's right shoulder a mean little squeeze, causing her to yelp, before getting off the bed. "The rest is up to you. I'll keep your morning meal warm for you whenever you're ready."

Bridgette picked up where Collum left off, working the soothing salve into her torso, neck, jaw, and finally down her legs. She didn't quite feel one-hundred percent, but the range of motion was significantly improved already. She eased herself out of bed and stretched, grimacing again at the movement, but knew it was essential to keeping those muscles from tightening again. The smells from the kitchen beckoned to her, and she shuffled out and down the hallway.

Collum was already dressed, similarly to how he'd been the day before, though his black tunic was sleeveless and laced up the front today. His leggings were thicker and looked suspiciously like denim, and his knee-high boots were black. His dark brown curls were loose and slightly damp, as if he'd just stepped from the shower, and only had time to run a towel through his hair. Bridgette found herself staring at him sitting at the table, a mug of hot tea in one hand as he mulled over a newspaper with the other.

She coughed a bit to alert him to her presence. "Sorry to interrupt. I can get my own, if you tell me where plates and cups are?"

Collum barely glanced up, but waved a hand in the general direction of cabinets by the stove. "Help yourself."

That's a bit dismissive, but whatever, she thought, fighting off annoyance. *This dude with his magic hands and his amazing ability to make me feel totally ignored, all in the same hour ...*

Bridgette decided then that she'd eat standing up, then go shower. If he didn't want her around while he read the news, she wasn't going to make him deal with her presence. It was her least favorite feeling, that sense of not being good or worthy enough, and around Collum it seemed to come up more often than not.

Three bites of scrambled eggs later, Bridgette found she didn't have much of an appetite anyway. She put the plate in the sink and walked to the bathroom, head held high as she tried to ignore the rising tears at the nagging idea she was just a nuisance to Collum. The thoughts plagued her through her shower, no matter how long she stood under the water to drown them out with a more rational portion of her brain.

When she finally emerged and wrapped herself in another fluffy towel, Bridgette was surprised to see that a note had been laid on the counter next to her clothes. It was from Collum — "Had to run a quick errand. Be back soon; try not to burn the place down while I'm gone." She rolled her eyes, then balled up the note and tossed it in the wastebasket. In the back of her mind, Bridgette vaguely remembered Aristoces telling the Samnung to reconvene this morning. She supposed Collum had gone off to meet with them, or at least make an appearance.

He wasn't back yet when she finished doing her hair and getting dressed, so she helped herself to exploring the rest of his abode. The only rooms she hadn't seen were his — the office, the bedroom, and the bathroom. She chanced a quick peek inside what was evidently his bedroom and was wholly unsurprised to see that the stately four-poster bed was made with military corners. Other than slightly more intricate furnishings and a larger space, the bedroom was quite similar to her own. The primary difference lay in that it had a dark-stained wooden door within that led to the office. She grinned and stepped forward to open it, anticipating the office to have a desk, a calendar, whatever Elves used instead of computers.

But what lay behind that door was otherworldly.

Bridgette gasped. She'd stepped from Collum's bedroom into a forest.

The floor under her bare feet was a carpet of soft, dew-damp moss and lichen. There were no walls: the forest seemed to go on infinitely; the ceiling was the sky outside. A soft breeze whispered through her hair, blowing back the reddish-blonde tendrils that hadn't quite made it into the hasty French braid she'd done a few minutes before. She was surrounded by trees, shrubs, and flowers, along with the faint tinkling cacophony of wind chimes, buzzing pollinators, and birdsong. It was, counting Fairevella, the most beautiful place Bridgette had ever seen. A large Fairy Circle of white-capped mushrooms lay to her right, and looped over the branch of one of the trees was an octagonal-shaped shelf laden with brightly colored crystals and gems of countless facets. It alone was still in the wind.

She wandered along what she presumed to be a pathway that led deeper into the trees, wondering if she was still inside or not. Air plants floated above her head, bobbing slightly in the wind, held inside shimmering glass containers of varying shapes and sizes. A large bird flew far overhead, and the further she walked, the louder the sounds of bubbling water became. Bridgette happened upon a creek bed as the source of that nourishing sound. Next to it, in a small clearing, was a worn area of dark, velvety soil. It was encircled by a lavish set of five-foot tall bushes unlike anything she'd laid eyes on before. Their leaves were fragrant and vaguely heart-shaped, each a hue ranging between pale lavender and nearly black aubergine. Stems of rich magenta and turquoise flowers rose betwixt the leaves, and of all things, a completely normal-looking blue and black butterfly was flitting about. Bridgette was mesmerized. She felt called to the little clearing and helped herself onto the ground, sitting cross-legged to study the insect, its iridescent wings an odd reminder of the Earth she'd left behind — had it only been yesterday morning?

She called up the lightness and felt herself float into the air, eye level with where the butterfly was perched on one of the floral stems. She watched intently as its little tongue uncurled to sip nectar from the flowers, and deep magenta pollen magnetized itself to its legs as it moved. She tilted her head sideways, just a bit, for a better look — but then, as if it realized she was there observing, the butterfly alighted and floated on the breeze toward her. She felt the smile as it warmed her face at the same time the butterfly came to land on an arm she didn't realize she'd stretched out for it.

What a curious place, she thought, the soft smile continuing to play on her lips. *I think I'm in love.*

"I think he likes you, too."

The voice startled Bridgette so thoroughly she nearly fell flat to the ground, but caught herself mid-plunge and whirled around in midair.

"Collum!" she cried out. "Holy shit, *how* are you so good at sneaking up on me?"

He laughed. "I should say you gave me a fright as well, Starshine. I was not prepared to come home and find not only that you weren't anywhere inside, but that you'd wandered into my office."

"Office. This is *not* an office, it's a fucking paradise."

"You truly have no filter, do you?" Collum chuckled. "I pride myself on making my work environment as pleasant an experience as possible, so yes, my office happens to be quite unusual compared to Earthly, human standards."

"You called this … your home office, and said today we would be going to your *actual* office?" Bridgette was slightly confused, but also pretty sure she was fine spending the whole day exploring this magical, not-quite-real forest of her companion's.

"Yes. The *actual* office of the fyrdwisa and fyrdestre is in the government building in Aelchanon, our capital city. It's a formal meeting space, though I do hope you find it equally enthralling," he said, somewhat dryly. "I rarely use it but thought it might be of interest to you as we explore the country today. Plus, I told Trystane I would show it to you, so I unfortunately owe him that promise."

"I want to spend all day here," she whispered, and reached out a hand to pull him into the air with her. "This is so … it's wonderful here, Collum. Can't I just stay?"

I wish, too. His lips didn't move, but Bridgette swore she heard him speak — and the shock caused her to drop them both.

"What?" he asked, alarmed. The look on her face was of both wonderment and disbelief. "Are you alright?"

Say something to me, she directed him with her thoughts. *I think … I think I heard you.*

Collum raised a brow. *There's no way. That's impossible.*

"No," Bridgette said, aloud this time. "It's not impossible. I don't know how it *is* possible, but I for sure can hear you. Tell me a secret and I'll repeat it back to you."

The Elf wasn't as confident, but he obliged: *I could hear you in the Samnung chamber yesterday. I do not hear such in that room. Until yesterday, when I heard you.*

Bridgette's brow furrowed. "Is it because I'm the Liluthuaé, that you could hear me?" she asked.

Collum resumed speaking as well. "I do not know. I do not know how this is possible. I've never been able to speak to anyone mind-to-mind like this."

Bridgette's heart was nearly beating out of her chest. "We're going to have *so* much fun playing pranks on everyone …"

"No, we are most assuredly not!" the Elf laughed. "Maybe Trystane. But no one else. I don't think it's a good idea for this to get out."

"Oh, come on!" Bridgette whined. "So I can't tell anyone I can fly, and now I can't tell anyone that I can talk to you without actually talking? Where's the fun in that?"

"The fun, Starshine, is that I get to teach you to hone these abilities."

"Can we practice them here? Or should we go back to Maluridae Wood?" Bridgette asked, scuffing a toe lightly in the soil.

"I suppose since you snooped and found my secret place, the cat's out of the bag, and we can practice here," Collum sighed reluctantly.

"I didn't mean to snoop …"

"Yes, you absolutely did. And I forgive you, but from now on, please *ask* someone before you open doors to their private chambers, will you? Something tells me anyone else you meet here is not going to be as easily giving grace to curious halfling minds."

Bridgette stuck her tongue out at him. "Fine. I promise. And I *am* sorry. Sort of. Sorry for exploring without permission. Not sorry that *this* is what I found."

He offered her his arm again in that gentlemanly gesture, but his smile was warm. "I'm not sure if I'm sorry you found it either, actually. Come now. Let me show you my home."

~ 18 ~

Collum led Bridgette out of his building on foot. When they stepped outside, it was onto a pebbled pathway surrounded by various conifer trees. A light misty rain fell around them, and fog was swirling. It was serene, silent but for the sound of those miniscule water droplets. Eerie, as if they were on top of a mountain alone with the Universe.

As Collum walked her down the path, she noticed the fog parted to make way, then closed back up behind them. *I hope we don't get too wet,* she thought, annoyed at the idea of arriving to the Elven capital soaked to the bone with mountain mist. *I wish it would stop.*

The two didn't say a word, nor hear each other's thoughts, as they made their way down the path toward a wider road. Bridgette found she didn't feel wet at all, despite being in the fog and mist. She wondered if the weather here was spelled to prevent Elves from being exposed to the elements instead of simply experiencing them, or perhaps Elves had innate magic that repelled it themselves.

Are you dry? she thought to Collum, afraid that if she spoke it would somehow break the serenity. *The weather out here is so different than it was in your … office.*

I am dry, Collum thought back, still intrigued by this ability to converse with her without speaking a word. He wondered how far a distance such a gift would travel. Typically, he needed to be in the same room with someone — unless it was someone with whom he had a covenant, which acted as a mental bridge — to hear their thoughts.

Why is it raining out here, but not in there? Bridgette thought in question.

Because my office is mine, and I happen to be in a good mood when I'm there. This weather is a bit morose for my taste, to be surrounded by it. Thus, I do not allow it to enter my place of solace, Collum responded. *Why does it matter if we're dry or not? It's just a bit of mist, it'll dry up long before we reach the Caisleán. The capitol building, that is. It is odd though, now you mention it, for the mist to not be touching us.*

"Hmm," Bridgette murmured. They'd reached the road by now, and Bridgette caught a hint of sunshine up ahead. She felt the gears start to whir in her brain, as if her sierwan gift was coming to her, but she shook it off. *Weird.*

It also seemed weird to her that no one else was out and about on the road, contrary to the previous day's visit to Fairevella. That, Collum explained, was because as fyrdwisa, he'd been granted access to a private route for coming and going. Especially with the concerns about Palna, the Samnung hadn't wanted his activity monitored — intentionally or by casual passerby.

"That's why the fog opens and closes behind us, then?" Bridgette surmised.

"Indeed," he grinned shrewdly. "I do love our beings, and I take my job to protect them very seriously. Do not misinterpret that. However, the position of fyrdwisa brings with it a certain … level of heaviness that is best dealt with in my own time and ways. It can be difficult to process and work through situations when one's solitude is constantly battered by well-meaning, but rather annoyingly constant, presence and pressure from those who wish to gossip or beg advice."

"Ah," Bridgette said, hoping she wasn't any part of that "annoyingly constant presence and pressure."

He stopped and looked her in the eye, grasping one shoulder tightly. Bridgette winced, still in some pain from the previous night of flying. "Bridgette Conner. Starshine, you are in no way annoying or pressurizing, and I take great pleasure in your constant presence right now. Do you understand? You're alright."

She nodded meekly. *Eavesdropper, you punk.*

He winked in response, and they continued down the road a few feet. Bridgette was surprised to see a pair of horses standing next to a wooden post marked with an elaborate golden "E".

"Are these for us?"

"They are," Collum answered. His eyes widened, and a slightly guilty expression came over his features. "I did not think to ask if you knew how to ride. I am sorry, Starshine. There are other ways, if you'd prefer."

Bridgette eyed the horses warily, unsure how to proceed, but didn't want to back down from a challenge. Not in front of Collum, and not when she was still alleged to have some death-defying task up ahead. *I can ride a damn horse.*

She took a deep breath, met Collum's gaze and said, "Let's do it. You can teach me, right?"

He demonstrated how to mount and hold the reins properly. The horse had a Western-esque saddle she recognized from movies, but the leather was deep brown with a regal quality. It was stamped with images of intricate interlocking knots, and adorned with gold and wood trim. Bridgette sat atop her horse and willed herself to be still, to not shake or show fear. Collum swung a leg easily onto the saddle of his horse, its coat so shiny black it was nearly blue. Her own mount was golden, and as Bridgette chanced a look down at the road, her eyes caught what was situated on her horse's poll.

It was not, she realized in awe, a horse at all.

"Holy shit," she breathed. She wanted desperately to reach out and touch the small twisting horn of varying shades of gold that wound up between the Unicorn's two ears, nested in the part of its fluffy platinum-blonde bangs, but she was afraid if she moved, she'd fall off.

"We *do* have horses, of course," Collum said, grinning. That same grin he had whenever something particularly amazed his companion about Heáhwolcen. "However, being part of the Samnung has a few benefits. This is Eloise, and this is Mithrilken."

Hearing their names, the golden and blue-black Unicorns straightened their necks a bit.

"I'm sitting on top of a *Unicorn*," Bridgette whispered.

"Yes, you are," the golden Unicorn whispered back mischievously, and Bridgette nearly lost her balance. "And we can talk, and hear you, Liluthuaé. But do nay worry; for we do nay spill the secrets with which we have been entrusted by our rídend — our sworn partners."

"I think I need a drink," Bridgette said, then switched to

speaking mind-to-mind. *I'm sitting on top of a talking Unicorn, Collum. I am about to* ride *a talking Unicorn.*

Yes, Starshine, you are. Eloise will take care of you. She's yours — a gift from the Samnung.

Mine? Bridgette could scarcely belief it. *Like … but I can't own a being like a Unicorn, can I? That seems like a trafficker or something.*

Not to own, Collum corrected. *But as your partner. Ride her, care for her, know her this week, and if you stay; if you* choose to stay, *of course, hers will be a covenant with you that breaks only upon death.*

That's morbid as fuck, Bundy.

Collum laughed, a jovial sound in the stillness of the misty air around them. "Come now, Starshine. Eloise won't let you fall off, but your ride will go significantly smoother if you grip her with your full legs, and guide as needed with your knees and calves." He clicked his tongue, and the four were off.

Mithrilken, whose horn was black rimmed with gold, and the Elf made a foreboding pair that morning, what with Collum's black tunic and boots melding into the Unicorn's blue-black hair. They seemed as of one body, moving easily together. Bridgette supposed that had to do partially with their covenant, but also with the time they'd ridden together, and the fact that Mithrilken wasn't a horse that needed guidance. Unicorns weren't pets or livestock, they were *beings* that chose whether or not to have a rídend.

"What do the Unicorns do that don't have riders?" Bridgette asked Eloise.

The Unicorn snorted. "Use the proper words, please, Liluthuaé. *Riders* are those who use equine forms for their own purposes. Rídend are those who breathe alongside Unicorns for life, working together for a better world. No Unicorn has a rider, but those who do nay choose to have rídend stay in their colonies. Some will fight, should need come of it. We are powerful beings in our own ways of physical force and metaphysical magic. Some choose to become téitheoir, healers, and work alongside beings of all kinds who chose that path. Though we cannay perform healing rituals in the same manner, our presence can provide strength, and our hair, horn, and hooves contain matla, the mighty power of the ancient ones, to be used in ritual as ingredients. Other Unicorns choose to simply *be*, and roam the world above the world for all their days."

"I see," Bridgette said. "I'm sorry for saying the wrong word, Eloise. Thank you for not kicking me off."

Mithrilken tossed his radiant mane and looked at her. "Eloise would do no such thing. She is but a young foal, barely old enough to take a rídend. It is a great honor for her to be with you, Liluthuaé."

"How long have you two been together?" Bridgette asked, aware that the question was of a relationship far deeper and far more intimate than any she'd experienced. Yet, anyway.

"Many decades," the blue-black Unicorn said lightly. "The fyrdwisa became my rídend when he was appointed fyrdestre."

"How many Unicorns have rídend?" the Elfling asked, still slightly baffled by the idea that she was talking to animals. Or animal-like beings, perhaps, was a better way to think of them.

"Many," Mithrilken answered. "One must be a great leader or of Elven blood to be rídend, though. Trystane, you have met. The fyrdestre, you will meet today. Various other leaders, including the Fairy ambassador to Eckenbourne, though as he is a winged being, his annwyl is more a symbolic gesture than most."

"Annwyl?" *So many new words to learn.*

"Yes. You are rídend. We are annwyl," Mithrilken said.

Each moment she spent in Heáhwolcen, Bridgette found something novel to process. Even the route they took to Aelchanon and the Caisleán now seemed otherworldly.

It IS otherworldly, she reminded herself. The road was hard-packed earth, wide enough for two carriages to pass with several feet between. It was lined on either side with faceted rocks in shades of gray and brown. On their left was a forest, and to their right seemed to be farmland: endless vistas of golden and green fields spanned the horizon to that side.

They hadn't passed anyone on the road yet, and Bridgette thought that mildly off-putting, although they'd finally reached what seemed to be the edge of the misty rain. The clouds parted slightly in the distance to allow rays of sunshine to pour through, illuminating the golden pastures and sparkling shades of lemon and lime onto the trees.

Why haven't we passed anyone yet? she thought to Collum.

I purposely reside on the outskirts of Aelchanon, in a more rural part of the country. Not a lot of beings live in this area. With it having so much farmland, usually only those who raise livestock and crops are here. We'll find more evidence of civilization the closer in we get, he answered. *Why are you speaking to me mind-to-mind?*

Bridgette blushed, glad the Unicorns couldn't see. *Because I am weirded out talking in front of them and knowing they can hear me. I'd rather talk just to you.*

The Elf smiled slightly to himself and gazed ahead. Because Bridgette had no riding experience, they were taking the road at a moderately-paced walk. It wasn't far from his apartment to Aelchanon, only an hour if he was to ride himself and be able to canter most of the way, but the reduced speed extended the journey. He realized it had been an age since he'd been able to take the road so slowly. Before he spent those months on Earth searching for the Liluthuaé, Collum didn't take time during the past two years to pay much attention to the land he'd chosen to live in. He was either at his apartment or at a government building, and his preferred method of travel was to evanesce. It was rare he even brought Mithrilken on something that wasn't a joyride or ceremony. Though, he thought, perhaps this first ride of Bridgette's was a ceremony of sorts.

That makes good hearing, Starshine, he thought to her. *I rather enjoy talking to you too, though I must say, it is still unusual for me to be able to communicate in such a way as this.*

Bridgette stifled a laugh — she didn't want to raise any questions from the Unicorns — and thought to him, *Why do you think you can? What makes me different than anyone else, other than this pre-destined world savior nonsense?*

It's not nonsense, Bridgette, Collum shot her a look. *You are destined to have a very important task ahead, and for the thousandth time, only if you choose to accept it. I do not know if you being the Liluthuaé has anything to do with our ability to communicate like this.*

You said earlier you were taking me to the University at some point. Could we ask a student or professor there about it? Bridgette thought back in question.

Collum considered this suggestion. *Yes, I think we could do that. Though it would behoove us to perhaps not mention it as a gift we share. Perhaps present it as curiosity to see if what we have is possible, and if so, how it may be. Simply a new-found being wondering if my gift can work both ways.*

Bridgette nodded in approval. *I like that.*

"Where all are you taking me today?" she asked, switching to spoken conversation.

"I told you, my favorite places. And a few less favorite places, which is why we're going to the Caisleán first," the Elf said. "It's a beautiful building, of course, don't mistake my thoughts there. However, a government building is not the most enjoyable attraction Eckenbourne has to offer, that's all."

"Where else?" she coaxed.

"You really do not give up, do you?" Collum laughed.

She flashed him a twin to the wicked grin of his that made her heart smolder. "I'm the Liluthuaé. I'm not supposed to give up, right?"

The Elf fought the urge to push her off her Unicorn.

Mithrilken and Eloise taught Bridgette much about Unicorn culture in Heáhwolcen during the rest of the journey. Even on Earth — and, to Bridgette's surprise, the Other Realms in Time that existed thanks to magic — Unicorns were partial to the various collectives of Elves. Most of the Elves in the world above the world came from habitats of mountain ranges and green forests, though elsewhere there lived Elves who thrived in the cold and, alternately, the warm sunshine. There were once also the Ealdaelfen, Mithrilken cautioned. He explained the Ealdealfen were a mysterious sect of "dark Elves" who practiced ill-intent ritual magic and spellcasting.

"So they're like, the Elven equivalent of Craft wizards?" Bridgette asked.

"A bit," Collum admitted. "But whereas Craft Wizardry is alive and well today, or so we think, the Ealdaelfen are purely mythological. Tales told to Elven children to keep them obeying their parents. Though they *did* exist millennia ago, Elven legend assures us the Ealdaelfen are long gone."

His certainty at this point struck the Elfling, and the knowledge of why came to her quickly. He saw her eyes become opalescent.

Collum ... Bridgette thought urgently to him. *They aren't gone. If there are Elves in Palna, the Ealdaelfen are very much alive and well.*

The Elf stared at her. *We will tell Trystane the moment we reach the Caisleán*, he thought back.

She nodded a silent response, eyes widened. In the short time since it had been given a name, Bridgette realized her sierwan gift was an intuition of sorts. She'd *always* had a strong intuition. Even seeing Collum that first time in the diner, she knew there was something to have her hackles up about. Though thankfully he wasn't the dangerous serial killer she joked about him being, he *was* a powerful creature in the physical, emotional, and magical senses. Being in Heáhwolcen, though, the sierwan gift gave her intuition about things she was wholly new to. This knowing about the dark Elves, when just a few days ago Elves didn't exist to her, was part of the ability that would take longest to get used to. She tried hard to put it out of her mind entirely for the time being: no need to focus on it until she could speak freely with Collum and Trystane.

A few minutes later, Bridgette noticed a shift in the scenery on the road. The forest was still there, now on both sides, and she could have sworn she heard the distant wailing of bagpipes. Butterflies and birds began to fill the air with movement, and the flora became slightly more magical than the wood they passed thus far.

"Look closer," Collum urged her quietly.

She did: what she was seeing wasn't just forest anymore, it was the yards and dwellings of Elven homesteads. Some built directly as treehouses, some that seemed to be mounds rising straight from the ground with trees and garden planted on what should be roofs. Others had a more traditionally human aesthetic that resembled log cabins or homes with plank siding. Each one was beautiful and seemed to blend perfectly into its surroundings. One wood-planked home was carved to look as though it was made of leaves rimmed in gold, and its chimney was patched with irregular shapes of vertically growing moss and lichen. Another home, one that looked like a mound, had been planted with a rainbow of flowers that cascaded from purple pansies at the top to blue hydrangea, then waves of English ivy and poufs of yellow and orange chrysanthemums. At the base of the home were brilliantly red roses, and the yard itself a grass with a distinctly maroon hue on one side of the blades. Bridgette realized Eloise had stopped walking so she could gaze upon it.

"You have nay seen a home like this before?" the Unicorn asked. Bridgette could hear the smile in her voice — Eloise, like Collum, seemed to take great pleasure in seeing their charge's amazement at the magic of this world.

"I haven't," the Elfling said, all thoughts of dark Elves gone from her mind now that she faced such majesty. "It's so … the rainbow is just seamless. It's like everything was perfectly planned to exist in harmony with everything around it."

"That is the Elven way," Eloise said. "The fyrdwisa will be

pleased you have taken to it so quickly, I think. The Elves do nay like to disturb Nature, but to be in balance with it. To live their lives alongside it rather than take it over. Though many humans on Earth come from a colonizing spirit, the desire to *own* and to *claim*, and unfortunately there are many a witch and wizard who fall prey to that mentality too, Elves and Fairies are quite opposite. It is their mission to preserve and protect."

"I see," Bridgette said. She wasn't quite sure she truly *saw*, per se, but the more time she spent here, she had no doubt she would. She understood to a certain extent that mindset about colonization — for years now, there had been discussions between human leaders and activists about whether or not ancient explorers and those who claimed to discover unknown land on Earth should be lauded the way they had been for centuries. Those explorers may have discovered worlds new to what they knew previously, but there were already people living there with traditions, cultures, and stories of their own that were simply ... destroyed in the spirit of claiming more and more land for kings and queens of old. Bridgette couldn't even imagine something like that happening here, if a curious human came to Heáhwolcen and thought it worthy of taking over. She felt an almost overwhelming sense of anger at that visualization, and silently swore to herself that she'd protect this place from any invading force, human or otherwise. It was too precious and too important to give up.

"Would you like to see more, Liluthuaé?"

Lost in her reverie, Bridgette had briefly forgotten she was riding a Unicorn and they had a purpose to their journey. "Oh! Yes, please. I'm so sorry — I kind of forgot we were stopped."

Eloise turned back to the road and continued their walk. Mithrilken had stopped a few paces ahead, and he and Collum patiently waited on their two companions to catch up.

"What do you think so far?" Collum asked.

"I've never seen anywhere like this. It's as if ... as if everything exists in such perfect harmony, and there's so much vibrancy and color and *life* everywhere. Each time I glance at something I have to do a double-take to see if it's natural or meant to *look* natural," Bridgette said, a smile pulling at the edges of her mouth. She knew it would bring that grin to Collum's face, and it did.

I love it when you smile like that at me, she thought to him. *And maybe "love" is a strong word there, but really, I do.*

He reached over and jabbed her shoulder slightly. *I'm just glad there's something endearing about me, considering a few days ago you were convinced I'd memorized your coffee shop order to come kill you with chai lattes.*

Fine. I won't say that around you. I'll keep all my sappy thoughts to myself, Bridgette thought in response, sticking her tongue out at him.

Colleagues and friends, Starshine. He didn't have to speak aloud for her to infer that cautious inflection. *But it does bring me joy to see you experience these new things, especially when they make you feel happiness.*

Bridgette pretended the statement didn't sting. How was it possible for someone to make her feel such an emotional range in such a short period of time? She didn't like it one bit.

"Is all of this Aelchanon?" she asked, in a hurry to change the subject.

"It is," Collum answered. "We do not have many cities in Eckenbourne. And even then, 'city' is not quite right for how they are organized. Eckenbourne is divided into sections, and each has a specific purpose. Aelchanon, for example, is business and government. Where I live is called Feormeham, which as you noticed is largely farmland. We also have Lisweald, where you'll find more nature than you will magical beings; Faustdúnleshire, toward the mountains; and lastly Estmereamel, the city of water."

"Estmereamel," Bridgette murmured, feeling another new word on her tongue. "So is that like, beaches?"

Collum chuckled. "We don't have beaches. Unlike Earth, Heáhwolcen isn't a globe. It is flat-surfaced. We're able to have weather similar to Earth because we are still within the same atmosphere, but it is impossible for us to have oceans in the clouds here as there isn't exactly a coast. Streams, lakes and ponds, where water can collect and flow — those we have a plenty."

"So how do you make sure people — er, beings — don't go off the edge and drop to Earth and die?" Bridgette asked, feeling slightly queasy. On Earth, the "edge of the world" was a myth. She'd never been anywhere, aside from a trip once to the cliff-filled Grand Canyon, where it was possible to simply fall off an edge.

The Elf laughed. "Mithrilken, Eloise, if you two do not mind, I'm going to take our Bright Star on a field trip."

The Unicorns stopped, and Collum helped Bridgette dismount. "Come on. I'll show you."

With that, he evanesced them somewhere very, very high up. Bridgette clutched at Collum's arm, caring not at all that she was so close to him. She had a feeling he wouldn't let her fall into the void or whatever it was happened if someone got too close to the edge of the continent.

"Welcome to the highest peak in Heáhwolcen," Collum lilted in a mock tour guide voice. "Hlafjordstiepel is the only place you can see almost everything. It's a very sacred place for magical beings, as it is the place closest to Ifrinnevatt and the spirits. We are surrounded by clouds and silence, and it is here that many come to center themselves should they need to escape from the stresses of daily life."

He turned pointed to one side. "Do you see that, over there? How there is blue sky above, but the land seems to blend into the clouds?"

Bridgette squinted and glanced toward the direction Collum pointed at. She could barely make out what looked more like stagnant fog than clouds. "I think so."

"That is what the edge of the world looks like. It is spelled and warded to protect us. We can walk to the edge, and if we were to reach out to touch it, our fingers would not pass through. We wouldn't be hurt; it is not an electrical charge; but only the elements can get through. Beings cannot. The clouds mark the rim of a magical dome that Artur Cromwell, Galdúr, and Aelys Frost put into place when our country was created."

Now that she heard that, Bridgette looked again at the fog,

and concentrated on following the arc to the other side. She noticed the sky shimmered imperceptibly, and realized Collum brought her here so she could *see* the dome itself. On the ground, she doubted it would be visible at all.

"Collum, what's that?" she pointed to the very top of the faint dome, where a barely visible reddish-hued circle met at the crest.

"It's the Meridian. The very center of the world above the world, and it's enforced with higher magics. It sits right above Palna," he explained quietly.

"Why is it red like that?"

"I'm not sure, actually, but I assume it's just the mark of the magics that seal it. The top of a dome is its most battered point, so it must be made the strongest to withstand the storm."

Bridgette studied Collum, who was staring upward at that red circle, lost in thoughts she couldn't hear. "That's metaphorical as hell, Bundy."

He glanced back down at the Elfling, who was still clutching his shirt in her fists for dear life. "It is, isn't it?"

The two stood silently for a few minutes. There weren't even the sounds of birds or wind up here, just utter, peaceful silence. Bridgette understood what Collum meant about beings coming to this place to center themselves.

"Sit with me," he said, gently pulling her down. Collum put his hands on either side of her cheeks, turning her face toward him. "I do not want to say anything to sway you either way when the Samnung explains what we must to you. But I need you to know that no matter what you decide, you are the most powerful, magical creature I have ever known. I barely know you, Bridgette Conner, and I know this about you. And I know you do not think this of yourself. For whatever reason, and it is not my place to pry and inquire, so I will not.

"Perhaps I am wrong for saying this, but I feel a very strong connection with you, and I infer that you feel this way too. It is so soon, far too soon, to feel that in most normal circumstances, and it concerns me that this is a sign that what we are experiencing is in no way normal. That perhaps all these *things* we have suspected about Palna and Craft magic are coming to pass, and it is necessary that things speed up so that we can work together better," Collum said. "Before I introduced myself to you, I took the time to learn things about you. As much as I could, without raising questions. What I learned is that you are kind, determined, and driven. You care deeply about people you allow into your space, and you are careful about who that is so you do not experience more hurt. You are loyal and believe the best in people, except for yourself.

"I heard you that night in the cottage," he admitted. "I wasn't listening to your thoughts, but I heard you crying. It was difficult to stand aside and not come to your aid. I know it concerns you that you cannot do magic. Yet. But not having performed a spell doesn't mean you're *not* who we know you to be. Spellwork takes time and practice. You can *fly*. You can speak to me mind-to-mind. You're a sierwan. Starshine, you truly are astonishing and incredible in so many ways. There will come times, many times, I am afraid, where you will question this about yourself because of what we must ask of you. But you must not let those negative things overcome what we know, what *I* know, to be true. Do you meditate?"

"Huh? Oh — no. I mean, I've tried but I can't really zone out like you're supposed to," Bridgette answered. Her voice was quiet: did Collum truly think all that about her?

"Let me show you how. And when those times of negativity come, all I ask is you take a moment to find yourself again before you make a knee-jerk reaction to close us off. Please."

"Okay …"

Collum demonstrated how to sit cross-legged, head tilted toward the sky with arms out, resting on either thigh, palms up and open. "Close your eyes and concentrate on your breathing. In through the nose, deeply, and hold it for just a moment before exhaling through your mouth. Feel your breath, feel the light and air around you. Clear your mind as you do this, over and over again, until all thoughts are exhaled and no more."

Bridgette did, and found it exceedingly difficult to ignore all the thoughts that immediately infiltrated her brain as she sat still.

But if she could ride a Unicorn, if she could evanesce to the top of the highest mountain on the continent, surely she could clear out her mind and be still. That seemed significantly less life-threatening.

The sun broke through the clouds above them, then, and suddenly Bridgette felt *much* more alive as the warmth hit her skin. She felt the smile form involuntarily on her face, and this time as she exhaled, she felt physically lighter. It was almost as though she was floating, though she felt the ground beneath her and knew she was still seated. But that feeling! She found she craved it, the almost out-of-bodyness that had enveloped her so briefly just now. A feeling of simply existing, letting what would be … be.

Foighne agus grásta, Collum's voice entered her mind. *Patience and grace.*

Neither one of those was a virtue Bridgette felt she possessed, and she had no idea why Collum sent those words to her. Yet in this still silence, feeling the misty touch of clouds contrast with the rays of sun shining on them, the Elfling had the oddest feeling of understanding what those words were supposed to mean.

~ 20 ~

Bridgette didn't know for how long the two of them sat at the top of Hlafjordstiepel, bathing in the clouds and sky-given gift of gold. Time seemed to fade away into irrelevance. Her vision became clouded with waves of colors, an internal kaleidoscope that glittered with lacy patterns of light and shadow, fire red, citron yellow, and ice blue. She felt free; one with the Universe and all that is, that was and ever would be.

How do you feel, Starshine? Collum thought to her. His mind-voice was a mere whisper, perfectly blending with the serenity of their mountaintop scene.

Like magic.

She slowly brought herself back to the world, and found Collum sitting with one leg outstretched, a soft smile starting on one side of his lips and those tidal pool eyes watching her even softer. "You are magic," he said quietly. "Let us go now. I feel we've abandoned our annwyl for a shade too long, and Trystane will be waiting."

He reached for her and evanesced them back to the road. It seemed an eternity since they'd gone to the mountain, and Bridgette was amazed at how renewed and refreshed she felt after their time there. Mithrilken and Eloise were still waiting for them, casually grazing in someone's front yard on bluish-tinged turf. A tiny Elf, who Bridgette thought couldn't be more than a toddler, was braiding their tails.

"Hello, Bridgette and Fyrdwisa Andoralain," Eloise said, lifting her head from the ground. "Please meet Starkardia, daughter of this house."

The girl giggled in delight, and Bridgette realized there was a full-grown Elf sitting a few feet away, watching them with mild curiosity.

"And I am Ethros, father of this daughter," he said, standing up to greet them. "Be welcome in my home, Fyrdwisa and sigewíf companion."

Collum smiled heartily and walked forward to embrace him. "Ethros — it is good to see you! It has been an age, I feel."

Ethros had creamy white skin and starkly contrasting dark auburn hair so long it brushed his belt. His eyes were as green as Trystane's, and he was the same height as Collum. "The fyrdwisa and I had many adventures together during our training," he explained to Bridgette. "But he continued his, and I chose to pursue a more creative path."

"Ethros is a seordwiph, and very skilled. He designs bladed weapons following traditional methods as old as the Fyrst," Collum explained. "If the deities bless us with the occasion, we will be to your studio in the future to commission a few items. This is Bridgette Conner, here as a guest of the Samnung for a time."

Ethros bowed, and Bridgette responded in kind. "It's nice to meet you," she said. "And your daughter is adorable!"

"I thank you," Ethros said, beaming at the child. She'd moved on to poking yellow chrysanthemums in Eloise's tail braids. "Starkardia is a gem, and we are glad the deities chose us as those to raise her spirit. I thank you too, for allowing her to entertain your steeds during your absence."

They chatted a few more moments, letting Starkardia finish her decorating, then Collum made it clear they must be on their way. Eloise promised the child she would return soon, and the four made their path back to the road to the Caisleán.

"We were nay worried, but we did wonder where the two of you got off to," Mithrilken commented once they were out of the others' earshot.

"I took Bridgette to Hlafjordstiepel. She wanted to see the edge of the world," Collum explained matter-of-factly. "And I taught her to meditate."

"A good place for that, one hears," Mithrilken said. "Did your experience provide you with any clarity?"

They both looked to Bridgette, who wasn't quite sure she wanted to share her experience yet. "Clarity? I'm not sure. But it was wonderful and peaceful. I feel very refreshed."

The Unicorn seemed to accept that answer, and they continued their walk into the heart of Aelchanon. A few minutes later, the Caisleán appeared before them. Like the Elven dwellings they passed on the road, at first it didn't appear to be a structure at all, so well did it meld into the trees. The closer they got, Bridgette realized why that was — the building was made entirely out of reflective glass seamed together with wood, over which great vines had been growing for a century or more. The glass mirrored the forest around it, and it wasn't until Bridgette saw her reflection that it struck her how the Caisleán was constructed. And what a reflection that was!

She and Collum made an imposing pair atop the Unicorns. Mithrilkin was a hand or so taller than Eloise, putting the top of Bridgette's head level with Collum's jawline. Their golden-rimmed horns gleamed in the shining glass, and Bridgette watched as the breeze blew loose strands of hair around her face, and how the reflection made the fyrdwisa's blue eyes shine even brighter. Had an Elven guard not chosen that moment to step out of the front door, Bridgette might have stared spellbound for an hour or two at the exterior.

"Holy shit," she breathed. "This is incredible."

She and Collum dismounted, and the Unicorns bounded off elsewhere. "I think that's enough riding for one day," the Elf told her, holding out his arm to loop through hers. "We'll walk or evanesce everywhere else today."

Or fly? she thought to him hopefully.

Nice try.

Somehow inside the Caisleán was even more enthralling than its exterior. Collum led Bridgette through the front double doors and into a scene she'd never imagined it possible to exist. There was a waterfall cascading down from the back wall — except it *wasn't* a wall, it was a veil of water with paths of stones to walk under and through — into a creekbed that trickled at their feet. Poufs designed to look like rocks were gathered at intervals to provide seating for meetings and those waiting to speak with Elven leadership. Birds chirped overhead and insects offered a soft cacophony of background noise. The variety of flora in this room was astounding: some Bridgette recognized, others entirely new and magical. The whole place smelled like woods after a fresh mountain rainfall.

This. Is. Actually. Insane. How can you not come to work here every day? Bridgette was baffled. She'd take this over the diner any day.

Because I like my office better. There generally aren't beings sitting outside my bedroom door waiting to talk to me like there tend to be here. But if you choose to stay, I imagine the Samnung would let you have an office wherever you'd like, including inside the Caisleán.

Bridgette rather liked that thought.

She followed Collum down one of the pebbled pathways to the waterfall, then through it and to the right. They seemed to be inside a mountain now, with doorways carved out from the rock face and glittering stalactites illuminating the ceiling above them. The floor under their feet was covered in soft moss, and the hallway was wide enough for three or four beings to stand at once. Trystane's door was the furthest down, lit softly by a candle burning on a sconce next to it. Collum knocked raptly, and the door swung open to reveal a female Elf with mahogany skin covered in tattoos of black flowers and lines. Her eyes were shades of gold and chocolate, and her black hair cropped short and shaved clean on one side.

"Fyrdwisa!" she exclaimed, forgetting professionalism and grabbing him in a giant hug. "Welcome back."

"Hello, Njahla. This is Bridgette Conner, a guest of the Samnung. This is Njahla, Trystane's advisor and, well, the being that keeps him in the right place at the right time, if we are speaking honestly," Collum said. "And I hope we are not too late to see him."

"Of course not," Njahla said, waving a hand in the air. "I wouldn't let him put anything else on the schedule today once he said you were planning to be here. Though in true Trystane fashion, he could not provide a time of your arrival, so he's back there reading something from Aristoces while he waited."

"Excellent. May we see ourselves back?" Collum asked.

Once Njahla nodded her permission, he led Bridgette through a room that made her think of a combination of bachelor pad, university professor, and vampire novelist. Trystane seemed to be a bookworm who favored deeply colored woods and the traditional gold of Eckenbourne. The elaborate

"E" was carved in several places, and though there was plenty of shelving, he preferred to organize in piles rather than giving everything its own place. Magical implements, crystals, and tools were scattered around, and at the back of the office suite, a massive skylight lit up where the Elven leader sat at an ornate desk, poring over a stack of pale blue papers.

"You seem busy," Collum commented, helping himself to a seat and motioning for Bridgette to join him on a second green velvet armchair.

"Hello, you two," Trystane said, breaking away from the papers and grinning at them. "Welcome to the Caisleán, Bridgette. What do you think of Eckenbourne so far? What have you seen?"

"Well," Bridgette began, "I rode a Unicorn, so that was unexpected —"

Both Elves laughed.

"— and Collum took me to the top of that really high mountain and we meditated for a while, and then here. It's so gorgeous, it really is. The Elven houses are just fascinating, and the Caisleán too. I couldn't believe we were even in a building until I saw my reflection in the glass outside. It's all so different here than it is in Fairevella," Bridgette continued.

"Good observation," Trystane said. "Because of their relationship with Earth, I've always thought the Fairies had a more human aesthetic to their architecture and fashion. Elves tend to stay true to what already is rather than what beings have made be."

"Eloise said something like that to me earlier, while I was admiring this one house that looked like it was made out of a flower rainbow. She mentioned that Elves like to live alongside Nature rather than take it over," Bridgette said, and explained how there were humans who thought similarly about what she referred to as a "colonizing mindset."

"I do not understand why some believe the concept of 'finders keepers' applies to things other than a spare sock discovered in the wash," Trystane said mildly, and Bridgette laughed hard at the metaphor. "For the Elves, just as a rídend cannot own its annwyl, we do not own that which we did not create. We are blessed with long life, and with those many years we are charged with using that time to care for and better the worlds around us."

"That's ... really nice," Bridgette said. "I think that's smart."

"You'll find that there are many amenities on Earth that we do not have here, for that reason," Collum said. "Magical beings do not waste. Everything is able to be reused or recycled in some way, so there is no 'garbage' in the sense of humans. And deity forbid we have any packaging or material that is non-biodegradable."

That fascinated Bridgette, and she wanted to ask more, but Collum kept speaking: "As much as I'm sure the Liluthuaé wants to know about our water filtration systems, we have more urgent matters to bring to your attention. We wanted to do this in person, since we were already coming to view the Caisleán today."

Trystane cocked his head. "Continue."

"As we rode, Mithrilken and I spoke of the Elven collectives, and the Ealdaelfen were brought up. We explained about this myth, and, well ..." He motioned for Bridgette to pick up where he left off.

"And it came to me that they're not a myth anymore," the Efling said quietly, eyes downcast. This seemed like terrible news, and it frightened her to have to make eye contact as she shared it. "If there are any Elves in Palna, they are Ealdaelfen. They may not be the same as those of the Elven myths, but they are being trained in Craft Wizardry."

"You know this for sure?" Trystane said, blanching. "The Ealdaelfen live?"

"I'm sure of it. I hadn't heard of them until today and the second I did, I knew this about them."

"Fuck," Trystane groaned, leaning back with his head in his hands. "This is not going to go over well."

"I'm sorry — "

"Stop apologizing," the two Elves said in unison.

"Geez, sorry for apologizing," Bridgette muttered under her

breath.

"It's not going to go over well firstly because, that's horrible news. Secondly, Nehemi is currently very anti-Elven legend, and something tells me if we come to the Samnung with news that our first living legend brings bad tidings about *another* legend that isn't supposed to exist, we're going to end up in a shouting match over what to do about it," Trystane clarified. "To be frank, I am not sure we *should* tell the Samnung this news."

"Would it make a difference if we did?" Collum asked. He waved his hands and summoned tea to the three of them. "Should we tell Aristoces, at least?"

"I don't think it would matter. Not yet. Once we determine how to handle Palna in general, I think it would be good knowledge to have, that perhaps it is more than just witches and wizards practicing magic of ill-intent. Outright walking into the Samnung in two days to tell them that a new breed of Ealdaelfen has been foretold? I think the queen might go for Bridgette's throat, or vice-versa," Trystane answered.

"What should we do, then?" Bridgette asked. She felt tired all of a sudden — the rejuvenating post-meditation glow seemed to melt away into the beginnings of despair.

"That," Trystane said, snapping his fingers and turning his tea into his preferred blend of cherry-red spirit, "is an excellent question I don't know the answer to."

~ 21 ~

The Elven leader shooed them out a little while later, instructing them to not tell anyone else about Bridgette's knowing of the Ealdaelfen. He promised them he would come up with a plan, but it likely would be many weeks before anything came of it.

So many secrets, Bridgette thought to Collum. *This mind-talk thing, the dad thing, the flying, some of the sierwan stuff. At this point I think you may just have to buy duct tape for me because I'm going to lose track of what all I'm not allowed to talk about.*

What is duct tape? Collum thought back.

Bridgette laughed aloud. "Never mind. It's an Earth thing. What are we doing now?"

"Walking down the hall so I can pick up some papers and introduce you to the fyrdestre, and then we're going to get lunch."

"Did you get to choose your fyrdestre?" the Elfling asked.

"Yes, and no. The fyrdestre process is very intense," Collum replied. "Remember what all I told you of the Fairy ambassadors and ambassadoras? It's similar. You spend many years in school learning diplomatic training, as well as military strategy, feoht classes, intense magical studies. Those who complete the required training for a career in becoming some sort of magical warrior, and wish to apply for the next fyrdestre position, must apprentice for a year, take qualifying examinations of both physical ability and knowledge, and regularly meet with the fyrdwisa and Elven leadership who will evaluate their progress. After this period of time, the top three to five young Elves who show the most promise become part of the Fyrdlytta. This is my network — those who report directly to me and those who are the most elite of our spies and soldiers. It is out of the Fyrdlytta that the fyrdwisa can choose his or her second, the fyrdestre."

"That was an incredibly long answer to that question," Bridgette said. "So you don't get to choose the pool of candidates, but you choose who fills the position from that pool?"

"Correct," the Elf said. "And as we do live an extended long time, sometimes the fyrdestre may choose to pursue a different path if the fyrdwisa is not ready to step aside. Should that happen, the selection process begins anew. I am grateful that I have not had to choose a second fyrdestre, but have had the same hand for my time as fyrdwisa."

"So who is he?"

"She," Collum corrected with a grin. "And you're about to meet her."

He placed his hand against his own office door, and it swung open at his touch. The office was plain and bland compared to Trystane's, and Collum's secret meadow office, but it served its purpose. Sitting at the smaller of the two desks in front of them was a female who looked a bit older than Collum. She wore a charcoal-colored eyepatch over her right eye. Her nearly black hair was curlier than his, and she had both lightly pointed ears and small iridescent horns sticking out from just above either side of her forehead. She wore a sleeveless tunic and leather leggings, and did not fear showing off her muscled arms and legs.

"Welcome back, comrade," she said, standing from her post. Her sepia-toned skin was tinged silver, and her square jaw and classically beautiful features made her an imposing figure. She turned her attention to Bridgette: "And you must be the Liluthuaé."

Bridgette felt suddenly small and unremarkable next to whoever this was.

"Hi," she said meekly. *Hi?! Deity fucking bless, get a grip on yourself, Conner.*

"Bridgette Conner, meet Fyrdestre Aurelias Parvhin. Aurelias, meet the Bright Star." Collum held his arms out in introduction.

What IS she? Bridgette thought to Collum, and he was standing near enough to tap her foot lightly with his in what was clearly a "shut up" moment.

Shit, sorry that was probably really rude. I've never seen a being like her, she apologized mind-to-mind.

That was *obnoxiously rude, and when you think of a more polite way to ask, I'm sure one of us will answer,* the Elf thought back to her, though his face remained smiling. *Please do not insult my second in command like that ever again.*

Great, Bridgette moaned inwardly. *Not even noon and I've pissed him off. Again.*

I'm not pissed —

Stop eavesdropping on my inner monologue.

"Why are you both standing there not moving?" Aurelias asked, raising the eyebrow not hidden behind her eyepatch. "I feel like you're talking, but neither of you is saying anything, and that is quite bizarre."

"Collum *is* quite bizarre, now that you mention it," Bridgette said sweetly, and the fyrdestre grinned at her.

"Two against one, Fyrdwisa. I like this Elf," Aurelias said.

"Elfling," Bridgette corrected. "My mother was an Elf and my father was a wizard."

"Both of us Elflings!" Aurelias exclaimed. "Oh, how exciting this will be. My father is an Elf and my mother half Elf, half Tiefling. Hence the horns — have you met a Tiefling yet?"

"She's met Bryten," Collum said, and Bridgette could hear him holding back a smile.

"Oh, that goon! Bryten's such fun, though he's *not* Tiefling, but has similar physical characteristics. Some Tieflings have pigmented skin, and my mother's heritage is shades of black and gray, so my Elven blood made me a bit silver," Aurelias babbled. Her slightly eccentric demeanor was a complete juxtaposition to her imposing physique, and Bridgette liked her already.

"What is it that the fyrdestre does?" Bridgette asked, eager to talk more to this new friend.

"Whatever the fyrdwisa doesn't want to do, usually," Aurelias joked, and Collum rolled his eyes. "He hates being at the office, so I come instead. Handle correspondence that is trivial, pass on notes that are of a more pressing nature, be the face of the office. Beings tend to know that if I like them, I'm more likely to figure out a way to get them an audience. Collum is also gone quite a lot, so I oversee the Fyrdlytta as needed in his stead. Usually he leaves instructions and I don't have to strategize behind the scenes though, which is helpful. I'm not sure I fully trust myself on that front yet."

Bridgette nodded. "That seems like a lot. He must depend heavily on you."

"Oh, he does," Aurelias said, winking at the Elf. "But it's all in good fun and work. Collum is amazing."

"You're off your rocker," Collum said, and Bridgette hoped neither one of them saw the slight blush that brushed her cheeks at Aurelias' comment. "I hate to stop by only to run back out, but I've promised Bridgette a day exploring Eckenbourne. We already are running a bit behind the schedule I had due to a side trip this morning to the mountains. I wanted her to see the Caisleán, but I didn't leave enough time for us to linger. I do need to grab a blank copy of letterhead, though, and did Magister Ephynius ever send us that report from his students? We're going to the University this week at some point and if I happened to run into him, I wanted to be prepared with questions."

Bridgette toned them out; she had no idea who Magister Ephynius was.

I wonder what it's like to live as an Elf all the time, she thought to herself. *To live here, to have all this magic and beauty around. To come to work in a place like this, or maybe Collum would let me work with him …*

Her thoughts trailed off, and Bridgette glanced over to make sure the fyrdwisa and fyrdestre were still engaged in conversation before allowing her next thoughts to even enter her conscious mind. *I wonder what it would be like to be with Collum all the time. Would he even like that? Would he ever let us move past this weird sometimes flirty friendship that we developed? Is it weird that friendship developed so fast to begin with? Is it weird that I've only known him for a little over a week and I want … more? That's probably not great …*

She struggled to keep a straight face as these thoughts rattled around in her brain. Bridgette tended to fall quickly — in love, in friendship, into a pattern of working until she burnt out — and more oft than not, she ended up hurt because of it. She had a feeling Collum wouldn't ever do anything intentionally to hurt her. Actually, she thought as her eyes shifted of their own accord, that's why he was setting boundaries to begin with. She did matter to him, no matter the strangeness of how quickly that developed, and hurting her was the last thing he wanted to do. Especially when it was more than his own friendship at stake.

This sucks. Bridgette hadn't realized her face fell, or that she'd managed to send that thought out, until a hand gently brushed her bicep.

What does, Starshine?

She didn't answer, perturbed that now she'd gone and blown her cover, but Collum turned back to tell Aurelias goodbye. Bridgette waved, plastering a fake smile on her face, and the Elf practically dragged her into the hallway.

What's going on? he asked her, mind-to-mind. *You were fine, then all of a sudden you looked as though you might start crying.*

I really don't want to talk about it, Collum. It's none of your business.

Technically we are thinking, not talking …

Bridgette groaned and cracked a half-smile. *You are such a punk. To be fair, I don't want to think about it either, because I have a bad talent of getting into my own head.*

I know.

She came clean later as the two waited for their lunch. The little café was, like everything in Heáhwolcen, straight out of a fairytale. Bridgette half-expected a Hobbit to come running out of the trees at this point, followed by dark, shadowy figures that in her momentary vision were the spirits of Ealdaelfen. Aelchanon's area of shops and eateries was much sparser than that of what she'd previously observed in Çeofilye: instead of bustling streets set aside for commerce, the Elves only put businesses in spots that they could seamlessly blend into Nature. She was now, for example, seated across from Collum on benches made of twisted vines, and the table between them was actually a large stump. The restaurant itself was inside the hollow of a tree the size of a Sequoia, though it had more of a pine look to its leaves. Each of the tables set up surrounding it was covered by an awning formed of tall, leafy potted plants, which provided shade and protection from light rains.

"I feel … like this is home," Bridgette said quietly, not

meeting Collum's gaze. He'd been watching her quietly since they left the Caisleán, waiting for her to share what was bothering her.

"That's not a thing to get in your head about," he said.

"No, I know. It's … it's not quite that." She struggled to find the right words for what she felt. "I feel at home here, but there are things I think I would want if I *did* live here. And it's so strange to feel so strongly about this place and these beings when I've known about them for what, just over a week? That's insane. It makes me question *everything*."

"There is nothing wrong with feeling a strong pull to something, Bridgette."

"But it's just so *fast*," she muttered, still not meeting his eyes. "Remember earlier, what you tried to get out of me about something my therapist said? I don't know a thing about your life growing up, but I was in and out of homes my whole life until I was thirteen. Nobody wanted me for very long. I would try so hard each time: maybe this would be the family. Maybe these people would want me and keep me and I'd finally have a home. Maybe I could spend more than a year at one school. When I was thirteen and I was taken in by this older couple, I was so scared that I'd spend the rest of my life homeless. Like, not on the streets necessarily, but without anyone to come home too. You age out of the system at eighteen. And people like to adopt babies and toddlers, not teenagers. The Simmonses, Doc and Martha, I was lucky to have been placed with them. But for the first three years I was there, I was terrified that they'd hit the three-year mark and be like, 'Oops, this was a terrible idea, this kid sucks.' Like all the others."

She played absentmindedly with her braid for a moment, remembering that constant feeling of being alone, abandoned.

"It always made me feel like I never would be enough. Or maybe I was too much, you know?" Bridgette continued. "So when I was in high school Doc and Martha got me in with this therapist friend of theirs, and he told me I had attachment issues. Which was pretty obvious, I know, but he made it sound like it was this horrible thing to become attached to things. And I don't like to be a horrible person, so I try really hard to give myself time before I become so enamored. Most of the time now it's fine, but sometimes …" She gestured wildly. "Sometimes it's easier said than done. And then I question if I'm rushing into things. Relationships, friendships, saving the world. You know. Just … everything."

Collum sighed. He wanted to comfort her, hug her, but knew that would probably only make her feel worse. The Elf instead gave himself a moment to think before responding.

"This morning I shared a similar thought with you, how unusual it is for us to have this strength of connection despite hardly knowing one another," he said thoughtfully. "But I do know this. Beings like you and I, we live a contradiction: constantly desiring love, but believing we are incapable of being loved. Thus, we come on hard and strong because that's how we love, and people run because they can't handle it. It perpetuates the myth."

Bridgette was biting her lip, internally praying to whatever deities existed that the Elf wasn't listening to her mind as he talked.

He wasn't, but the look on her face gave him a hint.

"Bridgette," Collum said — not quite a question, not quite a command. She glanced up in response, eyes wary.

"The fun part?" he continued. "The fun part is that eventually, someone comes around and absorbs that love. Wraps themselves in it like it's a blanket and thrives because of it. Just … be patient."

She nodded, lost in thought that he couldn't hear. Her mental abilities mystified him: sometimes Bridgette's inner voice would come to him loud and clear, as it did when she was in the Samnung chamber. But other times, like now, it was veiled. He heard nothing, but his ears rang as though there were something *to* be heard, should he tune into the right frequency.

~ 22 ~

That night, as she lounged again in the exquisite guest bath at Collum's apartment, Bridgette struggled to stay out of her own mind. She pulled a vial of lavender oil from the basket he'd brought her the previous evening, following the instructions to add several drops to the steaming water she soaked in, but it was almost as if her head was too far gone to be tugged back into the dreamlike reality of Heáhwolcen.

His words at lunch bugged her for reasons she couldn't quite place. Was he telling her to back off, for the umpteenth time? Was he saying they were similar in their desires? Was he reassuring her that there was nothing wrong with her?

"I *hate* this," she muttered to herself, putting her head in her hands, letting the ends of her hair tilt forward into the hot bathwater. By "this," she meant the incessant questioning inner monologue she'd been plagued with most of her life. It was a struggle for the small rational side of her brain to talk herself down sometimes, and when she succeeded, the result meant emotional exhaustion and a strong desire to lay in bed.

Now was not the time for "this."

Unable to relax, Bridgette heaved herself out of the tub and drained the water, the soft scent of lavender swirling out with it. She slipped not into pajamas, but into a clean pair of leggings and an oversized gray sweater. The Elfling had a feeling that though lavender might not do to take her mind off whatever plagued it, practicing flying just might. She still ached from before, and the added work from riding Eloise hadn't helped, but the dull burn of her body craved more. Plus, the zig-zagging of her thought pattern needed a distraction to focus on.

"Collum?" she called, stepping from the bathroom.

He appeared down the hallway. "Ready?"

"Yes."

Collum reached a hand for her, and she practically flew to him, so long and agile was her running leap. "Would you like to go to the wood, or do you want to stay here?"

"Here, please," Bridgette said, taking his hand in hers.

She hadn't been herself, not quite, the rest of the afternoon. Collum as fyrdwisa noticed this with concern; Collum as her friend noticed with alarm. It was a frustrating conundrum he'd found himself in — as he revealed on Hlafjordstiepel that morning — to have such a connection with her, so soon after *actually* meeting her. Normally his charges didn't have this effect on him, but the Elf found he cared deeply not only for her as a magical entity, but as a being he wanted in his life. There was not a sense of protection, another odd realization. Rather, a deep, burning sense of some deeper emotion. He didn't like that at all.

He also didn't like how quickly Bridgette seemed attuned to his mood shifts, even at times when he'd shrouded his thoughts from her.

"What's wrong?" she asked, pausing in his bedroom. She gave him a quizzical look. His eyes had gone far away, his expression hardened. His thoughts completely muted.

"Nothing," he lied. "Just thinking about my office becoming a training ground for mythical magical beings."

Bridgette smiled softly. He knew she didn't fully buy the fib, but he also knew she wouldn't press him to open up right now. The Elfling might be able to get all sorts of information out of him in a general sense, but she respected his privacy the way he did hers. A mutual, unspoken understanding.

"I think you need to call it something besides an office," she replied.

"I think *you* need to stop thinking of everything in comparison to how humans live."

Fair enough.

She rolled her eyes as they stepped into the hidden paradise he'd created. Bridgette followed Collum not down to the clearing he'd found her at before, but down a slightly different path further up the creek. The air was cool and chill, the light breeze softly blowing at her hair. She'd left it down and in its natural waves tonight — having her hair pulled back so often in braids or ponytails lately was likely to start giving her headaches. There wasn't a moon in Collum's office, but the sky above gleamed with blinking light from stars that caught in her reddish-blonde hair and gave it the effect of being lit on fire. The Elf noticed.

Bridgette *was* flickering flame. Or perhaps she was the match that must be lit, and Heáhwolcen's plight the flint to strike it against. He watched her out of the corner of his eye as they walked upstream. She seemed to be taking it all in; the scents and what little could be seen in the enchanted darkness that surrounded them. Collum loved to watch her experience magic. It was so new to her that the simplest things, things he'd grown up with and were old hat, mesmerized the Elfling. The same starlight that caused her hair to gleam alighted the opalescent flecks in her lilac eyes, and if photography existed in this world above the world, Collum found himself wishing this to be the image captured of the Liluthuaé.

"I hope," he said quietly, "that one day, all magical creatures and beings will see you as I do."

"What?" Bridgette stopped, taken aback. *The hell does that mean?*

"I mean you, right now, in this moment, so enthralled by everything around you. So desirous of more of it," Collum clarified. "The way the starlight catches in your hair and your eyes as you breathe this air and experience this world. It bothers me to think of you only being seen as this … *savior*, as you keep calling it. I don't want anyone to see you as a figurehead or a character. I want them to see you for who you are."

She raised an eyebrow. "Sweet-talking me, Bundy?"

He barked out a laugh. "No, not quite. I wish *you* could see yourself the way you are right now, without that ridiculous wall that I know you just threw up in your mind."

Bridgette scowled. *How did you know I did that?* she asked, mind-to-mind.

I can feel when you block me out, of course, Collum thought back to her. *We all do it unconsciously. Although I dare say that perhaps you do it intentionally more oft than not, to keep me from hearing what you're thinking.*

Me?! Keep the nosy serial killer Elf out of my head?! As if. Who would do such a thing? Bridgette thought to him teasingly, a wry smile forming on her lips.

He rolled his eyes and gave her shoulder a slight squeeze of companionship. "Are you ready?"

"Yes. What are we working on tonight?" she replied out loud, putting the impending soreness out of her head.

Collum thought for a moment. "Hmm. Last night was ascending and descending. Do you feel comfortable with that?"

Bridgette shrugged. "I guess? I mean, neither of us have really ever flown before without an airplane involved, so who the fuck knows what the comfort level should be."

"A fair point," he conceded. "In feoht — that's essentially our work in fighting and weaponry — the first few weeks of training, no matter if one is in the Fairy Mîleta, the Fyrdlytta, the Cailleach of Endorsa or the Bondrie Bródenmael, everyone works on essentials. Footwork. The basics. Typically two to four weeks of this type of training is required. Some become bored with it, or their egos demand that they are better than their sibling fighters. Those beings do not proceed with training. Each section of our Fórsaí Armada must work individually and together as a whole for there to be any level of effectiveness in what we do, and we cannot afford to have unfocused warriors. Or those who are not dedicated to protecting their siblings with their own self."

"So, what, we keep working on whatever the flying basics are?" Bridgette asked.

"I think that would be best. Now, you still must use your full limbs to move around, but what if this is a skill you can master over time, and you are able to control your movement entirely with your mind?" Collum mused. "Perhaps not to ascend and descend, but to change direction and speed midair."

"That makes sense."

Again, the two spent most of the night at this task of flight practice. Bridgette tried several times to move herself without moving, but nothing came of it.

Not yet, Collum thought to her encouragingly. *Stop doubting yourself.*

She stuck her tongue at him from fifteen feet above his head. *Stop eavesdropping on me.*

Stop thinking negative thoughts and perhaps I won't feel so compelled to intervene.

"Such a punk," Bridgette muttered, but she grinned as she rolled her eyes. She tilted her head upward, and a bit of knowledge filled her mind: standing — or floating — still would get her nowhere. But combining a slight movement with the will to put herself somewhere else? Now that could prove a fruitful blend.

She took a long, deep breath and, at the same time she exhaled quickly, shrugged her shoulders forcefully downward. Her body shot up into the air, and both she and Collum shouted.

What the fucking fuck! I figured it out I think — her thoughts were briefly a jumble of exuberant half-sentences that threw Collum for a loop.

What just happened? he thought to her. She was so far up now he could barely see her, even with his extraordinary Elven vision.

I knew how to move without moving, the Elfling responded in her mind. *I think you're going to have to teach me more about meditating. It was like, I had to breathe the right way, think a certain way, and move my shoulders with intention. And suddenly now I can't see you and I got here* fast.

Will you come down now, please? It gives me a bit of worry to not be able to see you. I've never flown to the ceiling of my office so I also do not know precisely how high you can go, Collum thought back. *This is quite disconcerting.*

Bridgette had no idea how far up she was. Everything above her sparkled slightly brighter; she was closer to the stars. But below, all she could see was cool, pitch-black night. To descend, she felt she needed to try the opposite of what she'd done to get so high. As she inhaled this time, she commanded her body to go downward, and she pointed her toes toward the ground for emphasis.

"Point your feet in the direction you want to throw" — a long-forgotten lesson from the year her foster parents forced her to be on a T-ball team.

Bridgette exhaled, but instead of shrugging in on the inhale and forcing her shoulders down as she breathed out, this time she pulled her shoulders up as her breath left her body. It worked — and she was both pleased and so surprised that she exhaled in a fast sense of relief. She slashed through the air, disoriented at doing so in the dark. There was a sudden sense of the ground coming up to meet her, and Bridgette instinctively formed her body to land in a crouch.

She hit with such force that the ground trembled.

Standing, her eyes wide, she looked at Collum directly in front of her. She'd missed squishing him by about six inches, and his expression mirrored what she felt hers likely was.

"Holy *shit*," she croaked out.

Bridgette swayed uneasily, and Collum reached out to steady her. "I think this is enough for tonight," he said gently, the tone of his voice masking his tumultuous emotions.

I think you're right, Bridgette thought to him, her inner voice sounding a bit woozy. *Will you bring me gingewinde when we get home?*

Home. She hadn't even realized exactly what she thought — her mind and body were in shock — but the Elf did. He fought the urge to smile in relief. "Home" meant she was leaning toward staying.

"Of course, Starshine."

Collum walked her back into the apartment, an arm around her waist to steady her. She seemed partly ready to give out at any moment, but he assumed she'd refuse him if he swooped her up and evanesced them back inside. Plus, Bridgette still felt as though evanescing knocked the wind out of her. Not the best feeling to have when she was already breathless from her not-quite-fall from the sky. So, walking it was.

He settled her on the couch, where she leaned forward to put her face between her knees as if to fight the urge to pass out. The Elf summoned a bottle of gingewinde.

"Drink this," he said quietly. "How do you feel?"

Bridgette practically inhaled half the bottle in one smooth gulp. "I don't know if I'm going to faint, honestly. Holy *shit*."

She put a hand to her forehead, and Collum had a thought. "May we try something?" he asked.

"As long as it doesn't involve me moving from this couch,

I'm game."

"We can speak to each other mind-to-mind. I wonder if we can … share memories? Image thoughts? With one another?" Collum mused. "If you are up to it, I would like to know what that was like, the extreme ascending and descending you did."

"Oh. Um, okay."

Bridgette took another long sip of gingewinde. She closed her eyes and began to breathe deeply, almost as if she were to enter the trance-like state she'd been in on Hlafjordstiepel. But not quite. For this, she wanted to maintain control of her thoughts and memories. She opened her mind fully to Collum and began to visualize the scenes from that evening: the walk into the night air, the normal flying she'd done. Then the velocity at which she'd gone so high up, the uncertainty with which she viewed the nothingness below her. Her attempt to put herself back down again, and her relief breathing out of her so fast that she lost all control. That feeling of spiraling downward, though she was dropping straight down, at an unprecedented speed. The force of the ground as she hit it with both her bodyweight and the weight of the magic she possessed. Unsteadily rising to her feet, and the warm, secure feeling of Collum's arm — *Fuck no, not that part.*

She broke off the shared memory without warning, and Collum blinked up at her. *How incredible,* he thought to her. *I could see, hear, and feel as you did. My heart is beating as though I was the one flying and falling.*

"Would *you* like a gingewinde?" the Elfling giggled shrewdly.

"I'm quite fine, though I might make tea shortly if you would like some. I do have a question for you," Collum said. "As you came back down, it was though you were overwhelmed with a sense of fear. Did you think you were going to get hurt?"

Bridgette shifted uncomfortably. "No. I couldn't see anything. It was so *dark*, and I knew I was falling, falling *fast*, but having that sensation and not being able to see anything was awful. I knew the ground had to be coming up and I kind of felt it before I hit it, but I didn't know how to slow myself down and I was so caught up in the feeling of falling …"

She put her head back between her knees. "Maybe we

should only fly in the daylight from now on."

Collum left her to regain her breath while he made them both a pot of tea in the kitchen. Tulsi, his personal favorite, seemed to fit the occasion, with a few drops of skullcap tincture added to each of their mugs. *A few more drops to Bridgette's, for good measure*, he thought to himself.

Bridgette gratefully accepted the proffered beverage and closed her eyes to breathe in the aroma and warmth.

"Thank you," she murmured. "Sorry that sent me in such a tailspin."

"Starshine, you really ought not to apologize for things beyond your control," Collum said, raising his brows as he sipped. "You have few truly poor habits. Your propensity for over-apologizing is one of them."

~ 23 ~

The next morning dawned bright and sunny, and Bridgette instantly felt her spirits lifted from the springlike weather that beamed inside her window. Collum hinted the day before he had a surprised planned for their excursion, and she practically bounced into the kitchen after slathering a bit more of his healing salve on her muscles.

"You're in a lighter mood," the Elf noted, grinning unabashedly. "The sunshine does you well."

"I told you, I don't like rain much. Or at least not the misty, dreary stuff we had to go through yesterday," Bridgette replied. "I've always liked sunshine and being warm."

Collum handed her a steaming crockware mug of coffee. He was determined that at least one day would not be fraught with ill happenings, as the past two had been. "Good. The weather is supposed to be like this for the rest of your visit."

"And what exactly does that mean for today?"

"We're going back to Fairevella, and we've been advised to wear something other than casual leggings, tunics and sweaters." He purposely added a theatrical air of mystery to his tone, and Bridgette chortled.

"Does that mean you're taking me shopping?" she asked.

"No, thankfully, it does not. I will do many things with you as my companion and colleague, but I do draw the line at shopping. I rarely even shop for myself," Collum said. "You can thank Trystane and Njahla for most everything in your wardrobe. And mine, come to think of it. They have quite the discerning eye for colors, fabrics, and textures that go with an individual's personality and attributes."

That explains all the blues you wear, Bridgette realized.

He winked in response. "What would you like for breakfast this morning? I can make eggs and bacon, or if you'd like a second cup of coffee that tastes far better than mine, we can make an early go for iced caife calabaza and honeycakes …" Collum let his voice trail off, knowing the moment Bridgette's eyes widened with glee that she'd choose the latter.

"What are those?" she asked expectantly. Any excuse to try new foods here was reason enough to forego the comfortable luxury of Collum cooking for her.

"A very traditional British-inspired take on coffee and coffee cake, popularized several decades ago by the Endorsan group that calls themselves the 'Modern Kitchen Witch Society'. They have a penchant for growing calabaza, a specific variety of pumpkin, and creating all sorts of delicacies from it. Iced caife calabaza is a sweet, milky beverage similar to coffee that is made of this pumpkin, and honeycakes are coiled vanilla buns dipped in honey, then sprinkled with a choice of toppings. I myself am quite partial to the take on savory and sweet, and prefer the toppings of bacon or hot pepper salt," Collum described.

Bridgette's mouth watered and her stomach let out a feral growl. "I want *those*."

"We can wear typical clothes to go for breakfast, then. I do recommend we evanesce though."

"That's fine," Bridgette said quickly. She didn't *mind* evanescing, but preferred to avoid it when possible. "I'll go get dressed and meet you back here in a few minutes."

She reappeared in the kitchen wearing the same sweater and leggings from the previous night, as well a giant grin. The very idea of sitting down to eat such a mythical-sounding breakfast was beyond her wildest dreams. Even at theme parks of her youth, where dishes had been given magically influenced names or were plated in such a way as to spellbind their eaters, the ingredients themselves were not borne of magic. Bridgette couldn't wait.

It was well-worth the discomfort of evanescing.

Where Elves lived within Nature itself and Fairies preferred a more colorful aesthetic that juxtaposed pleasingly with modern clean lines and a sort of minimalism, Endorsa was clearly the country most influenced by what were considered "human" tastes. The village they evanesced into, Bridgette noticed after catching her breath, was filled with examples of Craftsman-inspired architecture. Homes, businesses, and restaurants all had exteriors of brick and wood with a rustic color palette, occasionally abbreviated with a pop of color on doors or shutters. It was easy to tell the businesses apart though: each had a placard above its door with the business name, and a flag of either peacock green, champagne, or royal navy flew from a bronze post out front if it was open. These seemed to be the Endorsan colors, as Bridgette remembered seeing Nehemi and Cloa wearing them in their dresses during the Samnung meeting.

The café that served as their destination was clearly a coffee shop — as if the bronze-painted words "Coffee Cauldron" weren't enough of a hint, the roasty scents of chocolate, caramel, and toffee emanating from its chimney sealed the deal. Bridgette wasn't a bit surprised when they walked in and three portly witches, each wearing a sage green dress covered with a khaki apron, were behind the counter and serving. She held back a laugh.

This is the most stereotypical thing, she thought to Collum. *If a bunch of middle-aged white women on Earth decided they were going to open a witch-themed coffee shop, this is literally what they would look like. I'm trying so hard not to crack up!*

Her remark was so unexpected that Collum had to start coughing to cover his own laughter.

"How can I help you, dears?" one of the witches, her straight white hair pulled back into a loose chignon, asked the duo. "Oh — hello, Fyrdwisa Andoralain!"

Collum was still cough-laughing, and he waved slightly in response as he struggled to come up for air. "Hello, Murthel."

"The fyrdwisa *never* brings a lady with him, my dear. You must be quite special!"

Though her remark was clearly meant in a grandmotherly, caring way, both Bridgette and Collum nearly lost it at this point. The Elf suddenly bothered to remember he had magic that could fix this, and a moment later, Bridgette breathed in the smell of honeysuckle, and found herself no longer holding in abundant laughter. As long as she didn't catch Collum's eye, anyway; she knew they would both double right back over the second she did.

"Murthel, this is Bridgette Conner. She's here in

Heáhwolcen for the first time, having grown up on Earth," the Elf said. "So in that sense, I suppose she is special."

The witch positively beamed. "How wonderful, Fyrdwisa! And what a treat for us, that you've brought her to the Coffee Cauldron as part of her visit!"

"I wouldn't dream of doing otherwise, Murthel. I do not mean to order for her, but Bridgette did seem quite intrigued by the idea of caife calabaza," Collum said.

"Yes, please!" Bridgette stepped up to the counter, still carefully looking straight ahead. "The largest size, and iced, please. And one of those honeycake things."

"Of course, my dear! And which topping would you like on your honeycake?" Murthel rattled off a lengthy list of possibilities. Bridgette was overwhelmed by half of them being unfamiliar — obviously ingredients of magical origin that weren't common on Earth — and the other half all sounding equally appetizing.

She looked at Collum then. *Help?* she thought to him, hoping the amused pleading sound translated mind-to-mind.

"As it's your first time, Stars — Bridgette — I recommend the lavender," he suggested. She nodded in agreement, and he followed up her order with his own.

"Please have a seat wherever you'd like, dears, and Teale will have those to you momentarily," Murthel said, waving her hand as Collum pulled a slim wallet from his belt. "Put that straight away, Fyrdwisa. You know you do not pay here."

"Murthel, you know I can't do that," he said, smiling, and handed her a piece of paper. "Put this to good use — I know Avengeline has been speaking with the Fairies about importing Madagascar vanilla, and that does not come without price."

The witch blushed and accepted his payment. Bridgette hadn't seen magical currency yet, and she was bursting to ask Collum about it. The paper was almost holographic and seemed to morph from light purple to seafoam depending on how the light hit it.

He sensed her curiosity and led her out to the coffee shop's back patio. Bridgette noticed that Collum preferred to sit outside if possible. She certainly didn't mind, especially since the sun was out today. Even more so since the atmosphere was so quaint. Mismatched terracotta flowerpots brimmed with the first blooms of spring along the low brick walls around them, and each of the tables had two to four chairs, none of them the same. It was charming, with almost a country air.

"You were going to ask me about money?" Collum teased lightly, drawing her back to the present.

"Yes," Bridgette said simply. "I haven't seen you pay for anything except for today."

"Economics are different here," Collum said. "Heáhwolcen doesn't have money, really. Most beings and businesses function on a common sense of mutual aid, in-kind payment, and bartering. For example, should the witches of this shop, Murthel, Teale, and Avengeline, want to purchase something within Heáhwolcen, they're likely to pay for it out of a trade rather than paper money or coin. Just as many of their customers will pay for their coffees, sandwiches, and sweets with ingredients."

He inclined his head toward the windows. "There's a table in there with two forest Dryads. They likely paid for their fare using things from their own trees, probably spring apples, that the witches will use for tarts and pies. Aurelias has a small garden of strawberries, and that's what she uses in spring. Teale, who does the baking here, likes her berries so much that there is a very limited run of strawberry crisp bars each year named for her. It's only those of us who work for the Samnung, or respective governing bodies in each country, who are paid any sort of 'cash' salary. Mostly because we have little time to do anything elsewise that could be used to produce goods to share."

"Magical … socialism?" Bridgette mused, an eyebrow raised.

Collum shrugged. "I suppose, though we simply do what works for us. It doesn't have a name or a theory. It makes sense to aid each other and foster as much equity and equality as possible. Many magical beings are so long-lived that the idea of centuries or millennia of accumulating wealth seems horribly selfish, when there are so many other fruitful things one can do with the time and talents they are blessed with."

"Huh. In the United States at least, that idea of economics never seems to go over well with a lot of politicians."

The Elf didn't know what to say to that. Thankfully, there was only a further moment of awkward silence between he and Bridgette, as the witch named Teale appeared, their drinks and plates of honeycakes floating above her head. She waved them gently down to the table with help from a knobby birch wand in her left hand. "Here you go, dears! How are you this morning, Fyrdwisa?"

Collum bowed his head graciously. "I'm quite well, Teale. I hope the three of you are as well. This is Bridgette Conner, here as a guest of the Samnung. She is somewhat of a coffee connoisseur having grown up on Earth, and aside from what I have at home, this will be her first true experience with caife."

Teale, who looked exactly like Murthel, except with more frazzled gray hair, gave her hands a little clap. "Oh, how delightful! It is wonderful to meet you, my dear. Do tell us what you think, will you?"

"I will," Bridgette promised, a little unsure of how to act. Murthel and Teale seemed almost preternaturally joyful, as if nothing could cause them unease or discomfort.

The witch tottered back toward the door, and Bridgette realized why that was the word that came to mind when describing her walk: Teale wore Victorian-style gray ankle boots that looked too small and too tightly laced for her feet.

Very witchy, she thought to Collum, raising an eyebrow.

Be nice. It's part of their charm.

Poor Teale walks as though she's going to break an ankle if she steps wrong on those shoes. They don't look like they fit her at all.

I'm going to wall you out if you only speak to me in your mind to make judgmental comments, Starshine, Collum warned her. She picked up on his tone, though he didn't speak aloud.

"I didn't mean to be judge-y," she muttered. "Sorry."

"You're forgiven," he replied quietly. "Now try that. I want to know what you think just as badly as Teale does."

Bridgette obliged, and picked up the ice-cold glass in front of her. She sipped, and her eyes widened with glee. "Does this come with free refills? I could drink this for eternity — I am never going to be able to drink a regular pumpkin spice latte ever again. You've ruined me, Bundy."

Collum's eyes twinkled. "I thought you'd like it," he said, taking a sip of his own. "And the honeycakes?"

Those were met with similar rave reviews. Even if she hadn't been brought to Heáhwolcen for this world-saving mission, she'd stay just for the food and drink, Bridgette thought to herself.

"Tell me what we're doing today," she instructed Collum, taking another bite of the sweet, doughnut-like honeycake. "Pretty please?"

"You'll see. And you'll enjoy it, I think."

"Will there be food?"

He chuckled. "Do all human-raised halflings have such a one-track mind? There will be food at the end, of course. And even if there wasn't, what sort of host would I be if I didn't ensure you had sufficient sustenance to save the world?"

She smirked and pretended to throw a bite of honeycake at him. "A really shitty one. But everyone knows that an event's only worth going to if there's good food. And even the crappy food here, if there is such a thing, is way better than food on Earth."

"I would agree to that, having survived on too many hotel breakfasts this past year," Collum said. "No one seems to understand how to use seasonings other than salt and pepper. Or sugar."

"What's in these things that makes them so ..." Bridgette struggled to find a word other than "addictive." That didn't seem quite appropriate for something as wonderful as the drink she was trying to make last longer than a handful of minutes.

"That, Starshine, is a Modern Kitchen Witch trade secret. I do know that it is milk-based, and it does use true calabaza extract, enhanced with spices that make it sweet, warm, and cozy all at the same time," Collum said helpfully. "And now that I've said that, I feel as though I am a walking advertisement for the beverage. But it *is* rather quaffable."

Bridgette laughed at his choice of adjective. "Do they have

to-go cups? Because I'm about to quaff this down, and I'd like a second …"

As if by magic, a metal tumbler with coordinating straw appeared in front of her. Collum winked: "Knowing you, I presumed you'd want another for the road."

~ 24 ~

Halfway across Heáhwolcen, as Bridgette dressed for their mysterious outing, another sort of dressing occurred. Emi-Joye Vetur stared at her reflection in the flawless glass mirror, watching as her mother flitted around, wrapping her platinum blonde braids in a complicated crown shape around her temples. The twenty-five-year-old Fairy could hardly believe this day had truly come, but as she felt twists of magic secure her braids in place, a kind of finality filled the air. Her rosy, bow-shaped lips broke into a soft smile, and her mother stepped back to admire their handiwork.

"There, my love," her mother crooned. "You look like a queen."

"I should hope I look like an ambassadora," Emi-Joye replied, still staring at herself. More than a decade after choosing her life's path, the time arrived to fulfill it. She was nearly as tall as an Elf now in her adulthood, with an androgynously thin build, but feminine characteristics to her features. Her skin was the lightest ivory, with a hint of natural blush to her cheeks, and her slightly upturned eyes held irises of whirling icy blue. Her heart-shaped face was accentuated today with the smallest amount of white shimmer on her eyelids and high cheekbones, as was her collarbone, which peeked out of the top of her low-cut, boatneck gown.

Her mother tightened the silver fasteners on either side of her daughter's shoulders, and Emi-Joye's iridescent wings stilled in anticipation. The time was nearing; soon they'd fly to the Maremóhr, where, in front of hundreds of magical beings, she would officially be installed as the Fairy ambassadora to the Antarctic. Her gown today, floor-length snow-white fabric studded with crystals and silver beads, fit the part. She did rather resemble what she imagined an ice queen might look like, now that she gave it further thought.

A knock at the dressing room door: her father entered and

beamed widely at the Fairy as she turned to face him.

"Ready?" he asked, the smile growing bigger.

Emi-Joye's eyes twinkled. "And so we go."

By the time they arrived at the stately ceremony hall, the Maremóhr, its seats were already filled to the point of overflowing. In keeping with tradition, Emi-Joye and her family, as well as her predecessor and his family, Fairy leadership, and other important beings would remain in the back until Aristoces, Fairy of All Fairies, called them forth.

Bridgette and Collum were seated in the audience, in the front section, no less, and the Elfling assumed they were here for a theatrical performance. She still hadn't been able to goad Collum into giving her any additional details, something he was exceedingly pleased about.

"You look stunning, Starshine," he'd said upon seeing her.

Njahla had selected the dress. It was considered traditionally Elven: boatneck collar, long sleeves that widened into flowing bells with jeweled cuffs and matching trim at the neckline, hip belt, and hem. The dress itself was a deep teal, and split just below each hip to reveal an underskirt of palest lilac — Bridgette knew her eyes had inspired that one. There were iridescent opals in the jeweled beading, and the Elfling had been presented with a golden circlet to wear over her hair. She felt resplendent, as if she'd walked out of a Renaissance painting into her fairytale world.

The fyrdwisa was dressed in equally formal attire. His leggings were dark charcoal gray leather, and his navy, high-necked, long-sleeved tunic was embroidered with a design of gold leaves and artful swirls. Over his shoulders Collum wore a gray vest-like piece of apparel that draped more like a cloak, and a gold-buckle belt was slung across his hips with silver, bronze, chrome, and gold chains looped down over his thighs. The elaborate golden "E" was embroidered on either shoulder of his tunic, and a series of symbols Bridgette didn't recognize was stitched down both arms. He, too, wore a gold circlet. Like Bridgette's, it had dainty but powerful antlers rising from a center jewel. Where hers was an opal, his was multifaceted azurite. His eyes had never looked so blue.

"If I look stunning, then you look like something out of a dream," she murmured, unable to look too long at his form. "I *feel* like an Elf now."

Collum's smile then was soft, as it was now that he took her in as they sat in the evergreen velvet seats of the Maremóhr. While he watched her, she stared around them. Every magical being was dressed in their version of traditional, formal attire. It was rather a sight to behold, and as always, he adored seeing her behold it for the first time. He hadn't told her that he'd be going onstage, much less that she'd accompany him, and perhaps that wasn't smart. But Collum hadn't wanted to give her anything to be nervous of. He had a feeling she didn't enjoy having attention brought her way, though this wouldn't be *that* sort of attention.

"Does everyone dress up to come see a play? Or the opera?" Bridgette asked him, breaking the reverie. "It's like I'm sitting with a bunch of royals come to see Shakespeare himself."

Collum knew of the human playwright, and realized what Bridgette thought of their situation. "We're not at a theater," he said, knowing that his teasing tone would only serve to irritate her further. "You'll see soon enough what this is all about."

I'm sticking my tongue out at you in my head, you punk, she chided him mind-to-mind. He grinned back at her.

Any further retort would have to wait. The lights in the auditorium dimmed expectantly, and an ethereal array of soft music began to play. A layer of velvet curtains drew open onstage to reveal a full band of Fairies, three in skin-tight mini dresses of pure white glitter that seemed almost painted on, and two in oversized white sleeveless shirts worn over glittering white leggings. All five were barefoot and wore elaborately crafted masquerade masks adorned with feathers and pearls. The two in leggings each manned floating keyboards that emitted sounds somewhere between a xylophone and a synthesizer, which harmonized incredibly with the mournful, deep draw of an upright bass wielded by one of the Fairies in a dress. The fourth

Fairy gently thrummed on a set of white drums covered in tanned hides, which gave off distinctive reverberations that echoed in the halls of the Marémohr. But it was the fifth Fairy, whose mask was equal parts masquerade face covering and full feathered headdress, who captivated Bridgette most. She held a pristine silver violin under her chin, and the bow she drew across its delicate strings was strung with what had to be Unicorn hair. It produced sounds the Elfling could only dream of creating with her Earthly wooden violin — and Bridgette closed her eyes, finding herself easily lost in this song's meditative charm. Her breath rose and fell to its softly evolving rhythm, and her head tilted back in her seat. She began to float mere centimeters into the air as she felt the song and her heartbeat rise to crescendo. The violinist was flying above them, her paper-thin orange monarch butterfly wings changing pace along with the notes she drew forth.

Bridgette felt wetness on her cheeks, and realized she was crying. She didn't care: this was the most beautiful performance she'd ever witnessed, and she'd be damned if she let a little thing like vanity ruin the moment. She let the tears gently caress their way down to her jawline, then her collarbone, as she absorbed the music with her full mind, body, and soul. The band reached its peak; that highest point of a song when masterpiece meets final brushstroke; and Bridgette felt the instruments begin to evoke gradually quieter sounds as they cascaded down from the summit. When she opened her eyes again, the violinist took a final draw across the strings, the signal for all five to join and rise in the air for a bow and applause.

She was sobbing openly now. *How are those sounds even possible?* she wondered, directing her question to Collum as they joined the rest of the audience in a standing ovation.

The fyrdwisa, who'd studiously blocked her thoughts so he could concentrate on the music himself, finally looked at Bridgette and realized she was crying. *Did you like it?* he asked, mind-to-mind.

Bridgette stared at him incredulously. "Did I *like* it?" she asked aloud. "Are you kidding? I don't think there are even words to describe any of that. I could listen to that forever. I want to play like that one day."

Another tear fell, and Collum resisted the urge to wipe it away. "If you choose to stay, you could, you know," he whispered, a soft half-smile playing on his lips. "After saving the world."

She shot him a sidelong glance. "Right. Save the world first, then play violin. Priorities."

Collum elbowed her gently in the ribs, and Bridgette was spared further provocation by the arrival of Aristoces, who was the last being she anticipated seeing onstage at a Fairy concert.

"Tráthnóna mistéireach, beings of Heáhwolcen," Aristoces said as she flew from between the two velvet curtains and onto the stage. The Fairy of All Fairies landed softly, and raised her chin and arms in a gesture of embrace and welcome. "A joyous and fair day to each of you, as we gather for such an occasion."

Bridgette was struck again by how regal Aristoces was: the pure personification of magic and power, of all that was old and wise. As she had been that day in the Samnung, Aristoces was dressed simply and tastefully — her pewter-colored, floor-length gown sparkled with subtle black and quartz crystals on the hem and neckline. Its understatement somehow made her seem even more becoming and influential. She wore a silver crown bedecked with aqua agate; small stones on either side gradually increasing to a large, polished-smooth piece in the center of her forehead. Her natural curls were in their afro style, with several pieces weighted down and wrapped with silver wire to gently frame her face.

Bridgette stood alongside the rest of the audience, and they bowed to the Fairy leader in unison. Aristoces inclined her head at the crowd, and Bridgette followed Collum's lead as they sat back down.

Does Aristoces do this at every Fairy concert? Bridgette asked Collum mind-to-mind. He didn't answer, preferring to keep her in the dark. She kicked at his ankle. *Bundy, you really can be a dick sometimes.*

The Fairy's warm smile drew Bridgette's attention back to the stage. Joyous power radiated from Aristoces, and she lifted herself into midair, hovering just above their heads.

"Friends and colleagues, it is with the greatest of pleasure that I welcome each of you here today. This is a time to honor the life's work of Ambassador Frosset, as he enters his new position as ambassador emeritus, and we welcome and install his successor," she said, extending an arm behind her.

Wait a minute … Bridgette's eyes widened, and she gazed open-mouthed at Collum. He was fighting a massive smile, feigning seriousness as he watched the proceedings. *This isn't a show or a concert! This is a ceremony!*

"We begin by welcoming Ambestre Esmerina Malvarma, second-in-command and now bonded partner to Ambassador Frosset, and their young Fae, Siofra and Ilayda," Aristoces continued.

An adult female Fairy and two younglings flew forward to join her. If what Bridgette and Collum wore was considered traditionally Elven, the traditionally Fairy fashion was similar, and yet, markedly different.

The females wore stunning gowns of flowing fabric. The ambassador's spouse had a thin silver chain across her hips. Each adult had contrasting, complementary-colored capes of rich velvet attached to silver fasteners at their shoulders. The females' dresses were either sleeveless or bell sleeves with slits cut from shoulder to elbow. Additional slits in the back made room for wings. Siofra and Ilayda couldn't have been more than middle-school age, Bridgette thought, though she wondered if Fairies and Elves aged the same way humans did. The same way Elflings did. She brushed away the next thought before it could even enter her mind — how *did* beings like her age?

The younglings are eleven and fourteen, Collum thought to her, sensing her questions. *Save your inquiries for afterward, please?*

She glanced up and nodded. *Thank you in advance, oh wise Fyrdwisa.*

He rolled his eyes in an exaggerated fashion, then turned to the stage. Aristoces was welcoming a delegation from Earth, and Bridgette was legitimately shocked to see seven humans walk onstage.

"Wilgiest, winedryhtenen! Be welcome, friends and comrades, in our world above the world. Beings of Heáhwolcen, I present to you the Earth delegation, representing the seven nations with original territorial claims to the Antarctic: Sigewíf Catalina Quiroga of Argentina, South America; Thighearna Noah Irwin of Australia, a nation on its own; Thighearna Agustín Muños of Chile, South America; Sigewíf Élodie Jacquot of France, Europe; Sigewíf Aroha Te Rauna of New Zealand, Oceania; Sigewíf Dagmar Nilsen, of Norway, Europe; and Thighearna Charles Brady, of the United Kingdom, Europe," Aristoces recited.

The seven humans looked ... normal, Bridgette thought, in dresses or suits as if they'd come straight from a government office. Each had a sash around one shoulder, decorated with those same runes that Collum wore on his sleeves. All seven were smiling in some level of wonderment, and Bridgette made a note to ask Collum how they were supposed to keep the existence of Heáhwolcen a secret if humans magicked up the portal every time there was a new Fairy ambassador installed.

The audience was invited to stand then, and applaud the humans, who bowed or curtsied in answer. The Antarctic delegation shifted to one side of the stage, and Aristoces waited until the din calmed before speaking again.

"It is now my utmost honor to acknowledge our own leadership, the Samnung, as they make their way into our space," she said gracefully. "Her Majesty Queen Nehemi of Endorsa, with her daughter Cloa, princess of Endorsa, and their borhond Kharis."

Nehemi, haughty as what Bridgette assumed to be usual, strode onto the stage, her head held high, proudly carrying the weight of her peacock crown. Her eyes were as sharp as her cheekbones today — she seemed to command the attention of

the room, a whining child who would pitch a temper tantrum
should she not be harped on. She was dressed similarly to how
she'd been at the Samnung meeting earlier in the week, but this
afternoon's long-sleeved gown was a vibrant shade of turquoise
that made both her bronze crown and red hair gleam. The
gown's underskirt and trim were of actual peacock feathers, and
pearls edged paisley swirls in the fabric throughout. Cloa
followed her, her dull dark brown hair as dull as those odd, gold-
green eyes. She was dressed in essentially the same garb as
Nehemi, and Bridgette resisted the urge to gag: it was as if the
queen dressed a miniature of herself, and treated the princess as
though she was a child and not sixteen. The Elfling added
"What's a borhond?" to her list of questions for after the
ceremony, as her gaze landed on Kharis.

"Representing the Sanguisuge coteries of our lands,
Verivol," Aristoces continued.

Brigette openly gaped at the beautiful being who effortlessly
glided onstage next. She already assumed Verivol was a bit of a
fashionista, and they did not disappoint today. The Sanguisuge
had done their full face of makeup to accentuate those ice-white
cheekbones, and a slash of black lipstick made for a stark contrast
of their unmistakable pearly canines as they smiled slyly. Verivol
was dressed as though going to a costume ball when Louis XIV
was king of France, except their ruffled blouse was cut in a V so
deep it crested at the hips, where a wide band of black leather
met it. Skin-tight crimson breeches and knee-high black leather
boots completed the outfit, as did Verivol's numerous jeweled
accessories, and fierce-looking pointed nails painted silver.

"Corria Deathhunter, first of her name, master
swordswoman of Bondrie," the Fairy introduced.

The physically powerful female strode forward, clad in
cherry-red leather that was elaborately stamped with a pattern
Bridgette couldn't quite make out. Corria's chrome armor shone
brighter than usual in the stagelights of the Maremóhr, and her
intense, almost black eyes seemed to evaluate the energy of the
room. The room had gotten extra hushed, seeing that deathly

sword sheathed at her side. Her black hair was done in a braid formation so elaborate it must have been entirely for show: there was no way her helmet would fit over it.

Then Aristoces said, "Representing the Elven lands of Eckenbourne, Ard Rialóir Trystane Eiríkr, Fyrdwisa Collum Andoralain, and Sigewíf Bridgette Conner."

~ 25 ~

"I'm sorry, what?" Bridgette looked dumbly at Collum, who had stopped fighting his grin and now held his hand out to her. "Did she actually just say my name?"

"She did, Starshine. Come on," he urged, instantly regretting keeping this part of the day a secret. "I should have told you. I'm sorry."

"You should have, you punk," she hissed, and shot a fake smile up at Nehemi, having noticed the queen watching her shrewdly. "Don't worry, I'll learn magic and figure out how to hex you or something for this."

Collum choked on a laugh and evanesced them the short distance to stand next to an absolutely dashing Trystane, who waited for them at the curtain opening. Though the Elves of Heáhwolcen didn't recognize a *king*, per se, Trystane as ard rialóir looked the part. He'd dyed his ice-blonde hair to a deeper shade with grayish brown undertones, and wore a gold crown like Collum's — larger and with a center stone of stunning green onyx, which shifted between shades of moss, gold, and taupe. The three walked onstage, Collum and Bridgette following their Elven leader, and stood next to Verivol.

"The final member of the Samnung to join us this day, Bryten, of no surname, representing the beings of the wood, the brook, and the mountain," Aristoces proclaimed.

Bryten, his horns shined to exquisite perfection, gleamed almost as bright as Corria's armor. He'd perhaps exaggerated the metallic tone of his skin with added cosmetics, because Bridgette could have sworn he looked covered in glitter. He also chose to forego a shirt entirely.

I don't think I've ever seen a government official purposely not wear a shirt. In public, Bridgette said to Collum, mind-to-mind.

Clearly you haven't attended enough Samnung meetings, Starshine. It's more of a shock to see the Baetalüan with a shirt on *than without,* the fyrdwisa responded likewise.

She grinned, watching as the shirtless, golden being took his place next to the master swordswoman, opposite the stage from where she and Collum stood. Next to come, parading straight down the outer two and central aisles of the Maremóhr, were Fairies carrying the flags of Fairevella, Heáhwolcen, and the seven Earth nations that collectively represented Antarctica. Though they were flying, the nine managed to structure their movements as if in a staccato military flag line, marching to a battlefield drum beat only they could hear. Once in their places, the audience turned hushed faces toward Aristoces, who beamed proudly and said, "Please stand as we welcome the ambassadora-select of the Antarctic, Emi-Joye Vetur, accompanied by her parents, Tula and Johannes."

The Elfling was mesmerized by the young Fairy who then flew from between the curtains to join Aristoces. Her parents flew a few feet behind her, and the audience stood reverently as a trumpet salute sounded overhead. Emi-Joye, wearing a snow-white gown, her platinum blonde braids in an elaborate crown shape around her head, was nearly beyond describable.

She looks like an ice queen, Bridgette thought to Collum. His elbow was linked around hers, and he gave her arm a slight squeeze of agreement.

"The process to become a Fairy ambassador or ambassadora is an intensive one, which no Fae youngling takes lightly," Aristoces said. "I first met Emi-Joye when she was a precocious child, hardly older than ten. She attended a ceremony very much like this one during an enrichment experience for her school, and following the festivities, instead of flying in formation with the rest of her classmates, Emi-Joye flew out of line and back to the stage to speak with me. She showed great confidence, diction, and a level of calm professionalism even at such an age. I do not consider myself an imposing individual, but it is uncommon for a young being to feel completely comfortable in speaking to me as she did then. At that moment, I knew this youngling would do many great things in her life.

"That she has. Emi-Joye Vetur exceeded every expectation set for her," Aristoces continued. "Be it academic evaluations, physical trials, or spiritual gifts, her ability to focus, strategize, and seek out the best in others served her well these twenty-five years. When she turned sixteen and requested a territory to work with, I at least was not surprised by her choice of the Antarctic. Seven nations on Earth proclaim lands here — and many more contribute to the work and research on this icy plain. To be the ambassador or ambassadora of *one* nation is stress enough for most Fae, but to have a minimum of seven to corral and assist at any given moment? It is not an easy feat, as Ambassador Frosset warned her."

Aristoces paused as the audience tittered. "Yet this youngling was up to the challenge and did not back down. Ever. When she made her request, Frosset had a number of years left before his century of service was complete, and Emi-Joye undertook her next years of training knowing that she would not take her position at age eighteen. This did not dissuade her. She welcomed the opportunity to become an apprentice ambassadora and grew from the tasks placed before her. There was never a moment of complaint, nor an instance of dissatisfaction at the years of work ahead of her before she became ambassadora. Emi-Joye Vetur attacked each challenge with an open mind, with precision and with a goal. These are valued qualities that are indeed taught and encouraged to anyone who wishes to follow this diplomatic path. However, Emi-Joye is naturally gifted in these qualities, more so than any diplomat I have seen in my many years. It is my utmost honor therefore to preside over this ceremony, and cape her before you all this day."

Aristoces bowed her head slightly, and the full slate of Samnung leaders moved to one side of the curtain opening, where three barefoot, shirtless male Fairies now emerged. One, who wore a pair of loose white pants that tightened at the ankles, positioned himself behind a standing cello. Another wore what must have been a kilt, a wrapped skirt-like bit of fabric in shades of sparkling blue that looked like early sunrise reflecting off the ocean. He carried a silver flute. The third, also in pants, though his were somewhere between navy blue and black, had a violin. A brief moment of fine-tuning strings later, the music began.

Bridgette found herself again swept away by the sounds the Fairies made. This song was vaguely familiar, mournful, and she struggled to place the sound.

It's whale song, Collum offered helpfully, mind-to-mind.

Her eyes widened, and she heard it now: the soft call-and-answer of one instrument to another, then joining together until all three played together in harmony. A conversation of kindred sea spirits.

Why are they playing whale sounds? Bridgette thought to Collum.

This part of the ceremony is reserved for traditional music or performance from the nation the ambassador or ambassadora will represent Fairevella to. As Antarctica is a bit of an outlier in terms of being a nation of humans, the song played now represents the creatures that call it home, he thought back. *It sweeps you away, doesn't it?*

She nodded imperceptibly — lest the whole of Heáhwolcen dignitaries find out the two of them could converse inside their heads — and tuned back into the song. It was winding down now, she could tell, and Bridgette wondered briefly if Emi-Joye would be able to commune with the animals as well as the humans in this difficult habitat.

The audience stood to applaud the trio, which grouped together and bowed before flying offstage. Aristoces alighted back into the air, waiting until the clapping calmed before speaking: "With the presentation of our new ambassadora comes the presentation of her new second — a right-hand being that will serve in the event she cannot; a crucial advisor who will handle the day-to-day as well as the extraordinary. For her second, Emi-Joye Vetur has selected Apostine, a Fairy of no surname. We welcome him now."

The male Fairy who then flitted out was Faeling — full-blooded Fairies most assuredly did not have horns, golden-hued metallic skin, and a thin, demonic tail that ended in spearpoint. Bridgette knew better than to rudely ask what he was; she'd already had that lecture once this week from Collum, but she *was* curious. The Faeling, with his golden beetle wings, had to be the same type of Fairy lineage of Galdúr and Aristoces, with insect wings rather than gossamer. She'd have sworn he was sort of like Bryten, though his horns were those of a ram and not the thinner, more delicately forged ones of the Samnung member. She remembered something Aurelias said: Tiefling.

A gentle tap on her foot confirmed what she'd figured out, and Bridgette knew Collum must have been listening to her talk it out inside her head. So Apostine's heritage was both Tiefling, whatever that was, and Fairy. He had the Fairy eyes, too, Bridgette noted, though the whorls that filled his irises were amber. He resembled a golden god the Elfling remembered seeing in history books of old Egypt.

Apostine looked positively disbelieving at his being the choice of second as Emi-Joye flew to stand next to him. Trystane stepped forward to join them.

"Apostine, of no surname, I implore you to repeat after me, and speak aloud your Hyldájj," the Elf said, his rich voice booming through the Maremóhr. The Faeling nodded proudly, and the corners of Emi-Joye's mouth turned up with mirrored pleasure.

Trystane spoke, and Apostine repeated, in a deep voice an octave as low as Hell itself: "I, Apostine, of no surname, step forward this day into the role of ambestre of the Antarctic, second to the Ambassadora Herself. I solemnly affirm that I will in this role, to the best of my ability, support and defend the morals and rituals of beings magical and non; that I will bear true faith and allegiance to the same. I state that I take this obligation freely, without mental, physical, spiritual, or magical reservation, or purpose of evasion, and with no ill-intent. I vow to well and faithfully perform the duties of this office I am about to enter, be I so blessed by deity and magicks old and new."

Upon finishing, the audience positively erupted, and Emi-Joye embraced Apostine in a hug. She kissed his cheek, and stood with a hand on both his shoulders, speaking to him in earnest — quietly enough so that only the two of them could hear. Trystane inclined his head at the pair, then stepped back into place beside Collum.

Bridgette felt slightly emotional watching the new ambestre and his soon-to-be ambassadora at the center of the stage. She felt even more so when a lyre was brought forth and presented to Apostine, who soared high into the domed ceiling of the Maremóhr on those golden wings, and began to play. The twinkling sounds of his strings echoed and seemed to endlessly wrap themselves around every being. Then, he began to sing, his voice low and haunting, drawing out each of those melodies longer than humanly possible:

> *"I've found a home,*
> *A vast space of intention*
> *I've found fam'ly,*
> *Both born and chosen*
> *I am I, yet much more."*

The song was simple, and Bridgette was struck to turn her head back to Emi-Joye, who was crying openly in front of them. Bryten, too, had tears in his eyes. She glanced at Collum, wanting to understand, despite her promise to hold all questions until the end.

As you worked out, Apostine is half-Tiefling. The Tiefling are magical beings of … complicated heritage, shall we say, he told her, mind-to-mind. *It is often that Tiefling younglings are abandoned at a young age. Apostine has no surname because it is the way of the Tiefling, but he was lucky in that after his mother disappeared, his Fairy father refused to let the male raise himself. He encouraged Apostine to learn all he could about his Tiefling heritage, and his Fae one, so that perhaps a new order could begin for the horned beings. It is known that because of their typical lack of parentage, Tieflings stay to themselves and often do not, firstly come out into society, but secondly acquire any sort of position. This is a momentous day for both Apostine and all Tieflings in existence, for him to not only come forth but to be so welcomed in a leadership position like this. The song he sang just now is a retelling of an ancient Tiefling poem, called* The Lament. *This poem was song or spoken word, depending on presentation, of sadness, loss, and solitude. To have it reclaimed in such a way, rewritten to be a song of grace instead of mourning, is …*

Collum's mind-voice trailed off, but Bridgette understood. This time, it was she who gently squeezed the elbow her arm was wrapped around.

She barely realized, having been caught up in Collum's history story, that a Fairy who must be Ambassador Frosset had been introduced. The male had a young face, but his dark brown hair was speckled with white and gray. He wore a sleeveless, glittering white tunic that draped to his knees, and soft gray leggings. A silver belt around his hips sparkled as light hit the various blue and gray crystals adorning it, and matching cuffs were around both of his muscular biceps. He was addressing the audience, and Bridgette tuned in to what must be his retirement speech.

"Cat, Élodie, Noah, Agustín, Charlie, Aroha, Dag — it has been my pleasure to work alongside you and your countries for a full century, and I look forward to serving with you in this new role as ambassador emeritus," the ambassador said, addressing the humans. "These past few years as Emi-Joye has come along as my apprentice have been both challenging and rewarding. You have come to know her as an intelligent, gifted Fairy who keeps me on my toes and in line. I look forward to seeing her relationship grow with each of you, and those who will follow in your stead, during her century of service.

"Beings of Heáhwolcen, perhaps you do not know this, but the Antarctic is an unusual territory to partner with," he continued, turning his attention to the crowd. It does not have true citizens; its citizens are its creatures. The Antarctic is a region of ice and snow, and of spirit and science. It is where Nature, deity, and other worlds link each into our own, and the research done here is vital to all. My role as ambassador has been to offer guidance regarding the changing climates on Earth. For those unaware, the temperatures on our allied planet have risen greatly during my term, and I have seen icemelt rise oceans and glacier unforge. The eight of us whose leadership rules this territory know the dangers that rising water poses to our human friends, though I must add the merfolk won't mind a bit!"

Titters rang out in the auditorium, and Frosset paused before continuing after his little joke.

"Emi-Joye Vetur steps from a role of learning to a role of leading today, with Apostine at her side. There is much still to learn, and much still to do, to prevent this drastic change in Antarctic climate from threatening those elsewhere on Earth. The research our leaders will preside over will change the course of history, and I could not imagine a better Fairy to see that to fruition," he finished.

As he and Emi-Joye both headed back to centerstage, the audience stood and applauded the retiring ambassador. This wasn't the wild applause after musical performances or Apostine's oath of office, his Hyldájj, Trystane called it, but a reverent noise of appreciation, and of respect. The clapping quieted, and all faces turned next to Nehemi as the regal queen of Endorsa strode forth.

~ 26 ~

This time it was Apostine who stepped to the side, and Emi-Joye turned to face the imposing queen. Nehemi was by no means a petite witch, but the Fairy was so tall that she had to look down upon her. Even still, the steely-eyed queen gave her the slightest of shudders.

"Emi-Joye Vetur, by the power vested in me as queen of Endorsa, leader of the Samnung of Heáhwolcen" — Bridgette felt Collum bristle slightly at that — "I implore you to repeat after me, and speak aloud your Hyldájj," Nehemi said. There was no kindness, no pride in that faintly Australian accent of hers.

Emi-Joye swallowed deeply, took a breath and nodded. Collum heard the Fairy's inner voice then, a slight tremble before she started repeating Nehemi's words.

"I, Emi-Joye Vetur, step forward this day into the role of ambassadora to the Antarctic. I solemnly affirm that I will in this role, to the best of my ability, support and defend the morals and rituals of beings magical and non; that I will bear true faith and allegiance to the same; that I will let no being or creature cause affront or harm to the territory placed in my charge; that I will work seamlessly and without malcontent with my fellow leaders toward our common goals. I state that I take this obligation freely, without mental, physical, spiritual, or magical reservation, or purpose of evasion, and with no ill-intent. I vow to well and faithfully perform the duties of this office I am about to enter, be I so blessed by deity and magicks old and new."

Tears were streaming down her face, down her parents' faces, as Emi-Joye looked determinedly at the crowd rising to its feet. Bridgette expected applause, but none came. It seemed as though they were waiting for something.

They were: there was one more step before Emi-Joye was truly the ambassadora. With a flick of her wand, Nehemi summoned forth a hooded, ice-blue velvet cape lined with white fur. Five white stars were painstakingly embroidered upon it. She handed the cape to Frosset, who flew into the air to display the cape before the full audience.

"I bestow upon you now, Emi-Joye Vetur, the Indryhtu Sciccel, an outward symbol of your office and commitment, your vow of duty to the beings of Heáhwolcen, the Fairies, and your territory," he said, and lowered himself down to fasten the cape to the silver bolts at Emi-Joye's shoulders. "Comrades, winedryhtenen, I present to you now Ambassadora Vetur."

If they erupted when Apostine took his oath, they exploded for Emi-Joye. Fairies in the audience didn't just stand, they flew into the air. Witches and wizards lifted lit wands or fingertips in salute. Beings with faintly animal characteristics were braying, howling, stomping hooved feet. A clamoring in the far back left of the Maremóhr — that was the Bondrie Guard, clattering sword to shield and chrome breastplate in her honor. And the Elves, oh! The Elves! Bridgette was crying now too, and she could have sworn Collum even teared up as he and Trystane joined their brethren in calling forth a flurry of glittering ice crystals to shower from the domed ceiling. A series of five star-shaped snowflakes swirled above Emi-Joye's head and descended upon her in a five-pointed crown. Nehemi, even, held her want aloft and bronze light shone upon the Fairy.

Emi-Joye noticed the weight upon her head from that ice crown and lifted her chin higher. She adjusted her cape slightly against the iridescent gossamer of her wings, then flew out in front of the stage, centering herself over the flag of Heáhwolcen in the center aisle. She closed her eyes and extended both arms out, the Elves' magical ice crystals hitting her skin and melting instantly, leaving no trace but for a titillating sensation of anticipation. She savored that feeling, and opened her eyes and mouth to address those gathered to celebrate this moment alongside her.

A whispered word amplified her voice so all could hear: "It is with the highest level of gratitude that I fly before you today, beings of Heáhwolcen, fellow Fae and our winedryhtenen of Earth. I am honored to have been spoken of so highly by Aristoces, Fairy of All Fairies, and by Ambassador-Emeritus Frosset Malvarma. I have indeed dreamt of this day since I was but ten, the earliest age a Fairy may begin to pursue this career. At that time, I knew of the roles ambassadors and ambasadoras played in our society. Also at that time, I thought it must have been quite a boring role to have."

Laughter, then, from the audience, as the ice crystals continued to shower around them. A snowfall fit for a snow queen.

"My school, as Aristoces mentioned, attended the installment of Ambassador Marcallus Gaccio, Fairy ambassador to Italy," Emi-Joye continued. "Marcallus was quite old to assume the role, in his forties, and my young friends were shocked by this. We had always been taught that the role begins at eighteen. And his had, of course! Eighteen was when Marcallus declared Italy to be his territory, and he was willing to work, to wait, to patiently assist until his time came to step forward officially. It was that special patience, the foighne agus grásta, as we call it in the old language, that called to me. That knowing of what was meant to be no matter the timeline, and willingness to accept that the timeline was not in his control. Marcallus seemed such a good being. He is kind, he is thoughtful, he is waving at me from the fourth row ..."

More laughter. Bridgette grinned up at the young Fairy, whose smile shone bright as she waved to her friend in the audience.

"I was young and perhaps not impulsive, but I tend to rise to challenges. What a challenge, then, to be willing to wait patiently without remorse! It was that reason I approached Aristoces that day, and made it known that I, too, wished to pursue this life," Emi-Joye said. "At ten, I hadn't a clue what I wished to grow into. Over the years, as I began to fervently immerse myself in my studies, I found certain things to be true. Art and music are beyond me. Deity help anyone I ever try to forge blades for; they're more like to get stabbed than their enemy. Though I love feoht training, a life of professional, physical combat is not my style. I enjoyed studying and learning, but I had no patience for teaching. Rather, I enjoyed studying and learning with the forethought of future application. I became enamored with science and its interaction with magic, and by the time I was sixteen, I knew what territory I wanted to request. And, as deity would have it, it was a territory with years yet of an ambassador in service to it.

"Antarctica — I cannot fully explain it, but it called to me," she said dreamily. "As I stared at and studied maps of Earth, trying to find the best fit for me, I kept finding myself drawn to the white expanse at the bottom of the globe. As far away, just about, from Heáhwolcen as its possible to get in this atmosphere, much to my mother's displeasure. I was apprehensive: so far, and so many humans in its leadership already, and so odd a citizenry! I even went to a leódrúne and had tarot read for me, to question and confirm what I knew to be true. And so it was that I declared the Antarctic as where I wanted to serve and represent the magical worlds. I learned much from the ambassador-emeritus since then and have much to learn still. He alluded to this previously, but there is still much to be done in that region, much to be done that has great cause to affect every life in this atmosphere, magical and non. I am honored that the spirits and deities, the gods of old and new, saw fit to groom me for such an influential role. I truly hope I serve each of you well, for the next hundred years, and many hundreds after."

Emi-Joye bowed, and the audience erupted again. The Elves changed the ice crystals all to stars, and the magical lights became silver and blue as the Fairy brought herself back down to the stage. This time, she stood right next to Aristoces, Apostine by her side.

A tall Fairy with light reddish-brown hair and lavender eyes rose from the audience. Aristoces introduced her from the stage: Skyanna Elixabete, famed Heáhwolcen poet. Skyanna cleared her throat, and spoke with a voice that rang joyfully around the Maremóhr: "The moon rises!" The audience echoed her call, then quieted for her recitation:

"The roots of the starflower run deep into the soil
Connecting the flower to the Earth.
The flower's roots steady the soil
The soil nourishes the flower

So does the Fairy connect the world above the world
To the Earth.
The Fairy heart is said to be like a star
A many-faceted crystal,
Shining light into even the darkest places
Reflecting light on the Earth
Like the moon in the night,
Leading us into the darkness
That approaches.
Let light shine from your heart —
Let your roots run deep —
Let your wings always bring you home."

As Skyanna resumed her seat and the audience applauded her work, Nehemi again took center stage. This time, Kharis joined her. Cloa remained on the sidelines, that glazed look still over her gold-green eyes.

"In accordance with the traditions of old, Nehemi, queen of Endorsa, will now lead us in a ritual of protection and prosperity for the new ambassadora, the new ambestre, and the territory they liaison with," Aristoces said. Everyone hushed and stilled, all eyes on the Endorsan delegation.

The queen raised her wand. "The witches and wizards of Heáhwolcen invite each of you to join in meditation. We ask you to close your eyes, to breathe deeply, to remove from your mind all expectations and thought," she said.

A soft tendril of windchimes began to play; Bridgette couldn't tell where the sound came from, but she obeyed. She began to feel herself getting lost in the chimes, trying to follow their song, losing all track of where she was. If it wasn't for Collum's arm wrapped around hers, she would have forgotten herself entirely.

As their audience stilled, and the only sounds in the Maremóhr were the windchimes, Kharis began walking toward the doors at the back of the hall. Simultaneously, a handful of witches and wizards rose from their seats and encircled the audience, the leadership on stage, the humans. Nehemi summoned forth a massive length of green ribbon, and the beings began passing it down and around, thrice encircling the whole of the gathering.

"We, the beings here gathered, invite the goddesses Tyche and Lakshmi, the god Mercury; the gods Vishnu and Apollo; the goddesses Bastet and Soteria; to now join us in this circle. Be welcome, bringers of prosperity, of good fortune, of protection from harm," Nehemi said, feeling the temperature quickly dip, then rise again, as invited spirits entered. "We call forth now the elements: the voracious wind of air, the bubbling brook waters, the stoic soil on which we stand, the eternal flame of Salamandaria. We call forth our brethren sisters and brothers, siblings of old and new, witches before and after, to join from the North, the South, the East, and the West; the four corners and the powers of three, be with us now in this moment of space, time, and infinity."

Bridgette was both lost in her trance and present in said moment. She felt herself rising from the stage, surrounded by soft breeze and misty rain. She was cold, then hot, then stabilized, and felt roots rise to bring her feet back down to the ground. How odd, to be lulled into this sleep-like state, but how pleasant it was to be here.

Kharis and three other wizards approached doors and windows, then began using their wands to draw five-pointed stars three times each on them. After the third time, the pentacle sigils glowed turquoise.

Nehemi began to recite the ritual spell, three times. Her voice was joined the second time by witches and wizards, then the third by everyone in the room. Even the humans felt compelled to join in, and Bridgette found herself muttering words she'd never heard before, wasn't sure how she knew them now, except perhaps because of the magic itself enveloping her:

> *"As their spirits grow, so strong and fine,*
> *May these Fae prosper from the Universe and divine.*
> *We cast this circle 'round them here,*
> *So nothing ill may interfere.*
> *Safety surround these Fae who stand*
> *Joy and luck be blessed their hands.*

Nothing evil enters here
Without our permission, given clear.
Safety surround those Earthly lands,
Joy and luck be blessed those icy sands.
Nothing evil enters there,
Without our permission, given clear.
And by the power of three times three,
As it is, so mote it be."

~ 27 ~

An almighty roar and a searing burn — ice or flame, the Elfling couldn't tell — and Bridgette was pulled suddenly back into reality. She blinked, the crowded Maremóhr coming into focus.

What was that? she thought to Collum, gripping his elbow tighter in her arm. *I think I'm reeling.*

Very powerful Old Magick, made more powerful by the fact that every single being here willingly participated in it and contributed energy toward it, Collum thought in response. *It can be a disconcerting sensation the first time one is part of such an undertaking.*

No shit, Sherlock. How do you know if the spell like, took, or whatever?

Collum shot her a raised-brow look. *Because it's a spell. It's magic. That's how.*

She frowned slightly, then turned back to look at Aristoces, who was yet again waiting for the audience's din to silence.

"In accordance with our highest and oldest traditions, we of Fairevella invite you to join us in standing for *Il Cantic*, the Song of the Fae. Please rise," the Fairy of All Fairies instructed.

The audience obliged, and side curtains rose to reveal the original five musicians, now joined by the trio that played whale song. Apostine and Emi-Joye joined hands, then soared into the dome and began to sing together. It was a language Bridgette didn't know, something as old as the Fairies themselves, with a joyful, slow melody. A singing voice entered her mind — Collum translated for her, and Bridgette fought the urge to melt on the spot. Forget the Fairies; it was that lilting brogue she didn't want to end as it sang:

> *Once upon a sky-bright morn,*
> *Sweet Sun coated earth from canopy to loam*
> *Inviting wing-ed beings of old*
> *Into the world, now theirs to roam*
>
> *Fallen angel, spirits and lore*
> *Myth and beetle, bird of shore*
> *Insect, bat, and butterfly*

Sparrow, eagle, all alight

To fly! To fly — to claim these skies
And in them form realms on high
Once upon this sky-bright morn,
Amidst the clouds, the Fae were born.

Well-met they were with storm and sea
Well-met they were with ground and breeze
Well-met they were with mage and fate
Well-met, they were a novel race

With human limbs they could climb and work
On metamorph wings they could soar
With mystic vein they harbored elements
In bright eyes could their magic whorl

They fly! They fly — they now claim these skies
And in them formed realms on high.
Each day begins a sky-bright morn
And so go the Fae, wing-ed protectors forsworn.

Collum stopped his song as Emi-Joye and Apostine took bows from their place in the dome, and the musicians whose haunting melodies accompanied them bowed from their spots on the main stage.

"Please remain in place as our new leaders exit the Maremóhr," Aristoces commanded. She flitted to one side as Emi-Joye and Apostine flew out, and before Bridgette could process what happened, Collum evanesced them to a giant green meadow. The rest of the Samnung joined them shortly, some evanescing, others arriving of their own accord. Bryten looked as though he'd sprinted; a fine mist of sweat beaded along his golden brow.

"What did you think, Liluthuaé?" the horned being asked, walking up to her.

"I think I'm still out of breath from *somebody* evanescing me without warning. Again!" Bridgette hissed, making Bryten chuckle. "But really, that was … I had no idea what we were even doing. I thought it was a concert! And then suddenly, Aristoces was there, and that music! Jeez, that *music*."

She remembered Bryten being her sole ally at the Samnung meeting, when Nehemi dismissed the idea of creative professions being professions. The Baetalü seemed to have the same thought, and he winked at her.

"I thought you'd like that part best," he said, somewhat smugly.

Verivol joined them then, smiling so that both their fangs showed. "It is good to see you again, Bright Star," they purred. "I must say, you looked quite shocked to be summoned onstage. Did our darling fyrdwisa not tell you what this day held?"

"No, the punk of a 'darling fyrdwisa' most certainly did not," Bridgette said, then grinned. "You both look insanely dashing. Everyone does, really. I feel like I'm in either a dream or a painting, or maybe both."

Bryten bowed to her. "And you as well, Liluthuaé. I think you'll enjoy this just as much as the music during the ceremony. Welcome to the after-soiree — where we'll have food *and* music." He winked again, then bounded off.

Verivol remained a moment longer. "You'll find, Bright Star, that there is much to learn about the ways of magic and magical beings. I do hope you remain curious, and do not hesitate to ask that which you do not know."

She blinked, not sure what prompted that remark. Next thing she knew, the Sanguisuge moved faster than light and was halfway across the meadow, speaking to a Fairy who seemed to be manning a carving station. *Probably asking for the rarest, bloodiest cut,* Bridgette thought. She wandered off to Collum and Trystane, who were a few paces behind her, grabbing drinks. Collum was, anyway. Trystane had yet another glass of burgundy liquid he'd clearly summoned to him.

"What even is that crap you're always drinking?" she asked, accepting a flute of sparkling wine from the fyrdwisa.

"My personal spirit collection," Trystane said, feigning offense at her calling it "crap". "I've quite refined the art of procuring it myself over the years, and ever since, nothing has been to my liking. If you choose to stay" — his voice lowered — "perhaps you and the fyrdwisa can join me in my home for a tasting."

Collum shot him a bemused look. "Trystane, I have been asking you for *decades* to do a tasting. My Starshine is here for all of three days and *she* gets an invite?"

"Perks of being the Bright Star," the Elven leader responded, raising his glass in mock salute. Bridgette bit her lip to keep from laughing.

Suddenly, both Elves looked up. Emi-Joye, Apostine, and their parents were flying in.

Do I get to meet them? she asked Collum, mind-to-mind.

Of course, Starshine, he replied, and she recalled how he'd just called her "*my* Starshine" to Trystane.

Stop it, Bridgette, she thought to herself, and began following the crowd to where the new ambassadora was coming in for landing. She took a long, heady sip of the sparkling wine, watching as the Fairies came to join the festivities.

Emi-Joye landed first and flitted a few inches off the ground, mostly to keep her cape and floor-length gown from dragging in the grass. "Hello, all!" she called out, her voice light and breathy. "I've had enough ceremony for one day. Let us feast!"

The crowd laughed, and the ambassadora led the way to begin eating. In addition to the carving station, there was a bar laden with fresh fruits and vegetables, berries and nuts; a table overflowing with platters of fish, oysters, and shrimp; baskets of bread scattered around; and a towering cake that glittered as if it was covered with more of that magic ice the Elves rained down in the Maremóhr. Bridgette helped herself to some of everything, sticking close to Collum's side. Not that she was the introverted, nervous type, but she felt somewhat intimidated by yet another majestic being with such power and influence.

The Elves and Bridgette sat together. After a few moments, they were joined by, of all beings, Cloa. She cradled the one-eyed cat Arctura in her arms, and hardly looked at them as she took a seat and gazed dimly around at the party.

"This seems nice," she said, and a faint smile appeared on her lips. "Where are we?"

Bridgette dropped her fork mid-bite, and it clattered loudly on the wooden table. She'd not heard Cloa speak before. Collum and Trystane exchanged surprised glances before Trystane answered the princess.

"This is the after-soiree to celebrate the new Fairy ambassadora," he said gently, as if talking to a child. "See her there, the Fairy with the white-blonde hair and the blue cape? That's her. That's Emi-Joye."

Cloa tilted her head to one side, considering — although it was hard for Bridgette to tell if she could really even *see* the ambassadora. "I should like to meet this Fairy," Cloa said finally, petting Arctura. "I should like to think we will be great friends."

Trystane nodded slowly. "I will … bring her to meet both of you," he said, then rose and began walking toward Emi-Joye and Apostine.

What the FUCK? Bridgette thought to Collum. *She can speak?*

Yes, he thought back warily. *But rarely does she. And even rarer does what she say make sense.*

Emi-Joye graciously accepted Trystane's request to please come meet the princess and the Samnung's guest. She flew over, a warm, welcoming smile already pulling at her lips.

"Hello, friends!" she said. "I thank you greatly for spending time at the ceremonies today, and for joining us now."

"Aristoces has told us much about you," Collum said, bowing his head. "Well-met, Ambassadora Vetur. This is Cloa, princess of Endorsa, and our guest, Bridgette Conner, visiting from Earth to learn about her magical heritage."

Her cover story, Bridgette remembered.

"Earth! How fascinating!" Emi-Joye's eyes lit up. "I should love to ask you many questions. And our witch princess! The honor is mine, sigewifs."

Bridgette had about a thousand questions she wanted to ask the Fairy too, but now was not the time. Especially when Cloa continued to speak in that dazed, not-wholly-focused way she did.

"Your name is lovely, Emi-Joye," she said, her eyes not meeting anyone else's. "I feel as if I know you, but perhaps we have yet to meet. Perhaps it is our spirits that know of one another. Perhaps it is the fates that brought us together this day."

Again, Bundy, what the fuck, Bridgette thought fervently. An odd energy began to fill the air around the three females, and she didn't like it one bit.

Emi-Joye, who had no idea that Cloa wasn't normally like this, took it all in stride. "It is always a warm feeling when kindred spirits find each other," she said, and knelt before the princess. "I feel as if we should be great friends, should we wish to try. Perhaps you can even come with me to my territory one day, and see the magic that is there."

"I should like that," Cloa replied, nodding slowly; still not making eye contact.

"Beannaithe a bheith!" the Fairy said. "Blessed be that should come to pass. And you," she turned to Bridgette, "are from which territory?"

"Uh, the United States," Bridgette said, awkwardly swallowing her mouthful of spicy grilled shrimp. "In Georgia."

Emi-Joye looked confused. "Georgia is in ... Europe."

"Oh! No, no. So, there *is* a country called Georgia, which is in Europe. But there is also a state in the United States called Georgia. I'm from that one," the Elfling replied good-naturedly. "It can be confusing for people who don't know."

"A new lesson I've learned then, today," the Fairy murmured appreciatively, but her eyes now weren't as bright as her voice. "I should see to the other guests for a time. Bridgette, Princess, I thank you for joining us. I have a feeling we shall be seeing much more of each other."

She flew off without fanfare, before Bridgette even could reply farewell. She felt unsettled from that energy, as if her sierwan gift was about to come forth, but it felt ... different. Something was wrong, something was horribly off, and she couldn't put her finger on what. The whole atmosphere of the party suddenly made her feel ill.

Can we go, please? she thought to Collum, nibbling a bite of peach.

He glanced at her, trying to not draw attention to their shared gift. *Of course, but why?*

I can't quite explain it. Something just doesn't … feel right. It's off, and I think I might be sick. I would really like to not puke in front of every important magical being ever, she responded in her mind, willing herself not to vomit from the near-pressurized aura that was beginning to surround her.

"Trystane, I think it would be best if we returned to Eckenbourne," Collum said quietly. "Now."

Trystane shot him a sharp look. "I'll join you."

The three evanesced without a further word, leaving Cloa idly petting Arctura at the abandoned table.

~ 28 ~

The Elfling made it about three steps into Collum's apartment after they appeared there before vomiting on the floor. Again, albeit in a slightly different spot this time than she'd done after being unable to pass through the Seolformúr.

"FUCK," she choked out, kneeling on the ground. "Collum, I am so sorry *again* —"

He was at her side in an instant, a wave of his hand and a word cleaning the mess up. "Don't worry about that," he said. "What happened?"

Trystane looked horrified. He hadn't been there the first time this happened; they'd met up with him later that night after she couldn't go through the gate. "What in the nine circles of Hellfire is happening, Bridgette?"

She scooped her knees into her chest and leaned against the wall, its coolness soothing her suddenly aching head and heated flesh.

"I think … no, maybe I don't think. I have no idea why, but like, when Emi-Joye came to the table, I started to feel sick. Not the same as that day at the Fairy gate; that was almost this force keeping me back. The longer Emi-Joye was there talking to Cloa, this was more like an … an aura. Like we were being surrounded by this energy that *should* have been good. You know, like friends meeting or something. 'Kindred spirits' or whatever the fuck she said," Bridgette mused, thinking she sounded rather ramble-y. "But there was something *wrong* with the energy. I don't know why; I don't know what. But I felt it, and … and did you two see Emi-Joye's face when she reacted and then left so suddenly? Guys, I'm willing to bet that whatever the hell it was, Emi-Joye felt it too, and felt the *wrongness* of it."

The Elfling looked stricken.

Trystane threw himself onto a corner of the couch and summoned a bottle of gingewinde from the kitchen. It floated toward Bridgette, who graciously opened it and chugged, much to the Elves' amusement.

"Do you think it was your sierwan gift?" Collum asked, leaning against the wall next to her.

She shook her head. "No. This was different. I mean, maybe knowing something was wrong was my sierwan thingy? I didn't feel my eyes do the shifty thing though. But feeling the energy itself was unlike anything I've ever felt before."

Collum rolled his eyes at her lackadaisical descriptions of her unusual gift: "the shifty thing" and "sierwan thingy." But he stared at the ceiling, pondering what it meant, and ran a hand through his dark hair. The sierwan gift was indeed a *knowing*, but it usually didn't have anything to do with perceiving unusual energies. At least, not from what he'd read on it. He was beginning to make a longer list of questions to ask the magisters at the University when they visited two days from now — the shared mental communication; the further reading-up on Liluthuaé lore from Magister Ephynius; perhaps some questions on the Ealdaelfen, too. Now this. *Deity help,* he thought to no one in particular.

Bridgette finished the final sips of gingewinde, then slowly got to her feet. She'd almost forgotten the Renaissance-esque dress she wore, and told the Elves she'd be back momentarily. She desperately wanted to change clothes and get into anything but this finery.

"What do you think?" Trystane asked quietly, once Bridgette was out of earshot. "Have you read anything about abilities like this before?"

The fyrdwisa came to join him on the couch, summoning a glass of his own as he did. "No. Well, many beings have abilities to sense or manipulate energies, myself included. I think this is different, if she's describing being able to physically feel things like forces and auras. And if Emi-Joye really was able to feel whatever this was tonight too … It was rather unusual, was it not, for her to disappear so quickly?"

Trystane nodded. "It seemed awkward and abrupt, which is very unlike Emi-Joye. I've not had much interaction with her, but during what I did have, she was pleasant and cordial. To leave while still at the beginning of a conversation, as she did tonight, flies in the face of those previous meetings. I dislike this all very much."

"I think we need to arrange for the two of them to spend time together," Collum mused. "I was going to bring Bridgette to the Samnung meeting with us tomorrow, but what if we forego that, and send the two into Endorsa to explore?"

"Not a terrible idea, except that Emi-Joye and Apostine are supposed to both attend the Samnung meeting," Trystane replied. He took a sip of his homemade spirit. "Perhaps I'll put a bug in Aristoces' ear. She'll take this very seriously, that Bridgette got sick again and felt another strange energy. Maybe after the meeting opening, the two can explore, and Apostine will represent their office. It's a formality, really, and if it's *that* necessary Emi-Joye attend a full meeting, she can do the one on Saturday instead."

"Deity *bless*, why do we have three full Samnung meetings this week?" Collum groaned. "That's not counting me having to dip in to file my report with Lucilla, who *still* hasn't forgiven me. And I think I'd rather go back to human hotels and continental breakfasts with cold scrambled eggs than listen to Nehemi for another damn minute. That woman … to borrow a phrase from Bridgette, 'I cannot deal.'"

The Elven leader chuckled. "She is one for excellent verbiage, the Bright Star. I like her immensely, Collum, and I hope she decides to stay. Even if the world isn't in nearly the sort of danger she's supposed to save us from, I enjoy her company. And her wonderful ability to drive Her Majesty the Queen insane with merely a look. She'll be quite a fun asset to have at our abundance of Samnung meetings. Which, I believe we had so many scheduled because she's only here for a week, and we have much to go over with her. Did you learn why you could hear her in the chamber? I'd forgotten until just now."

"No," Collum said. Not evasively, because he *hadn't* figured that out, but he had no inclination to clue Trystane in that there was more to the story there.

"Hmmm," the Elf said. "This is all so irregular. I realize we are dealing with a legend brought to life, and unprecedented things come with that. However, the sheer *amount* of things that have happened since Bridgette arrived here is astounding. She is a sierwan, she can commune with you when others cannot, she can sense forces beyond our understanding. Yet, the female can do no magic whatsoever in terms of spellwork. Even accidental magic! Cloa has even accidentally performed spells before. And she's dafter than a doornail. I truly cannot make head nor tails of it all."

Collum sensed Bridgette about to emerge, and shot Trystane a warning glance. "I think you'd be right to ask Aristoces about Emi-Joye tomorrow," he said.

"What about Emi-Joye?" Bridgette asked as she came into the living room, refreshed and clad in less formal attire.

"Trystane and I were talking about what happened tonight, about your mention that perhaps Emi-Joye felt and reacted to your same energy," Collum said. "We'd like to investigate this situation further and think a good start would be to send the two of you off exploring Endorsa together instead of attending the full Samnung meeting as originally planned."

"A day without interacting with Nehemi? Ugh. Sold," Bridgette said dramatically, throwing herself on the couch next to Collum.

Trystane's eyes glittered. *See? I told you so,* he thought to the fyrdwisa.

Collum rolled his eyes, and sent a thought to Bridgette: *You've quite impressed our leader with your outstanding wit and ability to piss off the queen.*

Bridgette's face didn't change as she thought back, *You ain't seen nothing yet, Bundy.*

But to Trystane, she said aloud, "Seriously though, what do you think me hanging out with the Fairy ambassadora to the Antarctic will do to figure out this weird energy thing?"

"Firstly, I'm curious to see if that energy is around Emi-Joye herself, or if it only comes out when the two of you are together.

Or, further, if it is when the three of you are gathered," Trystane said, referring to Cloa. "You were around Cloa at your first Samnung meeting, and that energy field, or aura as you called it, did not manifest?"

"Nope," Bridgette replied. "But all three of us were on the stage together today with the Samnung and the human leadership, and I didn't feel it then."

"There were many energies taking place simultaneously at those times, though," Collum said thoughtfully. "I could detect utmost joy and triumph, not to mention all the magics being performed. Perhaps, if this aura was there, it was masked by everything else."

"Yeah, maybe. But I couldn't feel any of the other stuff you just mentioned," the Elfling responded, stumped. "What would it mean if it's something that comes up when she's alone with me?"

"Before you talk to Aristoces, a suggestion," Collum said, looking at Trystane. "Perhaps we should test that theory first, by arranging for Emi-Joye and Bridgette to have contact in the hall. Without Cloa present. Then we can see if it is something between she and the Bright Star, before sending them off together and causing her to get sick again."

"A fair idea," Trystane agreed. "I will see to it, Bridgette, if you are comfortable with that."

"I think so. But what if it doesn't, and then we go into the Samnung chamber with Cloa, and it comes up again?" She groaned. "And then what if I puke in front of *everyone*?"

~ 29 ~

A non-worry, as it turned out: Princess Cloa wasn't at the Samnung meeting the next day.

"She's ill," Nehemi spat, when Collum inquired of her whereabouts. "Something she ate at that after-soiree when she was sitting with you three."

Oh, fuck, Bridgette thought to Collum as she outwardly morphed her face into platonic concern rather than despair. *Ohhhh fuuuuck.*

Ask Emi-Joye the moment you two get out of Cyneham Breonna. Ask her about the aura or whatever you want to call it. If it made you sick, Cloa's sick, and she felt it too? There's something much bigger going on here, and it worries me. The fyrdwisa, too, kept a straight face as he thought this to Bridgette, but his fists were clenched beneath the table. He wished Trystane shared the same gift; the Elf hadn't come into the room yet and missed the unsettling snap from the queen.

Aristoces had indeed granted her ambassadora permission to leave the chamber, Liluthuaé in tow. She'd briefed Emi-Joye the night before about Bridgette's true reason for visiting, and the Fairy had even more questions to beseech her new companion as the two were dismissed. They walked — well, Bridgette walked; Emi-Joye flew — down the stairs and out the foyer door into the sunny spring day.

"Where would you like to explore?" the Fairy asked, her jovial demeanor back in full. "I can show you historic sites, we can go shopping, we can eat and drink, perhaps take in a performance!"

The Fairy seemed so delighted that the Elfling hated to put a damper on her spirit. But she had an assignment, so Bridgette stopped walking, closed her eyes and took a deep breath like she had that morning on Hlafjordstiepel. "Somewhere we can talk. Privately."

Emi-Joye looked concerned and narrowed those whorls of icy blue. "Alright then. A drink it is. Do you trust me?"

"What?"

"Do you trust me?" the Fairy asked again. "Because to go

where I would like to take you, we're going to have to fly. And it is ill-advised for me to fly those who do not give their consent."

"Oh — I mean, yes, of course. Fly me to the moon," Bridgette quipped.

"As you say," Emi-Joye said. She looped an arm around Bridgette's waist and lifted them both into the sky, shocking the Elfling thoroughly with how strong she was. The two were quiet for the duration of the flight, in part because Bridgette was fascinated by how different her flying was compared to Emi-Joye's. The Fairy didn't seem to use her body at all: the full work was done by her wings, fifth and sixth limbs controlled by muscles Bridgette didn't possess.

Emi-Joye landed in front of a nondescript tavern on the outskirts of Galdúr, and the two walked inside to find the magical equivalent of a traffic jam. There were bodies everywhere: at tables, at the bar, standing wherever room could be found. Bridgette felt somewhat claustrophobic and looked pleadingly at Emi-Joye.

"Seriously? We can hardly move," she griped. "How are we supposed to find privacy in here?"

"We hide in plain sight, of course," the Fairy responded. "If we snuck off somewhere isolated, it would raise questions as to where the new ambassadora and the Samnung's guest went off to. So I brought us to the busiest place I could think of, which is this fine establishment."

"Fine establishment" might have been a tad of an overstatement. The tavern was constructed entirely out of wood, and though it was painted nicely enough on the outside, the interior was dingy and dim with worn yellow lighting. The floor was also sticky, coated in centuries' worth of spilled beer and worse.

"Great …" Bridgette muttered in response. She followed Emi-Joye deeper into the crowd, amazed that no one bumped into anyone's wings, until they reached the far end of the resin-coated wooden bar. A wizard was there manning the register as well as the wells.

"Hello, Sheridan," Emi-Joye said, a sly smile parting her full lips at the sight of the man, whose imposingly muscled arms were hard not to stare at. "Mind if we take the back table?"

Sheridan, who had messy light brown hair and dark brown eyes under a pair of brooding brows, grinned at her voice, though he didn't look up from the glasses he'd spelled a rag to polish. "The usual to eat and drink, Em?"

"My usual, yes, and whatever the Elfling would like."

He looked up and noticed Bridgette standing behind his friend. A wave of his hand sent menus floating toward her, and she selected a beer and sandwich from the list.

As the females walked to what apparently was Emi-Joye's preferred seat, Bridgette realized how used she'd grown to being able to speak mind-to-mind with Collum. It was disconcerting now, after days of that option being available to her, for it to be non-existent. To have been able to converse like that would have been useful given the noise they found themselves in.

"What *is* this place?" Bridgette asked, raising her voice slightly to make sure the Fairy heard her. She got a sharp look of reproach in response.

"Keep your voice low, Bridgette," Emi-Joye said, her voice suddenly serious and barely audible above the din. "This is Taberna Körtz, one of the oldest businesses in Endorsa and all of Heáhwolcen. It was founded by some of the original wizards who ascended the portal after Artur Cromwell and Galdúr Iontach an Chéad Cheannaire first created the world above the world."

"What is that you said after Galdúr?" Bridgette questioned. She'd never heard Collum or Trystane mention the Aziza having a surname, much less one that sounded so complicated to pronounce.

"You likely won't have heard it outside official documents and the Fae," Emi-Joye said, a bit kinder now. "It is what we call him, and it means 'the great first king.' He couldn't be Fairy of All Fairies, as Aristoces is now, for that was a Fairy that existed elsewhere at his same time. So he chose a title, egged on by Felicity and the Cromwell children. The youngest who came with them, their second son, called Galdúr 'King of the Fairies,' as he was the first such being the boy had seen. A bit of an inside joke, if you will, between them all."

"That's … fascinating," the Elfling mused. "All of this is."

"Culture shock, no doubt," Emi-Joye replied. "What is it you wish to talk about, that we must meet in secret and discuss outside of prying ears?"

Bridgette still wasn't sure they were truly in privacy here, so she kept her voice low as instructed, and searched carefully for the right words to say.

"Yesterday, at the after-party — soiree, or whatever — when you were there with Cloa and I, did you feel … strange, at all?"

Emi-Joye narrowed her gray-blonde, perfectly arched brows. "What do you mean, 'strange'?"

"Strange like, sick? Out of nowhere, maybe? Or just unsettled?"

Two plates of food and two pints appeared in front of them, and Bridgette jumped back, startled. She'd expected to see them floating their way, not simply exist where her elbows had been propped seconds before.

The Fairy chuckled. "The tables here are enchanted. Saves the staff a bit of a hassle as they don't have to navigate the crowd, and there's no worrying of over-indulgent patrons grabbing a sandwich from midair as it is sent toward a table."

"Oh," was all Bridgette could think to say, as she eyed her sandwich.

"Why do you want to know if I felt strange yesterday?" Emi-Joye asked, though she'd yet to answer the original question.

Bridgette swallowed her bite of corned beef on toast. "Yesterday when you, Cloa, and I were talking, well, first of all it was weird for Cloa to talk to begin with. She doesn't speak coherently that often."

The Fairy raised a brow. "You have my curiosity."

"Well," Bridgette was struggling for words again, "I started to feel this weird energy surround us. It's very hard to describe. More of an aura, kind of. It was something that felt as if it *should* have been positive, but it was like, tainted. Something was shielding it from being a true positive energy, and it was like that positivity was trying to break through this barrier. It made me feel unsettled, and sick. Actually sick; I threw up just about the second we got back to Collum's apartment afterward. And today, you didn't hear it, but Nehemi said Cloa wasn't at the Samnung because she was sick too. Nehemi said it was something she ate, but after I got so sick and felt that energy, it made me wonder. It made all three of us wonder: me, Collum, and Trystane."

Emi-Joye was deathly silent. She didn't meet Bridgette's eyes, and seemed to be concentrating on picking seeds out of her sandwich bread. The Elfling quietly finished her own sandwich and beer, waiting for the Fairy to say something.

"I would not say I felt an aura," Emi-Joye said slowly. "But there came to me a sense of great anxiousness, the more we three spoke. The conversation needed to end, and so mote it be."

"So you *did* feel something?" Bridgette pressed, leaning forward onto the table. "But it was different from what I felt, it sounds like."

"How were you able to feel this aura, as you call it?"

The Elfling paused, unsure if she should reveal her sierwan gift before the rest of the Samnung knew about it. She supposed it was alright though, if Aristoces trusted the ambassadora enough to tell her about Bridgette being the Liluthuaé.

"Do you know what a sierwan is?" Bridgette breathed, flicking her eyes around to make double-sure no one was listening. "I don't know if that's a whole magical world thing or just an Elf thing."

"The sierwen of times long past were of great service to their leaders during war times. They are only Elves or Elflings —" Emi-Joye stopped, realization dawning on her. "You're a sierwan. That's how you could feel this aura."

"Well, no, actually, it's not, but yes, I am."

"Explain," the Fairy instructed, turning her attention back to her sandwich.

"The whole sierwan thing, it's like a *knowing*. I can't explain how or why I know things, just these knowledge and truth bombs get dropped into my brain and I can make sense of things, connect dots, that others can't. It's really weird, honestly," Bridgette said. "Everyone has their gut feelings, their intuitions, right? This is that, but way stronger. And I don't have to search for meanings behind it, because the meanings and context arrive with it most of the time. But this ability to sense these energies is something different, and that's what we're trying to figure out."

"What do you mean, 'these energies'? Have you felt this before?"

"Once. The first or second day I was here and we went to Fairevella, we were supposed to go to that big fancy palace place —"

"The Seledreám," Emi-Joye interrupted, then bade Bridgette continue.

"Right. The Seledreám. So we got there and there's that guarded gate, the Seolformúr, which Collum told me is supposed to keep out magic of ill-intent, Craft wizards, all that jazz. Only, there was a physical energy barrier against *me*, too. Being a sierwan meant I knew *why* that barrier was there, but didn't explain how I could feel the barrier. So that's the difference between the sierwan knowing and this ability to feel off-energies," Bridgette rambled. "And I got sick after that happened, too."

Emi-Joye took another moment to process. Sensing Bridgette's impatience for a response, she finally said, "There are always multiple energies at play in every situation. Perhaps different beings simply intuit them differently."

"Seriously?" Bridgette stared at her, wide-eyed. "*That's* what you have to say about this? 'Different people see things differently'? Come freaking *on*, Emi-Joye. You know there's more to it than that. It's not normal for three people to all feel something off and two of them get sick from it."

The Fairy looked at her, and there was an iciness to her eyes that had nothing to do with her ambassadoraship. "Perhaps Cloa ate a bad shellfish. Perhaps your anxiety manifests with physical illness. There does not always need to be something sinister at play, Bridgette. Rational explanations must be considered instead of jumping to dire conclusions."

Bridgette wished she could evanesce right back to the Samnung chamber. She didn't understand how Emi-Joye could just ... not care! It made her furious.

"Rational explanations? Wow, what a thing to bring up as we sit here in a magical café that defies rationality!" Bridgette hissed. "You know what? Screw you, and your fucking ambassadora crap. You know there's something bigger happening, and you're either too scared to admit it, or you don't trust anyone enough to talk it through. I'm going to figure this out, with or without your help."

She stood up and forced her way through the crowd, back to the door, fuming the whole way.

~ 30 ~

The vibrant sunshine outside blinded Bridgette momentarily — it had been so dark and dank inside the tavern — and her mind grasped at straws. She had no idea where she was, but she'd be damned if she went back inside Taberna Körtz and admit that to Emi-Joye.

She turned on her heel and began wandering the streets of Galdúr, equally eager to take in Endorsa and to distract herself from the anger at Emi-Joye brushing aside something she *had* to know was important. Bridgette didn't need to be a sierwan to know that's precisely what the Fairy was doing in there!

Fucking hell, she fumed inside her head, wishing again that she could evanesce, or that Collum would magically appear next to her. *This is insane. I don't just get sick out of nowhere and I'm not even allergic to any food. Something's going on and somebody doesn't want me to know about it.*

Her angry steps took her vaguely in the direction she remembered them flying earlier, past various aged buildings in what she assumed was the "old town" side of the capital city. The longer she walked, the newer her surroundings appeared, until finally she reached the heart of Galdúr's bustling commerce center. As in the village where the Coffee Cauldron was, the buildings here were assuredly human-inspired. Though magic could have kept them pristine and new, Bridgette knew that their exteriors had been allowed to show age — a homage to the centuries past in which they were built. Not quite as old as the area where the tavern was though; this was perhaps more 1800s than 1690s. She felt as though she was walking through downtown Nashville, as if her apartment building and campus were just around the corner.

A shop caught her eye: blinking crystals hung from its windows, catching and redirecting the sunlight in dazzling rainbows across the road. Bridgette paused, mesmerized. *What the hell*, she decided, and strolled inside. A female with skin whiter than snow, and curly hair dyed a brilliant shade of firetruck red, was arranging small burlap bags of herbs on a display shelf.

"Tráthnóna mistéireach, friend!" she said to Bridgette, and smiled so that her two elongated, pearly white canines were easily visible. "What brings you in today?"

Bridgette, caught off-guard by being face-to-face with a Sanguisuge instead of a witch, blinked and gathered herself. "I was just kind of, well, wandering, really. Your crystals in the window caught my eye and I figured why not come in."

"A walk-about is good medicine for the spirit," the female said. "I am Lymerian. Who are you?"

"Bridgette Conner," Bridgette answered. "Is this your shop?"

Lymerian smiled, the corners of her black eyes turning up as well as her lips. "Well met, Bridgette Conner. Yes, this is my shop. I specialize in the Old Magicks — the rituals, the things that require more than just a wand and spellwork."

"So like that thing Nehemi did yesterday at the ambassadora installation?" Bridgette asked, biting her lip at the thought of Emi-Joye again. "That was a ritual, right?"

"*Queen* Nehemi, friend. I suppose it was, though I was not there."

Bridgette bristled at the correction, but reminded herself that Lymerian clearly lived in Endorsa and probably *had* to address the witch as such. "Ah. It was a weird thing to be part of."

She paused at the crystals, her back to the Sanguisuge. "So are you a witch too, since you do that kind of magic?"

"No, friend, but one does not have to be a witch to do rituals. Magic is within us all. I lack the ability to utilize my hands and wands for harnessing energy, but what I do not have in wandskill, I make up for in other ways," Lymerian said.

"Other ways?"

"Yes, friend. The Old Magicks require a lifetime of knowledge: of crystal lore, of herbal properties, of colors, shapes, and mystic geometries. Ritual magic may be performed by any being, but the true Old Magicks, the predecessors to that which you were likely part of at the Maremóhr, are the manifestation of existence. They are the ways of balance, of light and dark, of elements and Nature, transcending the time and space we have been placed in. They are what connects us all, and it is through that connection that energies may be gathered and redirected for specific purposes, much more powerful than what can be produced by a witch or wizard holding a wand." Lymerian's voice was a bit rueful, Bridgette thought: perhaps the Sanguisuge wasn't as much of a Nehemi sympathizer as her earlier remark indicated.

"How does someone know if they're proficient in the Old Magicks?" Bridgette asked her.

"There are signs," Lymerian said simply. "If the Universe, the deities, the magicks themselves have chosen you, you will know."

"Ah," Bridgette said, though her thoughts were roiling. *Guess that is a 'no' for me then.*

"You have questions, friend, that I cannot answer," Lymerian said, suddenly at Bridgette's side, a hand on one arm. She lifted Bridgette's chin up so that her black eyes met the lilac ones of the Elfling. "Only the higher powers, the Universe, can do that. But heed this: You have spent so much of your life worrying about many things that in the grand scheme have little to no meaning. Be not anxious about these unknowns. Focus instead, Bridgette Conner, on those which bring you joy. And take comfort in knowing there is much in this world, in this moment of space and time, in all the moments of space and time, that no being can or will understand. It means you need not fret about trying to understand — we must each of us accept that it is beyond comprehension. Accept this, know this, trust this: and it is then that you will find your magic."

"Um, thanks?" Bridgette said, a sudden desire to get out of the shop overtaking her brain. "I should probably get back now, but the person I came here with kind of ditched me. How can I get back to Cyneham Breonna?"

Lymerian smiled gently, as if she knew Bridgette was unsettled by her breathy instructions and pointy teeth. "It is not far, but the roads can be confusing to those unfamiliar with our city. Allow me, friend, to draw you a map."

Bridgette shivered involuntarily as she and her scrap paper map re-entered the sunlit outdoors a short while later. Lymerian's illustration was straightforward and easy to follow — a good thing; Bridgette had never been great with directions — and she hoped it wouldn't take too long before she wound back up at the Samnung chamber. How she would explain to the fyrdwisa, Trystane and Aristoces as to where Emi-Joye was though … she hadn't figured that out yet.

She didn't know how much time had passed since they'd arrived at Cyneham Breonna that morning, and she hoped Collum wouldn't be *too* terribly put out with her for leaving the Fairy and wandering the streets of Endorsa alone.

He probably will though, Bridgette thought miserably. Collum had an astounding ability to worry about her wellbeing more so than his own. She wondered how close she'd have to be for him to hear her mind-to-mind. In a hope to avoid having to see the full Samnung, maybe she could send a thought to him, let him know she was outside and she wanted to go back to his apartment now.

An unexpected voice called to her from behind, and Bridgette whirled to see Eloise at the edge of the pasture along the road. "Well met, Bridgette Conner," the Unicorn said. "I did nay expect to see you here. Where are you going, and why are you alone?"

"Well, I didn't exactly plan to be here, first off," Bridgette said, walking over to her golden annwyl. She ran her fingers through Eloise's silky mane. "I technically should probably go back to Cyneham Breonna, but I would *really* like to avoid the Samnung if at all humanly possible."

"I can help with that, should you like," Eloise said. She nuzzled Bridgette's hair with her strong muzzle. "Would you like to be transported back to Eckenbourne?"

"Yes please!" Bridgette could scarcely believe her luck. "To Collum's apartment, if we can?"

"Then let us go." Eloise let the Elfling grip her mane and pull herself up, riding bareback for the trip.

It was a lengthy jaunt, partly because Bridgette had neither a saddle nor the magic to spell a barrier between her legs and the Unicorn's sides. And partly because they were on the side of Endorsa furthest from Eckenbourne, and further still from Collum's apartment. But the ride was soothing, in its own way. Eloise didn't ask questions or demand answers. She seemed to know that the Elfling was troubled and needed to process something, unpack the day, without interruption or unsolicited thoughts and advice. Eventually they made it back, Bridgette's legs sore from straddling, and she gratefully hugged the Unicorn around her neck.

"Thank you, Eloise. I appreciate this more than you know," she murmured, and turned to walk the path. "Hopefully Collum won't murder me on sight for disappearing today."

Bridgette reached his door and knocked. No answer. *Shit. He's not home yet*, she thought, and sat down to wait for him, her back against the hallway wall. She didn't realize she'd fallen asleep until the fyrdwisa's voice startled her awake.

"Where in the seven hells have you been?!" he asked, clearly exasperated. "We have been looking for you for *hours*, Bridgette!"

"Sorry?" she grumbled. "I've been waiting here for a while …"

He shook his head and placed his hand upon the door, unlocking it with his touch. Collum ushered her inside, followed by Trystane.

How could you be so fool — Collum stopped his thought, but it was too late. Bridgette looked at him, shock and hurt evident on her face.

"Bridgette —" he called fruitlessly after her as she darted to her bedroom. "Shit."

"She's safe, Collum, and that's what matters," Trystane said gently. He took his regular seat on the couch, and summoned two bottles from the kitchen. "She'll come out in a moment once she's collected herself. Or once you go to the door and apologize for whatever you said or did to send her scurrying."

Not about to tell you that, Collum thought to himself. He strained his mind for Bridgette's, but it was as if he and Trystane were the only ones in the apartment. Not a whisper of thought to pick up on.

"She doesn't like to be worried about," he said, accepting his dark beer. "And she doesn't like to upset anyone. I suppose being awoken with me cursing at her was perhaps not the best reaction, given these things I know of her psyche."

"Likely not," Trystane said, a smirk playing on his lips. "Go say you're sorry, Fyrdwisa. That's an order. I won't have you losing the Bright Star because of some silly little spat between the two of you."

"Fine," Collum said, and eased himself down the hall, groaning inwardly. "Bridgette?"

Silence.

He closed his eyes. *Bridgette, please come out,* he thought to her. *I'm sorry. I shouldn't have said that. You're not a fool; I was worried and sometimes when I worry about you in particular, I lose a bit of myself in the process. Please come back to the living room and let us three talk.*

"Fine," she finally answered from behind her door. "But I'm coming out to talk to Trystane, *not* to you, Collum."

He blinked. She rarely called him anything other than Bundy. He'd messed up this time.

Bridgette didn't make eye contact as she stalked from behind the door, pushing it open so hard it nearly knocked him backward. "What do you two want?"

"We want to talk to you, Bridgette, about what you did today and where you went," Trystane said, cocking a brow up. "Sit and drink with us, and let us chat."

"Stop being such a formal dick, Trystane," Bridgette snapped, surprising herself with her short fuse. "I'm so over this. Some days you want me to save the world; some days you act like I'm a porcelain doll, this fragile thing that you have to walk on eggshells around. Just pick one, dammit."

"As you wish," the Elf practically growled, all traces of professionalism suddenly gone. "Where the seven hells have you been all day? Why didn't you come back to the Samnung chamber? What did you and Emi-Joye talk about? Where *is* that deity-blasted Fairy?"

Bridgette smiled, pleased that she'd touched a nerve. She

replied with a somewhat aloof explanation: "Emi-Joye flew us to this tavern. We talked, she was super unhelpful and kind of a bitch, so I left and walked back through Galdúr. I went into this crystal shop owned by a Sanguisuge, then got a map to Cyneham Breonna and on my walk there ran into Eloise, the Unicorn. She offered to take me back here, so … here I am. I didn't come back to the Samnung chamber because I was pissed off at all of you, and especially Emi-Joye. We talked about *nothing* because that's all she gave me when I told her everything from yesterday. And I haven't seen her since I left the table. I don't know where she is and frankly, I do not care."

"I want to know more about what she didn't talk about," Collum said, his tidal pool eyes meeting hers. She felt the apology then; knew he really was sorry. Not sorry for worrying, but sorry for making her feel pain about it.

Bridgette sighed. "She admitted to feeling anxious and said 'the conversation had to end,' so she ended it. And then she proceeded to make me feel like I was crazy for having this talk with her. She said something about there being a rational explanation, like Cloa ate a bad shrimp, and that not everything had to have 'dire circumstances.'"

"She knows more than she's letting on," Trystane said, inferring immediately. "But *why*?"

"I don't know. I did most of the talking. She wanted to know how I felt the aura yesterday, so I told her, and I told her about being a sierwan, so she could understand the difference between my knowing things and this tangible feeling of energies," Bridgette answered. "Well. She figured out I was a sierwan, actually, I didn't tell her outright. But I definitely picked up on her knowing more than she was willing to let on about her mysterious anxiousness that happened at the same time as the aura."

Collum groaned, sinking back onto the couch in feigned annoyance. "The University magisters are going to charge us tuition for the number of questions we'll have to ask them tomorrow."

~ 31 ~

Though Bridgette forgave Collum the previous evening, she was noticeably stuffier with him Thursday morning, the fyrdwisa thought. It was as if their relationship had reverted somewhat to that morning at the cottage in Danvers, when she was still wary of trusting him as she'd come to in the days since. She accepted his offer of eggs, toast, and hot coffee with a curt "Thanks," and barely said another word to him at the breakfast table.

"Deity bless, Bridgette, what is wrong with you today?" he finally asked, unable to stand the strained silence any longer. "I know you know how sorry I am for yesterday."

She pricked her fried egg, letting the golden yolk flood across the gray earthenware plate. "I don't like making you angry, and I'm embarrassed that you got so mad at me. And now I'm worried I'm going to upset you again."

The Elf put his head in his hands, frustrated but trying not to show it. "Starshine, I wasn't angry *at* you. I was worried about you and reacted poorly. I didn't mean to embarrass you. And we cannot *do* this song and dance of worrying about upsetting the other. It has happened several times in the weeks we've known each other and we don't quite acknowledge it, but we should. We are each our own being, and I care very much that you are happy, but I'm not going to walk around on eggshells to make you that way. Nor should you."

Bridgette sipped her coffee, eyes downcast. "Can I ask you something? A favor, kind of?"

"Of course."

"Will you tell me if I do something wrong, to make you angry, or if I'm just like … too much? And not hide it from me or walk on eggshells about it?"

"Provided I am not barred by the Samnung from doing so, I will never hide anything from you, Bridgette. I promise. I am one-hundred percent honest and transparent with you as often as I can be," Collum said.

"And if you're going to leave, or you want me to leave and

leave you alone, will you tell me that, too?"

His brows furrowed. "Where is this coming from?"

She swirled a toast point in the thickening yolk. "I'm scared I'm going to do something to make you go away. Or make you want me to go away. Like I'll make you mad, or not be a good enough witch or Elfling or screw something up with the Samnung. And you won't want anything to do with me anymore, and it's the same thing over and over again like it has been my whole life. Find something wonderful and manage to fuck it up no matter how hard I try not to."

Collum was next to her before she realized he moved; his hands grasped her wrists, forcing her to look at him. Her eyes were dim and pained. Terrified. All because of one night thinking she'd upset him.

Seven fucking hells, this woman …

"Bridgette. You are *fine*. I don't know how to convince you of this. You have no need to be afraid of me leaving or wanting you to go away. Beings get angry, and they forgive each other. You were angry with me yesterday, and I didn't like that at all, but you didn't stay that way, right? Please allow me that same grace if I am ever upset with you, Starshine. You're going to have to try quite hard to fuck anything up with me, okay?"

He sent those tendrils of honeysuckle and vanilla wafting over both of them, and Bridgette took a deep breath, feeling the truth of his words fill her lungs along with the sweet scents. "Okay."

Collum squeezed her wrists gently before letting them fall back to her lap. "I promise. You are fine."

"Thank you," Bridgette said quietly. "I trust you. And I appreciate you."

He resisted the urge to hug her. "I trust you, Starshine. And I appreciate you, too. Let me fix you something different to eat — there's no way that egg yolk is anything but cold and nasty after letting it sit there while we talked."

She answered him with a soft lopsided grin, and a moment later he was frying up two more eggs. As he'd resisted the desire to embrace her, she resisted the desire to dream. It was comfortable, so comfortable, to be with him like this. Dangerously comfortable, and no matter what Collum said about her being fine … it didn't seem right to allow herself *these* dreams.

Bridgette ate her fresh fried eggs still in silence, though a markedly looser one than earlier, and gave her companion a quick squeeze at his waist as she walked by him to get dressed.

"What is appropriate attire for a trip to your alma mater?" she joked, her normal attitude slowly making its way back. "Do Elves wear varsity logo sweatshirts?"

"No, they most assuredly do not," Collum answered cockily. "They wear normal clothing and reserve gaudy designs and sportsball for humankind."

"Normal clothing? Fancy leggings and oversized shirts are not 'normal.'"

"Fine, then. Go put on your magical being costume and meet me back in the living room in an hour, please," Collum laughed, pushing her gently down the hallway. "I'll be the one in 'fancy leggings' waiting by the door."

He was in fancy leggings. As their visit to the University was somewhat considered official Samnung business, Collum wore attire that — if what he wore to Emi-Joye's ceremony was formal — could ostensibly be called Elven business casual. Bridgette gave him a sarcastic once-over and he grinned wickedly back before extending an arm to her, ready to evanesce the two of them to the University.

She was grateful he took them just outside the gates of the grounds, allowing her to catch her breath from the jolting travel before being face-to-face with anyone else. During the pause, Collum briefed her on what to expect inside.

"Firstly, we are meeting with Magister Ephynius, who is the highest-ranking educator in histories of magic. He is a wizard, and a bit deaf in one ear, but strongly dislikes being talked to in a loud voice unless he asks you to do so. Most of what I want to know can be directed to him at first, at least, and we can go from there if he recommends a different magister or student to speak with," Collum said. "I do not mean to patronize, but if you don't mind, I would like to lead the discussions with him — and as you see fit, and especially should your sierwan gift become evident, you chime in with comments or questions. Magister Ephynius does not know your true nature, though when I arrive with a brand-new Elfling asking about the Liluthuaé legends, it's possible he'll put two and two together. But he is not the gossiping type and will keep this knowledge to himself."

"Is it okay if he knows I'm a sierwan?" Bridgette asked.

Collum considered. "I think so. Emi-Joye already knows, and is not a member of the Samnung, so I don't think it will be horrible for anyone of Magister Ephynius' stature to find out as well. Do not bring it up though," he cautioned. "As with Emi-Joye yesterday, perhaps it will be best if it is self-determined rather than revealed."

The Elfling nodded. "Let's go to class, Bundy."

He glared at her, but there was a twinkle in those tidal pool eyes. "If you call me Bundy in front of anyone at the University, I will personally ensure you attend the bland Ostara ceremonies in Endorsa tomorrow as Queen Nehemi's aide instead of the parties in Fairevella as a joyous participant."

She stuck her tongue out at him, and accepted his lead across the cobblestoned road that led to the wrought iron gates of what was colloquially known as "the University," though the official name inscribed across the entry, shining in polished Endorsan bronze, read "Prifysgol Grantabrych Draíochta."

The hell does that mean? Bridgette asked in her mind.

It's old English, Welsh and Irish — Prifysgol Grantabrych are essentially synonyms that both mean 'university,' or 'place of higher learning.' 'Draíochta' is magic, the Elf answered.

So it's a university of magic. How ... original.

He elbowed her in the rib. *Don't make me laugh in front of Magister Ephynius!*

She grinned as they reached the gate and walked onto the sprawling, soft green lawn at the front of the school. Buildings and green space, dotted with trees as old as Heáhwolcen, seemed to stretch for miles. The human architectural influence on the buildings was notable: someone, wizard or Fairy or Elf, had undoubtedly been an Ivy League student during their time on Earth.

"What do people — I mean, beings — study here?" Bridgette asked, aloud this time.

"Many things," Collum said. "I don't mean to sound aloof. It's simply true. We have students of business, of history, of specific magics, of Nature, of the spirit realms. Engineering, too, of sorts. Other types of magic not found here; ancient species and languages."

"What did *you* study?"

"Two things" — he laughed as Bridgette called him an overachiever — "The inner workings of the mind, so I could better understand and utilize my innate abilities. And secondly, I studied diplomacy and communications."

"Well then, big man on campus."

He laughed again. "It was a long time ago, and I continue to learn despite holding two degrees."

The first building in front of them was of deep brown brick accented with white columns, white balconies and an impressive white clocktower at the roof. Like the buildings Bridgette came across near Lymerian's shop, it was spelled to appear aged and worn, though no damage could ever truly be done to its exterior in a place created by magic. This building, Collum explained, was home to the expansive library and administrative offices.

She didn't say it out loud, but Bridgette reveled in the thought of arriving at such a place. As exciting as Emi-Joye's installment had been, and as amazing as it was to meet these many different types of beings, the thought of setting foot in a magical university was enthralling. She'd grown up with various fantasy novels that depicted magical schools and the students who learned there, but to truly be faced with one was the most unreal experience of the entire trip so far.

Magister Ephynius greeted them just inside the doors of the brown brick building. He was a tall, thin man, and were it not for his round ears and considerably un-opalescent amber eyes, Bridgette would have pegged him for an Elfling on height alone. He didn't *look* old, per se, but as age could be spelled on and off buildings, it likely could be that way for faces, too. In human years, she'd think him in his sixties, and probably the type of man who would have gone to Woodstock. The magister had long, frizzy gray-blonde hair pulled back in a messy bun, peachy-pink skin, and wore oversized shabby robes that resembled a well-loved housecoat. He had an air about him that was equally carefree and intently sharp, as though he only had opinions on certain things, and on those things, he would not waiver.

"Ah, Fyrdwisa Andoralain! A pleasure to welcome you back at last!" he cried out, beckoning them in. "And you must be Bridgette Conner, yes? The Elfling from Earth?"

News travels fast in these parts, she muttered mind-to-mind. Collum snorted in response.

"It is our pleasure to be welcomed with such a receipt," he said, answering the magister's embrace. They were the same height, though Ephynius' bun made him look taller. "I appreciate you taking the time to speak with us this day. Between the two of us, we have many questions we'd like to have answered, and perhaps some stories to share."

Magister Ephynius nodded gleefully. "To my chambers, then!"

He led them down a hall and a sharp ninety-degree turn, and with a start, Bridgette realized that this entire building encased layers and layers of books, surrounded by levels of offices arranged in a rectangular fashion. Ground level, where they entered from, was in roughly the middle of the floors: they rose high toward the sky and descended into darker basement floors. A balcony on each level allowed whoever was standing there to look into the hundreds of shelves, floating balls of light illuminating them at various intervals. Ladders could reach to a point, especially from the lower levels and several feet beyond the floor on which Bridgette stood, and then Fairies came into play. Bridgette watched as one received word that a book was needed, and he flew from a barely visible desk all the way up to the highest level, scanning quickly for the desired tome.

This is fucking magical, she said in her head. *Can I just ... live here?*

The soft smile played at Collum's lips. For once, he hadn't been watching her take in the library — he'd been distracted by answering questions from the magister about his recent travels to Earth — but he heard the wonder in her inner voice, and squeezed her arm in acknowledgement as they walked down the hall.

Truly, Magister Ephynius' office could not have looked more like a hoard of books and papers. Stacks upon stacks, some shelved and some floating in midair, others on the floor, allowed for a one-being-wide path from the aged wooden door back to his desk and a hideous burgundy sofa. Bridgette was reminded of a musty old antique shop: clearly whatever magic kept his skin from showing age was not applied to the atmosphere of his inner sanctum.

Magister Ephynius seemed to realize this, and with a quick wave of a wand he pulled from inside his robes, made the coating of dust on the sofa dissipate. He motioned for them to have a seat, then summoned tea.

As he poured hot water into tiny gray teacups, the magister settled into educator mode. "I'm quite intrigued by the list of questions you hinted to, Fyrdwisa. Where would you like to begin?"

Collum accepted his tea, shot a quick sideways glance to Bridgette, and said, "First, I want to know everything you know about the Elven Liluthuaé legends."

The magister blinked. "I mean no disrespect, Fyrdwisa, but you have come to me with this request prior, and I shared with you then all that I continue to know now. It is legend. I can direct you to specific books, of course, that talk about Ylda and the Fyrst, but those are volumes both I and students of Elven lore have read."

"There is nothing else known about the legends?" Collum refused to accept defeat so easily.

"In our library, no."

"Are there other libraries in Heáhwolcen? Or a different historian to talk to?" Bridgette offered.

"No, Sigewíf. Not that would be nearly as detailed as what

we have here."

"So where can we go then?" she asked.

Magister Ephynius smiled. "To your home world, of course. There are still Elves, very well-hidden, on Earth, and with them the ancient of most ancient books. Aelys Frost and her followers were not the only group of Elves there; just the first to choose to follow Artur Cromwell and Galdúr. They would be most likely to have the knowledge you seek."

"Speaking of knowledge we seek, and ancient beings on Earth, can we also ask you about the Druids?" Bridgette blurted out, forgetting that Collum had requested to ask the questions. *Oops.*

He nudged his leg against hers, a silent acknowledgement and note of forgiveness.

"Ah, Druidic magicks! The most ancient, some would say, to have been practiced by those of human descent," Magister Ephynius said, his eyes gleaming in the soft light. "What is it you wish to know of these?"

"Well," Bridgette stammered, realizing now she had to ask, since she'd brought it up, "It's about Palna. And the walls. Some of the Samnung members think that the inner wall inside Palna, that the citizens put up themselves, is counteracting the magic of the main barrier. These Samnung members also think that using Druidic ritual with their collective magics might strengthen the main wall and maybe even break the Palnan inside one down for good, neutralizing any threat they might pose."

Her plan had seemed *far* more confident when she was brainstorming to Collum and Trystane, she thought.

A pipe appeared out of nowhere, and Magister Ephynius puffed on it for a moment. The patchouli-scented smoke only furthered Bridgette's vision of him at Woodstock.

"You would like me to share my opinion on this, yes?" he clarified.

Bridgette and Collum nodded. Magister Ephynius slowly nodded too, as if considering what to say next.

"There are no Druids here. They would not come, and have never shown true desire to join us in this world above the world.

Thus over the centuries, much was lost between those of us who are here and those of us who are not. 'Us,' of course, being the practicing witches and wizards of Heáhwolcen and of Earth. There has not been direct contact, to my knowledge, between the magical beings of Heáhwolcen and the Druids for at least one hundred years," he said. "That is not to say they would not be open to it. But they would not come here, I do not think."

"Okay, they can't imbue the walls with spells in-person. But could they teach like, Nehemi and Kharis?" Bridgette asked.

"*Queen* Nehemi," Magister Ephynius corrected her. "That is possible. But it is impossible to say in full confidence that, firstly, they would be open to such a thing, and secondly, that it would work. Thirdly, you must find the True Druids."

~ 32 ~

Bridgette stared blankly at the scholar. "What do you mean, 'the True Druids?' There *are* still Druids on Earth, right? Like, they do the whole ceremony thing at Stonehenge every year?"

Magister Ephynius smiled mysteriously. "There are Druids, yes. But one must consider that those who profess to be Druid may not, in fact, be imbued with the same magickal powers as the Druids of which you speak."

"What the magister means, Starsh — Bridgette — is that there are humans who cannot perform *actual* Druidic ritual or magick, because they simply are not gifted in those ways. But they still live their lives in Druidic tradition and call themselves as such," Collum clarified. "I would gather from that caveat, then, that the Druids we seek are … not looking to be sought after."

"You gather correctly, Fyrdwisa," Magister Ephynius said gravely. "But it can be done. Like your Elven kind, the Druids are very much eager to stay out of the spotlight, particularly that of the humans. I do not think they mind at all that there are human Druids, to help them hide."

Something about the way he said that stirred Bridgette's mind, and she shot a thought to Collum: *The leader of the human Druids knows how to find the magical ones.*

But her face remained thoughtful, and she nodded. "When I get back to Earth, I'll definitely have to do some research on that. Maybe I can go to Stonehenge myself and take a look around."

The Elf changed the subject quickly before an awkward silence began, and their shared gift accidentally revealed itself. "The last historical thing. I wanted to ask about the Ealdaelfen. Theirs was not lore I studied, except to have grown up with youngling bedtime stories featuring these dark and evil twisted Elves as villains."

"That is, finally, something I can assist you with," Magister Ephynius said, a smile unexpectedly lighting up his face, giving some luster to his amber eyes. "The Ealdaelfen are more, much more, than lore and childhood storybooks."

He settled back into his creaky burgundy chair, which matched the sofa Collum and Bridgette sat on. *Storytime,* Bridgette thought to herself.

"You are familiar, of course, with Craft Wizardry, yes?" His guests nodded, and Magister Ephynius began.

"Millennia ago, when Elves were created, they were made with only good intent in their veins. Elves of old were one with Nature — they were once called the Ealdgecynd for it. But with Nature and within the Universe, within the time and space we occupy, there is a natural desire for that which is opposite of what is meant to exist. Over time, there were born Elves who wished to commune with deeper, darker elements. Things of Earth, and things not of Earth. They are still Elves; they are not a separate form of being as an Elf and a Fairy are. But a faction grew. They called themselves the Ealdaelfen and believed themselves to be a higher form of Elf. More noble of birth, though *all* Elves are descended from Ceannairí Álfar, and thus deserving of *more.* They wished to be worshipped, as they saw Earthly deities, not shunned or feared, and hidden away in the woods and moors and mountains. They communed with hellspirits and their sole intent was not ensuring balance and existence, but to create chaos … and then rid the world of it, leaving destruction in their path to dominance. For in their minds, if no one *knew* they were the source of the entropy, it would only seem right to idolize those who cleared it away.

"Some Elves ignored the danger posed by the Ealdaelfen, saying these tidings would never come to pass, for they had not been forbode," Ephynius said. "Others sympathized with them, but did not wish to cause harm. For was it not the purpose of an Elf's existence to ensure balance? 'Ah,' said the Ealdaelfen, 'And what is balance without an opposing force to challenge that which cannot be, so what is meant can be born?' It was this way they gained followers, and began to procure this chaos in small amounts. Snippets here and there. Nothing major. It was not until an Ealdaelfen who called himself the Raisarch tried to subjugate the rest who held his ideology that it all fell apart. The

Raisarch decided that it was not enough for *all* Ealdaelfen to become the superior models of Elven life. He wanted to be the supreme leader, a patriarch of all Elves — Ealdaelfen or no. It is unknown precisely what occurred, but he attempted ritual magick of the most ill kind."

Bridgette had a feeling Magister Ephynius was not being entirely truthful in saying nobody knew what happened, but she chose not to interrupt.

"Unlike the smaller spells and rituals that had been performed, this was the first sign of true chaos to come to the Earth," the magister continued. "It resulted in the remainder of the Elves taking on the Ealdaelfen in spell, might, and blade on the battlefield, the first time such a thing of brutality befell these beings. The Ealdaelfen were defeated, and those that remained chose to retreat far from the green surface their siblings inhabited. They isolated in caves, underground, far from the public eye. It is not known what happened to the Raisarch, but so awful was his magick that it and the Ealdaelfen became the youngling stories our friend Collum grew up with. A warning to the little ones that should they attempt to use magic in such a way, they will be found wanting — and sent to live out the rest of their days alone in the dark caverns and crypts with these shadowed, vile creatures as their only companions."

Collum shook his head and sipped at his tea. "It certainly scared me straight as a youngling. There is nothing to fear of the dark itself, but when you are a child and imagine living in the dark, alone and haunted by evil? I shudder at the memory."

"So what, these are like, deviled Elves?" Bridgette asked. Collum elbowed her, not amused at her terrible pun.

"The devil is a being associated with specific Earthly religions. Ill-intent, darkness, evil, whichever term you prefer, can befall the mind of anyone, human or magical," Magister Ephynius said patiently, her joke lost on him entirely.

"Has there ever been a revival of the Ealdaelfen?" Bridgette questioned. "Like, what happened to them over all the years after their defeat?"

"Elves are not meant to truly be isolated in the sense that the Ealdaelfen were. Though they do not tend to have large families, or gather in great numbers, Elves still find joy in companionship and associating with others. They likely went mad and perished of their own accord," the magister said, and Bridgette shivered at the thought.

Her head was not something she wanted to be alone with, even if she won some great war, much less been on the losing side.

Collum broke the long moment of silence that followed, asking for the magister's suggestion on who to speak with regarding energies and auras.

"An interesting inquiry," he remarked, tapping a finger idly against his pipe. "I would suggest speaking to Magister Basira. She studies the intersection of physical and mental energies, though I believe her work is more centered on the conjuring of and calling upon spirits."

They found her in the library, a younger witch with light brown skin, soulful dark eyes, and black curls streaked with honey-gold. She seemed quite enthused that Magister Ephynius had thought of her, and cleared off a mound of books at a table to make room for Collum and Bridgette.

"Fyrdwisa, it is an honor to meet you!" she said. "What can I do for you and your companion?"

"The honor is mine, to work with a scholar such as yourself on this matter, Magister Basira," Collum said graciously. "But the reason we wanted to speak with you is all Bridgette."

The Elfling nodded. "I can't do spells, but during my time here in Heáhwolcen we learned that I can … *feel* energies, like invisible physical barriers, and auras, sometimes. Nobody else can, or if they can, they won't admit to it. We're wondering why that's happening, and what it means. And why I can feel physical forces sometimes, but more spiritual ones at other times."

The magister blinked, perplexed.

"These are gifts I have not heard of before," Magister Basira remarked. "When you say you could *feel* a physical force, can you

- 233 -

describe that in more detail?"

"Yes. So, there's the magical gate, the Seolformúr in Fairevella, which is spelled against magic of ill-intent. I didn't mean Fairies any harm and I don't have any ill-intent for them. And like I said, I can't do magic," Bridgette said, chuckling. "But I got up to the gate and it was almost as if I could feel the spell itself, an invisible force keeping me back. It made me sick to my stomach being near that energy. Then this other time a couple of days later, I was around some new people. We were fine when it was only a couple of us by ourselves, but when we were together as a whole group, I couldn't feel a physical force, but some of us definitely felt unease and it made a couple of us sick after. That's what I've been calling the aura."

"It is possible for magic to be *felt* in certain circumstances. If it is powerful enough magic, and the being itself is powerful as well, the being can determine where magic is or has been. But I have never before heard of such a gift causing an individual to become ill while that gift is manifested," Magister Basira mused. "I would suggest asking a member of the Samnung to take you to other places in Heáhwolcen that are similarly protected as the Seolfurmúr is, and see if you can firstly sense a spell in place, and secondly how that affects you physically and mentally. The auras, though. Many of us have an intuition. This is known. It is most unusual for there to be collective intuition in a group setting, unless someone in that setting is deliberately causing some harm. For example, should the fyrdwisa pull his dagger at this moment in a menacing manner, I would imagine it would cause an air of unease at our table. But for the fyrdwisa to simply sit here and think about pulling his dagger, neither of us would know, and there would be no unease."

Collum and Bridgette jointly chose not to share a glance at that. They were possibly the *only* instance in which one would know if the other was about to pull a dagger.

"Is there such a thing as *that*, then?" Bridgette asked. "Where people can sense each other's thoughts and actions, and be able to communicate them to one another?"

"That, yes," Magister Basira said quickly. "It is exceedingly rare. It's more common for a being to be able to sense thoughts or feelings, and far less so for a pair of beings to share such things with one another. Hold on for a moment — I want to get something for reference."

She stepped back from the table and darted off between the never-ending rows of shelves.

Bridgette turned to Collum and asked, "Is there anywhere else in Heáhwolcen we could go to test the energy theory? To see if I can sense powerful magic in general, or if it was just the gate and I deciding we'll be forever at odds with each other?"

He grinned. "That is by far the most powerful here, but we can still test it. Aristoces, Trystane, and Queen Nehemi I'm sure will gladly enchant various objects and see if you can detect anything. I'll buy you caife calabaza once a week for the rest of your life if you feel anything of Nehemi's, but specifically lie and say the magic she has must not be powerful enough for the legendary Liluthuaé to feel."

"You are a *punk*, Bundy," Bridgette said, laughing. "You're on. Although the satisfaction alone of annoying her might be worth it, even if there weren't endless caife calabazas in the mix."

By the time Magister Basira returned, Bridgette had nearly forgotten why they were sitting at the table in the first place. She'd been practicing her voice inflections for telling the queen of Endorsa that her magic was wimpy compared to that produced by the great Fairy of All Fairies and the most dashing Elven leader she'd ever laid eyes on.

Collum was nearly doubled over with laughter, but resumed his professional demeanor swiftly as the magister approached, a hefty purple book cradled in one arm.

"It took me a moment, but I found it!" Magister Basira said proudly, flipping the book open and scanning down a page. "Here, look. The ísenwaer."

Collum leaned over her shoulder and read aloud: "'The ísenwaer is a rare psychological partnership wherein two individuals are able to not only detect one another's sentiments and emotions, but communicate via silent channel between their minds. It is different from the individual gift to detect a being's inner mind. Instances of the ísenwaer have included both those with previously existing psychological gifts and those with this being their only one.'"

He chewed the inside of his cheek. "Does this book say anything about how beings are able to do this? Must they have some sort of connection to each other, or is it at random?"

Magister Basira skimmed the next few pages. "It seems that it's so rare, no firm conclusions have been made. However, what *is* known of mind-magic is that when souls meant to be forged meet, they are much more in tune to one another in general. It would make sense that such a connection would make the ísenwaer that much more powerful."

"How is it different from the covenant things, like what Collum has on his wrists?" Bridgette asked. "Aren't those kind of connections and thought-sharing?"

"In a way, yes," Magister Basira said. "But they are communication channels. Say you and I had a covenant together, Bridgette. You could think you wanted to ask me for this book. I couldn't simply pick up on that thought. Through our communication channel though, the covenant, you could specifically reach out to me and send a message, asking me to bring you this book. When I receive the message, I can touch my end of the covenant, hear or see what you have said, and reply in kind. The ísenwaer is different because it requires no such channel. I would only open my mind to send a thought to you, and you would receive it immediately and be able to reply likewise."

"A fine gift that would be," Bridgette quipped.

"Indeed," Collum agreed, standing from the table. "Magister Basira, I thank you for your time, your research and your suggestion to test Bridgette's ability to sense great power. It is my hope we will be able to do this sooner rather than later."

"My pleasure, Fyrdwisa and Miss Conner." She turned her eyes back to her own stack of books, and the two walked out toward the University grounds.

~ 33 ~

"That was … illuminating," Bridgette said quietly as they reached the wooden library doors, hefting them open to enter the bright outdoors again. "Mostly because of what Magister Ephynius *didn't* tell us."

"Indeed," Collum said again. "So what have we learned, and how can we go from here, Starshine sierwan?"

She smiled at the unexpected moniker. "Well. Apparently the stuff we *really* want to know about the Liluthuaé legend and Druidic magick are on Earth. And there's something fishy to me about what he didn't say about the Ealdaelfen. Like he knows more than he's letting on about what happened to them and the Raisarch. I'm sure some of them did die, by suicide or whatever, isolated in caves like that, but —"

Bridgette stilled as soon as the words were out of her mouth. Her eyes wide and opal. She whirled toward Collum and a storm of knowing flowed from her mind to his, only a handful of them full sentences that he could process: *That's how there are Ealdaelfen in Palna. That one evil Craft wizard guy you talked about recruited them. They wanted to be worshipped like gods, and he wanted all of humankind to pay for thousands of years of magical persecution. So he brought them, years and years ago, to this country of his. But, fuck, Elves are immortal, right?* She looked panicked. *Collum … what if the Raisarch is in Palna?*

He closed his eyes and took a deep breath as her thoughts continued to free-flow too quickly for him to pick up on them all. Collum wondered what it must look like to students passing by: an Elf and an Elfling, standing in the middle of a lawn, seeming to just stare wide-eyed at each other for minutes on end.

This is why I'm here. His mind jolted back to Bridgette's at that.

"What?" he asked aloud.

"We don't need to find the Earth Elves. We need to find Trystane. And probably Aristoces," Bridgette replied, her voice firm despite her reverberating heartbeat. "Can you summon them? To the wood again? This is really important and I don't think it can wait."

"Then to Maluridae Wood we shall go," Collum said, extending an arm toward her. "I'll summon them when we arrive."

Trystane and Aristoces were mystified by the middle of the day request for their presence in the wood, but still they came. Collum sealed their circle, then he and Bridgette began to talk about what they learned from Magister Ephynius, and what Bridgette's sierwan gift revealed.

Thankfully, Collum thought to himself, Bridgette had time to gather her thoughts now and share details in a much more coherent manner than how she'd told him earlier.

"Aristoces, the other day — I don't know if Trystane told you or not — I had a knowing come to me that there are Ealdaelfen in Palna. I'd never heard of Ealdaelfen before, but Collum and apparently most Elven kids grow up with horror stories they star in," Bridgette began, noting the Fairy's raised eyebrows at the revelation. "We asked Magister Ephynius today what he knew about them, but didn't tell him that I'm a sierwan or that I had this knowledge of them being very alive and well. He told us that they were pretty much the Craft wizard version of Elves — very intent on doing magic of ill-intent, but because they're Elves, their magic is different. It's less spellwork and more like, working directly with Nature. Anyway, Magister Ephynius said that after this great war between the Ealdaelfen and the rest of the Elves, the Ealdaelfen were defeated and forced into isolated caves where, he figured, they went crazy and died. Including the Raisarch, who is the self-proclaimed leader of the Ealdaelfen.

"Except," Bridgette continued, "I felt like there was something weird about the way that Magister Ephynius just kind of brushed off the fact that a whole bunch of Elves like, killed themselves out of madness. The way he said it was kind of like, maybe he knew — or thought he knew? — something he shouldn't, and didn't want to share in case it wasn't true. But the knowledge that came to me after we talked to him was that the Ealdaelfen are alive, at least some of them, because that Craft wizard dude went into the caves and recruited them to come to Palna. The Ealdaelfen wanted to be worshipped like gods; he wanted to kill all the humans because they were so horrible to magical beings. So it … it makes sense, if you think about it, that they would feel drawn to his cause.

"That's when I decided we needed to talk to you two, because this …" Bridgette paused and took a deep sigh. "This is why I'm here. The Ealdaelfen represent chaos. Evil, ill-intent, all that shit. They've disrupted the balance of Nature and the Universe so much that there's a real threat, especially combined with Craft magic in Palna and the already pissed-off beings that are walled in there. The balance has to be restored somehow."

"And that's why the Liluthuaé came to be in this time," Trystane finished for her. He considered what she'd told them. "Most of this about the threat in Palna we knew, though, Bridgette. While I appreciate your urgency in wanting to share this information … it's largely nothing new, nothing to be alarmed over. Yet."

Bridgette groaned. "But it *is*, Trystane, don't you get it? If the Ealdaelfen are working their nasty rituals and those are enforced with, or enforcing, equally ill-intentioned Craft magic, Palna is preparing for *war*. Magister Ephynius said the Ealdaelfen originally had this philosophy that if they created havoc, but nobody realized it was them, they could fix all the broken crap and suddenly the world has these magical saviors to worship and adore. That inner wall was created by them as a way to showcase to Palnans that 'oh no look, the Fairies and the Elves and the non-Craft wizards all hate us, so they made their barrier even stronger, woe are we!' And now they are gaining sympathy from citizens who aren't Ealdaelfen, and maybe weren't even Craft wizards, to illegally learn Craft magic, so they can break through both walls and take down the beings who put them there. Take over the world, you know the drill from there, I'm sure. So yeah, I'd say it's something to be alarmed over."

A moment's silence followed, as the Elves and Fairy of All Fairies took in what Bridgette insisted was full truth.

"This makes sense to me," Aristoces said. "We have long known that the Liluthuaé would come to exist when there was a threat to all magic. Now that we know, or believe we know, what is happening through those walls, how do we proceed?"

"Bridgette had a thought on this when she first arrived in Heáhwolcen," Trystane said slowly. "I mentioned to her that Nehemi and Kharis believed that perhaps Druidic magick could be used to strengthen our barrier, and her suggestion was to speak directly to those beings to ask how this could be made possible."

"I think that would be step one," Bridgette agreed. "Go to Earth and find what Magister Ephynius called 'True Druids.' Apparently the Druids I'm used to seeing, the ones who come to Stonehenge in England and do all the ceremonial things, are humans who practice a Druidic lifestyle but can't perform the same level of magick. Magister Ephynius hinted though, and my sierwan gift confirmed it, that the leader of these human Druids is a mask. He or she protects the secrets of the True Druids, and by gaining this person's trust, we can reach the Druids who can help us. They may not want to come to Heáhwolcen, but they might be able to tell us ways to use their rituals with the magical beings we *do* have to combine and magnify the power until it completely blocks out that of Craft Wizardry, or at least takes down that inner wall.

"While all of that is happening down on Earth, we can't just leave the wall unprotected," Bridgette said. "The Bondrie Guard isn't equipped to fight with magic, or at least not as well as they are with weapons. When I first came up with this idea I didn't know about the whole army that Heáhwolcen has, but I think sending some of them to assist the Bondrie Guard might be helpful. Especially once we figure out how exactly to counteract the Craft spells — I doubt they'll go down easy, and everyone needs to be prepared for the worst, just in case," Bridgette said.

"What happens when the inner wall is defeated?" Aristoces

asked. "I assume you have thought of this, otherwise you would not have brought it up."

"There are two options. One, Palna can keep being basically a prison, and it goes back to having only the outer wall. And maybe throw some more people in there to monitor the situation so that it doesn't get to this level of dissent again," Bridgette explained. "Option two, once the inner wall is down, the bad folk get weeded out. Sent somewhere else far away from Earth and Heáhwolcen. Don't ask me where though, I haven't figured that out yet. Not all Palnans are these terrible wizards and Elves and what have you, probably. It's been locked inside itself for generations, so there have to be some younger beings who don't agree with the thoughts of those who got them in trouble in the first place. So we get rid of the icky ones, and welcome Palna back into the fold of Heáhwolcen as its own country again."

Most of this plan she'd accidentally created days earlier, before anyone realized she was a sierwan, but now that she said it out loud, Bridgette believed for the first time that she actually knew what she was talking about.

"You have given this much thought," Aristoces remarked. She looked to the Elves. "Which would you rather see: Palna as its own entity, or Palna as it was meant to exist following its defeat?"

"Its own country," Collum said. "I was not sure at first, when Bridgette originally mentioned this possibility. But I have never been fond of the fact that at the center of the world above the world there is a place that is hardly better than a prison."

"I agree," Trystane said. "However, I caution us all: None of us, *none* of us, has ever known a Palna without the influence of Craft Wizardry. Collum, and I too, really, were too young at the time of the Ingefeoht to remember much of what happened, much less what it was like when Palna was an open country as our own are. Palna was founded on the principles of this magic. Is it possible for a peace and openness to exist between our five countries, as well as our comrades on Earth, knowing this? Is it possible for Palna to exist *without* Craft magic being involved?"

We need to do research on Craft Wizardry itself, Bridgette thought to Collum. *I want to know how it functions. What makes it different from … whatever the opposite of Craft is. What makes it detectable by the Seolfurmúr. Whether it is taught, or a genetic predisposition, or a combination of the two. But I have a feeling we can't just waltz back into the University library and say, 'Hey Magister Ephinyus, we would like to learn Craft now please thanks.'*

"All excellent questions that must be investigated before we proceed," Collum said, both answering Trystane's question and acknowledging Bridgette's points. "This would be incredibly sensitive research, though, Trystane. And I fear that it will require more than a visit to the University. Did the modern Samnung ever learn what happened to the Elusive Grimoire?"

Bridgette snorted. "The 'Elusive Grimoire?' Did you guys actually swipe that name from a fairytale?"

"We did not," Collum said patiently, professionalism winning out over his desire to poke her in the ribs for the jibe. "Baize Sammael had a great Grimoire of Craft Wizardry, full of rituals and spells. It consisted of several volumes, quite old, passed down from many generations of his family and added to by each. After the Ingefeoht, when Baize Sammael was defeated, the Grimoire was taken for safekeeping by the Samnung at the time, and its location was a secret that died with the then-king of Endorsa. Only a select few know it is positively still in existence, but magical beings did not let its legends die out as Baize himself did. They search for it still to this day, and as years went on, the Grimoire became somewhat of a treasure hunt, much like the humans and their Holy Grail. As no one has found it — because wherever it is hidden, it is hidden well — it became known over time as the Elusive Grimoire, as it has eluded capture for most of my lifetime."

"… Oh," was all Bridgette said, feeling somewhat mollified.

Trystane smiled at her. "Oh, you're going to love this part. Endorsa is the safekeeper of the Elusive Grimoire. Although Nehemi does not know precisely where it is hidden, those volumes are indeed tucked safely away in her territory. Why don't you ask her about them, Liluthuaé?"

He knew Bridgette wouldn't dare say anything negative about the queen in front of Aristoces, but her eyes flashed dangerously as if to accept the challenge.

"I could do that," she agreed. "How exactly would I bring something like that up? I don't think I could really walk up to Nehemi out of the blue and ask nicely if she happened to know where the Elusive Grimoire of Craft Wizardry is, as I'd like to borrow it and — wait, why are we wanting to find this thing, anyway? You didn't explain that part," she said accusatorily to Collum.

"We need to know our enemy," he said simply. "Trystane is correct in that none of us knows whether Palna can exist without the influence of Craft magic, so I believe it is important to learn all we can about this type of work. Not to learn to use it ourselves, of course, but have an understanding of what it is, where it comes from, how it differs from other magics."

He was essentially repeating Bridgette's thoughts aloud now, but in such a way as to make it seem like he'd come up with them — and thus not give away their shared gift, the newly-named ísenwaer.

"Got it. So, my first official task as Liluthuaé is to walk up to someone who does not like neither myself nor the fact I exist to begin with, and ask her if I can maybe borrow these evil, magical books so I can learn about the evil magic and therefore fight the evil magic?" Bridgette said, only half-joking.

Collum and Trystane nodded, and she chuckled. "I think I'd rather save the world ten times over than ask Queen Nehemi if I can borrow her secret spellbooks."

~ 34 ~

Later that afternoon, once the four had a firm plan set in place for Saturday's Samnung meeting, Bridgette and Collum returned to his apartment with a few hours clear of tours and official business.

He felt an odd freedom at this. Though his original plan had been for them to spend all day at the University, that was foiled by more important matters than touring old buildings.

There will be plenty of time for that in the months to come, he thought to himself.

Collum could hardly believe the week was nearing its end. Tomorrow they'd go to Fairevella for its Ostara celebrations, and Saturday would likely be an all-day affair with the Samnung.

Especially if she stays. Seven fucking hells, I hope she stays, he thought, watching the Elfling as she wandered into the kitchen, jabbering on about trying more of his "magic juices" to see what witchy powers might assert themselves next. *I'm not sure I can fathom what will happen if she doesn't.*

The past two years of his life had been dedicated to Bridgette Conner, even though he'd only truly known her for the better part of two weeks. It had been forebode, of course, that the Liluthuaé would be born, but both birth mother and Bridgette disappeared before that happened, and Collum assumed they were dead. Either during childbirth, as the Elfling hadn't been birthed by a midwife or medical magister anywhere in Heáhwolcen, or killed by whatever enemies had struck and killed Nehemi's parents and the previous fyrdwisa. When the Samnung found out the Liluthuaé was firstly alive and secondly, being raised as a human on Earth, he was immediately dispatched to find her. Once he finally discovered her in the diner, it had been his next mission to learn all he could about her.

Bridgette called him "Bundy" as a joke, but in truth, if Collum *had* born ill-intent toward her, the actions he took in seeking her could very well have been those of a murderous maniac obsessed with his target. Collum had never before been sent to find an ally. Any previous search of his was for specific information or an enemy, typically a Palnan sympathist who was trying to start precisely the type of wall breakdown and re-assimilation he, Trystane, Aristoces, and Bridgette were about to suggest to the leaders of Heáhwolcen. So, when it came to gaining Bridgette's trust, the fyrdwisa had no previous experience on what to do. Hence how he came to "stalk" her, then find her in a way that was, looking back on it, more like a narcissistic male cornering prey than that of a diplomat hoping to bring an expatriate home.

After devoting so much of his recent life to this Elfling he barely knew, to have her choose to go back to Earth would be devastating. He put in so much work to find her, and they had too much hold and sway over one another than he cared to admit aloud. Collum chose to enforce a certain distance between them. They had a purpose, he and the Liluthuaé, and nothing could get in the way of that if she chose to stay.

Collum noticed early on that boundaries were hard for Bridgette to both set and accept. She felt boundaries placed on her were signs of discontent, signs — especially where he was concerned — that she'd done something wrong or made him angry, and she feared doing anything that would make him leave. The strange connection that formed between them was equally strained and magnetic, and having the ísenwaer did not help. Both of them had become so accustomed to having each other's mind within reach this week that, on the few times they'd been without the other, there had been an odd silence in their heads. Bridgette noticed this when she was with Emi-Joye, and Collum when he'd been at the Samnung without her. Despite decades of being fyrdwisa and previously fyrdestre, and as such being accustomed to his gifts being blocked with the chamber spells, one single meeting with her head brimming with questions before him? It was as if his whole existence changed.

He both craved and resisted this. Her companionship, her snark, her mind … they all fascinated him, but he was wary of letting himself indulge that fascination. *We have a job to do,* he reminded himself, for what seemed the millionth time since that night at the coffee shop, when she took his revelation of thought-hearing with such stride and wit that he immediately warmed to her — Liluthuaé or no.

Bridgette returned from the kitchen then, and he realized she'd been asking him something.

"Hello? You alive in there, Bundy?" she asked. "What's wrong?"

"I was thinking," he said simply.

"Obviously. About what?"

"About you."

That was not the answer she expected. Bridgette blinked. "Like ... is that good?"

Collum shrugged and reached out a hand for the second bottle she held. "You and that overthinking mind of yours. Why must me thinking about you be good or bad? Can I not just think about you without an intention associated with it?"

"Whatever, weirdo," she grumbled, curling up in her usual spot on the sofa. "What magical activity do you have planned for us next?"

He walked over to lean against the wall across from her. "I do not know that it is magical, per se, but I can cook for us, and then I suggest we relax to our own devices for the evening. Ostara is going to be quite a busy day tomorrow."

"Can I ask you questions about it while you cook?" Bridgette asked, sitting up straighter, that gleam in her lilac eyes hinting she had *plenty* of questions to occupy them.

Collum grinned. "Of course, Starshine."

She wanted to know everything. He knew this already; had heard the queries brimming the moment he mentioned the holiday again. But Collum never wanted to spoil a surprise. He enjoyed it too much, watching the Bright Star take in every first in Heáhwolcen. Seeing her cry at Emi-Joye's installation was unexpected. The Elf knew Bridgette's love for music, how it spoke to her and how she could in turn speak through it, though he hadn't heard her play yet, but he hadn't realized the emotional effect Fae music would have on her.

So Bridgette asked, and between butterflying chicken and roasting root vegetables, he answered with as little detail as he could muster. His back was toward her, but he sensed her annoyance at his evasiveness — and she knew exactly what he was doing.

"You know, Bundy, it's really rude to take someone to a foreign country and then keep her itinerary a secret. If only I knew a way to retaliate …"

The way she said that made him whip around, spatula in hand, to find the Elfling floating cross-legged at the ceiling, a bottle of *very* pricey Fae wine in her hands, dangling dangerously over the hardwood floor.

"It would be a *shame* if this just … fell, wouldn't it?" she said wickedly, the opalescent flecks in her eyes shining brighter than the sun.

"Oh, you little — " he swatted at her feet with the spatula, and she kicked back, laughing.

"Tell me what to expect tomorrow, you punk! Otherwise, this bottle is going the way of the direwolf."

Collum narrowed his brows dangerously. *Two can play at this game.*

He summoned the bottle straight from her hands, and she gasped in surprise.

You sly, sly fox, Collum Andoralain.

And then she flew straight at him, tackling him against the wall as they each grappled for the bottle, laughing and half-heartedly blocking and hitting at each other, until their cores hurt from the play. Collum uncorked the bottle with a spell, and suddenly he was pouring mouthfuls alternately between her lips, then his.

The Fae wine was complex, Bridgette realized, once she stopped giggling long enough to savor it on her palate. It was sweet at first, rounding out with grassy green apple and a clean minerality as she swallowed. There was almost a saltiness to it, a freshness, that made her think of uncorking a bottle as she sat on the fishing pier at her favorite beach.

You like it, then, I suppose? Collum asked, mind-to-mind.

She shared the sensory memory with him, like she had that night of the near-flying disaster: an image and the feeling of her perched on the edge of the old wooden dock, shoes by her side, bare legs and feet dangling over the edge above the glistening turquoise Gulf waters. She sent him the sounds of gulls cawing, of waves hitting the rocks and sand to her left, of boat motors tremoring past toward the causeway. The sight of the many sunsets she, Doc, and Martha had shared on this exact spot for so many years, the three of them nearby on a wooden bench, waiting for the ephemeral "green flash" moment as blazing sun met stark horizon. The scents of salt-worn air, the feel of the warm breeze as the day died down.

That's what this wine makes me think of. The only other place I think I could ever call home, she thought to him. *You said you don't have beaches in Heáhwolcen. If you ever wanted to, you could come with me here one day. I would really like to show you this world, the way you've shown me yours.*

Ours, Starshine. This whole world is ours.

She smiled softly, and opened her mouth for him to pour more wine for her, drinking it from the bottle as if they were two college students, and not a nearly two-hundred-year-old Elven warrior-spy and his twenty-two-year-old misfit Elfling companion about to attempt to save these shared worlds of theirs.

Perhaps it was the wine, or the playfulness of letting both their guards down, but Collum felt more at ease that night than he had in what seemed an age. Being fyrdwisa in a time of relative peace was not exactly exciting, but it had its moments. Usually his main job — prior to finding Bridgette — seemed to be maintaining decorum in the Samnung chamber when Nehemi inevitably did or said something to annoy Trystane, or his best friend and Elven leader intentionally said or did something to goad the queen into losing her shit.

This, though. This moment of joy, with Bridgette in his kitchen, was something he did not expect when being sent to find the Liluthuaé.

It was unusual for anyone, save Trystane, to be a guest in this apartment. Collum had no family anymore; his parents had chosen to cross into the spirit realm together nearly a century ago and give their bodies back to soil, sky, and sea. Though Elves were in theory immortal, they could choose to surrender their physical forms. His parents had done so when his father was found to have a wasting disease that no magic could cure. It was a rare thing, for an Elf to have such an illness, but not out of the realm of possibility. After much discussion, and heartbreak on all accounts, Collum urged his mother to join her beloved partner in taking that final adventure. He was fyrdestre by then and had his work and the Fyrdlytta to keep him busy. The fyrdwisa promised to take care of him. Trystane, who had long been like an older brother to him, made the same vow.

And assured that her only offspring would be well-cared for, his mother agreed.

That was the longest, hardest day Collum could remember, and most of the details were fogged with pain. His parents had looked their most resplendent, even though by this time his father was barely able to walk unaided. The ritual was performed, and the whole of the Samnung, the Fyrdlytta, plus most of the Fórsaí Armada itself, was present for it, out of respect for his position as fyrdestre. He remembered finding the absolute beauty in the aches of his heart, remembered the gleaming golden light as his parents' spirit forms were welcomed from the earthen foundation of Heáhwolcen into the mysterious spirit world of Ifrinnevatt.

Losing his parents was difficult for Collum to process — perhaps he'd not fully done so yet, even a century later — and he'd thrown himself into his work to keep the grief at bay. He wondered now, sitting on his kitchen floor next to this gleeful, wicked little Elfling, sharing a bottle of Fae wine and eating chicken and cubed turnips straight from their respective pans, if his mother and father would be proud of him. A thought that had never before occurred to him; what they would think of him now. Would they be proud of him, the fyrdwisa, who spent the greater part of two years on Earth to find a living legend? Would they worry for his safety if he shared with them the plan he'd helped concoct earlier, to begin dismantling the Palnan walls? He wished he could ask them what they knew of Craft Wizardry — they'd been alive during the Ingefeoht, and his father, a great storyteller, lived alongside the Fyrdlytta and chronicled the war for their history books.

"Deity bless," Collum blanched, nearly dropping a piece of chicken. He turned to Bridgette, this time a light gleaming in *his* eyes, and grasped both of her hands in his. "Starshine, I think I've had a revelation."

She cocked a brow. "Aren't I supposed to be the sierwan in these parts?"

"Yes, you wicked thing," he said, squeezing her fingers. "But I've just been thinking about my parents. They are no longer of this earthen plane; they long ago crossed into the spirit world. My father was a historian, a great storyteller, and I remembered that he lived alongside the Fyrdlytta during the Ingefeoht. The battle fought over Craft Wizardry. What was published formally in the history books is common knowledge, so there is nothing to be gained by reading those. He would have kept diaries, though, notebooks, his personal thoughts and references, sketches, that sort of thing, to help him as he wrote. I wonder if there is something in one of those unpublished works of his that could help us? Either help us find the Elusive Grimoire, or perhaps answer some of our questions about Craft Wizardry itself. My father was always very thorough in his work, and it is quite possible … if there were Craft prisoners taken, he may have spoken with them, and recorded these details for his personal use."

Bridgette leaned forward and kissed him on the cheek. "You're fucking brilliant, Bundy."

~ 35 ~

He pulled away from her affection, the wine not having inhibited *all* his boundaries with her, but still smiled broadly. "I'm not sure where my father would have put those things — when he and my mother crossed over, many of their personal possessions were distributed to benefit everyone. I only kept a few things of theirs, and it has been so long since I've gone through them, I'm not sure that his diaries are there. But they must be *somewhere* in Heáhwolcen. I'm sure we'll see Aurelias tomorrow at the Ostara celebrations — I'll ask her to start digging around the office and the Caisleán itself, and put a word in with the Fyrdlytta commanders. If I don't have my father's records, they're in storage somewhere, tucked in a box and forgotten."

"You're waxing mighty poetically about your father's diaries," Bridgette said, swiping another sip of the wine. "I accused you of quoting Shakespeare once and I think you just did it again."

Collum snatched the wine back. "An Elfling by any other name —"

"— would still punch you if you didn't tell her what she was doing tomorrow!" Bridgette interrupted, laughing as he held the wine bottle over their heads. "Seriously, Bundy. The last time you surprised me I ended up going on-fucking-stage at an official government ceremony with zero mental preparation. *Please* do not do that to me again!"

Oh! That's why she is so insistent, Collum thought to himself, a little dumbfounded that he hadn't realized this before.

"I'm sorry," he said aloud, and meant it. "I didn't think about that aspect of it. I don't want to spoil everything, and I don't want you going in with expectations, but I assure you that neither of us will have anything to do with the ceremonies themselves. We are simply going as revelers to enjoy the holiday, and you'll get to observe some more Fairy traditions. And yes, before you ask, there will be traditional food!"

"Thank you. And do I get to wear a fancy outfit again?"

"Only if you would like to. It is customary to dress in more spring colors on Ostara, as it is the Spring Equinox. Njahla will have put a few options in your dresser and closet, I believe."

"I bet you a caife calabaza they're some shade of purple."

"You don't have anything to pay for a caife calabaza with, Starshine, so it's a good thing I'm not going to take you up on the bet. You'd lose. I happen to know that Njahla was considering either gold or shades of green for you to wear on Ostara, as there was so much purple in your formal gown," Collum said. "Though some Elves are rather fond of having signature colors, Njahla wasn't sure how you would feel about that, and chose options to complement your eyes, hair, and skin tone."

"I don't mind wearing purple," Bridgette said sheepishly. "But green and gold are nice, too. I can't believe you guys went to all this trouble to freaking clothe me while I'm here."

"I assure you, finding the correct size of clothing was somewhat a chore," Collum said slyly.

The Elfling's jaw dropped. "What. Are. You. Talking. About."

Collum laughed so hard at her expression that his stomach muscles burned. "Nothing so risqué as what just came into your mind, Starshine. I merely happened to be in the same store as you were and observed which size clothing you purchased."

"Yeah, fucker, because you were *stalking me*," Bridgette cried out, laughing too. "Of all the Elves in Heáhwolcen, how did I get stuck with the one who thinks it's perfectly acceptable to follow a girl around in shops to see what size leggings she wears?!"

"You're lucky, I suppose," Collum retorted, those tidal pool eyes twinkling brightly.

She gave him a half-smile. "I suppose so, too."

The two sat there for what seemed like hours, talking and laughing, and eating a second helping of chicken each, as if they'd known each other their whole lives but had missed valuable time catching up. Collum told her about his parents, the not-so-painful parts, and about growing up as an Elf in this magical space. He shared with her some of the Ealdaelfen stories that his mother read to him, or in his father's case, orated, as a youngling. Bridgette, in turn, relayed more about the Simmonses, avoiding the earlier childhood memories of being in the foster system. She told him of the books she read growing up that had fictional magic, magical schools, and worlds hidden within their pages, and how the expectations she'd had affected her perceptions of Heáhwolcen.

"I was honestly shocked to see that the University was more like Harvard in the States than it was this old British castle," Bridgette said, chuckling. "After reading all of these books, everything just seemed like it was supposed to be so … English!"

"You must remember, though, that Heáhwolcen was founded by American colonists and freed slaves," Collum reminded her. "Witches and wizards, magical beings of all cultures came to be here as time went on. Where Fairies and Elves tend to be concentrated in Europe and the African continent, some in Asia, witches and wizards come from every single background on Earth. As they came to our world above the world, they did so with their cultures in tow, and Endorsa in particular — Bondrie to a lesser extent — became of so many cultures that no one reigns supreme. The older architecture though were by far the most classic that pulled from European and American design, because those are the nationalities of beings who were here first."

"It's fascinating," Bridgette replied. "America, you'd think anyway, is supposed to be this giant melting pot of ideas and cultures because of all the different immigrant groups that came there. It was supposed to be this country of equality and opportunity. But the older I get, and maybe it's just how society itself has developed too, the more I see that's not *really* the case. Like, yeah there are a whole bunch of microcosms of culture spread around. But sometimes I think 'American' culture is just … a culture of appropriating other cultures. Even, no offense to Artur Cromwell, the English colonists who came here like, stole land from the indigenous humans who were already there. And it just kept on and kept on like that until it's so ingrained in how everything in America operates that to call it out is seen as, like, you're trying to *start* something rather than *stop* an unfair system."

"Indigenous humans and magical beings," Collum corrected. "Native American peoples have their own forms of magic that were sometimes fully ripped from them by white settlers and colonists. Artur Cromwell, from what we know of him, tried very hard to not be part of those situations. Once Heáhwolcen was founded, it was to several indigenous groups that he first visited, knowing them to have magic, and letting them know this world is theirs, too, should they like to come."

"And did they?"

"Some did."

Heáhwolcen, Bridgette thought as she readied for bed a short while later, challenged everything she believed. The existence of magic. The economics of paying in kind more so than in cash or coin! And the fact that such a system *worked* here! What it meant to truly be a multicultural place, though the Elfling wasn't naïve enough to assume it was always perfectly so, especially given that Palna was some sort of prison.

Heáhwolcen challenged her feeling of belonging, too.

Each day she was here, she felt more at home. Which terrified her as much as it excited her. She tried not to dwell too much on the "terrified" aspect as she tucked herself into Collum's guest bed. It wouldn't do to end such a good day with anxious thoughts.

He woke her gently what seemed far too early the next morning, calling her softly mind-to-mind: *Breakfast is ready, Starshine. There's hot tea and coffee, your choice, and I made cinnamon buns with sweet venison sausage.*

Her stomach grumbled, and she hastily ran a brush through her hair before entering the hall. "That all sounds incredible. As usual," she said, her voice groggy from not nearly enough sleep.

"I've already eaten, so I'll leave you be for the morning," Collum said.

"What? Why?" *Did I do something wrong —*

"You didn't do anything wrong, Starshine. I want to make sure I talk to Aurelias about my father's diaries, and though I know she'll be at Ostara, I also know that my fyrdestre enjoys revelry as much as any Fae, and I would prefer to give her these instructions while she is of sound mind to receive them," Collum said, interrupting Bridgette's tendency to blame herself for whatever ailed him. Even if nothing ailed him, as was the case at this moment.

"Oh."

He gave her a half-grin. "I'll be back soon, don't worry. We should plan to be in Fairevella around noon, so I will return with enough time to change into my Equinox finery."

Bridgette dug into her breakfast as he evanesced to the Caíslean, and yet again found herself nearly overcome with the flavors of food in this magical place. Collum's cinnamon buns were baked in such a way to be perfectly crisped on the outside, and gooey in the middle. She tasted not only cinnamon, but nutmeg and allspice, and just a hint of nuttiness: far better texture and flavor than any of the cinnamon buns she'd grown up with. The sausage was the meat human butchers could only dream of making, with its smooth texture and refined spice blend that resulted in a smokey, sweet quality.

I'd move here for the food alone, she thought to herself.

Once the breakfast dishes were washed and put away, Bridgette wandered into Collum's office. She doubted he would mind — and in fact, she presumed this is where he figured she'd go! — since they'd spent time there together already. Bridgette wondered how often Collum stayed in his little piece of paradise when he didn't have a temporary houseguest. She hadn't seen him go in here alone the whole time she'd been here, though, granted, it was attached to his bedroom, and he always seemed to rise much earlier than she did.

Bridgette took one step from his hardwood floor onto the soft moss, then leapt into the air. She closed her eyes, feeling the gently swaying breeze as she pushed past it, through it, higher and higher. The sunshine was warm, and she relished it. She slowed her ascent and curled into a cross-legged, seated position.

That was how Collum found her: floating far above him, meditating deeply. He felt her mind the moment he evanesced into the living room, no clear thoughts; simply peace emanating from her presence. He stood for a minute, taking in that feeling, before telling her he was back. *Starshine,* he whispered mind-to-mind. *Come get ready.*

She emerged a few moments later, a cloyingly sweet smile on her face as if she'd just woken from a long nap. "Welcome home. What did Aurelias say?"

"She is unaware of anything matching that description in our office. However, she is going to speak to the Fyrdlytta this coming week and ask where such possessions might be. She also suggested speaking to those who published the history texts that contain my father's reports. Those authors, if they are still with us, may have powerful insight as well, and might know where his notes are," Collum reported.

"That's a really good idea," Bridgette said. "Is she going to meet us at Ostara?"

"We'll likely run into her, yes. Aurelias is hard to miss."

The Elfling grinned, hopeful about possibly seeing her new friend again. "Meet you back here in an hour?"

Collum nodded, and the two went their separate ways to dress. Bridgette's closet had indeed included an outfit fit for the Spring Equinox: buttery yellow leggings that sparkled in the sunlight, and a semi-fitted sleeveless white tunic with matching butter fabric at the collar, the shoulders, and the high-low hemline. It was belted with a length of golden rope. She split her hair into two braids coiled around her head, which felt rather spring princess-y, put on a bit of makeup, then returned to Collum.

Njahla clearly played up blue being Collum's signature color, and it was evidenced by the shining navy leggings and white-and-navy tunic that looked quite similar to Bridgette's, though it wasn't belted and had an even hemline. His laced up the front with sparkling strands of navy and gold, and that familiar elaborate "E" was embroidered over the heart.

"Off we go," Collum said mischievously, and whisked them away into whorls of inky dark.

They landed just beyond the crowd — Bridgette could see

thousands of beings gathering the next street over — to catch their breath and ready themselves to enter the throng.

Collum hadn't been lying about everyone bringing food, and she realized with a start that they hadn't. Then she remembered everyone in Heáhwolcen except herself could do magic, and suddenly stacked trays of cinnamon buns were balanced in Collum's hand.

That's why you were up so early, she thought to him. He winked, and led her between the gaily decorated homes and shops in Çeofilye's center square. Tables were lined all over, each laden with dishes and serving utensils. The desserts were further down from where they arrived, which allowed Bridgette a chance to really take in the celebration as they walked through.

Everyone was in some semblance of pastel or brightly colored attire. Even Verivol, Bridgette was surprised to note, was dressed out of their usual gothic color palette in silvery gray and pearl white.

"Bright Star!" they said jovially as Bridgette and Collum approached. "How good to see the both of you. We missed you at the Samnung meeting, Bridgette."

She was confused for a moment before realizing Verivol meant the meeting she and Emi-Joye disappeared from, then never returned to. "Oh! Yeah, sorry about that. Girl talk, you know. We just kind of got involved and that sort of thing."

Verivol cocked an eyebrow at her, as if to say they knew she was lying, but wasn't planning to be the one to tell the secret. "I hope it was a fruitful exchange."

Bridgette rolled her eyes, since her gig was clearly up. "Rotten fruit."

The Sanguisuge broke into a wide grin, fangs on full display. "You are a gem, Bridgette Conner."

"She rather is, isn't she?" Collum piped in, hands empty after situating the cinnamon buns. "Verivol, a pleasure. Would you join us?"

"Join us for what?" Bridgette asked, but the answer was soon clear. They'd arrived just in time for the great feast to begin.

Aristoces flew high above the crowd in the center of the

square, her voice magically enhanced to project through the din. "Tráthnóna mistéireach!" she called out, and her audience fed the greeting back. "Fáilte, all! A beautiful day this is to celebrate the Spring Equinox, to honor the life well-lived of the Goddess Eostre; to commemorate the cycle of birth and rebirth! We begin this celebration with a feast: to nourish our souls and selves so we may enter the cycle anew of strong mind and body. Let us savor the fruits of our labors of harvest, of creation, and eat!"

The mass move of magical beings to hundreds of tables was the most orderly mad rush for food Bridgette had ever seen.

Their table, once they made their way through the line, was overflowing with options. Bridgette overfilled her plate; she couldn't decide what looked best and decided to have a small portion of everything, with the exception of soup that looked like warmed, spiced blood. Music filled the air from various artists playing instruments around the streets of Çeofilye. The atmosphere was lively, joyful, and so colorful! As they moved away from the food tables and toward a massive open green space where blankets had been set out for picnics, the air began to smell of sweet blossoms and perfumed florals.

The entire scene screamed "spring," and Bridgette couldn't help but wonder why anyone in Endorsa would prefer boring ceremonies to this sort of festivity.

~ 36 ~

The true festivity, though, had yet to begin. A group of Fairies, which Collum explained was part of the city's beautification committee for holidays, began coming around with goblets of Fae wine for guests who wished to partake. Bridgette gladly took a glass, enjoying the crispness of its pear and apricot flavors, chilled and spelled to remain the perfect drinking temperature. She watched as beings got up from their picnics, abandoning remnants of food, and began to dance.

"Come on," she said to Collum, attempting to pull him to his feet. He shook his head and laughed, so Bridgette reached for Verivol instead, who rose to join her.

Collum watched as the Sanguisuge and Elfling moved to the vibrant sounds of flute and violin, and realized that in the two years since he'd attended an Ostara celebration in Fairevella, he'd forgotten a key component of Fairy celebrations and Fae wine: the glasses were enchanted to automatically refill.

Wonderful. He rolled his eyes, laid back on the blanket and stared at the sky, watching as Fairies flew overhead. They danced with their wings and bodies in the air as their non-winged comrades twirled and dipped on the ground below. It truly was a majestic sight: glittering wings of gossamer, iridescent wings with crinkled texture, the insane array of insect wings carried by the Aziza, and the darkness of the rare Fairies who had animal-like bat wings. It was only when Aristoces alighted and the music died down that Collum even remembered where he was and what he was doing, so lost had his wine-mind been in the Fairies' wings.

"As this day grows long and our revelry begins, let us welcome our Goddess into our midst with open arms! Let us accept from her these gifts of promise for a fertile spring, with fields ripe of grain and fruit, with beasts giving us new life and good meat!" she crowed.

The Fae wine and spring sun suited Aristoces. She never shied from radiating her full power, but something about the way the golden rays reflected through the fiery orange portion of her butterfly wings exemplified it; gave it a physical manifestation around her as she invited the Goddess Eostre into their fold. This was when the theatrics would begin, and Collum glanced to where Verivol and Bridgette watched the scene unfold.

A Fairy was chosen each year to represent the Goddess and be glamoured into a larger-than-life golden March hare. This year's hare hopped around the corner on cue, a crown of pink roses and white daisies around her ears. Behind the hare were Fairies who'd earlier passed out the Fae wine, dressed now in ceremonial garb — long, flowing dresses in pastel hues of Fairevella's customary seafoam, lime, and turquoise. These Fairies had crowns of flowers in their hair too, and delicately placed similar adornments on every being equipped to carry offspring.

The Goddess Eostre was known for bringing things to life each Spring Equinox, Collum sent the thought to Bridgette, who was clapping and cheering for the approaching parade. *What these Fairies are doing is a symbolic gesture of her traipse around Earth on this long day, awakening both flora and fauna. The Fairy glamoured as a March hare is a representation of the Goddess herself, as she was known to carry such a creature with her.*

Bridgette turned from watching the hare and its line of Fairies to look back at him, an impish grin plastered on her face from the drink and the dancing. *You just want to see me in a flower crown, don't you?*

I am cutting you off from Fae wine, Starshine. But he grinned. The flowers did suit her — the adornment fit perfectly atop the braid crown she'd given herself that morning, and the pink roses complemented her flushed cheeks.

As the music began to pick up again, the crowd danced together toward the center of the square, where a post had been erected. Fairies started this traditional dance, grasping ends of long glittering ribbons that flowed from the top of the pole, flying in-between, over and under one another as they braided and twisted the multicolored strands into elaborate shapes in time to the music. A bright flash, from Aristoces' hand most likely, and suddenly smaller ribbons were raining down on the crowd, and all the beings assembled there were dancing with ribbons flowing from their own hands.

Collum took a rare moment to use his gifts and listen to the thoughts of Fairies in the sky: he would have liked to be up there, too, watching the interplay of colors and movement down below.

Are you eavesdropping, Bundy?

He jolted back to reality to find Bridgette nowhere in sight, but her laughing voice filling his mind. *What?* he thought back to her.

I could hear you try to listen in on some of the Fairies in the air, silly! I wish it wasn't a secret I could fly. I'd like to be up there too.

Where are you in this crowd, Starshine?

She danced out from the swarm, her hair coming loose from its braids, and a turquoise ribbon wrapped around each wrist. Collum smiled that soft smile — she looked positively radiant.

"Come dance with me?" It was equally a plea and a question.

"I don't enjoy dancing the way you do," he answered. "But I am very glad you seem to be enjoying yourself."

"What's the point of coming to a celebration like this and *not* dancing?" Bridgette asked, perplexed. She settled next to him on the blanket, catching her breath for the first time in what seemed like hours.

"The food, of course," Collum joked, poking fun at her. She stuck her tongue out at him. "I much prefer to watch than to participate. Be a fly on the wall, as the humans say."

"For a spy, I guess that's pretty on-brand," Bridgette commented. "If you change your mind though, I'll be in that general direction." She gestured to her left, back to where she'd come from a few minutes earlier.

"Have fun, Starshine. I'll be here."

Bridgette grinned, the corners of her lilac eyes crinkling with joy. He was very glad he'd brought her, just to see her happy like this. She'd changed in many ways this week — maybe it was just how comfortable she'd become with him, or maybe it was Heáhwolcen as a whole, but Bridgette seemed more at ease with herself. Less stressed, less questioning her every move as it related to someone else's perception of her, for the most part.

Collum lost himself in the music again, watching beings of every background and culture join with more food and wine, more twists and twirls and airborne dancefloor couplings. As the sun reached its setting point, Aristoces flew once more into the sky and called forth again the Fairies and the hare. They came out, the Fairies with baskets of wrapped treats on each arm, and tossed handfuls into the air around them. Beings jumped and leapt forward to catch one, Bridgette included. She may have accidentally allowed herself to fly *just* a little bit to reach higher than she normally would have been able, but this was the part of Ostara that most intrigued her: she really wanted to eat one of these Fairy fortune cookies. "Frihtri," Collum had called them.

Treat in hand, she darted back to find Collum on the blanket, his own frihtri next to him, unopened. They'd long ago lost Verivol to the revelers, but neither minded. Bridgette was perfectly content to sit here and exchange fortunes and good tidings with her Elf companion, just the two of them.

Tell me about the true fortune cookies on Earth, Collum instructed her, mind-to-mind. *I would like to do this properly for once in my life.*

"Well," Bridgette spoke aloud, knowing it might raise suspicion if she and Collum just stared at each other too long in silence, "They're these little cookies that are given out at Chinese and sometimes other Asian cuisine restaurants in America. Lots of times in restaurants when you get your bill at the end of the meal, they will give you a peppermint or something as an after-dinner treat. And this is the version of that in lots of Americanized Chinese places. Each cookie has a 'fortune' inside of it and for the most part it's just like, a little saying, pretty generic. It has lucky numbers on it too, so sometimes people who play the lottery will use those numbers in their choices for a big draw."

Collum's expression indicated he had no idea what a lottery was, and for once, Bridgette got to be the one to say she'd explain something later.

"Anyway, as I said, it's usually something pretty generic. Like, 'you'll make someone laugh today' or 'great money is coming your way,'" she said. "But they're all just for fun."

"How do you enjoy them in a group setting?" Collum asked.

Bridgette shrugged. "Usually we just take turns opening them and reading them out loud. But I have this superstition thing that your fortune won't come true unless you eat the whole cookie. Some people just like to break open the cookie, read the paper and toss it away. Not me."

"Would you like to go first?" Collum asked.

She gently unwrapped the gauzy packaging on the beautiful cookie. It was shaped like the fortune cookies she was familiar with, but dusted with edible glitter and scented of vanilla and almonds. She cracked it open, pulled out the roll of linen that was inside, and gasped.

The fabric was blank at first, then warmed in her hands to reveal a poem:

> *Be not impatient, O Bright Star*
> *The deities know of who you are*
> *A plan ahead for you is set*
> *Though it will not be realized yet*
> *Trust in that which the Universe decrees*
> *As it is, so mote it be.*

"How the fuck does this cookie know I am the Bright Star?" Bridgette whispered, her voice barely audible above the din. "And what the hell does this even mean?"

She shivered and read the poem out loud to Collum, her eyes wide with caution.

"The difference is that ours are, well, actually fortunes in the frihtri," Collum said, trying not to laugh at how afraid she looked. "Each being who opens one is given a blessing or suggestion just for them, because of how the spell works."

"But who sets the spell?" Bridgette asked, clearly about to freak out. Magic was still *so* new to her, Collum realized. She was still operating under the impression that spells had to be cast by someone or something, and did not understand that enchanted objects — like the fortune paper — pulled power and knowing from the Universal magic around it, from Nature, to "know" and "reveal."

He tried to explain this, but she still seemed unsure. And then Bridgette ate her cookie — partially because of her superstition, but more because she wanted to know how good it would be compared to the rather cardboard-y fortune cookies of her Earth upbringing. As predicted, "divine" wasn't a good enough word for it.

Collum opened his next, and he furrowed his brow. He wasn't about to tell Bridgette that he usually avoided frihtri, preferring to keep his future a complete surprise instead of having any sort of expectation that he must wait for. What was revealed on his own paper was precisely an example of this:

> Blue of eyes and dark of heart,
> Your future is an arrow-dart
> Striding from the midnight veil
> Into the light through seven hells
> You will not see it hurling
> But fast indeed it comes
> And you will at first refuse it
> Until your soul doth mourn
> The arrow strikes deep and quick
> Wounds you with its sharpened tip
> Heal you will and heal you must
> Before the pieces can be picked up.

"That sounds … morbid," Bridgette said, wrinkling her nose. "I don't know if you should eat your cookie. Maybe that's not a fortune you want to come true."

Collum's stomach churned. "It sounds as though something aims to break my heart."

Bridgette groaned. "*Definitely* don't eat the cookie."

"You ate yours, and I don't know that I'd like your fortune either," Collum said, summoning courage as he put the treat in his mouth. "We'll face these uncertain futures together, then."

She rolled her eyes and laid down with her head languidly in his lap. "Whatever you say, Bundy. Whatever you say."

As the sky darkened further, and Bridgette's breathing deepened, the Elf realized she'd fallen asleep like that. He looked down to see her flower crown askew, her lips slightly parted against his thigh. One hand rested lazily across his knee. He leaned down and whispered to her, "I'm taking us home now," and quietly evanesced them to her bedroom, where he laid her on top of her comforter and let her sleep the night through.

When Bridgette woke, Ostara seemed like a dream — a very lurid, beautiful dream with promise and hope and light at the end. She only vaguely remembered falling asleep on Collum's lap, and wasn't sure if it was part of the dream or a memory. She sat up, rubbing her eyes, and felt a strange tightness in her chest. Today was her last full day of this trip. Tomorrow she'd be going … home. If Nashville, if Earth, could even really be considered home anymore.

She'd never felt more at odds with herself. They'd be headed to the Samnung after breakfast, and she knew, even though Trystane and Collum had tried to ease her mind about the situation, that the leaders of Heáhwolcen would want an answer. Would she go back, not just to finish the semester out, but *really* go back? Or would she stay, take on this still-vague threat, in whatever way she could?

Bridgette shook her head to clear it. *Fuck*, she thought to herself, then reached her mind out for Collum. *Can we fly this morning?*

Yesterday's meditation was one thing, but not since flying with Emi-Joye had she taken time to work her muscles to hold herself in the air and really practice the motions. And even that time … Emi-Joye had been doing the flying. She yearned to lift higher than a few inches off her bed, and she needed to focus on something to clear her head from the undefinable tumult currently holding it hostage.

Collum was at her door moments later, a curious cocked smile on his face. She knew that the Elf could hear fear, or perhaps uncertainty, when she'd asked for him.

"Of course, but we haven't much time," he warned her. "Not if you want to fly, eat breakfast, and look presentable before we evanesce to Galdúr."

"Even a few minutes would be good, I think. My head is not

in a great place," Bridgette admitted. "I'm so stressed out about being at the Samnung today. I just want to focus on literally anything else besides being stressed out and anxious."

"Then let us go," Collum said, beckoning toward his room.

For the next hour, Bridgette didn't care about breakfast, and tried hard not to care about the Samnung either. She was loathe to admit how much she wanted to avoid the entire concept of being the Liluthuaé. The impending decision was entirely terrifying to her, and she wanted her mind cleared of it. She wanted to fly, to be free, to be in the air and out of the way, with nothing holding her to the ground except the ísenwaer and the Elf she shared it with. But all too soon, he gently coaxed her down — she couldn't avoid who she was forever.

Bridgette purposely took an actual age to get dressed, slowly pulling on tan leather leggings and a creamy knit sweater made of velvet yarn. She opted for the cowboy boots that she'd come to Heáhwolcen wearing, instead of the leather Elven-style boots she'd rather enjoyed wearing since. There was a sort of comfort in those well-worn shoes that she felt she would need for the next few hours.

Collum and Bridgette, owing largely to her slow departure, were the last to arrive at Cyneham Breonna that morning, joining most of the officials in the small lobby. When they walked into the chamber, there was a new Elf seated at the Samnung table: she had dark reddish-brown hair, porcelain skin nearly as light as Emi-Joye's, and her eyes were a purplish gray with that unmistakable opalescent sparkle. She was dressed in a full-length, formal velvet gown of a green so dark it was nearly black, and she radiated grace and power that rivaled that of Aristoces. Her eyes were shrewd and watchful — and they fell on Collum the moment he and Bridgette stepped through the door.

Collum stopped dead, and his grip around Bridgette's bicep became deathly tight. The sealed chamber walls had kept him from hearing the Elf inside the moment they'd walked into the building. *What in the seven fucking hells is* she *doing here?*

Bridgette didn't react outwardly, but shot a thought to him, sensing his sudden tension.

Who is that? she thought to him.
He couldn't answer. He didn't know how to.

~ 37 ~

Even Nehemi was somewhat rattled by the stranger's presence, Bridgette noted. The queen wore a dress of burgundy and cream today — complemented, of course, by Cloa's similar attire of cream hemmed in gold ribbon — but her demeanor was more cautious than spiteful. Whoever this Elf was, she was important. And Bridgette wondered how she'd not known about her before.

Who is she? she asked Collum again, mind-to-mind. And again, he ignored her. Pointedly ignored her. The sierwan knowledge came to her — he knew precisely who this woman was. She was important to Bridgette's task, and he was … not terrified, but strongly against the idea of her being near the Elfling before Bridgette made her decision.

As the rest of the Samnung filed in, and exchanged glances as they, too, saw the Elf at the table, Bridgette's wariness only grew stronger. She didn't like this atmosphere one bit, nor did anyone else, from what she could tell. The female clearly wasn't supposed to be here, but she was also evidently of such stature or importance that they couldn't kick her out.

Which did not bode well for how the rest of the afternoon would unfold.

Though no one was speaking as they usually would, aside from hushed whispers between Verivol and Bryten, Nehemi still rose to call the Samnung to order as if nothing was amiss.

"Fáilte, all," the queen said, bowing her head ceremoniously to the new Elf. "As you can see, the Samnung is joined today in a most wondrous surprise by a being who we have not seen in some time. When it became known to her that the Liluthuaé had indeed arrived in Heáhwolcen, she very much wanted to meet her and share a piece of this story. Should it please all of us, I bade her do so now."

Collum swallowed hard. It most certainly did *not* please him. There had been no time, no warning! But he had to try, before Bridgette was completely blindsided in front of the entire

Samnung, to tell her what was about to happen.

Starshine, I am so sorry — you have no *idea how sorry —*

But he was interrupted by the Elf rising smoothly to her feet, addressing them all as one. The fyrdwisa felt his heartbeat quicken: he was no sierwan, but he knew that whatever happened in the next few minutes would be crucial to Bridgette's choice. And he had no way to warn her what she was about to hear.

He already knew this story. He'd played a starring role.

"Friends, ceannairí, I am grateful for your audience this day," she said. Her voice was reserved, but Bridgette again sensed great power hiding there. "For those who do not know me, or do not recall — as it has been indeed, per Queen Nehemi's words, some time since I've entered this chamber — my name is Mohreen Conner."

Bridgette's soul went cold and her eyes went opal. She didn't hear much of what Mohreen said next, as Collum's soothing voice entered her mind: *Breathe, Bridgette. I'm so sorry. I didn't know she was coming —*

Collum knew Bridgette's next words before they even left her brain.

You knew? You knew my mother … and you knew that she was alive? That she was here?

Though Bridgette's words were mind-to-mind, he heard the sting. The betrayal. And his heart ached. The fyrdwisa didn't know what to say to her, how to apologize for this one. How to explain that he *couldn't* apologize because, just as with her father's origins, he'd been sworn to secrecy on point of death. Collum Andoralain was many things, but he wasn't infallible, nor was he the type of being to risk his entire world's safety for the sake of one Elfling's mental wellbeing. Even *this* Elfling. But he hadn't counted on the complicating factor. Though Bridgette didn't know her father, it was no secret her mother birthed her on Earth and disappeared, leaving her to the mercy of the American foster care system.

Bridgette Conner had been left, alone, as a newborn — and

more than twenty years later was now face-to-face with the female who instilled in her those deeply ingrained fears of abandonment, those constant brooding anxious thoughts. Her head at this moment was being pulled in too many directions for Collum to follow. She was spiraling inside, though her body and blank stare did not give any indication of her mental turmoil. He curled her fingers between his and held tight, urging her to listen; even as he hated himself for putting her through this pain.

Mohreen's eyes met hers, and Bridgette forced herself to look; to break her mind from Collum's and pay attention to what was being shared with her. She thought this was an out-of-body experience: her head felt so distant, every movement methodical as she turned her head toward her mother's.

Her mother's.

A face she had long imagined, but never dared dwell too much on. This was the face of the woman who carried her developing form, then chose to leave her. Abandon her. Run away, and not look back for more than two decades. The face of the woman who — Bridgette shivered, and secretly hoped Collum was listening — fucked a Craft wizard and was so disgusted by the child that would be born, she left it for dead with nothing but a note that said she hoped Bridgette would understand one day.

She fought the urge to panic, to vomit. To run, right then. But she felt Collum's fingers squeeze hers a smidge tighter: an apology, encouragement, presence.

No. She wouldn't run. This time, for once, she would be brave. She was the Liluthuaé, after all, whatever the seven hells that might mean in this circumstance.

So Bridgette looked, hard now, at Mohreen. Calculating her every move with those lilac eyes.

"Why are you here?" she asked, her voice barely above a whisper; the anguish and anger both equally evident as she interrupted her mother's words.

Mohreen looked somewhat taken aback. "I am here because you are here, my daughter."

Let her talk, Collum said sharply, mind-to-mind. *Do not fight her, or me for that matter, here.*

The last thing they needed was an all-out shouting match down the table. The last time that had happened, Trystane had left gauges across the wood and Corria Deathhunter had pulled her sword on Nehemi, defending the Elf's side of whatever the argument had been over. Collum shuddered at the memory: a scene like that, and Bridgette would be lost to them. He refused to consider that as even a possibility.

The Elfling listened to him, by some small miracle of deity and spirit. She continued to stare at Mohreen, silent and forceful in her attempt to create an air of discomfort in the room.

"I am here," Mohreen continued after a moment, "because you are the Liluthuaé, and you are born of my womb. Because the time has now come for you to come into your destiny, and I wanted to ensure that you knew the full story of what happened and how you came to be."

Bridgette wanted to leap across the table and choke the new Elf. *Collum, I can't just sit here and take this. She was gone for more than twenty years. Twenty-two fucking years. And now she just shows up and I'm supposed to listen to her? Forgive her?*

He was squeezing her hand so hard in his that he was afraid he would break one of their fingers. Her heartbeat was rattling in her chest, and though her breathing was even, it was deep and angry. There was agony flowing through her veins.

"When I was much younger, I specialized in theater. I even graduated from a school of the arts on Earth, a renowned school of the arts. I was an actress of the highest caliber," Mohreen said, and Bridgette thought she sounded rather high on herself. "Returning to Heáhwolcen, I did not want to work in theater, though. It held no interest for me, to act out the legends of goddesses and beings past. I wanted my work to have purpose, and so I approached the Samnung. I was not trained in any sort of combat, so being part of the Fórsaí Armada was not possible. But I was determined, and so I begged over and over, after multiple audiences, to be of use to them in some way. Palna was growing restless within its walls, not for the first time, and I wanted to aid in solving the problem.

"I happened to be in attendance at one meeting in which Master Swordsman Druan Heart of Stones suggested the idea of calming the dissent via encouraging good behavior," the Elf continued. "This sparked an idea of my own: I remembered watching film of soldiers in the Earth's world wars as human women danced onstage and performed shows for them, to 'boost morale,' they called it. The master swordsman's thought melded with my own, and I proposed a similar concept. We would send in theater troupes, artisans, encourage some form of trade and the arts, but the moment Palnans began to start beating down their walls again, the positive reinforcement would be ripped away."

That sounds like a fucking torture chamber, Bridgette thought to Collum. *Or something that parents do to teach kids to behave.*

A brash description, but it is apt, Collum responded, mind-to-mind. Hearing Bridgette think that made him question every decision he'd made at that ill-fated meeting. He shuddered inwardly.

"King Hermann liked this idea, and suggested a further step," Mohreen continued, unaware of the secret conversation happening under her nose. "He offered that in addition, the Samnung periodically send in individuals who weren't there for morale boosting, but rather, to reinforce Palna's position in our world — that the evil beings who inhabit it are threats to the greater Universe, and do not deserve to see the light of day outside its walls. There would be spies sent in under the guise of being prisoners, criminals from elsewhere in Heáhwolcen, who were in Palna to work off their sentences. Because they weren't government officials, and were considered 'ill-intentioned,' it was thought that perhaps Palnans would be more willing to talk colloquially to them and share things that the Fairy ambassador or other liaisons could not."

Bridgette stared in open horror at the philosophy the previous generation of leaders had of Palna and its citizens.

"What the actual f —"

But Mohreen kept talking, as though Bridgette hadn't spoken at all. "My theater troupe was in Palna regularly, but we were unable to do much information gathering. So I asked the Samnung, after several months of going back and forth, if I could be sent in with the prison guise. By this time, those beings had gathered enough information to give a muddy idea as to what was happening in Palna. Ydessa and Eryth Tinuviel were plotting … something. The Samnung wanted to know what. I offered to be the sacrificial lamb."

I refuse to acknowledge anyone who calls herself a 'sacrificial lamb' as my birth mother, Bridgette thought to Collum, her tone icy. *I hate her.*

Mohreen detailed how she'd been given a new disguise for this next task. She would be assigned not directly to either of the Tinuviels, but rather, to a garden work detail that worked around the Palnan palace residence. She would be in close proximity to both of them, but to the servants as well. And servants talked.

"I had this position for several years, going back and forth to Palna to work in the gardens. My crime was theft, which was why I kept getting sent back," Mohreen described. "The servants asked what it was like 'out there' and I got very adept at lying. I created a second Heáhwolcen that was much more like the Earth I'd gone to university at than the world above the world actually is. We have barely any crime here, but with generations of beings having no contact with the outside, how was any Palnan housekeeper or shrub-clipper to know this? That period of my life was almost an out-of-body experience. I was a second Elf in Heáhwolcen, a filtered version of myself that had a rough streak, but was very good at sweeping patios and arranging flowers. One evening, I was lucky enough to be assigned to work an outdoor event that the Tinuviels hosted. Finally, after years of being this entire other Elf, I would be close enough to speak with the two beings I most wished to know. The character I played was intentionally attractive, and Eryth took the bait."

Bridgette's eyes shifted. Her heart skipped a beat.

And now she knew. Her father wasn't just any Craft wizard. Her father was Eryth Tinuviel, the illegally-practicing Craft leader of Palna. Collum hadn't moved his hand from hers, but when he knew she had put the dots together, he slid their grasped fists into his lap and cupped his other hand around them. This was not how he imagined her finding out … any of her story.

Mohreen was looking at her, seeing her put two and two together. "Your father is the ruler of the most dangerous country in all the worlds, Bridgette."

"And you wanted to get rid of me for it." Bridgette's words were cold.

"The dalliance went … further than I intentioned," Mohreen said evasively. "When I learned I was with child, I knew it had gone too far. The fyrdestre was my contact during my time in Palna. And through our covenant together I asked him to remove me from the situation. He came with me to the birth healer, and it was there we learned I could not terminate this pregnancy. The Elfling that would be born was forbode to be the Liluthuaé, and we could not lose it."

Bridgette thought she was going to be sick. She didn't realize she was crying at first, and she hated it. Hated that the entire Samnung was watching her lose her mind, her history, her stability. Collum hadn't told her any of this. Hadn't mentioned that he'd been her mother's contact while she was doing whatever she was doing with Palnan gardens and Eryth Tinuviel. Definitely hadn't bothered to remark he'd been with her mother when she tried to have an abortion, because she — the lust-child of an Elven spy and the most deadly wizard alive — wasn't supposed to have even existed.

But what sense of humor the Universe had: even in the womb, the Liluthuaé was a balance to the chaotic coupling.

~ 38 ~

"This is all so fucked up," Bridgette breathed.

Mohreen acted as though she hadn't heard the remark. "I was hidden away after that, and largely forgotten about. Which made it quite easy to spirit you away after you made your entrance onto this earthen plane. I hid you so that Eryth Tinuviel could never find you, and I hid myself so that no one would come looking."

"You *abandoned* me on a *different planet*," Bridgette hissed. "You could have stayed there, too, assumed a different identity, if you're such a good actress. But instead, you left a newborn baby with a *note* like it's 1923 and I was some unwanted child."

She refused to acknowledge aloud that she, in actuality, had perhaps been unwanted — and only carried to term to further prove Mohreen's role in life as a "sacrificial lamb."

"The thought did not occur to me at the time," Mohreen said, raising a brow. "I was most concerned with the safety of the Liluthuaé and keeping her existence a secret."

"What did you do after you dropped your baby off on Earth? Did you ever try to come looking for me?" Bridgette was angry now, not bothering to keep her tone calm.

"I returned to Heáhwolcen and resumed a quiet life deep in the woods. I believe the fyrdestre thought I was dead. The covenant between us had been ended when I returned from Palna, so he had no way to contact me unless he searched for me directly," Mohreen answered.

"We did think you were dead." Trystane's voice was an unexpected force from the other side of the table. "Had we had any inclination otherwise, we would have found the both of you far sooner, as was the initial plan before you disappeared. The Liluthuaé could have been protected *here*, raised *here*, whether by you or any other being, and come into her power and might properly instead of having a weeklong crash course at age twenty-two."

Bridgette wished she could speak to Trystane like she could to Collum; send him a silent thanks for having her back at that moment. But instead, she spoke aloud to Mohreen. "Do you have any idea what it was like for me to grow up like I did? Do you have any idea what it's like to know your whole life that your mother abandoned you, and then in foster care live in constant fear that everyone else is going to do the same thing? That you are constantly unwanted, and you feel like you have to prove yourself to everyone around you, so they won't disappear?"

"You were in no danger from being discovered by the Tinuviels, and that was all I was concerned with. You are an Elfling and daughter of two very powerful beings. I knew you could handle yourself," the new Elf responded, as if Bridgette should have known these obvious answers.

She doesn't know I have exactly zero powers, Bridgette realized.

Collum squeezed her hand. *Let us keep it that way.*

"Despite the challenges she was faced with for the life you left her to, Mohreen, Bridgette has grown to become a force to be reckoned with," Collum said. "She is kind and daring, and gives much to both this world and to Earth. When you came to us two years ago and shared that both of you were alive, I wondered then what prompted you to do so. Why that moment? It was a question you never answered. I believe Bridgette, and the Samnung, deserve to hear it now."

Something flickered in Mohreen's grayed eyes. "There were rumors starting again, of what was happening in Palna. And there is talk in the wood that perhaps the Samnung is not strong enough on its own to hold the prison together."

"It's not a prison, it's an entire *country*," the Elfling corrected. "Most of the beings locked up in there didn't do anything wrong except be born there."

Mohreen's chief talent outside of acting seemed to be pretending others weren't talking when she wanted to be the center of attention.

"I heard these rumors and knew that if the birth healer had been right, that the Liluthuaé was among us, and she alone, my daughter, could save us all," the Elf said. "I determined the time was nigh to return to the Samnung and explain where she was."

Bridgette stood up abruptly, jerking her hand from Collum's

with surprising strength, and left the chamber. He shook his head at Mohreen, then followed the Elfling out. She was in the bathroom dry heaving over the toilet when he found her. The fyrdwisa wet a cloth and put it across her forehead, then sat on the floor next to her. They seemed to be doing a lot of this lately, he thought.

Talk to me, Starshine, he urged her, mind-to-mind.

It's all so much. So much to take in. Bridgette sounded utterly broken in her mind-voice. *My mother is alive. You knew her and you even knew that she was here. My father is Eryth fucking Tinuviel, and all I know about him is that's a really bad person to be related to. My mother is also a frigid bitch who cares more about her reputation than her child. And today … today I'm supposed to make this giant, life-altering decision about whether or not I'm sticking around and working with the Samnung. And Collum! Look what the Samnung and my mother did together. They reinforced this idea of Palna being a prison. They essentially sent her to be a whore for them. Collum, I can't do magic like my mother can. So what the fuck am I supposed to do? Sleep around and maybe try to birth a better alternative?*

Collum closed his eyes and leaned his head against the wall, pulling her close. "I am so sorry, Starshine," he whispered to her. "For everything. For keeping these secrets from you and for the pain and grief that I, and the Samnung, caused you. I don't ever want you to feel as though we've led you on, because we, I especially, would never do that to you. You are a powerful being, Bridgette Conner. Mohreen does not matter. Her choices brought you here, but you are not her and this Samnung is not the same as the one she worked with. Aristoces, Kharis, and I were the only ones who were there at that time. And I'll be damned if I let anyone send you to Palna under the guise of prisoner or whore or anything else without your full and informed consent to do so. Mohreen made her choices and her choices do not need to be yours."

He truly hated himself in that moment, knowing the grief that had been laid bare because of what he'd kept hidden. Hated that he couldn't be a better comfort for Bridgette, because he'd been part of the cause of her anguish to begin with.

They didn't know how long they sat on the cold bathroom floor, not saying a word, just processing the morning's events. It was Bridgette who shifted her weight and decided to get up, claiming that her tailbone was aching after sitting for so long.

"Are you ready to go back inside?" Collum asked her.

She shook her head. "No, but I'm going to. You're right, that her choices aren't mine. And this is a different time, under a different set of leaders. We can do this together. Whatever 'this' is."

Collum stood to join her. "Then let us go."

No one said a word as the two re-entered and took their seats again. Mohreen was studying them, hard. "It is my understanding that today you must decide what to do with yourself. That the Samnung is giving you an option."

Bridgette nodded. "They are. I can either stick around and save the world, or I don't have to. With *this* Samnung, things are different."

A big emphasis there, Collum noted. The rest of the Samnung did too. Even Nehemi gave a slow nod of approval.

"I caution you, daughter mine, that when one involves herself in government affairs, the concept of 'choice' becomes very vague," Mohreen said. She smirked. "But how very noble of you to assume otherwise. When you align yourself with a mission, you do so at the cost of all that is dear to you. Your fyrdwisa knows this now, I'm sure."

Suddenly Mohreen's presence made an awful lot of sense to Collum.

"Bridgette knows that I was under strict orders, on threat of death, to not reveal certain information until the right time came to pass. She knows I am incredibly sorry that I could not do so," he said.

"And I accepted his apologies," Bridgette added quickly, lest Mohreen try to get another word in. "I don't know why you came here today. You've caused a lot of harm here, and given me way too much to think about."

The new Elf rose to her full height, impressive under the weighty fabric of her gown. "Then I hope you make the right

decision, Liluthuaé." She walked out without another word, and
the room heaved a collective sigh of relief.

Bridgette leaned into Collum and tried hard not to start
crying again. *What a fucking day.*

"Bright Star, this is not how we planned on you learning the
additional information about your story," Corria Deathhunter
said after a few minutes of silence. "You are right that Mohreen's
choices are not yours. I cannot imagine the difficulty you must be
experiencing with all that just unfolded, and all that we must ask
of you. There is no clear plan of attack, no firm timeline, yet we
are asking for this alliance."

"Will you join us?" Trystane asked. His voice was quiet, his
tone even, though Bridgette knew there was both hope and
unspoken imploring behind those words.

The Samnung members sat around their circular table, all
eyes on her. Even the fog-like wisps of formless Spirit in the
corner seemed to be watching, taking the moment in. This was
it. It was do or die. Fight or flight.

Corria Deathhunter was right: they didn't know what the
plan was. Bridgette would be agreeing to a role she didn't know
how to play, because no parts had yet been assigned. Her
heartbeat quickened, and there was a sudden tightness in her
chest. The panic. She knew that feeling all too well, and Collum
knew it too; but in the warded magic of the chamber room, there
would be no calming spell to ease her nerves.

She didn't know what to do. To stay seemed impossible:
what if she failed? To go seemed to ensure failure: could she do
that, break her own heart and run from this magic place?

All Bridgette wanted to do was to run. Far, far away, where
no one needed her. Though her heart's greatest desire was to be
needed; to feel valued and appreciated, this was too much. This
was the greatest burden the Samnung would ever ask any single
being to shoulder, and they were asking *her*. She didn't feel
worthy of this task, especially not after what just happened with
Mohreen. She didn't feel capable of taking it on. She realized
she'd been holding her breath, her eyes swimming and
unfocused. Bridgette felt Collum's thoughts tickle her mind, but

she managed to block him out. To hear what he was thinking right now was too painful. To let him hear this inner monologue of despair was somehow worse.

I don't belong here.

"I can't." The words choked out of her as she released that long-held lungful of air, and she backed away. *You fucking coward.* She could picture Mohreen's shrewd, blinking eyes taking in the room.

The Samnung members' reactions were swift. Aristoces and Trystane glanced at each other. Verivol buried their face in their hands, and Bryten leaned back on his stool, staring at the ceiling. Corria Deathhunter turned away. Kharis looked downcast, and Nehemi offered a simpering grin. Cloa seemed to take in a change in the atmosphere and tilted her head slightly, as if to process what was going on. Even Arctura's behavior altered: the cat let out a hiss, eyes locked onto Bridgette's form.

But it was Collum whose reaction was the worst. In the split-second after she spoke, his eyes dulled and his own breath seemed to catch in his chest. Just for a moment.

The moment was long enough. The pain and disappointment Bridgette saw flicker in those tidal pool eyes nearly broke her, and the humiliation sent her mind reeling. *Run,* a little voice inside seemed to whisper.

And so she did. Before any of them could catch on, Bridgette bolted out of the chamber, down the stairs and into the greenery-covered foyer of Cyneham Breonna. She ran past Lucilla, who gave her a startled look, and out the double doors into the streets of Galdúr. She had no idea how to get to the portal. She didn't even know where it was. She simply knew she needed to go back.

As if in answer, she heard hoofbeats appearing behind her. Bridgette had a sudden vision of Collum riding Mithrilken to come after her, but she quickly squashed that thought from her mind. *He is no more,* she told herself. *You stabbed him in the worst way. There is no returning now, not to him.*

The hoofbeats, though, weren't Mithrilken's. They belonged to Eloise, and in about three seconds the golden Unicorn overtook Bridgette's stride and halted the Elfling in her path.

"Where is it you need to go?" Eloise asked, taking in Bridgette's strained, terrified expression. "You do nay want to remain?"

"No. Please, go away. I just … I can't do this. I can't fucking do this. I have to get out of here," Bridgette said, glancing around to make sure she wasn't being followed. If she didn't leave this moment, she'd change her mind and have to go skulking back to eat crow she did not want to taste. "I'm going to the portal."

"You can nay get there very quickly on those two legs, Liluthuaé. Allow me," Eloise offered, and tilted her head and horn down in a bow. Bridgette gratefully clamored on.

"I'm so sorry. I know I'm letting everyone down but I *can't do this*," she emphasized again, as the Unicorn took off at a near-gallop. "I'll only manage to get everyone killed and I'd rather have no part in that. I don't know what it is like to be in a war. I can't even do *magic*, Eloise. They may call me the Liluthuaé or the Bright Star or what the hell ever, but this is not … I'm not who they want me to be."

"That is the choice you have made," Eloise said simply, and Bridgette wondered which choice she referred to. "I will take you to the portal, and once there, you will need to find Geongre Akiko to procure your documents. No one will question you, and you can go forward from there."

The Elfling nodded, gripping Eloise's mane in her hands. *Go forward, because there is no going back.*

LATER

~ 39 ~

Bridgette sat in class, unable to find a comfortable position in which to prop her arms during the lecture. Her head ached and her shoulders were tense, and she found it difficult to pay attention as the professor droned on about the appropriate angle at which to flick a baton when conducting an orchestral piece.

I do not. Fucking. Care, Bridgette thought. *Why am I even here?*

She loathed this class. She, now that she thought about it, loathed much of what she'd returned to for these past few months. The endless doldrum of scholars talking about theory. The repetitive grind of waking up, attending class, coming home to practice, going to sleep; over and over again until the weekend, when "attending class" was replaced with "serve world-famous Wafflewiches". It was only those moments when she was alone with her violin that Bridgette felt somewhat alive, her heart stirring the smallest bit at the mournful and elative sounds she produced pulling her bow across the strings. She sat, now, in this stupid orchestra auditorium, not caring about batons or angles — she would be *playing*, why should she learn to direct? — and began to mimic chords and finger placement with her left hand, playing a silent melody that only she could hear.

Bridgette had very little experience composing music. She'd never written anything down, never charted a note. But this piece … this wasn't designed for scholarly endeavors. This was pure emotion. Every night after class, after she finished her necessary practice and recorded any required audio, she put her digital recorder in her bookbag and retreated to her porch. There, in the dark, surrounded by a circle of flickering candles and various plants she managed not to kill, she closed her eyes and played. The notes came to her without thinking. This composition was soft and gentle in parts, hard and fast vivid musical imagery in others. Some nights, the song was short. Others, she called upon that feeling of lightness and hovered in midair, playing until long after midnight.

There was no rhyme or reason to this piece. It constantly evolved, weaving with it the long-suffering confusion and sense of belonging and loss, the aching of soul that eroded her the longer she stayed here. This endless melody told of dreams and love, magic and Unicorns and Fairies. She imagined when she played that ribbons of shimmering seafoam and lime green flowed from her fingers, tracing amongst an imaginary audience, surrounding them with the whole world above the world that she so longed to go back to.

But I can't go back, she thought, coming suddenly to reality. Back to the stiff-backed auditorium chair, with that muddy old man up front still waving a baton she rather would like to shove down his throat. *Stop it. It's not the old dude's fault he's so miserable. Or that* I'm *so miserable.*

The Elfling had tucked *him* away, far away, in a corner of her mind. She tried not to think about him. It hurt too much. He made it clear that he was her friend, her colleague and confidant, but could not and likely, she presumed, did not want to be anything but. Bridgette forced herself to avoid remembering that look on his face when she left the Samnung. He'd looked — despite himself, despite all the gallantry and emotionlessness required of him as fyrdwisa when a wartime decision must be made — his eyes clouded. Those wonderful, majestically blue eyes lost their luster. For just a moment, but it was enough. She'd hurt him so deeply by being so afraid, and it was that humiliation, knowing she'd scarred him; that was what kept her here. Pinned to this seat in this class she hated.

Her mind drifted again.

What did she have to do today? There was a test tomorrow. Or perhaps the day after? Time seemed irrelevant. Why had she chosen to take a full load of summer classes? Oh. Right. Because she had nothing better to do. Nowhere to go *home* to, though she had managed to keep up a conversation with her foster parents every week. At least, she thought it was a week. Maybe it was more. How close was she to finals, again?

A rapping noise brought her again back to reality, and Bridgette realized she'd started to doze off. She *also* realized she'd started to levitate off her seat. Not enough for anyone to notice except for her, thankfully. That would have been difficult to explain. The rapping noise this time was the professor tapping his baton on a podium at the head of the stage. He seemed to be demonstrating how to call the audience to attention, to let them know a new piece was about to begin. Or something to that nature, anyway. Bridgette wanted to go back to sleep. She briefly contemplated feigning ill — getting up and running out of class, off campus, and back to her apartment. Come to think of it, she didn't feel right at all. She again thought to the previous night, how restless she'd been, struck with myriad dreams that woke her, but she couldn't remember a thing about them.

Weird, she thought, glancing up to see the clock. *Ugh. How much more time am I stuck here for?*

The clock wasn't working. *Just my fucking luck.*

Bridgette shifted again in her seat and glanced to her right. The student sitting there was furiously taking notes, trying to write down every word out of the professor's mouth. The older woman to her left was doing the same thing on a laptop. The Elfling just wanted a nap. She gave in to faking sick and grabbed her backpack from the floor to make a run for it.

She made it about three steps from the end of her row before her head throbbed so hard it blinded her with pain, and she fell straight to the floor. When she came to, a flurry of students was circled around her, and the professor was right over her face.

"Miss Conner? Are you feeling okay? You took quite a fall."

Bridgette shook her head numbly. *Shit. Maybe I'm actually sick.* "I ... don't feel good. I need to go home now."

"Would you like for Mister Ardmore to accompany you?" the professor asked. His face was concerned, and he motioned next to him, indicating a wiry freshman with curly brown hair. Curly brown hair and blue, blue eyes.

Bridgette almost fainted. Collum's face came to her clear as day, and the shock of seeing what she'd tucked away for nearly four months was unexpected. She blanched, then shook her head again. "No. No. I just ... I need to go now."

She scrambled unsteadily to her feet and leaned against the wall. "I'll be fine. I just need something to eat, and a nap. And some ibuprofen."

Bridgette had little memory of how she made it back to her apartment without falling over again. She vaguely recalled crossing the street by the coffee shop and forgetting to check for oncoming traffic. But she was back in her own four walls, and her heart was beating out of her chest in terror and anguish that she'd tried so very, very hard to deny existed or needed to be released. *Why did he come to me like that? Why did seeing him … why did it do this to me?*

She clutched her hands over her heart and sank to the floor, head still throbbing. She wished she could summon a pill bottle or banish the pain, but having spent barely a week on the magical continent, there had been no time to learn any sort of spell casting. Assuming, of course, she was capable of doing so. No one had figured that out yet.

Bridgette tried unsuccessfully to ease her rapid heartbeat. She tried deep breathing, like Collum had shown her. But that just made her think about *him*, and she struggled to mentally box him neatly back up. She started to cry, out of frustration; out of the miserable headache that wouldn't go away; out of despair.

What is wrong *with me?*

She buried her face in her hands, shoving the heels of her palms into her eyes to ebb the flow of tears. Collum's face kept coming into her mind's eye. *Why? Why can't he just go back in his corner in my head and leave me alone?*

Bridgette, eyes still closed, took a deep breath in and as she exhaled, the vision of Collum inside her head suddenly zoomed out. The whole Samnung stood there, staring curiously at her, as if they could see her. She knew they couldn't, but it was … an unusual sensation. The Collum-in-her-head stepped forward, and she allowed herself to bring him into focus and to swim inside his tidal pool eyes. Just for a moment. Just this once. His brow was furrowed, and she wanted so badly to reach out and touch him, but she couldn't. He wasn't real. This was the Collum she pretended she didn't dream about, have nightmares worrying over.

"Liluthuaé," the Collum-in-her-head seemed to whisper. And

in real life, Bridgette felt her closed eyes move. She hadn't felt
that in months and almost forgot what it was like, as if her
eyeballs gently brushed the inside of her eyelids. The knowledge
flew into her so quickly that she struggled to process it all, and it
came very disconnected. Something was wrong. She should have
known that, sierwan or not, the second Collum-in-her-head
called her "Liluthuaé." He never called her that. She was
Starshine. She was only Liluthuaé to him when … when they
needed the Liluthuaé.

"Mother. Fucker."

Bridgette was packing her bag before she was aware of her
actions. She didn't even know if she had enough money for a
plane ticket. Hell, she didn't know if there *was* a plane to catch.
But she had to get back to Heáhwolcen. She had to get back to
Collum, and do what little she could to help, whatever the
danger was that caused her gift to manifest so suddenly.

The hired car seemed to take an age to reach her apartment,
and then to turn around and deposit her at the nearby airport.
The Elfling practically flew to the check-in gate, eyeing the list of
incoming and outgoing flights intently for anything that would
put her within a hundred miles of the old Salem Village. There
was a flight to Boston departing in half an hour, and Bridgette
ran to the nearest kiosk, praying to whatever magical spirits and
deities she could think of that somehow there would be an open
seat.

I have to get on this plane, she thought desperately.

It wasn't a cheap ticket, but she had a feeling Earthly money
wouldn't be needed in her hands for some time to come. It was
worth the spend, Bridgette decided.

She was grateful for long summer nights when the plane
pulled onto the New England tarmac. The sun was just
beginning to set, the sky glittering with rich shades of cotton
candy pink and blue. Bridgette pulled her phone out of her
pocket and looked to see what time Endicott Park stopped
allowing visitors.

Sheee-it. By the time she got from Boston to Danvers, she'd
have missed it. *First thing tomorrow.*

The Elfling could, however, still get to Danvers tonight, and she knew that she'd also be able to stay in that little cottage the Samnung owned. She hurried to the front of the airport where taxis and hired cars drove in and out, searching for passengers, and hailed the first cab she saw.

"Where to, miss?" the gruffy driver said. His cab smelled noticeably like stale cigarettes, despite its prominently placed "No Smoking" sign in the windshield.

"Um, Danvers, please," Bridgette said.

"That's not very specific," the driver urged. "Can I have an address?"

"Uh …" Bridgette had no idea what the address of the cottage was. "The Witchcraft Memorial, please."

"It's early for Halloween, isn't it?"

"Not for Halloween. I mean. I'm not going there for costumes and stuff. I'm going to be staying near there," she fumbled the words. *Just take me to the damn place.*

Bridgette was grateful that the driver opened the door to her then, and drove without small talk. She tried to pay attention to the radio, her window rolled down to blow out the cigarette smell, but the driver seemed to favor news talk stations instead of music. She found the discussions of the day morose and disheartening. Something about the president refusing to denounce the leader of a white supremacist organization; hurricane predictions for the Gulf Coast; a bit of a dire look at the country's economic situation and unemployment rate that contradicted reports from the nation's leadership.

Well, that all sounds horrifically sucky.

When the taxi finally pulled up at the memorial, it was nearly pitch-black dark out. The driver seemed concerned about leaving her there, but Bridgette turned the flashlight on her cell phone and pointed up at the light post. "I'll be fine!" she assured him, slightly mollified that he was worried for her safety.

So am I, if we're being honest here …

She closed her eyes and willed herself to remember, in reverse, how they'd driven that morning from the cottage to Endicott Park. The memorial had been on the way, she recalled.

And for the first time in such a way, she summoned her sierwan gift. Bridgette turned inward, focusing her energy on the shifting feel of her eyes and the intent of knowing where the cottage was. The route came to her, and she began to walk. About a quarter-mile down the road, though, she wondered if it wouldn't be faster to figure out how to evanesce, if that was even possible on Earth.

Hmm. I mean, I can fly here, so why couldn't I try? Collum once explained what happens when one evanesces: it was a kind of out-of-body experience where one willed oneself into nonexistence *here* and simultaneously into existence *elsewhere*. Bridgette cringed. Evanescing was somewhat actual magic. Not a spell, but something she would only be able to do if she had magical abilities. *What a fucking conundrum.*

But she could try. The worst that could happen is she would just look slightly stupid, standing on the sidewalk with a suitcase, eyes closed in the dark. Bridgette called upon her feeling of lightness, hoping that perhaps might speed things up, and envisioned herself twisting into nothing until the cottage came into view.

After several minutes of not moving, she decided perhaps a Plan B was necessary. She rolled her eyes, gripped her suitcase with one hand, and propelled herself into the air with the other arm. Slightly unsteady, as she hadn't pushed herself off balanced, the Elfling rose headfirst into the foggy New England night. She didn't want to get too high — she still had to see where she was going — but she needed to stay well out of sight before she kicked off new-age rumors about witches in Salem.

That would be fun to explain to the Samnung, she thought, imagining Nehemi's ire if she had to go stand before them and sheepishly talk about how she could firstly, fly without wings, and secondly, had been stupid enough to fly where humans could see. Collum's face flashed into her mind again, with that wicked grin she adored so much. He'd probably kick her under the table, and just to be mean, send her a thought that would make her laugh while she was supposed to be apologizing for her actions. *Always such a punk. Fuck, I cannot wait to see you.*

Bridgette flew idly, taking care to stay just at the cloudline.

She could fade upward if a human was on the streets below, preventing it from seeing her. She knew the cottage wasn't far at all, and she let her sierwan knowledge guide her route.

The cottage emerged below her, and Bridgette made triple sure no one was possibly watching as she brought herself down from the air and onto the walkway. The porch lights were on, as if expecting her, and she eyed the key box warily.

Now how do I get into you? she wondered.

In answer, one number on each of the six numerical dials seemed to come into sharper focus. The Elfling grinned and rolled the combination: a key fob dropped to her feet.

~ 40 ~

The cottage was just as she remembered. Time, it seemed, had frozen the little place, and after locking the door and claiming "her" bedroom again, Bridgette went downstairs to examine the gigantic bookshelf. Some of the books were clearly of magical origin, with titles discussing things of ritual, herbs, and spells. A handful were in languages she didn't recognize, but surprisingly, the greatest portion were classic fiction and biographical works of human nature.

Guess the magical beings don't want to be culturally inept when they visit.

She pulled out a worn copy of a title she recognized — "The Hobbit" — and opened it to find an inscription on the inside front cover.

"To our darling Collum. May you never lose hope in the journey ahead. We love you. Mum and Da."

Bridgette slammed the book shut and shoved it back on the shelf. *Why is Collum's book from his parents on this shelf. In a cottage that belongs to the Samnung.*

Because Collum skirted the truth, a little voice inside her head whispered. It made perfect sense for the fyrdwisa to maintain a residence on Earth, if not more than one, the same way Fairy ambassadors and ambassadoras did in their respective territories. Yes, technically the cottage belonged to the Samnung, because Collum was part of the Samnung.

Bridgette rolled her eyes, and sent a thought she knew would never find its recipient. *You punk, Bundy. You could have just told me you owned a house.*

The last time she'd been here, Bridgette had a panic attack in the bathroom. Tonight, she hoped, would be significantly less traumatic, despite the revelation she had that Collum owned the damn place. And it was. She slept better curled up in sheets, which she could have sworn smelled like honeysuckle, than she had in a dozen weeks.

Bridgette woke to her stomach rumbling, and she wished

Collum was in the kitchen cooking. Her heart seemed to skip a beat at the thought of seeing him again, and she shook it off. There was no sense in delaying. She needed to get to the portal immediately, though perhaps she'd stop for coffee first.

She wasted no time getting ready and stuffing the key fob back in the lockbox, rolling her suitcase down the pathway back to the sidewalk. The walk to the coffee shop she'd spotted all those months ago was short, and the iced beverage in her hand made the significantly longer walk to Endicott Park go by a little faster.

What will they do when I get there? Hell, what will I *do when I get there?* Bridgette wondered. She was nervous. What if the Samnung didn't want her anymore, since she'd said "no" before?

You can't think like that, she told herself. She vaguely wondered if she managed to spell herself into walking quicker, because it didn't seem to take long at all for the park to come into sight before her. This time, the visitor's center was open for sure, and as she entered, a perky female park ranger greeted her.

"I'm here to tour the archives," Bridgette said, remembering what Collum told the ranger when they'd initially gone to Heáhwolcen.

The ranger, just like before, inclined her head and took Bridgette to the marked door. She was surprised to see significantly less activity in the portal chamber, and immediately approached the front desk. A bored young Fairy sat there, tracing sigils in the air with a strand of glitter coming from his forefinger.

"Can I help you?" he asked, not making eye contact.

"I need to go to Heáhwolcen," Bridgette announced. "Immediately."

He paused and glanced up at her, eyeing her from head to lightly pointed ears to the very Elf-like leather boots she'd pulled on a few minutes before. "I'm going to need to see your documents."

"I don't have documents. I just need to go there and see the Samnung. Like, right now."

The Fairy gave her a very dramatic teenage look. "Lady,

that's not how this works. You can't just go to the world above the world. You have to have travel documents that give you permission and detail your route and the purpose of your visit."

Bridgette growled, and the Fairy pulled back.

"Listen, kid. You are going to let me through this gate and up that portal within the next five minutes, or I will personally tell Aristoces you prevented me from going."

The Fairy narrowed his eyes — they were stormy gray whorls — in response. "I happen to work for Aristoces, thank you, and I happen to know she would never, ever allow anyone to depart from or arrive into Heáhwolcen without cause or proof of purpose. You need to produce your travel documents or go back to whence you came."

I do not have fucking time for this. Bridgette slammed a fist onto the Fairy's desk, and he jumped back. "You will bring me Geongre Akiko, and you will tell her that Bridgette Conner is coming home. You will do this *now*, or so help me I will *cut you*."

"I see no weapons on you. You're feinting."

Having never done magic in her life, Bridgette was as surprised as the Fairy was to find herself pulling a small, amethyst-jeweled dagger out of thin air. "Watch me, you glittering bug. Get me Geongre Akiko, fucking *now*."

Where the HELL did this knife come from? she thought rapidly as the Fairy flitted quickly upward. The look on her face was menacing, but her mind was whirling. *Did I just summon something?*

She didn't have much time to think about it past that, as the Fairy returned with another. Geongre Akiko's hair was jet black today instead of bright blue, but she wore the same lime green headband in it. The lead travel deputy lit up with surprise when she saw Bridgette standing impatiently before the desk.

"It *is* you!" she exclaimed, issuing a quick curtsy. The male Fairy's eyes wove between them, unsure what to do.

"I need to go back, now," Bridgette said urgently. "Please. I don't think I've ever had whatever documents this kid thinks I need. Not even that time with Collum. And I'm so sorry I can't stay to explain. In fact, I don't know that I could fully explain even if I wanted to. I just felt … something isn't right, but what *is* right is that I need to be there."

Akiko tensed and nodded. "Of course, Sigewíf. We will make an opening in the next departure. Come with me, and I apologize for the behavior of Luthus. He was enforcing protocol, of course, but I'm sure he could have done so in a more professional manner."

The male Fairy looked pissed, and Bridgette flashed him a slightly evil half-smile. "Apology accepted."

The hilt of the jeweled dagger was still visible in her hand.

Bridgette followed Akiko to a short line radiating from the glimmering magic portal. "Do you wish me to dispatch a notice to the Samnung?" the Fairy asked her. Bridgette shook her head, nearly at the point of tapping her feet with urgency.

"No; thank you though. I just need to go there immediately. Collum will know what to do." *Or at least, I hope so.*

Akiko handed Bridgette a small folder. "Present this to the Fairy at the gateway. And do not be afraid to take the portal alone. You're safe here, and oh! We are so glad to have you home."

The Elfling fought back a rush of emotion she hadn't expected as she gratefully accepted the folder of likely forged travel documents. "Thank you, Geongre Akiko. I appreciate you so much for all of this."

The Fairy gave her one last smile before she flew back toward the front of the terminal. Bridgette turned to face the portal and took a deep breath as she handed the folder to the gateway guard. She stepped forward onto the portal floor, and a few moments later, felt herself hoisted into the air by an invisible pulley, bringing her to the home she so desperately wanted to be back in.

A set of windchimes alerted her that she'd arrived, and Bridgette stepped uncertainly out of the portal into the arrival chamber. *Well. This was about as far ahead as I thought*, she said to herself, realizing she had no way to get to ... wherever she should be going. *I have to find Collum.*

He couldn't hear her, or at least she didn't think he could, unless he happened to be in whatever building the arrival chamber was in Fairevella. She didn't want to risk going out and wandering the streets of the Fairy realm either, and have the news of her arrival ruined by reaching the Samnung before she found him. Not that many Fairies knew *what* she was, though. Bridgette chewed on the inside of one cheek, considering her options. She turned to her left and approached the check-in desk.

"Hi!" she said brightly to the Fairy who sat there. He had skin so white it was almost translucent, dotted with tattoos that resembled snake scales. His hair was vivid red and hung nearly to his shoulders, and his large wings were scarlet and bat-like.

"Hello," he said mildly. "How may I help you?"

"I need to find the fyrdwisa. Or get to Eckenbourne, but I can't evanesce. Or fly," she added hurriedly, knowing full well how much a lie *that* was.

The Fairy smiled, revealing teeth even whiter than his skin. "I see. I do not know the comings and goings of the fyrdwisa, but I am happy to hire you a carriage transportation to Eckenbourne, if that would be of assistance."

"Yes! Oh my goodness, yes. Thank you," Bridgette said, reaching out with a sudden urge to grasp his hands in thanks. "You can't like, summon one of the Unicorns, can you?"

The red-headed Fairy chuckled. "Are you rídend?"

Bridgette blushed. "Not quite. I didn't do the covenant thing, so I don't know if I technically am? But if I had done it, my annwyl would have been a golden Unicorn named Eloise …"

"One moment, please. I'll see what I can do." He spread his bat wings and flew off down a hallway, leaving Bridgette unsure of how to proceed.

She waited for what seemed like an eternity, but finally the Fairy came back, a big smile on his face. "Eloise will be waiting outside for you shortly."

"Really?!" She could hardly believe it. "How did you manage that?"

"I am Geongrestre Etreyn. I believe you know Geongre Akiko, yes? I am studying under her leadership to become geongre when the time comes for her to pass her role on," he said, grinning. "We have the ability to bring in a variety of transportation that other travel deputies do not have access to. Including the Unicorns."

The Elfling could have hugged him. "Thank you. Thank you *so* much, Etreyn."

He winked and inclined his head, indicating that her ride was nearing. "You are so welcome, Liluthuaé."

She didn't give a thought about Geongrestre Etreyn somehow knowing what she was, and she practically ran to the front doors. Eloise wasn't saddled, but she was waiting just outside for the Elfling to find her. "I did nay think you would be gone for so long, Liluthuaé," she said.

"I didn't think I would come back," Bridgette responded honestly. "I need to see Collum, please. Right away. Can you … do you know where he is?"

The Unicorn bowed her head. "Get on. I'll be as fast as I can, but you must hold tight. It'll still be a decent journey into the heart of Eckenbourne."

"Fast" was a bit of an understatement. Eloise took the route at a full gallop, the Elfling's suitcase mounted to her rump, and Bridgette prayed her muscles would help her hold on. The cool wind blew by, and she felt her braids come fully undone, her reddish-blonde hair flowing behind her as they rode.

"The fyrdwisa has missed you, Liluthuaé," the Unicorn observed. Bridgette had no idea how she could talk while traveling at this pace.

"Has he, now?"

"He did nay think you would return either. He will be most surprised when you knock at his door."

Bridgette fought back a grin at the thought. *He's probably going to kill me.*

Eloise pulled to a halt at the secret entrance to Collum's apartment. Bridgette's body ached from holding on to the Unicorn, and she wondered if the Elf would be so kind as to offer her some of that salve he gave her after flying lessons. She peeled herself off Eloise's back and gave her a hug around the neck. "Thank you."

The Unicorn nuzzled her fondly in return. "Go give the fyrdwisa the shock of his life, Sigewíf."

Bridgette gulped down clean air and tried to calm her beating heart. She had no idea what she was about to walk into. Would Collum really be shocked to see her? Would he be happy, or angry? The uncertainty of the situation brought unexpected anxiety to the surface of Bridgette's mind, and she fought to keep it under control. Now was not the time to start panicking. She began the walk up the path, noting it was silent except for the occasional bird chirp or tender windchime in the distance.

A brief walk later, Collum's dark-stained wooden door stood before her. Bridgette stepped backward. *How am I getting cold feet? Why now? It's just Collum. Who probably will be annoyed that I am even here.*

She raised a fist and knocked sharply, squinting her eyes shut in silent prayer that if Collum was home, he wasn't ready to murder her for leaving when the Samnung, when the magical world, needed her most.

Bridgette heard the lock turn inside, and the door opened to reveal Collum Andoralain, tall and trim in his dark navy leggings and a sleeveless gray tunic belted at the waist with gold and navy cord. He was barefoot, and his wavy hair had been cut shorter than she remembered. But those tidal blue eyes were the same, and they widened in disbelief as they took in the being that stood in the doorway.

"Hey," Bridgette said weakly, suddenly feeling like she might drop straight to the floor.

"How —"

But he didn't let himself finish the question. Collum glanced quickly to either side of the hallway, and pulled the Elfling inside his apartment. He put a hand on either of her shoulders and studied her at arm's length. Her hair was disheveled, her eyes sunken. She looked like she'd lost weight, and somehow gained a very lovely dagger that matched her eyes. She was also dressed in clearly Elven boots, which he remembered putting in the cottage for her …

How are you here? he thought to her. *How did you get in the cottage?*

The lockbox is coded, and I decoded it, silly. I bought a plane ticket to Boston, got a ride to Salem, flew to the cottage, walked to the portal and magicked myself up with a little help from Geongre Akiko, and then when I got here the geongrestre secured Eloise to take me from Fairevella to your apartment, she responded mind-to-mind.

"Please explain what you mean when you say you 'flew to the cottage,'" Collum said aloud, a hint of suspicion in his voice.

Shit. "Um. I got tired of walking so I just … flew there …" she said sheepishly. "Oh. And I managed to summon a dagger, and I still can't evanesce. That was what I tried first, and when that didn't work I decided to fly."

"You summoned a dagger while trying to evanesce?"

"No, I summoned a dagger when I was threatening to cut the little bitch Fairy who wouldn't let me into the portal without travel documents."

Collum barked out a laugh, and then couldn't stop. He doubled over. "Deity save us, Starshine, you never cease to astonish me."

~ 41 ~

Bridgette could hardly believe the reception she'd gotten. She expected Collum to be angry beyond words with her — hurt because she'd left, shocked she'd come back, and furious that she'd put him through the entire rigamarole. Laughter; so much laughter; was the complete opposite of the reunion she'd imagined. And she'd done a lot of imagining in the hours since she decided to fuck it all and jump on a plane to Boston.

"Are you … aren't you angry with me?" she whispered, stepping back from the arms that were wrapped around her torso. "For leaving?"

Collum became serious, though the opalescent flecks in his blue eyes still glistened. "Of course not. How could I be angry with you? You were given a choice, and you made your choice. I will be forthright in saying it is not the choice I'd have preferred you make, but it was *yours* and therefore ours as the Samnung, and mine as your fyrdwisa and friend, to respect."

Her heart sang a bit. She was right; he wished she'd stayed.

"I really missed you," she said quietly, not meeting his eyes.

Not nearly as much as I missed you, he thought to himself, though his only outward answer was to embrace her again.

Collum didn't know if he would ever be able to express to her what it was like to lose her that day: for one second, her to be there; the two of them curled against each other on that cold bathroom floor, readying for the battle ahead; and the next moment, she was bolting out of the Samnung chamber as if Baize Sammael himself had evanesced there to chase her. He knew she'd seen his sadness when she vocalized her choice. And a part of him hated that. Despite all his careful planning, his complete intentions to be her platonic companion, her leader in their task … he'd let his emotions get the better of him for a split second. But it had been enough, and he spent the next twelve weeks wondering what her seeing that had done.

It was hard for him to know that she'd, perhaps not regret, but definitely question, if her actions had been the most reasonable in that moment. It was harder still for him to consider that his reaction would compound how she processed the events of that day. Bridgette darting away and disappearing for months was one of the most difficult situations he'd ever found himself in, and it was a situation he quite actually could not allow himself to be in.

Bridgette Conner was supposed to be his task. A companion, yes, but first and foremost, a task. They had a job to do, and he could not allow anything to compromise that.

And yet he very nearly had. He knew this, because watching her slip away was the most painful thing he'd ever witnessed. And because of who she was to him, because of who she was born to be … he let her go.

The fyrdwisa of Heáhwolcen watched the Lilluthuaé as she stepped beyond his reach, mental or physical. Collum Andoralain, who occasionally answered to the nickname "Bundy" and enjoyed secret flying lessons and a second voice inside his head, let his Starshine go.

The echo of it sounded in his ears for days on end: *I let her go.*

He knew this was the best decision for her. She'd made her choice, and he had to respect it, no matter how hard it was. No matter how much he hated every second of her being gone.

The Samnung was in collective shock in the minutes after Bridgette left. They all watched her run out of the chamber as if chased by a ghost. Collum, truth be told, had feared the exact scenario coming to pass when he stepped into the room that day and saw Mohreen sitting there. For a brief moment, when they were on that bathroom floor, he thought perhaps they'd summited the worst, and she'd face her own fears just to spite her birth mother. But everything about that day had been too much for her to process all at once. He wished that Corria Deathhunter and Trystane hadn't asked her to stay. Not right after all that. He wished that they'd recessed; let everything process. The flight he'd booked for them from Beverly back to Nashville hadn't been until noon Sunday: plenty of time for Bridgette to take in, talk through, and mull over what happened with Mohreen and what she'd learned, before making a rational decision.

Collum knew, too, that his own actions had played a major part in her bolting. She placed so much trust in him in the short time they'd known each other, and he betrayed it all. Between that, and Mohreen showing up, and the pressure she felt … had he been in the same position, Collum wasn't sure he wouldn't have run, too. Run away from the necessity of being needed.

So for twelve weeks, he wondered.

Wondered what Bridgette got up to during the day. Was she happy? Was she still taking classes? Was she doubling down on her studies in the aftermath of deciding to honor her human upbringing instead of her magical heritage? Did she question her choice? Did she miss Heáhwolcen? Did she … miss *him*?

It was excruciating. Collum became very adept at compartmentalizing, as Bridgette had, their time together. He'd tucked her away as she'd hidden him aside, determined to focus on his work. But where Bridgette had become engrossed in her music, Collum chose to concentrate specifically on his own healing. He'd realized the night before Ostara that there had been some significant processing he'd failed to do for far too long, and that sense of loss was only building with the Liluthuaé's sudden departure.

His fellow Samnung members hadn't said a word to him as he walked out of the chamber, mere minutes after Bridgette disappeared. He didn't make eye contact with any of them, not even Trystane. He didn't know what to say in that moment. He didn't know what to *think*. He was both numb and feeling too much all at once, and it was unbearable.

Collum evanesced the second the door closed behind him, and when he opened his eyes back in the apartment, an emptiness loomed in front of him. It was the same emptiness he'd experienced at those Samnung meetings without Bridgette: the quiet of being the only one constantly in his own head. The quiet of being the only one constantly in his own apartment.

She was still everywhere, though. The guest bedroom sheets

were rumpled. Where he was strict "military corners," as she'd
called it, making the bed was not Bridgette's strong suit. Nor was,
apparently, sweeping the errant strands of red-blonde hair from
the bathroom floor after a bath or shower or deity help her,
brushing the damn mane. She'd left without any of her
belongings save the clothes she wore and the small pack that
contained her phone and wallet. Not that she'd brought much,
but her original bag was still … here.

Collum gently closed the doors to her room and bathroom
and stepped away. The apartment even smelled like her. There
were still dirty dishes in the sink from the night before Ostara,
when they'd imbibed that expensive Fae wine and fed each other
dinner sitting on his kitchen floor. He swore he felt her; swore
that if he turned just a hair faster he'd see her slip around a
corner; but the rational part of his mind hit overdrive and told
him it was only wishful thinking.

I can't be in this place.

Even his office, his one deity-damned place of solitude, was
haunted by Bridgette Conner. Tainted by the memories of flying
lessons and peaceful meditation. A sickening feeling rose in
Collum's gut. He'd felt similar to this when his parents were
gone, but that was markedly different. They'd planned for that.
This was sudden. Jarring. *Where the fuck do I go now?*

Aurelias had done a double-take the next morning when she
arrived at the Caisleán.

"What on Galdúr's wings are *you* doing here?" the halfling
asked, in clear shock, but her shrewd intellect quickly turned her
tone to one of command. "Are you sick? You look sick. You look
like you haven't slept since Ostara. And where's Bridgette? Is *she*
sick?"

The words choked in the bottom of Collum's throat. "She's
gone."

"What?" Aurelias' jaw dropped. "What do you mean? Your
flight's not for hours yet; I double-checked before I came in —"

"She left." His tone was terse, unyielding. Aurelias didn't

question him further, but kept shooting concerned glances his way as the two went about their daily duties. She had, anyway: Collum was so not used to sitting at a desk to do paperwork that he was going equally as stir-crazy staring at reports as he had been in his apartment. It didn't help that his reports were all about his time on Earth, searching for Bridgette, and he was due to submit one at some point about her week in Heáhwolcen. And how the week ended a day early.

The Elf couldn't stand it. He threw his pen down and looked at Aurelias. "Will you be able to handle things if I go away for a bit?" he asked, already knowing her answer.

"Of course, Fyrdwisa. If there is anything —"

He cut her off. "My gratitude, Fyrdestre." And just as quickly as Bridgette had darted out of his sight, he evanesced out of Aurelias'.

Collum spent the next eight weeks on Hlafjordstiepel, camped out at the top of both worlds. He knew Aurelias would have told Trystane, who would have told the Samnung, what happened that morning after Bridgette's departure. He knew they wouldn't summon him unless it was absolutely vital. There was no one to disturb him here, then.

He needed to clear his mind. To process and grieve, and do the long-overdue healing that had plagued him since his parents' walk into the spirit realm ... then turn and do the same for the Liluthuaé. It was not an easy process, to confront these hard memories, then to question how he'd responded to them happening. It was difficult to dredge up things he wasn't proud of, coping mechanisms that led him to build walls and become so closed-off and focused that for many years, everyone save Trystane, Aurelias, and occasionally Aristoces and Njahla saw him as only a pillar of strength and leadership. No emotion, which made for a decent Armada commander, but a much less decent friend.

The Elf focused completely on himself for those weeks. Day in and day out, he meditated: breathing in all that he had to be grateful for, exhaling the pain and memories that did not serve him. He sat in stillness and let his mind wander as it willed, bringing difficult thoughts to light, finding a silver lining in them, tucking that away deep in the recesses of his consciousness as he let the rest go. He stretched his body and mind in ways he hadn't done in a century, the connection between brain and skeleton and muscle tissue forging anew. He allowed himself to feel strong emotion — pain, anger, deep sadness — and did not hide the physical responses they brought to the surface.

For eight weeks straight, he did these things, before waking one morning and feeling … whole. It was something he'd forgotten the feeling of. It wasn't happiness, necessarily, but for the first time in decades, Collum Andoralain felt peace within him. He returned to the apartment that day and found Trystane had arranged for it to be cleaned. The place was fully his again, though he was careful not to spend too much time on the guest wing just yet. During the ensuing four weeks, those weeks where he missed Bridgette fiercely, but accepted and respected the boundary she'd set — a feeling of loss he knew in time would fade, though she would never be gone entirely from his life or mind — Collum faced his daily life with renewed vigor and spirit. He was active and attentive at Samnung meetings and with the Fyrdlytta. He attended his training courses daily and supplemented the battle-ready physical work with mental exercises each morning and evening. It was hard and daunting, but Collum had faced his worst Self on the mountaintop, and he'd learned to give himself grace. He forgave his parents, something he wasn't even aware he needed to do, for putting on him the sense of loss and abandonment he'd realized Bridgette felt about Mohreen. He forgave himself for becoming such a stone-faced Elf instead of who he truly was. He forgave himself for what he'd done with Mohreen and the Samnung as fyrdestre. He forgave Bridgette, too, for leaving — and he let himself feel that sting still, and let himself wish she was still here.

Collum learned to appreciate the tiny glimpses of Starshine that still shone from time to time. A golden glint on the side of a building would be the sheen of her hair in the sunlight. He began drinking his caife calabazas iced, and purposely started a weekly ritual of spending time with the three witch sisters in their café. Each time he smelled anything remotely like vanilla or honeysuckle, he smiled before he realized the expression was on his face. He knew she was still *here*. Somewhere, far below, and he let himself wonder those questions of her wellbeing, while trusting that the Universe, spirits, and deities knew exactly what they were doing. He trusted that she was well. That he would be, too.

And after twelve weeks of this peace, grace, forgiveness, and healing, opening the door to find a disheveled Bridgette Conner standing in front of it was the last thing Collum could possibly have expected.

"I missed you, too," he finally said aloud, and wondered how long they'd been standing there in silence. Time had become irrelevant these past weeks.

"It was weird being the only voice inside my head," Bridgette said. She hadn't let go of him. "It was too quiet."

"Things were assuredly quieter here, too, without your constant taunting and questioning," Collum responded. "Samnung meetings became boring again."

The Elfling looked up at him, a devilish look in those lilac eyes. "They're about to get seven hells of a lot more interesting, then."

~ 42 ~

Collum threw back his head in laughter again. He felt so much lighter now! Lighter even than he'd felt after his eight weeks of solitude. "I don't know who's going to have the better reaction, Starshine. You're in luck, arriving on a Wednesday. This is our regular Samnung meeting day, and I have to be there soon, if you'd like to join me."

"Let's go give 'em hell, Bundy."

She had enough time to freshen up, though she'd have to wear human clothes. There hadn't been any Elven ones in the cottage, save the boots, and Njahla had done quite a thorough job of removing most traces of her from the guest wing of Collum's apartment. But as Bridgette started unpacking her toiletries, she noticed Trystane's second had skipped something.

Is this … the same toothbrush? she thought, mostly to herself, though she didn't mind if Collum heard. She fingered the wooden handle, intricately carved, and its cream-colored bristles.

Collum blinked. He'd been in his room, and had forgotten indeed what it was like to have her voice chiming in his head. It was the same toothbrush — a silly thing, but he didn't want his apartment entirely void of her. She'd ogled over the simple tool, for Elves didn't let even simple things exist belied of beauty. Collum had pretended not to hear her that very first night in Heáhwolcen, all those months ago, as she examined it in wonder. Njahla didn't miss it in her cleaning — she glamoured it so it wouldn't be seen until he was ready.

Of course, he thought back to Bridgette, grinning to himself. *You liked it so much, I couldn't just let it go.*

Those words stopped him for a moment: *like I let you go,* he thought to himself now.

Bridgette smiled. *I'm glad you kept it.*

So am I, Starshine.

The two reconvened in the living room a short while later. Bridgette still looked as though she hadn't slept well for three months, but she'd tamed her hair into a long braid down her back, and donned the most Elven-esque clothes she'd packed.

Collum was his usual portrait-perfect self. A black belt with gold chain lay across his hips, strung with what looked to be his wallet pouch and knife sheath.

"Oh!" Bridgette gasped. "Can I bring my swanky dagger?"

Collum laughed. "Of course, Starshine."

She darted back to her room to get it, and when she returned, Collum waited with a simple blue belt and sheath for her to wear it on. "This was the closest color I had in a belt that might fit you," he said apologetically, tying the straps closed at her side.

"Thanks, Bundy," she said. "It matches your eyes."

He rolled those eyes at her in answer. "Let us go."

The fyrdwisa hoped he'd timed their arrival perfectly, so that everyone save the two of them would be seated in the chamber. The Samnung had come to expect this of him by now, arriving just a few minutes past time to be seated. Collum, as healed as he was, still found small talk and pre-meeting chatter uncomfortable.

Indeed, he evanesced them to an empty seating area outside of the chamber. "Are you ready?" he asked, turning to meet Bridgette's eyes.

They were hesitant, but she breathed in deeply, and in response the Elf — without even thinking — calmed her with those favored scents of hers. She opened her eyes and straightened her shoulders. "As ready as I'll ever be."

With that, Collum opened the chamber door, and stilled Bridgette's entrance with a hand outstretched behind him. "I apologize for my lateness, your majesties and ceannairí. There has been a development that required urgent attention."

He cocked his head and ushered the Liluthuaé inside — then wished beyond words that he could hear the Samnung members' thoughts as they realized what the aforementioned development was.

Trystane shot them a look of utter glee. "Welcome home, Bright Star."

Verivol was up from the table in an instant, wrapping their arms around Bridgette and lifting her into the air as they'd done dancing and reveling at Ostara. "It has not been the same without you!" the Sanguisuge said. "We are glad to have you back."

"I'm glad to be back." She paused, looking at Collum softly. "To be home."

Verivol positively beamed then, squeezing her within an inch of her life. "Tell us, Bright Star. What made you change your mind?"

She realized then that she hadn't even told Collum why she'd come back. They'd been so caught up in seeing one another again that she hadn't made it that far. He hadn't asked, either.

Deity bless, I told Geongre Akiko more about why I'm here than I have even you, she thought to Collum as Verivol set her to the ground.

Someone summoned another stool, and Bridgette took in the rest of the Samnung as she sat. Cloa, in true form, hadn't even registered her presence, though the cat had. Arctura watched her with narrowed eyes, making Bridgette shiver. Everyone else shared an expression caught somewhere between utter surprise and delight, save Nehemi, who predictably looked as though a bit of roadkill had walked through the door.

"Yes," the queen commanded. "Do tell us why you've returned."

Trystane and Collum exchanged a fleeting glance as Bridgette met Nehemi's cold eyes, as if to say, "... here we go."

"I was sitting in one of my classes — one of my *music classes* —" she added emphasis just to bait the queen, "and started to feel sick. I hadn't been sleeping well and at first I thought it was just that. Maybe I was falling asleep, or something. So I got up to leave class and pretty much passed out standing up. The professor offered to have a classmate help me to my room, but I refused the help. I had a vision when I got back though. I saw the fyrdwisa's face, and it was as if he was calling to me. He called me 'Liluthuaé,' which he rarely does unless it's official business. Then my vision blurred and zoomed out, and suddenly all of you were there, and he called to me again. I knew then that something was horribly, horribly wrong."

She paused, taking a deep breath. "I'd been struggling for a while with my decision to leave when I did, and how I did, but I wasn't ... I wasn't ready for what you asked. I don't have any of my shit together, so how the hell was I supposed to be this world savior for everyone else? Then Mohreen was there, making it even harder and it was ... that whole day was so much and I couldn't handle it. But this was different. I wasn't being thrust into something I was unprepared to accept. I was being called. So I came."

Nehemi narrowed her eyes even more. "You had a vision?"

"Yes." *Oh shit — I forgot they don't know* — she thought furtively to Collum, keeping her face expressionless.

Collum nudged her foot under the table in acknowledgement. "Yes, she did," he spoke up. "Our Liluthuaé is a sierwan."

Nehemi's skin paled. "A sierwan. And how long have you known this, Fyrdwisa?"

"It became evident during her visit," he replied. "However, as she departed without prior planning, it did not seem relevant to share that information with the Samnung at large."

"The fyrdwisa kept that information on a need-to-know basis on my orders," Trystane piped up, having their backs like always. "As we continue to be unsure of what precisely the danger is, I made the call that this ability not be publicized for fear of potential retribution."

Yeah, retribution from fucking Nehemi, Bridgette thought shrewdly to Collum, who tamped her foot in silent response.

I swear to Hecate if you make me laugh, Starshine ...

They're going to lose their shit when they find out I can fly.

Collum ignored her glib comment and spoke aloud, addressing the room. "A sierwan is a gifted Elf or Elfling who is able to ... connect the dots, shall we say, when others are unable to. They have no control over what triggers a knowing to come to them, and many times these things are provided without context. Sierwen were very powerful hands of former Elven rulers, and were quite valuable strategists in times of war. Although I could never in my wildest dreams have imagined the

Liluthuaé would be a sierwan, the gift makes much sense knowing it now. It will undoubtedly play a great role as our knowledge around Palna grows and we formulate our plans."

"But you say this knowing cannot be controlled?" Corria Deathhunter inquired. "How can it be of service to us in planning?"

"I can't control it, that's true, but I've noticed a kind of pattern as to when it appears," Bridgette said. "I can't use it to, for example, cheat on a test in school — to know the answer. But I can call it forth to remember forgotten knowledge, or knowledge I am privy to parts of already, which is how I got to Collum's cottage the other night. And it appears on its own sometimes when I'm trying to work out an issue in my own head, and other times when there's, it's hard to explain, but it's as if the sierwan gift is a way for the spirit world to tell me things I need to know as the Liluthuaé."

Should I tell them about the Ealdealfen? she asked Collum, mind-to-mind. *I feel like they will want an example of this kind of thing.*

"Bridgette knows of her legend, by now," Collum said aloud, hoping Bridgette would understand he was going to tackle this for her. "She knows that the Liluthuaé's presence is ordained by the spirits and deities; that only they would know when she needed to be born after Ylda's great departure. It would make sense that they would also find a way to guide her in this life, so that her calling may be fulfilled. While in private conversation with Trystane and myself, Bridgette revealed things that she could not have otherwise known about Elven and magical culture. She raised questions based on these 'knowings,' as we have come to call them, which she and I later were able to bring up to magisters at the University. Now that the Bright Star has returned, I hope we are able to further research the answers we were given, and perhaps see what other knowledge they might spring forth."

That seemed to satisfy Nehemi, at least for the moment. The Endorsan queen loosened her shoulders somewhat, but her gaze stayed fixed on Bridgette. "This vision. It provided you with no other context?"

Bridgette shook her head. "No. Usually when something comes forth there … isn't any context. But this is also the first time I had a visual knowing. Everything else has just been information that comes to my head. I just knew something was wrong and that it was time to come back."

"But nothing is wrong," Nehemi said, shoulders stiffening again. She lifted her chin. "Things are unchanged. The wards and walls are secure. We've not had any blasts of errant magic. Are you simply here to cause us to panic and accept what you say as truth?"

It was Bridgette's turn to narrow her eyes, and she cocked her head to one side. Collum felt the wave of anger wash over her, and saw her eyes visibly darken. He froze as she spoke, in a voice that was hers but not hers: "I am Truth, your majesty."

Collum glanced at Trystane, to see if he'd noticed the change in Bridgette — no one else seemed to have, except Nehemi, seated directly across from the Elfling. Her nostrils flared. It didn't look even as though anyone heard her speak except for the two of them. *What in the seven hells*, he mused, unsure what was happening. But as soon as the odd exchange began, it was over, Bridgette blinking as though nothing at all occurred. Nehemi, too, eyelids fluttering as if emerging from a trance.

We need to go, before anyone suspects anything, he thought to Bridgette.

Suspects what? Bridgette asked, mind-to-mind. He realized she had no idea what had just happened.

That you … what just happened with you and Nehemi? Collum thought back, though it was an incomplete thought. He wasn't sure how to describe what he'd seen happen, much less explain how he'd seen it and no one else had.

Collum was intensely uneasy. How had no one else noticed the momentary, perceptible shift in Bridgette's eyes? In her tone? In the way that she commanded Nehemi, of all beings? How had the two individuals engaged in the unusual exchange not noticed themselves?

"Are you going to answer me, Liluthuaé, or just continue to

stare blankly in my direction?" Nehemi said, interrupting the silent conversation happening before her. "I'll ask you again: Are you here to cause us panic?"

"No, you idiot," Bridgette snapped before she realized what she'd said. *Fuck.*

The queen leered across the table, her eyes blazing. Every word she spoke next was in a tone so icy, Collum swore the temperature of the chamber dropped a few degrees. "Idiot, Bridgette? I dare say I'm the smartest being in the room, as I'm the only one bothering to investigate these claims further instead of accepting them as the blatant deity-foresworn truth. You barge back in here after months of absence and claim to have this mysterious knowledge that — despite centuries of magic in this room! — only you, a half-human not even twenty-three years of age, are privy to. For all we know, you are an agent of Craft magic sent to influence us!"

Bridgette fumed, and rose halfway off of her stool.

It was Bryten who spoke up, intervening before the exchange got somehow more heated.

"It doesn't matter so much the reasons and the past. It matters that the Bright Star, who for deity's sake, Nehemi, is *not* a Craft witch, is back," the Baetalüan said, somewhat sternly, in the queen's direction. "Now that she is with us again, I propose we discuss how to move forward with our plans."

Bryten turned to Bridgette. "Since you've been gone, as her majesty implied, exactly nothing out of the ordinary has happened, to any of our knowledge. Perhaps this is good. Perhaps not. The larger perceived threat continues to exist, of course, but with the lack of action from Palna or Palnan sympathists in the rest of Heáhwolcen, we question what actions to take."

The Elfling nodded her understanding and shook her head slightly to calm herself. "It doesn't make sense to take tangible action when, in the public's eye, the action could be perceived as one without cause."

"Precisely," Bryten said.

Bridgette nodded gravely. To Collum, she shared a thought:

This is about to get really crazy, isn't it?

Buckle up, Starshine, he thought back idly.

"The last thing we want to do is accidentally spark the very fight we're trying to prevent," Corria Deathhunter offered. "Perhaps these knowings of yours will help us in understanding what it is we are not seeing."

Bridgette glanced her way, then met each member of the Samnung's eyes: a final acknowledgement and acceptance of working with them in official capacity. She ended with Nehemi, lilac irises bright with challenge. "Perhaps they will. Count me in."

~ 43 ~

Neither Collum nor Bridgette was in the least surprised when Trystane evanesced into the living room an hour after they did that afternoon, a flurry of evergreen whirls announcing his arrival. Just like the two companions, the Elven leader felt at home in the apartment, where he could be fully himself and unfiltered. Which meant the moment his form became corporeal in their midst, he reached for Bridgette and promptly lifted her into the air in a giant, most un-ceannairí-like hug, and kissed her on the cheek as he set her down.

Her peals of laughter lit up the room, and Collum felt his breath catch. He'd forgotten in her absence what it was like to have a joyful noise of that caliber in his ears.

"Bright Star, you could not fathom how much we missed you," Trystane said. "Nor how shocked we were to have you walk into the Samnung chamber. I had a suspicion you would be back —"

Collum interrupted: "A suspicion based entirely on his weeks of plotting how to sneak down the portal to come get you himself."

"— Okay, that might have been the case —"

"It was assuredly the case."

"Deity damn you, Collum Andoralain, I am speaking!" Trystane's eyes gleamed with good-natured joviality despite his vague attempt at scolding the fyrdwisa. "As I was saying, Bridgette —"

The Elfling kissed him on the cheek, too. "I knew as soon as I was gone that I'd fucked up, Trystane. But I didn't know how to go back in that room without humiliating myself, and I was angry that I cared so much about everyone else's opinion of me. This is my home. This is where the fates decided to put me. Embarrassed or not, I'm done being the type of person who sidesteps her calling."

The fyrdwisa could have kissed her. He slung an arm casually around her shoulders instead, tucking that desire far within. "You've changed, Starshine."

She responded with a soft half-smile. "Have I?"

"You have," Trystane said, casually flipping a hand and summoning all three of them bottles of crisp apple ale from the kitchen. "You are much more sure of yourself. It is indeed as if you've chosen both subconsciously and consciously to accept what the fates chose for you, and the confidence shows."

"It assuredly showed in the Samnung meeting," Collum murmured. "What was that stare-down with Nehemi and the 'truth' phrase?"

Both Trystane and Bridgette looked at him blankly.

Collum groaned inwardly. He'd been afraid of this, and both of them just confirmed his suspicions. "When you and Nehemi were facing off, when she accused you of lying, you stared her down as if she was nothing. Your eyes shifted, but not the sierwan shift to opals. They became deep purple, for but a moment, and you told her, 'I am Truth.' Spoken as if the word was capitalized, with extreme emphasis. Then you both blinked and as soon as it occurred, it was over."

"Say what now?" Bridgette arched an eyebrow. "I did what?"

The Elf repeated his story. "Apparently I'm the only one who saw it happen, and I could not tell you why."

She shot him a quick, knowing glance. *The ísenwaer.*

That was her sierwan gift sharing a realization, he knew — and hoped Trystane hadn't noticed the millisecond shift in her eyes — but clearly neither one of them knew *why* their shared bond allowed him to witness the momentary exchange. Another visit to the University and Magister Basira might soon be in their future.

Trystane sipped his ale. "That is most unusual, Fyrdwisa."

It was most unusual too for Trystane to swap to official titles in the middle of his living room.

"Do you know of this happening?" Collum asked him.

The Elven leader bit his bottom lip in concentration. Clearly what he wanted to say was delicate information, and Collum could tell he wanted to avoid revealing this to Bridgette for some reason.

I'll tell you later, but now would be an excellent time for you to need to use the bathroom, Collum thought quickly to Bridgette. She slipped down the hallway with a promise of a speedy return, and he swapped his focus to Trystane.

"What?"

"This is a strange time we are living in, Collum," Trystane murmured, his voice barely above a whisper. "Already there are three instances of resurgence of ancient legends as old as the Elves themselves: the birth of the Liluthuaé, the rise of a sierwan, the return of the Ealdaelfen. It all centers around Bridgette, and it is all coming up so quickly it's nigh impossible to keep track. I feel as though every time we think we've figured out one aspect of her character as legend, something else comes to light."

Collum thought guiltily of the ísenwaer and Bridgette's ability to fly, but said nothing. He only nodded.

"In your studies, did you ever learn of the Maylemaegus?" Trystane asked carefully. When Collum shook his head, he explained. "The Maylemaegus is the ... for lack of a better term, Universal presence and power. It *is* power. Therefore it is exceedingly difficult to explain. It is the collective virtues, moments, and elements from which magic and collective thought are originally derived. We all, in some way, are thus connected to this concept of Maylemaegus."

He frowned. Collum was unused to seeing Trystane struggle so for an explanation.

"There is ... another legend, and it is so mythical it's a bit ridiculous, even for magical beings to believe in. But there was once a hint that certain beings would be the Maylemaegus brought to life," Trystane continued carefully. "*Truth* is Maylemaegus."

Collum's eyes widened slightly. He understood. "You think the Liluthuaé is one of these beings."

The Elven leader nodded. "It would make absolute sense, *if* this is a true thing. But you hearing her say that today, on top of all else we know about Bridgette ... I am leaning toward believing it."

"How did you know of this?" Collum asked, simultaneously sending a thought to Bridgette that she should find a reason to keep to her room for a few more minutes. "And how do I not?"

"Because I'm a quarter-century older and wiser," Trystane quipped, grinning to lighten the mood. "But actually because several decades ago, I found a chest of documents that Aelys Frost transported to Heáhwolcen. I rummaged through them and read a few of the more interesting pages."

Collum froze. "I would very much like to see that chest of documents, Trystane."

"I'll have them brought from storage to the Caisleán in the morning, then."

The conversation was over, but the two small-talked until Bridgette returned, pretending nothing out of the ordinary had been happening.

Except for all three, it was exactly the opposite: Bridgette hadn't been privy yet to what Trystane and Collum discussed in her absence, but she'd spent the last fifteen minutes stuck in her head, mulling over what Bryten said to her during the Samnung meeting. They knew *something* was up, but couldn't do anything stupid and — as Corria Deathhunter mentioned — accidentally be the spark to a conflict they very much would prefer to prevent. Bridgette hadn't met Ulerion, the Fairy ambassador to Palna who'd apparently disappeared, but she did know that without his reports back to the Samnung, there had been about a year where no firm knowledge of the country had reached the greater government.

Bridgette seethed momentarily at that, the idea that the Samnung had spirits waft in and out as they please from Iffrinevatt, but deity forbid *Palna*, a country of sentient magical beings, be represented in the chamber. There was much to unpack about the entire Palna situation in her mind. She didn't have the full context, didn't truly understand why it was deemed acceptable to blame an entire citizenry for the faults and actions of its — admittedly — horrible former leader, and the despicable behavior of its current rulers, but deep in her heart, Bridgette knew that to continue allowing Palna to exist in its current space was both ineffective and cruel. There had to be a better way, especially in a place like Heáhwolcen, where so many different cultures, beings, and magics coexisted relatively peacefully.

And so, when she resumed her spot on the couch with her Elven brethren, the Liluthuaé took a deep breath and revealed her plan.

"I think …" Bridgette bit her lip. "I think I know what we need to do."

"About?" Trystane asked. He finished the ale and summoned a glass of his liquor.

"About Palna. About figuring out what's going on, and how we can solve it."

Trystane cocked his head. Usually when Bridgette knew things, she seemed far more confident in herself. "Is this a sierwan knowing?"

"No," she said, picking at her nails. "I don't think it is. My eyes didn't shift. It just seems like the right thing."

"Do tell us, in that case," the Elven leader encouraged her.

It *did* feel right, this plan she was formulating in her mind. She took another deep breath. "I need to follow in Mohreen's footsteps."

A pause.

"Come again?" Collum said politely. Surely he hadn't heard her correctly.

"I need to follow in Mohreen's footsteps," Bridgette repeated, feeling more sure of the idea as she spoke it out loud again. "We need to know what's happening in Palna. The Fairy ambassador disappeared, which is sketchy to begin with, and worse, it means we've lost our key source of important information. So I'll go instead."

"Absolutely not," Collum replied immediately. Trystane's brows rose, but he said nothing.

"Why not?" Bridgette accosted her companion. "Am I not up to the challenge?"

"At this moment, no," he said. "Why in seven hells would you think this is a good idea?"

"Because it's been decades since any sort of program like this existed. It's time to extend a hand, especially since — aside from rumor — nothing actually bad has happened between Palna and the rest of Heáhwolcen," Bridgette explained. "I'll go in as an exchange student studying something, but really what I'm studying is the inner workings of the government there. See if I can find out what's happening, where the potential for Craft Wizardry and Ealdaelfen magic is building, and at what rate."

Collum opened his mouth to object again, but Trystane raised a hand. "I don't disagree with this train of thought, Bright Star. But we cannot send you in entirely unprepared, and there exists the complication that you cannot perform magic."

A slight sting to this truth. But Bridgette smiled ruefully at the thought. "For once, that might be to our benefit. If Palna is supposed to be this country where no magic is taking place, I'll fit right in. They won't see me as a threat, because I can't do magic, and they might be more willing to trust me. At least trust me enough to let me make a friend or two and get the gist of what's going on, what they think of the rest of Heáhwolcen."

"An exchange program though," Trystane mused. "Would that not imply that a Palnan citizen of similar age would then come to the University?"

"I guess?" Bridgette hadn't given that part much thought. "But would that be so bad? To open the door? Like, are we really going to keep Palnans locked up in Palna for the rest of eternity?"

Collum didn't miss the "we" she'd let slip. "We've discussed this topic previously, and I don't think anyone's thoughts on it have changed," he said. "I believe the exchange portion is out entirely. We don't even know if Palna has anything similar to the University."

"Then we need to read every Fairy ambassador report from Palna since its outer wall went up," Bridgette said firmly. This time, her eyes did shift. "We need to know everything we can about this country that no one except the Fairies have been to in twenty-some-odd years."

Collum hadn't missed her eyes going from opalescent lilac to lilac opal. He closed his eyes, partly because he was praying this knowing wouldn't turn out to be true, but simultaneously realizing it was … and that was a *lot* of paperwork to go through. Given that he'd just requested to receive a chest of centuries-old Elven documents too, the fyrdwisa had a feeling he'd be doing more reading in the next few weeks than he had since his time at the University.

Seven fucking hells, Starshine, what did you just sign us up for?

"I'll put in a request with Aristoces first thing in the morning," Trystane said. "I'm not sure we'll be able to get them all at once, of course, as that's more than a century's worth of reports. She should be able to send some of the more recent ones with Seamund though."

"Seamund?" Bridgette asked.

"The Fairy ambassador to Eckenbourne," Trystane clarified. "Though Aristoces and I have an extraordinarily close relationship, most of the time outside of Samnung meetings and direct Samnung-related business, my contact with Fairevella is handled via Seamund."

"Gotcha," the Elfling replied. She rose from the couch and began to pace the living room, a tell-tale sign she was solidifying their plan. "Seamund can bring us enough to start with, and I'm assuming over time will be able to bring all of it. Honestly, the more we know about Palna, Craft magic, and Baize Sammael, the better."

Bridgette stopped pacing suddenly and blinked. "Holy shit. Do you remember that last time we went to Maluridae Wood, before Ostara? We never got to put any of that plan into place because Mohreen was at the Samnung meeting and threw all of us a giant loop. Fucking hell, there is *so* much we have to do!" she practically wailed.

Collum raised an eyebrow. "We are not in any particular rush, Starshine. It's more important we take our time and do this as best we can, rather than jump right in with no preparation."

She looked at Trystane. "I need to sleep on this. Really work it out, before I start rambling and making no sense. Can we meet with you tomorrow? I want to really have a plan in my head before throwing it all out there helter-skelter."

"Of course. It would behoove us to have Aurelias and Njahla present as well," Trystane said. "Shall we say, the Caisleán at eleven in the morning? Collum, I should be able to let you know the status of those documents at that time as well, and it will allow me to speak with Seamund about the Palnan ambassador reports."

Collum and Bridgette agreed, and Trystane evanesced without further ado.

The Elfling slumped on the couch, feeling exhausted from what had become quite a long two days, and mentally drained from all the thoughts refusing to coalesce inside her brain.

"I feel like I'm talking in circles," she moaned. "Like, we had this plan, this plan never got put into place, and now there's all this extra stuff that just came to me. I think I need one of those fancy boards they have on crime shows where they put all the pictures, maps, and theories up to physically connect the dots."

Collum's cocked head told her he had no idea what she was talking about.

"Never mind," Bridgette chuckled. "A piece of paper will work, I guess. And some of that bath magic stuff?" she added hopefully.

"I'll fetch you some paper and pen, and the bath oils are all in your cabinet. Sleep well — don't cause yourself undue stress. We will figure this out and move forward," Collum said. He stretched his arms out, and a moment later, the needed office supplies appeared in front of her, as did a large slab of stained ironwood.

"It's to lay across the sides of the bath," Collum explained. "So you have a surface to bare down on while you write."

Bridgette was touched. She hadn't thought of that. She also hadn't thought about food, and her stomach grumbled. There had been a small luncheon during the Samnung meeting, but it was about time for a more substantial evening meal.

Collum grinned. "I'll make you a sandwich."

I could so get used to this, Bridgette thought to him a while later, thoroughly soaking in the bath. She'd followed one of the spells on the kit, though she felt silly saying the incantation aloud — did it matter that it was only words, when they couldn't be imbued with the necessary magic? — but the resulting luxuriousness of rose quartz and pink sea salt, the scents of peony and tulsi, the endless bubbles reaching above her breasts … Even if it was only in the metaphorical sense, this was the most magical bath she'd ever experienced. Collum had delivered her sandwich, and Bridgette munched, eyes closed, while trying to organize her thoughts enough to put them on paper.

What should be a fairly straightforward plan was inherently compromised by nearly two centuries of history she needed to study. The preparation alone for what she must do would be time-consuming, and both mentally and physically taxing. As a student, exchange or no, she needed to understand at least the basics of Palnan history, preferably from a lens that wasn't clouded by hatred of Craft Wizardry. There was the Elusive Grimoire, but going on an Endorsan treasure hunt was a low priority. The best she could do was read the reports and histories she had access to.

That was step one: become a bookworm.

Step two would require more planning and outside assistance. They *had* to find the Druids. If Bridgette could get into Palna, if she could learn about the two walls from the inside, combining that with whatever knowledge she gleaned from the Druids could be the key to unlocking that particular barrier — pun intended.

Step three, figure out her cover story. Why was she going to Palna, especially if there wasn't some form of higher education institution there? The story had to be absolutely foolproof. That, Bridgette knew, was essential. Though she knew nothing of Craft magic, she had a suspicion that anyone skilled in the practice would be able to sniff out a lie faster than she could speak it aloud.

Step four, become a temporary Palnan citizen, with a plan for getting out once the necessary knowledge was acquired.

Finally, step five: dismantle the wall and …

And what?

Bridgette put her head in her hands. They kept getting to this particular point of contention and getting stuck. Trystane had been right, all those months ago, when he said that nobody knew how or if Palna could exist without Craft magic. She wished her sierwan gift would send her some magical knowledge, but her eyes remained stubbornly normal. Either it wasn't time for her to know this particular step yet, for whatever deity-damned reason, or it was something that depended on what happened with the previous four. *Fuck.*

She stared at the list she'd made, and heaved herself out of the tub. Bridgette had a feeling Collum wasn't asleep yet, perhaps waiting to see if she wanted to fly, but she'd rarely wanted to sleep so badly in her life.

Her body ached, her brain ached, and she didn't bother putting on pajamas before throwing herself underneath the downy comforter. It was the first restful night Bridgette could remember having in months, and the bonus thought of waking up to Collum's cooking had her rising with a broad smile as soon as the watery dawn light reached her window.

I missed this, she thought to him, slipping into her sleepclothes to walk out into civilization.

Missed what? his snarky response came, the teasing tone evident even in their mind-speak.

"Missed you cooking for me first thing in the morning," she said out loud, padding into the kitchen. "I'm so sick of world-famous Wafflewiches, I'd have willingly eaten a shoe if it meant you'd come make me bacon and eggs."

"You wouldn't have had to eat a shoe, Starshine. I would gladly have made you breakfast, lunch and dinner, all you had to do was ask," Collum said. "However, as we have a morning meeting with our Elven delegation, I thought perhaps we could dress early and visit the Coffee Cauldron beforehand?"

"Say no more!" Bridgette exclaimed, eager beyond reason to have a cup of that iced deliciousness in her hands again.

She dressed swiftly, again putting on rather Earthly clothes of jeans and a loose-fitting tank top. At some point, she'd have to go out and find or buy Elven leggings, tunics, and that sort of fashion again. Maybe she could convince both the fyrdestre and Njahla to come with her, the first for comic relief and the second for her sense of style. Both, because Bridgette had no idea where or how to begin shopping in Elven stores.

Collum whisked the two of them away to Endorsa, arriving directly in front of the coffee shop. Bridgette caught her breath from evanescing, sighing deeply to inhale the wondrous bakery scents that she'd so missed for three long months. The campus coffee shop was one thing, but the Coffee Cauldron was a level all on its own — her regular go-to was lackluster every time she thought about the exact drink that was about to make its way into her hands.

The three sisters were dressed in short-sleeved sky blue dresses under their khaki aprons, and they could not have been more delighted to see Bridgette. She didn't know that Collum had been making frequent trips to see them while she'd been gone, so she didn't realize their joy wasn't directed at her, so much as it was the effects she had on her companion.

"Hello, dear!" Murthel cried, clasping her hands in front of her. She ran from behind the counter and wrapped the Elfling in a strong hug, despite being nearly a foot shorter. "We were wondering when you would visit again!"

This seems to be a common theme, Bridgette thought shrewdly to Collum. To Murthel, Teale, and Avengeline, who'd joined them, she gave a genuine thanks, grasping each of their hands in turn.

"Avengeline, I know you've probably had your share of Earthen coffee beverages, but I assure you: there is nothing like caife calabaza in Nashville, Tennessee! Even if the fates hadn't decided to bring me back, I would have found a way to return just for you three and your treats," she said.

The witch tittered. "You're a gem, Sigewíf! It's no wonder the fyrdwisa enjoys your company so. He's a changed Elf when you're around."

"Is he, now?" Bridgette asked, smirking at her companion. "If he is, it's only because I drive him crazy enough to make him laugh, because it would be highly unprofessional of him to throttle a guest of the Samnung."

Collum threw back his head and did laugh at that. "Bridgette speaks truth, my friends. There are times where I am highly tempted to do such a thing."

She smiled warmly up at him, still surprised by how those tidal pool eyes could envelope her whole soul without even trying. "What can I say, it's a well-honed talent."

He punched her lightly on the shoulder. "Friends, we unfortunately cannot spend the morning here, as we have to return to the Caisleán for a meeting with Trystane. Today's breakfast must be a bit on the run, but I assure you, there will be plenty of time for us to come and enjoy a carefree day on the patio with your creations to fuel us."

Murthel scurried back behind the counter to take their orders — two iced caife calabazas, of course, the largest size for Bridgette and a smaller cup for Collum — and spout off the day's specials. Teale's latest idea was to offer weekly featured honeycake toppings, given the variety of late spring and early summer produce coming into season, and thus far it had been well-received. That week's offerings were cardamom-kumquat and spicy chile-peach, and the companions took one of each with intent to share.

"Are we going to evanesce with food in our hands?" Bridgette asked, accepting their goodies. "That seems … risky."

"You have an utter lack of faith in magic sometimes, Starshine," Collum grinned at her. "We have a bag for the honeycakes, and will each hold our drink in one hand. You can hold me with the other; I'm not going to drop you somewhere in transit."

"Oh."

They disappeared into the familiar inky whirls, and reappeared a short distance from the Caisleán. "We still have a few minutes before we need to go inside, so I thought it would be nice to picnic," Collum explained, pointing to a grassy field to their right. "Especially since I was a dolt and did not bother to bring Trystane anything."

"Epic fail," Bridgette said, walking to the grass. She hopped the low-lying rail fence and settled cross-legged in the sun, beckoning for the Elf to please hand her the honeycakes. "Which one should we eat first?"

The two dined in near silence for a while, surrounded by chirping birds and that constant, distant peal of windchimes. It was quite warm in June, and Bridgette wondered if Elves ever wore shorts: July and August would be sweltering, she could already tell. She laid back in the grass, arms tucked under her head, and felt the golden sun ease its way across her as the morning wore on.

"Bundy, what do you do as fyrdwisa when you're not searching for mythical Elven creatures?" she asked. Her eyes were closed; her voice sounded almost pensive.

Collum stretched out to lay next to her. "Many things. It depends on the day. Some days it's filing reports. Making sure Trystane and Nehemi don't kill each other, that seems to happen fairly often. I train, I meditate, I travel to liaison with whatever beings may need to be liaised with. Oversee the Fyrdlytta; read and study. Keep you in check, of course."

She grinned. "Punk."

"In truth, being fyrdwisa has been a relatively non-adventurous job for me. Once things were settled with Nehemi as queen of Endorsa, and until Mohreen showed back up to surprise us, there was a long period of near-doldrum. I'm not complaining, believe me — the last thing I desire is conflict — but compared to the Fairy ambassadors and ambassadoras, who are constantly traveling to and from Earth? It was pretty boring," Collum said. "I jumped at the chance to go to Earth myself for the first time in decades."

"Are you scared? About all this with Palna, and with me?"

He considered that. "Scared, no. Apprehensive, of course. There are, as you've mentioned, as Trystane will probably mention again today, many unknowns. As I said, I do not desire conflict. Many of us who are active in governing affairs and combat training were too young to recall the Ingefeot. None of us alive now, at least not in Heáhwolcen, are old enough to remember the Ealdaelfen in their prime. And as Magister Ephynius hinted, there is only so much history that is preserved in the world above the world. Some still resides in Elven communities elsewhere."

Collum remembered then that he hadn't told Bridgette about his conversation the previous evening. He furrowed his brow. "Now that I say that, though, I'd forgotten Trystane is to procure some documents for me. Last night, when you stepped away, he shared with me that several years ago, he came into possession of Elven histories that belonged to Aelys Frost. When Trystane mentioned this, he did so by way of sharing a legend I've never heard of, but one that he'd found skimming those documents in passing. I'm very curious to know what exactly is in those documents, and what Elven history Aelys Frost managed to smuggle up to Heáhwolcen."

Bridgette propped herself up on her shoulders. "What do you mean, 'smuggle'?"

"Aelys Frost led one of many communities of Elves on Earth, and one of countless communities of Elves that exist in all the other instances of time and space. None of our histories will be truly complete because we are only able to study the background of what we are descended from," Collum explained. "Aelys Frost, however, was not *the* prime leader of the Earthen Elves when she led her dúnaelfen to Heáhwolcen. Many thought she was on a fool's errand to go, but her community's habitat was under siege by humans. They came up the original portal soon after Artur Cromwell and Galdúr opened it, much to the dismay of Elves who preferred to remain separate from other magical beings. They were harangued, distrusted from then on, until the Ingefeot, when Fairy ambassadors came to restore peace and build an allyship. But between the moment Aelys Frost made the decision to leave Earth, and the time the Fairies visited, she was shunned, for lack of a better word. And so any records she brought with her were essentially seen as stolen in the eyes of all other Elves on Earth. It's probably why whatever these documents are were hidden in a chest for almost two hundred years."

"Why didn't Trystane want me to know this chest existed?" Bridgette demanded. "Why couldn't he have said that while I was in the room?"

"Firstly, Starshine, and I mean this truly: do not let him know that you are aware of its existence yet," Collum cautioned her. "I'm sure he knows you'll find out soon enough. You asked me a few minutes ago if I was scared, and again, I am not, but I think Trystane is more uncertain of the future than I am. The legend he read in those documents may have something to do with your spat with Nehemi yesterday, but he's ... to be honest, a bit anxious after so many stories have come to be true in recent times. I believe he wants me to do as much research as I can to find out if there's anything else that might surprise us, before it jumps out of the storybooks into our midst."

Bridgette relaxed a bit. "Oh. I won't say anything, promise."

Collum glanced up at the sun. "It's almost time. Are you ready with this plan of yours?"

"No," she admitted, grinning faintly. "I've only got like, half of it figured out. The final part depends on how the rest of it goes. I'm not sure if Trystane, or anyone else, will like that."

The Elf wasn't either. He sighed. "We knew we were going into this with myriad unknowns. It only makes sense to add a few more to the mix."

~ 45 ~

Njahla wasn't at all shocked to see Bridgette when she opened the door to Trystane's office that morning. She was shocked, however, as was Collum, when the Elfling wrapped her in a hug and invited her on a shopping excursion whenever time allowed for that to happen.

"You picked out the best clothes and you didn't even know me — and I don't know where to begin shopping for Elven clothes — so I would be honored if you and Aurelias would come with me," Bridgette explained, her eyes bright.

"Of course," Njahla stammered, blinking. "I cannot speak for the fyrdestre, but it would be mine honor."

"Now that we've settled that," Collum murmured, ushering the two females inside. Sitting in front of Trystane was a massive stack of papers on his desk. Collum's shrewd eyes didn't miss the weathered ashwood chest that was semi-hidden on the floor.

The stack of pages was multicolored, and Bridgette asked the relevance.

"In terms of the Fairy ambassador reports, it appears we will be reading backwards. Seamund was easily able to bring us the past ten years' worth of documents, but will need time to access the rest. Ulerion has been — was? — ambassador for only thirty years before his disappearance, and he's quite an eccentric bloke. He frequently color-coded his reports, but would change colors without warning based on his mood. Hence," Trystane paused to shuffle through some of the papers, "these pink ones are pink because they were written in spring, but *these* are pink because he apparently believed they were of urgent nature, and *this* top section is pink because Lucilla got pissed off for some reason and purposely only gave everyone in the Samnung pink paper for a month."

Collum cringed; that would be his fault.

"Great," Bridgette said. "So now not only do we have to read this dude's reports, but we have to decode his random color scheme? Awesome. Exactly how I planned on saving the world."

Aurelias evanesced into the office then, and having

accidentally mis-calculated her arrival position, nearly sent the stack of papers flying as she whirled into existence on top of Trystane's desk.

"Whoops!" she said, jumping down and noting the panicked expression of all four faces in front of her. "What'd I miss?"

"Just the fact that you almost sent ten years' worth of Ulerion's already hectic reports scattering into unorganized oblivion, nothing major," Trystane muttered. "Could you perhaps evanesce into the hall from now on, Aurelias?"

"Sure, chief," the fyrdestre said, bowing her horned head slightly at him. She turned to Collum. "Didn't bother to bring anyone else caife calabaza, or caife mokka, I see."

Leave it to Aurelias to point that out, he thought to Bridgette.

"My apologies, Fyrdestre. The Bright Star awoke and begged for a visit to the Coffee Cauldron," Collum said out loud.

Bridgette shot him an annoyed glare, but said nothing.

"You can bring me one tomorrow then, when we're sitting down in a quilting circle to read these damn things," Aurelias said sweetly, conjuring up a stool to perch on. "And Njahla prefers tea to caife, don't forget."

"I won't," he promised, rolling his eyes. They *would* have quite the task ahead of them, and caffeine would be a welcome help.

"Well then. Now that we're all here, Bright Star, the floor is yours," Trystane said. He casually leaned back in his chair, fingers interlaced behind his head. "Tell us what we're doing."

Way to put me on the spot, Bridgette thought.

She took a deep breath and started talking. When she finished laying out her plan, it was met with thoughtful silence. Trystane spoke first after a long moment.

"We can begin the first two steps simultaneously," he said carefully. "If the four of you are tackling the reading, you can do so head-on at first. I will, meanwhile, work with Geongre Akiko to arrange for travel to Wales, where it sounds the best place to begin searching for the Druids. I am not sure off the top of my head who the ambassador is, but he or she will likely be asked to accompany Bridgette and Collum. Meanwhile, Njahla and

Aurelias can continue the research here, and I'll take a turn or two."

He turned to face his advisor and the fyrdestre. "I am about to reveal information to you that must stay within these walls: There is a significant connection between Bridgette and Emi-Joye Vetur, the Fairy ambassadora to the Antarctic. I believe it will be prudent for her and her second, Apostine, to join in on this research as well. The more eyes, the faster we can whittle down what promises to be an inordinate amount of paperwork."

The two females nodded.

"What once they return from Earth with the Druidic knowledge?" Njahla asked.

"Then we prepare for Bridgette to go to Palna," Trystane said simply.

Collum's throat went dry. He knew this was coming; he'd been preparing himself to hear it ever since Bridgette brought it up the previous evening. But the thought of her in that place would never make him feel comfortable. Perhaps, he realized, that was a prejudice of sorts: he'd been raised and conditioned to know very little of Palna except for its Craft history. Nonetheless, until he knew different, he doubted he'd be fully able to trust that any sort of positive environment existed within those walled borders.

"Prepare how?" he asked, looking at his leader.

"Figure out my cover story, first off," Bridgette said. "Don't freak out, Collum. By the time I get there, we'll have had plenty of time to do that. Like you said yesterday, we're not on a specific timeline here and we're not going to rush into things."

She felt odd, being the one comforting Collum instead of vice-versa.

Why are you so scared of me going? she thought to him, tuning out Njahla and Aurelias offering suggestions as to her soon-to-be feigned identity.

We don't know what we're putting you into, he said back, mind-to-mind.

You never knew what you were putting me into, and you were the one who brought me here, she reminded him gently. *Trust me, I'm fucking terrified, but this is the only way.*

Collum promised himself he'd make the preparations be as long-lasting and as thorough as possible.

"Your preparations need to include more than your cover story," he said aloud. "We need you to be proficient in protecting yourself, just in case, and I feel it would be prudent to work on your mind-strength as well."

"Mind-strength?" Bridgette questioned.

"Yup," Aurelias said. "Mind-strength means that in case one of the Tinuviels or someone they're close to is able to do what the fyrdwisa does, to hear your inner monologue, you can block them out. Most of the time you won't know who might be trying to listen in on your thoughts, because you're *not* gifted like Collum, but you can put up mental barriers as defenses."

"Mind-strength will also give you greater control over your reactions to things," Trystane added. "If you hear something of interest to your journey, or something that the Samnung would need to know, you can absorb that knowledge without having it show in your body language or facial expression."

Bridgette groaned inwardly. She was terrible at that — Collum half the time tuned her out for privacy, but knew her thoughts anyway through sheer familiarity with her posture and those damn eyes of hers.

Those damn eyes. *Shit.*

"I'm going to have to keep them from knowing I'm a sierwan," she said. "How the fuck do we do that?"

Nobody had given it much thought.

"Are magic contact lenses a thing?" Bridgette asked. "Or can you like, glamour me or something, so that the shift doesn't show?"

"We can try that," Trystane said. "We will probably have to enlist some aid for a glamour of that nature, though. When we share our plan with the Samnung at large, perhaps Nehemi or Kharis can perform that task."

"Who's going to tell the Samnung?" Bridgette queried. "I don't know that Nehemi will take anything well from me at the moment."

Trystane rolled his eyes, losing the ceannaíri demeanor for a moment. "That would tend to happen when you call a ruling queen an idiot."

Njahla and Aurelias glanced at one another, but said nothing.

"We can add it to the agenda for next week's meeting," Collum said. "I'll do the talking, and it will give me time to speak with the various commanders to flesh out our physical training plan."

Everyone agreed, and Trystane rose to bid the three visitors farewell. "Aurelias, Bridgette, I'll trust you two to transport the reports — by *walking*," he added pointedly. "Collum, I have a package for you as well, though you may want to send it home for review."

They split up as such: the two females heading down to Collum's main office, and Collum back to his apartment.

Bridgette used the momentary alone time to invite Aurelias on the shopping trip she'd proposed to Njahla.

"Njahla has a perfect eye for color and texture. I love everything that she picked out for my first trip, and she didn't know a thing about me then except what sizes I wore and the color of my hair and eyes. I trust your opinion too, trying on things and being honest about whether something looks good on or just in theory," she explained. "Maybe it's silly, but I think we'd have fun."

"We'd have a brilliant time!" Aurelias said excitely. "I'm in. It sounds far better than the other task you've signed me up for."

"Sorry about that," Bridgette replied. "I meant mostly for it to be a me and Collum thing, but Trystane sort of expanded the invite."

The fyrdestre chortled. "It'll be fine. We can each take a year and work from there."

Bridgette frowned. "I wish we could start from the beginning instead of the end. You and Collum know what to look for, but I don't. I'm worried I'll miss something in whatever I'm reading, because I don't have the full context of Palna's history memorized."

"Are you or are you not a sierwan?" Aurelias asked pointedly, quietly, so no one else would overhear. She smirked at her fellow Elfling.

"Fair point," Bridgette said, grinning back. "I guess I'll know what's important when I see it."

The two settled down and Aurelias handed Bridgette a pen and opulent leather-bound notebook with a lilac opal closure.

Seeing Bridgette's impressed look, she shrugged. "When Trystane said we'd probably need writing supplies for the Liluthuaé's project, I figured we could spare no expense."

"Sheesh," Bridgette said. "Thanks."

She reached for the top-most section of colored pages, but felt uncomfortable in the office setting. It was so … *sterile*. "Can I take this outside? Collum and I sat on the grass this morning and it was easier for me to focus out there."

Aurelias, grabbing the next year's worth of reports, smiled at her. "Wow. You really are two of a kind," she said. "I've known the fyrdwisa his whole life and he's never been one to enjoy being, as he puts it, 'trapped in a room.' He'll probably join you, honestly."

Perfect.

Bridgette smiled back and slipped out the door. She made her way to the grassy field and laid on her stomach, tempted to roll up the legs of her jeans so her skin could absorb some of the sun that bared down on her. The most recent year's worth of reports wasn't even a full year, as it was during the past twelve months that Ulerion had disappeared. She wondered vaguely if there would be some hint as to why that might have happened, and she flipped back to the previous January to start researching in some semblance of chronological order.

A Summation of Goings and Sights, as Reported on the 2nd Day of the First Month of the Year Two Thousand Seventeen
Prepared and Respectfully Submitted to Aristoces, Fairy of All Fairies, and the governing officials of Fairevella. by Ulerion Mewt

> Tráthnóna mistéireach, ceannairí mine! It is with great pleasure I wish you a blessed start to this newest year from within our most unusual country of Palna. I traveled this past week to a city new to me, a shock, truly, having been its ambassador for multiple decades! But Ydessa and Eryth are wont to keep their secrets, as we know, and it took much pleading for me to make this possible. Larivuria - pronounced lAR-eh-vu-free-ah - is positively wonderous! It is entirely different from anywhere else I have traveled to in Heáhwolcen and in Palna itself. By some small miracle, Palna has an entire beach. A true beach, with waves in the ocean, sand, and shells, I believe I even saw a shark! The magic that once dwelled here truly is astounding, ceannairí mine.

Bridgette's reading was interrupted both by her eyes shifting and by the presence of Collum joining her on the grass. "Found anything?" he asked, and he knew her answer as she turned to face him.

"Collum," she began slowly, "How well do these reports usually get read by whoever is supposed to read them when they get turned in?"

He blinked. "I'm not sure. Why do you ask?"

She chewed on her lip. "Because when we were on the mountain that day, you said there were no such things as beaches and oceans in Heáhwolcen. But on January 2, 2017, Ulerion submitted a report about visiting a beach. In Palna."

"What?" Collum said sharply.

She handed him the paper and watched him read, peeking over his shoulder to get to the parts she hadn't taken in yet:

> I have heard of beaches before, but never with mine own eyes had I seen anything of the sort! Sohli guided me on a full shopping expedition before we went, as typical clothing isn't suited for such an environment. I traded robes for short breeches, and it was encouraged for males to not even wear shirts! Curiously though, I could not fly there; I

could only be transported via Ydessa and Eryth's private methods, but it was much worth the hassle. I loved it! I do wish there was some place like this in Fairevella, or perhaps even Endorsa, where the sun shines all day and there are such creatures and beings to enjoy. It was a most pleasant way to ring in the new year for Sohli and I. I declare, even my wings seemed to shine more after spending so much time there. Most of this past week was spent basking and learning about the different creatures that inhabit these waters, the likes of which you could not even imagine.

The Tinuviels arranged for lessons in aquaculture and aquatic horticulture, and we attended lectures aplenty on fishes, saltwater, sea-faring mammals and birds. It was most fascinating, and should the occasion arise, an excellent opportunity for expanded studies for the University to offer in our home country! There are magical creatures that reside here, though I am told no merfolk, although if merfolk were to know of Larivuria, I have no doubt they would thrive here. All of the eateries and shops offer shells and fish, scallops and shrimp, seaweed greens even! These are things we could not otherwise import except through our Earthly allied trade agreements, but could you imagine, ceannairí, if we could trade within Palna for these items as we do our fellow Heáhwolcen countries!

To ring in the new year, Sohli and I stayed up so very late with the citizens and travelers of this city. There were fireworks of an array of colors, shooting up and out over the horizon, for an age after the witching hour! It is my hope that we can bring this custom into the greater Heáhwolcen, for such a spectacle would delight so many of our citizens. I'm off to visit a new restaurant with Sohli - commerce is so abundant here! - and wish you well.

Respectfully yours and blessed be.
Wy árung,

Ulerion Mewt

"Who is Sohli, and what the hell are these private transportation methods that the Tinuviels have at their disposal?" Collum asked no one in particular. "And where, *where*, is this damned beach?"

Bridgette ran a hand through her hair, loosening her braid to let the strawberry-blonde waves blow in the summer breeze. "I don't think it's in Palna."

He looked at her, unasked questions filling those tidal pool eyes. "What do you mean?"

"I'm not sure," she admitted. "But it's ... elsewhere." She knew this to be true, but her sierwan gift provided no additional background.

Collum stood up and reached for her hand. "Come on. We're going to the University. We need to find a map."

~ 46 ~

"A map of Palna?" Bridgette asked. "Does that even exist?"

"It does if you know where to look," Collum said smugly. "Which I do, but you are not to breathe a word of this to anyone. If anyone asks, the knowledge we are about to come by is through your sierwan gift. Understood?"

"Sheesh, Bundy, sure thing. Take me to your mysterious map gallery."

They evanesced not onto the grounds before the stately library building, but instead directly inside a decrepit stone structure that Bridgette was shocked even existed on the gorgeous campus. Every other building in Heáhwolcen, save that tavern Emi-Joye flew her to, only *looked* old, but whatever careful preserving spells had been placed elsewhere had clearly skipped over this … place.

"Welcome, Starshine, to the Coven House of Wand and Sword."

"Where *are* we? I thought you said we were going to the University. Pretty sure this is a shed."

Collum smiled broadly. "It is a shed, unless you know how to remove the glamour."

He waved a hand and whispered an incantation Bridgette didn't catch, and suddenly the two of them stood in a circular room lined with centuries-old worn gray stone, full of dark velvet chairs and leather sofas, with a half-moon-shaped bar across from them. The room was scattered with beings, and as Bridgette looked up and around, she noted an iron spiral staircase that went up two additional levels, each a thin balcony that ran around the circumference of the walls, with ample small tables and more velvet seating arrangements. The room was dimly lit, comfortable with floating candles, and had the air of a very old, very secret attic space.

She realized her jaw had dropped only when Collum slipped two fingers under her chin to close her gaping mouth.

Collum's smile hadn't left his face. "Come have a drink with me," he said, leading her to the bar.

"Fyrdwisa! Fáilte, friend!" The young bartender, either a Teifling or a Baetalüan by the horns protruding from his fiery red curls, practically jumped over the counter at the two companions. "What brings you to the House today?"

"Nonóir es linne," Collum replied in formal greeting. "The honor is ours. Two standards, please."

Whatever that meant sent the bartender snapping and waving his hands for a minute, setting ingredients to make themselves into a pair of matching cocktails right before Bridgette's astonished eyes. As the magic worked itself into fruition, the bartender again turned to face the Elf.

"You ordered the standard, yet avoided my question, Fyrdwisa," he said.

"My companion and I have need of the Alcove. Is it currently reserved?" Collum asked, quietly and casually.

"It is not," the bartender responded.

"Please make sure we are not seen, in that event, and that it is thusly reserved the remainder of the afternoon." Collum summoned the two glasses to him, and cocked his head as a sign for Bridgette to follow him.

Where are we going? she asked, mind-to-mind.

When we get to the foot of the stairs, drink your full drink and lean against the wall. Do not say anything to anyone; do not draw attention to us, Collum instructed back to her.

Not until you —

Just do it, Bridgette. Please.

She gave him a dour look, but trailed after him to the bottom of the spiral staircase. She leaned against the stones, started to sip whatever a "standard" was, and found the taste so revolting she almost spat it out.

The faster you drink it, the less you'll notice the taste, Collum thought to her.

Indeed, his glass was practically being chugged, and his eyes near watering from the bitter tang. Bridgette swallowed hard and gulped the liquid down, trying not to let it sit on her tongue too long. She felt the stone wall become smooth, melt away, and then they really were standing in a musty-smelling old attic.

"Will you *please* explain what is happening?" she snapped.

"Yes, but please keep your voice down. I don't want anyone overhearing us," Collum whispered. "In fact, I'd much prefer we just … use the ísenwaer, if you don't mind."

Fine, Bridgette thought to him immediately. *What is all this bullshit about? What did you just make me drink? You know, on Earth they teach women not to just blindly accept drinks in case they're drugged, and this seems like a pretty awful trip already.*

Collum glared at her. *Would you please trust me, Starshine?*

I do trust you, Bundy. *But I would still like to know what we're doing and where we are.*

He sighed. *As I said, we are in the Coven House of Wand and Sword. It's a very prestigious organization at the University, in that it exists only in the minds of those who know of its existence. Think of it as the student organization version of the Maluridae Wood, which as you know has a similar construct.*

So it's a secret society? Bridgette asked, mind-to-mind. This made sense to her: after all, it had been clear from the start that the University's architecture was inspired by Ivy League colleges on Earth. Those had not-so-secret societies galore.

Essentially, Collum thought to her. *Once you are part of the Coven, you are a member for life, and its membership … perks, shall we say, are at your disposal. The standard is a potion that allows members and their guests to visit areas outside of the common bar. It is a little-known fact that prior to the Ingefeoht, Baize Sammael himself frequented the Coven House to speak to members. As he was not a member himself, he was only invited on select meeting nights — to spark debate, take part in conversation, that sort of thing — and only saw certain portions of the House. All non-members are required to be escorted, and only select ranks of members can bring their guests anywhere within the House without question.*

I take it you're a member of select rank? Bridgette guessed.

Collum's eyes gleaming was answer enough, but he continued: *What is even a littler-known fact is that a fellow member of select rank once showed Baize Sammael more than they should have, and he therefore had knowledge of a few places he shouldn't. This member came into possession of certain artifacts during one of his visits, and he requested they be put where they'd be kept safe. I do not know this to be more than rumor, but it is belief among those who know that whatever Baize Sammael hid here was tucked away so that if war came to Palna — as it eventually did — some Craft things would be preserved.*

The Elusive Grimoire? Bridgette's eyes widened as her mindspeak interrupted his.

He shook his head. *No, that he kept with him until the Ingefeoht,* Collum thought to her. *Though it's in Endorsa, it assuredly would not have been hidden in a place frequented daily by curious college students and graduates. This would have been things that had importance to him, but could be easily overlooked. Like a map.*

Bridgette gazed around them at everything stowed in this attic. There were hundreds of boxes, of *things*, everywhere, in no particular form of organization. *How are we going to find a map in all of this?*

Because I found it when I was a student, and I hid it myself.

Oh, that wicked grin!

"And you thought you'd wait until now to casually reveal you know the whereabouts of Baize Sammael's map of Palna?" Bridgette hissed aloud, trying to decide whether to punch him or laugh at his devilish, youthful behavior.

In truth, I hadn't thought about it in many years, Collum thought to her. *I didn't take too close of a look at it — I was afraid of being walked in on. When I found it I was firstly not supposed to be in the Alcove, but secondly on a time-crunched hunt for something entirely different. However, I do not remember there being any mention of a beach on that map, and I want to be one-thousand percent sure. Ulerion and I weren't by any means more than the most casual of colleagues, but I know he would not lie in his reports. He went to a beach for the new year celebration last January, and we need to find out where.*

She watched quietly as he navigated the towers of boxes and dusty things, whispering various spells as he went, until he was so far back in the attic, she couldn't see him. She felt strangely alone, as if a presence she couldn't see was keeping watch over her. It made her shiver, and she wished Collum would hurry up and return to her sight range.

Come here, he thought to her from the other end of the attic. *Don't trip over anything though.*

Bridgette rolled her eyes and carefully picked her way back toward him. *Where are you?*

Take a left.

She did, and found the Elf unfurling a very old, very yellowed piece of vellum on the floor in front of them. The light was incredibly dim in this area of the attic, and though Collum had full Elven eyesight, Bridgette couldn't quite make out the same level of detail. He snapped his fingers and a tiny blue flame appeared above them, emitting a soft white glow that lit up the faded lines and letters on the paper.

What was the name of the city in Ulerion's report? Collum thought to her, scanning the map.

Larivuria, Bridgette responded, spelling it out for him. She knelt next to the Elf, joining the visual search now that she could see clearer.

Palna was a roughly circular-shaped country. The map didn't show the rest of Heáhwolcen in detail, but pointed out where Fairevella, Endorsa, and Eckenbourne were. Bondrie was founded after the Ingefeoht, so it didn't exist at the time the map had been drawn.

The map was decently large and detailed. It wasn't topographical, but whoever drew it made sure to illustrate various landmarks: the mountain range that began dead center and trailed northwest, between the border of Endorsa and Fairevella, for example. A bold pentacle marked the capital city of Düoria, located southeast of the mountains, nearer the original border of Palna and Eckenbourne. There were forests and lakes, streams and what appeared to be areas reserved for housing and business. But no Larivuria, and no beach.

Maybe Ulerion was wrong, Bridgette thought to Collum. *If he'd never seen a beach, maybe they took him to one of the lakes? This one to the north is pretty far from the capital. Plus the lakes aren't named on here. Maybe this one is named Larivuria, or maybe one of these other cities or towns had its name changed over the years. I mean, when was this map made? It had to be before the 1860s, if it was before the Ingefeoht.*

Bridgette spoke sense, he knew, but something still felt off to the Elf.

Try something for me? he asked, mind-to-mind.

She looked at him. *Anything. Well, except if it involves spiders.*

Collum chuckled. *Not at all. You can call forth your sierwan gift, yes?*

Theoretically … Her mind-voice was hesitant, and she gave him a long look. *I've only done it that one time, when I used it to remember the way to the cottage. Which, by the way, it would have been nice for you to tell me was* yours, *not the Samnung's.*

He punched her lightly in the shoulder. *My apologies, Bright Star.*

You're forgiven. What trouble are we about to get into now?

I wonder if, since you are in the presence of something that belonged to Baize Sammael, you can use that to trigger your sierwan gift.

Bridgette understood immediately. *You want me to see if I can find where he might have hidden what all else is rumored to be hidden here?*

Precisely.

She frowned, and her eyes met his. "I don't know," she whispered out loud. "There's nothing … special about this map. Not that I can feel."

Collum knew she meant "feel" in the sense of auras and intangible barriers she'd been privy to noticing. *Try*, he urged her, mind-to-mind.

Bridgette sighed deeply, then closed her eyes and willed herself to breathe in and out, concentrating on the map in front of her. She touched it, brushed her fingers lightly at the edge, and opened her mind in case there was any sort of spirit or presence that might like to make itself known, to share knowledge with her. After several minutes of silent outreach, she grounded herself back inside the attic and gave Collum a sorrowful look.

Nothing, she thought to him.

It was worth a try, Collum thought back kindly. He rolled up the map and said aloud, "Oscuro." The vellum disappeared in an instant.

Why do you do some magic with spells, and some without? Bridgette asked him, mind-to-mind.

Spells I use more often I'm able to do a bit of mental shorthand, like the scent-casting, he thought back. *I will it to be, and it is so. But in instances like this, where I don't want the map to be visible, but I also don't want to lose it, a specific word or incantation is more helpful in producing the intentional magic. I could have silently willed the map to disappear, but that could have been misconstrued by the universal powers as making it gone forever. By using a deception spell, I glamoured the map to not be seen, but is still carried with my person until I reveal it again.*

Magic is intense, Bridgette thought to him. *I'd probably fuck it right up from the start.*

"You'd learn — we all do," Collum said out loud. "We need to go back to the Caisleán. I suppose it would be helpful for me to also indulge in a stack of those papers, wouldn't it?"

"No shit, Sherlock."

Aurelias was still in the office when the two appeared there, evanescing with much more precision than she'd done that morning. "Where in the seven hells have you two been all day?" she asked.

"Bridgette came across something that I wanted to clarify, so we went to the University," Collum said simply. "We came back for but a moment; I need to get my share of these things."

The fyrdestre handed him a stack, along with a notebook and pen of his own. "Bridgette has the most recent year, I have the one before. Njahla already came for hers, so you have … 2014, it looks like."

"Have you found anything interesting yet?" Bridgette asked her.

"I don't think so," Aurelias replied. "Ulerion likes to write about fashion a lot. I don't think I ever met him; I'd remember him. He seems very colorful."

"He is," Collum said. "I met him a few times. Ulerion came to several Samnung meetings after the death of King Hermann and Queen Lalora, but it's been quite some time since I've seen him. I believe his hair changed color more often than Geongre Akiko's, and that's saying something."

"He sounds like quite a character," Aurelias mused. "Do you think we'll find him?"

"To my knowledge, it's been very hush-hush that he disappeared to begin with," Collum said, hoping there were no prying ears in the hallway. It had been a while since he'd checked the strength on his sensory wards in the Caisleán office, as he was rarely there. "I'm sure we will, though. He probably hasn't disappeared anyway. From the little Bridgette's read already, he was enthralled with several of the cities there that are so unlike the rest of Heáhwolcen. The Tinuviels could have granted him citizenship."

Aurelias clapped him on the shoulder. "That's the spirit, chief. How often are we going to meet to compare notes?"

"You and Njahla can alert me either when you've finished a year's worth, or in the event you find something that is particularly pertinent to our overall research," Collum said. "We can gather all together every few weeks, unless something else comes up."

His fyrdestre nodded, and Collum evanesced he and Bridgette back to his apartment in time to make a hearty evening meal.

~ 47 ~

Their schedule became somewhat routine for a time. Most mornings, Collum would either fix breakfast or leave ingredients for Bridgette if he was gone when she woke. On occasion, they would go into Endorsa for caife calabaza. Usually those were the days they met Trystane, Njahla, and Aurelias at the Caisleán, and Collum made sure to bring back drinks for his Elven comrades. The greater part of the daytime was spent reading for Bridgette, and Collum alternated between his normal fyrdwisa duties and assisting in the research.

Samnung meetings interrupted the norm, but Bridgette took to skipping them after the one when the Elves and Elfling shared their plan. Corria Deathhunter and Aristoces reacted as Trystane had, with quiet reservation that this made sense, and would be the right way forward. Verivol and Bryten were strongly opposed to the concept of the Liluthuaé going anywhere near Palna, and the Sanguisuge actually bared their fangs when Nehemi praised the idea.

Bridgette was somewhat shocked that Nehemi sided with her on this, but realized that of course the queen would: putting Bridgette in charge of strategizing would surely mean if anything went wrong, the Bright Star would be blamed. And if she was harmed in any way, it'd be her own fault. A big opportunity for Nehemi to gloat and tell her fellow Samnung members, "I told you so."

Verivol said as much as they hissed in disagreement with her. "You're only hoping to get her killed."

It was Bridgette who'd calmed them, and Bryten. She stood up to command the room's attention, and said, "While I'm entirely sure that's true, Verivol, we have the problem of not knowing what is happening inside both of those walls, and this is my solution. Palnan officials will be weird about a stranger coming in anyway, but they're going to be real quiet and extra sneaky if someone from the Samnung shows up. It makes the most sense for me to be the one."

She turned to Verivol specifically then, a half-smile playing on her lips. "Thanks for having my back, Verivol. I mean it. But you guys kind of showed up on my doorstep to tell me I was destined to save the world, so it would be really nice if I could like, I don't know, maybe … do it now that I've decided it's worth doing?"

That was that: but the interaction rattled the Elfling, and she told Collum she didn't want to go back unless she had something to share.

"It was like … they put all this faith in me back in the spring, but now that I'm here and doing the damn thing, they have *zero* trust in me," she muttered one morning, swirling a wooden stirring spoon in her mug to blend iced coffee and sweet cream. "It started to make me second-guess if this was the right thing, even though I *know* it's the right way to go about everything. I don't like that, so I'd just rather not go at all."

Instead, she used the time that Collum was in Endorsa each Wednesday to hide away in his paradise of a home office, letting herself breathe methodically into a trance-like state. When he arrived home, he'd go and get her, and their reading, eating, or whatever mundane task the day held began again in earnest.

Bridgette filled her ornate notebook with notes, and sketches when she got bored. It didn't take her long to read Ulerion's reports. They were mostly short, weekly updates. But as she'd suspected, she lacked context. Ulerion would mention various names and other places, ceremonies and foods, and *lots* of fashion — apparently in Palna, which was largely inhabited by witches and wizards, it was commonplace for individuals to dress in much brighter colors and wildly textured fabrics than elsewhere in Heáhwolcen. There was absolutely nothing traditional about the traditions of that place, Bridgette decided. It was as if Baize Sammael had shunned the historical pretenses of magicks of old in an attempt to create an entire culture around his new magic of Craft Wizardry.

Half the time as Bridgette read through a report, she'd have to pause to go look something up. One page — which quickly expanded to four pages and counting — of her notebook was dedicated to names she didn't know. An appendix of sorts. Going into this research, Bridgette was only familiar with Ulerion and the Tinuviels. The ambassador had a habit of name-dropping every few sentences, and the mysterious Sohli was mentioned quite often, but she had no idea who any of them were.

She'd taken to asking Collum to evanesce her to the University at least once a week, and those days she didn't read anything new in Ulerion's reports. Rather, she scoured library shelves and — in her words — pestered Magister Ephynius for as much information as she could glean. Which unfortunately, but not unexpectedly, was not much at all.

Though Ulerion's reports were somewhat eccentric and scattered, the Elfling began to paint a mental picture of what Palna must look like. It seemed a drier climate with a set rainy season, rather than the noted seasonal changes of the rest of Heáhwolcen. Bridgette figured that must have something to do with the magic in the barrier. The country appeared to operate as well as any of the other four would, should it exist only in its own bubble without access to trade or outside influence. There were unusual phrases Ulerion would use occasionally, and Bridgette researched those as well: she didn't know if they were common among all magical beings, or if they were a dialect that evolved in the years since the barrier went up.

Despite her constant hope otherwise, Bridgette hadn't spotted anything that caused her sierwan gift to manifest. Even skimming the others' notes hadn't caused the tell-tale sign of opal eyes. And her companions read so much faster than she did! They, of course, had the benefit of knowing what may be significant enough to note, and didn't seem to care about Ulerion's penchant for writing in a casual tone. It was as if he expected whoever else read his reports to automatically know who and where he was speaking of. None of them did, save a few random names Collum and Trystane remembered from Mohreen's days of spying for them.

It was thus with a frustrated air that Bridgette emerged in the middle of a Tuesday in late July, hair half-falling out of a messy tousle she'd arranged on her head, and slammed a folder of reports at the kitchen table where Collum sat. He jolted: he'd been so caught up in his own task of reading that day's newspaper that he'd blocked out all other minds from his own.

"What?" he asked immediately. "What have you found?"

She threw herself — a very haggard human version of herself, wearing denim leggings and an oversized T-shirt from the diner — into the chair across from him.

"Nothing. I have found *nothing.*"

Collum's sharp eyes softened, and he smiled slightly. "You're frustrated."

"Really? What on Earth could have given that away?" she snapped, but her tone wasn't angry. "Yes, I'm frustrated. I'm so far behind everyone else. You guys are like, practically whittled down into the 1990s and I'm still on my same year. Which isn't even a full year."

"That doesn't matter. You're doing a far more thorough job of researching than any of us are, Starshine."

"Well, yeah, but I still don't *know* anything," she said. "I keep reading through these stupid things, having to stop every five seconds to write something down or go look something up. None of it is helpful to what we need to do."

"But it's helpful to you," Collum said quietly. "You've spent these last weeks learning about Palna. Its culture, its cities. This is good knowledge for you to have before you go in there, is it not?"

"… Oh." She hadn't thought of it that way. "I guess you're right."

"I am right." He cocked an eyebrow playfully. "Why don't we take a break today?"

"And do what?"

"Well," Collum said, sounding a bit guilty, "I feel a terrible host. When you first came back, it was shortly before the Midsummer holiday, and we became so engrossed in our task that I did not even think to break from it to attend the ceremonies and celebrations."

Bridgette rolled her eyes. "That was nice of you."

"I am, therefore, not going to let Lammas pass us by. The official holiday is tomorrow, August 1st, but I already decided we'd take today and be part of the preparation, too."

She knew he was patiently waiting for her to ask what Lammas was: "You know I have no idea; just freaking tell me!"

He laughed. "Lammas is the first of the harvest celebrations. It honors the goddesses Demeter and Ceres, and the grudai, the season's first grains. It is, in true form, Trystane's favorite holiday, as there is *much* drinking involved."

"Grains equal beer and whiskey; I get it."

"And bread. There is a lot of bread."

"What are the preparations we get to be part of today?" Bridgette asked, sitting up in her chair. Ulerion's reports were already forgotten in the excitement of doing something new.

"We'll be going into Endorsa and helping the bakers," Collum replied. "And, my favorite part of being fyrdwisa in relative peace-time, taste-testing the food and drink along with the Samnung."

"Yes. I am in," Bridgette said. "What do I wear and when are we leaving?"

Because the holiday fell on a Wednesday that year, Collum explained as they strode into Galdúr, the Samnung cancelled its meeting for the week as they would all be together for the Lammas tasting. It was an honor for each of the bakers, brewers, distillers, and artisans to have a member of the Samnung bless their wares.

"Bless them? Do we have to like, do a spell?" Bridgette recalled that day at the Maremóhr when she was swept away into the trance of Nehemi's ritual. She didn't feel certain she was up to being that light-headed for the rest of the day, especially after blessing countless items for the ceremonies.

"Yes and no," Collum said. "One of us will likely say an incantation, but it is ceremonial. As religious humans tend to do before beginning a meal."

"Ohh — so literally just a blessing. I can do that," Bridgette said.

Collum led her to the Mimea Botanicci, the sprawling botanical garden that surrounded the grounds of Cyneham Breonna and Deu Medgar. Though she'd seen the gardens before — it was hard to miss them, given that the Cyneham Breonna foyer was somewhat of an extended exhibit — she'd yet to explore them otherwise. Today would be an experience: the soft floral scents were intermingled with warmth, butter and herbs, citrus and spice.

The rest of the Samnung members were waiting for them, dressed in casual clothing except for Nehemi and Cloa, who wore flowing gowns of gold and their coordinating crown and tiara. Even Arctura had a golden collar, and Bridgette could tell the strange cat was displeased with the adornment.

Just follow our lead, Collum said, mind-to-mind. To the Samnung, he offered greetings out loud, and the group walked into the fray. The artisans were arranged as they would be the following day for the main celebration, when all beings of Heáhwolcen who wished to partake would arrive. There was a section for sweet breads and pastries, aisles of savory loaves and butters, a handful of Elves offering dishes of cultivated wild rice. Interspersed throughout were the brewers and distillers, handing out tiny earthenware cups to be sipped from — unless, Collum told Bridgette, a being brought with them an ale horn or their own container that could be filled.

"This is amazing," she murmured. The two were at the back of the Samnung group, watching as Trystane, Aristoces, Nehemi, and Corria Deathhunter alternated as to who would take the first bite or sip and offer praise and thanks. After the Samnung leader did this, the rest were able to partake if they wished. There were dozens of food artisans, and Bridgette lost track of where they were in the gardens the longer they were there. She tried ales and lagers that had such clarity in their light wheated hues; nibbled the most rustic of crusty breads spread with herbed butters. She noticed that ingredients and textures tended to vary based on a maker's magical background, and it astounded her thoroughly.

This loaf of raisin bread is literally glittering, she thought to Collum at one Fairy's table. *And that one next to us has blue crust!*

Blue cornflower ground and added into the dough, he noted, mind-to-mind. *The Fairies do rather enjoy adding more flair than you'll find at the*

Elven booths.

Most curious to Bridgette were the breads from Bondrie. They were more on the savory side and flattened instead of loaved. There were corn and blue corn, wheat and rye, but all had the appearance more of fluffy pancakes or thin tortillas than what Bridgette considered bread.

She asked Collum about it, and he explained that most of Bondrie's citizens hailed from warrior or soldier backgrounds. They were used to living straight off the land and roaming nomadically rather than having houses even in the Elven sense. The food traditions of their peoples were things that could be easily prepared, cooked, cured, and preserved using the heat of the natural sun or over a fire. Or, of course, eaten raw once cleaned.

They are not primitive, nor are they tribal, Collum warned her, mind-to-mind. *Do not address them as such, despite what your Earth history may have taught you. We'll go into Bondrie at some point and Corria Deathhunter will show and tell you of the beings she leads.*

The colonizer mindset, Bridgette thought to herself. She wondered how often it came up in Heáhwolcen, when the descendants of English and American colonists as witches and wizards lived side-by-side with beings she suspected were the descendants of magical indigenous peoples.

"How will tomorrow be different?" Bridgette asked, accepting a tiny cup of amber ale from a Bondrie wizard. He did not hand them things, but rather used a mangled twist of white branch to lift and direct each cup. Nor did he smile with his teeth, but the crinkles around his coal-black eyes were indicative of how pleased he was to be sharing his beverages.

"Firstly, there will be likely as many beings here as there were at Fairevella's Ostara celebration," Collum said, sipping from his own cup. "Deity bless, this is delicious! Secondly, there will be an opening ceremony which will require us to be on stage" — he indicated a platform visible in front of them — "though Nehemi will do most of the speaking. There will also probably be a ritual blessing, but it will not be near as intensive as the one during Emi-Joye's installation. Other than that, it will be much eating and drinking, and there will be performances throughout the day."

"Bread, booze, music. I can dig it," Bridgette said, finishing the amber ale. Collum gave her a bemused look, as he was wont to do when she dropped a modern human expression in the middle of the magical realm.

"It means I'm very excited for more free food," she clarified. "Who wouldn't be?"

~ 48 ~

Perhaps it was Bridgette's preoccupation with the task she'd avoided for two days, and perhaps it was spending so much time in the shadow of the Endorsan queen, but Lammas would not go down in history as her favorite celebration in Heáhwolcen — despite the free food. She much preferred the freedom of dancing at Ostara to the feigned ceremonies that preceded the granary festival, and liked flower crowns more than the linen wrap dresses and tops they each had to wear. Allegedly the garb was to honor the "traditional" attire of farmers of old, but Bridgette was pretty sure it was just an excuse for Nehemi to make everyone else look like shit while she and Cloa shone onstage.

Indeed, the Endorsan royalty wore wrap dresses, tied expertly across one hip with the ends of the tie draping beautifully down the length of their legs. Foregoing their usual crowns, both the queen and princess had circlets of meadowsweet pinned to their hair. Each of the Samnung leaders also had a woven capelet draped around their shoulders in colors complimentary to their wraps. Bridgette was grateful for Aristoces, Verivol, and Bryten: it was as if the three of them intentionally dressed themselves in such a way as to poke fun at this strange attire. Aristoces' wrap did not have sleeves, and instead was wound tightly across her bust, tying artfully at the side for a high-low hem effect over a floor-length skirt. Ostensibly her top was to allow more freedom of movement in her wings, as sleeved tops did not suit that well. Bryten was predictably shirtless, but wore a length of woven linen tied around his hips at the top of his leggings. And Verivol wore a wrap dress that rivaled Nehemi's, dyed a rich shade of plum wine that matched Bridgette's. Verivol tied their dress in such a way that it opened down the front, revealing their pearlescent white, muscled chest and legs clad in mustard-gold leggings.

"You're amazing," Bridgette whispered to the Sanguisuge. "You and Bryten. I fucking love it."

Nehemi, predictably, scowled upon seeing them. She took in Bryten, then Verivol, slowly up and down, looking as though she smelled something horrible in front of her and wanted to see where the stench radiated from.

"It is an affront to our agrarian ancestors for the two of you to wear your traditional garments in such a manner," she murmured angrily.

Verivol smirked, showing their fangs. "The Sanguisuges of old had little need for agrarian lifestyles, Your Majesty."

She didn't respond, and turned on her heels, gracefully ascending the staircase to the raised stage.

The rest of the Samnung followed, and Bridgette found herself trailing at the back with Collum and Cloa. The princess closed her eyes as they walked, taking deep sniffs of the heady, aromatic air around them. She and Kharis hadn't been at the tasting, Bridgette recalled.

"Where were you yesterday?" the Elfling asked before she could stop herself.

Cloa turned her head. Those glassy, glazed eyes of dull greenish hazel met Bridgette's, and the princess spoke in that singsong, dreamlike manner of hers: "I was at my studies."

"Studying what?" The Elfling found she had an urge to get the young witch to talk, to come out of her shell. "Magic?"

"Languages and mathematics, penmanship and history, runes and culinary arts," Cloa said, a shy smile pulling up one corner of her mouth, though her eyes were unfocused again. "It is unseemly for a princess to study the raw arts."

The fuck is a 'raw art?' Bridgette asked Collum, mind-to-mind. When he didn't respond, she realized he was listening just as closely to their conversation. She asked the princess instead.

"What do you mean, 'raw arts?'"

But as the three of them ascended the staircase, she found she'd have to wait for an answer regardless. The vast crowd assembled at the Mimea Botanicci began to hush in anticipation of Queen Nehemi presiding over the Lammas tables.

Bridgette didn't care about the ceremony: she was far more interested in decoding the perhaps fifteen words Cloa had spoken to her, so she again beseeched Collum in silent question to explain.

Is Cloa not allowed to study magic?

He glanced at her, just barely. *I do not know. I've never thought to question what the princess does or does not study.*

She just told me, when I asked her about it, that it's 'unseemly' for a princess to study whatever the hell 'the raw arts' are. I'm going to take that as a 'no.'

Why does this bother you so, Starshine?

It was hard for Bridgette to keep their secret for a moment. She nearly whipped her head to Collum and shouted at him, but managed to put her angst aside just in time. *It bothers me because she's a witch, Collum. And not just a witch, but the one I guess who is supposed to rule Endorsa if Nehemi ever kicks the bucket. How is she supposed to prepare for that without being trained? It would be different if she was a kid, I guess, but she's what, sixteen? Shouldn't she be learning to cast spells and do rituals like the one we're about to be part of?*

Ah. The Elf understood, at least in part. He supposed it was odd, perhaps, that Cloa wasn't being outwardly taught magic — though the term "raw arts" befuddled him. The only childhood magical education he had experience with was his own, and his parents began honing him in his abilities at a young age. But Elven magic was different in some ways than witchcraft, because of Elves' deep connection with Nature: Elves did not need spells to the same extent that human-descended beings did. The Universe understood Elven, and Fairy, magic in its collective subconscious, much better than it did witchcraft.

However, for Cloa to be any semblance of a witch, she *would* need tutelage in the subject. Not only did witches and wizards need to learn to control and direct their magics, they had a much greater necessity for memorizing what must be endless spells and wand motions. A never-ending dance with the Universe, magic was. Where Elves, Fairies, and certain other beings were born into the perfect partnership — one moves, the other moves with them — witchcraft had to first become acquainted. There was a courtship, a learning of one to the other, the awkward phases of stepping on toes and unintended consequences, before *finally* they meshed and could dance together in unison and with grace.

Cloa has done magic, he thought back to Bridgette, after long moments of considering. *I have seen her accidentally perform spells, and she did not seem to realize what was happening. Nehemi did, though, and chastised her, now that I think about it. Not a true scolding, but more the reaction of an exasperated parent whose child is misbehaving. Perhaps whatever ails Cloa causes her magic to behave differently, so it is best for her not to utilize it.*

Bridgette processed that; her thoughts interrupted by Nehemi beginning the ritual blessing of Lammas. She hadn't paid a lick of attention to the ceremony at hand and was caught off-guard by the queen inviting the goddesses Demeter and Ceres into their midst. Lammas was also an occasion for the four elements to be brought forth. In the northern, southern, eastern, and western regions of the garden, great bowl-shaped vessels were filled with either softly rippling water, sky-licking flames, mounds of colored earth, or silvered phantom breezes.

The Elfling willingly gave herself over to the magic as it enveloped them, though she paid little mind to what Nehemi said in the blessing itself. Her head was elsewhere, wondering what was so wrong with their princess that she could not be allowed to perform the magic she'd been born into. Bridgette felt — and she shuddered at the words, remembering that day of the strange aura — an odd form of kindred spirit for the strange girl. She did indeed want to be this girl's friend, her protector, although in that moment she was unsure if the protection would be from whatever shadowed Heáhwolcen … or protection from the vile, overshadowing presence that was Queen Nehemi.

Following the ceremony as they descended the staircase, Bridgette again tried to talk to Cloa.

"Tell me about the raw arts?" she asked. "Please, I mean. I've never heard of that before."

The princess gave her another dreamy stare. "It is unseemly for a princess to study the raw arts."

Is she a robot? Bridgette thought to Collum, but to Cloa, she said, "Yes, I heard you say that already. But that doesn't tell me what the raw arts *are*."

Cloa looked at her, considering, and Bridgette swore she saw an odd gleam flicker in the glassy eyes, flicker so quickly she decided she imagined it. But Cloa held her gaze more intensely than she had before, and tilted her head to one side. She said, or sang, rather:

"Artists with brushes some do paint,
Artists with clay, vessels do make.
Artists with tools, things they create.
Artists without, are stronger in mind
And do not rely on tools of any kind."

Bridgette did not have a clue what the princess was on about. "So what, magic is a raw art because it requires you to use a tool? A wand?"

The princess said nothing, but pet a purring Arctura in a noncommittal response. Bridgette wasn't even sure Cloa was paying attention to her anymore. She turned to Collum, a few steps behind them as they stepped onto the gravel pathway to begin walking through the garden.

A little help, please? Can't you hear her thoughts?

He gave her a bemused look. *I can, but Princess Cloa ... does not think in the same way others do. Her mind is a cacophony of voices, and unfortunately they make as little sense as what she speaks aloud does.*

The princess has multiple personalities? Bridgette thought to him incredulously. Well *that* certainly explained a reluctance to let her do magic, given from what the Elfling had seen about multiple personality disorders on television shows ...

No. His thought back to her was so sharp that Bridgette thought Collum had spoken aloud. She whipped her head to him, eyes wide.

No, he continued, his thought-voice softer. *She does not have a multiple personality disorder, nor does she have multiple personalities any more than the average being does. Cloa is one being, but with the ability to have much going on in her mind at one time. The voices are all hers, simultaneous branches of thought from the same neural tree. She constantly has, of all things, music humming in the background of her mind, too.*

It is as though she is unable to compartmentalize, perhaps, he continued, mind-to-mind. *If you imagine the mind as a file cabinet, think of hers as having all or most of the drawers open to rifle through at the same time. Cloa is able to flit between her drawers and back again within seconds of one another, whereas you and I are much better at closing almost every drawer before focusing on one or two. Perhaps one is in the forefront, and there is another partially open that we can think about, but just as quickly dismiss until we are able to give it our full attention. Because of this, because she has so many threads of thought and inner monologue, it is difficult for me to decipher. But when she spoke to you, there was only a ... a muffled buzzing noise in the background. She put her full attention on answering you, but just as quickly as she did, she was back in her clutter of file cabinets.*

As much as Bridgette wanted this knowledge, and still wanted to know what was off about the princess, it made her uncomfortable to now have it stuck in her own brain. She chose to go with Collum and walk the festival, hoping more bread and beer would take her mind off trying to figure Cloa out. They had a bit of an upper hand compared to most of the beings there, having mapped it out the previous day, and were able to make quick work of visiting their favorite booths.

The actual Lammas celebrations were slightly different than the Samnung tasting day, as several tables were set up now with earthenware mugs and platters for beings to take with them and pile high with treats. Periodically, someone would come by to pick up dirtied dishes and drop off freshly cleaned ones, grabbing snacks of their own as they did so.

It was a merry atmosphere, and Bridgette did like the gleeful music playing, but felt oddly constrained in Endorsa.

There was a pomp and circumstance here that she could have lived without, and after a few hours of endless strolling, being introduced to Elves and Fairies and witches and entire new-to-her species of beings, Bridgette thought she was going to lose her mind.

I really hate this, she confided to Collum via the ísenwaer.

He shot a look at her. *What?*

This small-talk. All these people. Or, beings, I mean, she thought back. *It's just so much going on, and it's all surface-level interaction. I want to get to know people and not talk about the weather, for Pete's sake. And I never thought I would willingly say this, but after two days of eating bread and beer, I could really go for a vegetable.*

Collum chuckled, putting an arm around the Elfling's shoulders. "Shall we venture into the shops of Galdúr?" he asked out loud.

"Whatever you want, so long as I'm out of this place," she grimaced.

Bridgette breathed a sigh of relief, one she hadn't realized she'd been holding in, the moment they were exited of the gardens. The air was fresh and clean, the faint sound of windchimes in the breeze filling the space in her ears.

"You're not going to be sick, are you?" Collum asked, concern washing over his face at her deep breaths.

"No," she replied. "I didn't feel like, the aura sickness or whatever it is. I just genuinely don't like networking-type events where I have to constantly be filtered and be *on* all the time. Pretending to be interested in the random day-to-day stuff people were saying in there to each other, and to us. I'd much rather have been able to talk with the artisans and bakers whose stuff I really liked. Asking their process, their history, that kind of thing."

"I see. So Ostara suited you better then, because it was all revelry?"

Bridgette grinned. "Yep."

"Duly noted," the fyrdwisa smiled back. "Though our duties with the Samnung do require a fair bit of, as you said, networking, I will do my best to ensure we make our appearances and then quietly leave when the opportunity arises."

She squeezed an arm around his waist. "Thanks, Bundy."

The streets they walked down seemed empty compared to the crowd left behind at Mimea Botanicci, but they were still bustling. A familiar face was suddenly at their side, and Bridgette started as Aurelias — sipping from a silver ale horn — threw an arm around her empty shoulder.

"Tráthnóna mistéireach!" Aurelias cried in feigned formality. "The great fyrdwisa and the Bright Star walk among us! Deity Dhaoibh, to what do we owe this great honor?"

Collum rolled his eyes. His fyrdestre could be *just* like

Bridgette sometimes, with the sass and sarcasm that oozed from both their mouths. Seven hells, it was probably why he could get along with the Bright Star so easily: he'd been doing this for decades by the time he was sent to find her.

"Hello, Aurelias," he laughed. "We were being rather stifled in the crowd."

"Oh, an escape! How very daring of you, Fyrdwisa!" Her visible eye glinted with merriment, aided by however much ale she'd been enjoying at the festival. "Where are we off to now?"

"*We*," Collum said pointedly, "are going shopping. You are welcome to join us, of course."

"Shopping?" Aurelias turned and pouted at Bridgette. "I thought you, I, and Njahla were supposed to go shopping for you!"

Bridgette smiled and freed herself from under both of their arms. "What the hell. Bring her too. Let's go spend all Collum's money on pretty leggings … and something besides this linen tunic from Hades."

"I hate the both of you," the fyrdwisa muttered, as Aurelias gave him a mischievous look, and evanesced back to procure their Elven comrade.

~ 49 ~

"Was Nehemi always like this?" Bridgette asked Collum several hours later, as they sipped chamomile tea under the night sky in his "office."

They'd spent the afternoon with Aurelias and Njahla, joyous and entirely frivolously, picking out a few pairs of leggings and fitted pants, plus tunics and tanks, for Bridgette. Collum paid for some with his Samnung wages; others, the shopkeepers either refused payment entirely — citing their fyrdwisa's job well-done as payment aplenty — or bartered with Bridgette on ways she could pay in kind. One had a son who wished to learn an instrument, and the violin student offered her expertise in exchange for a handwoven silk wrap top that was similar to the Lammas outfit she wore, but of a much finer fabric and tie-dyed coral pattern.

Collum was caught off-guard by her question, having been lost in his own mind, which was very far from the Queen of Endorsa. "Like what?"

"She's so haughty and pompous, like she's better than everyone else for some reason. And not necessarily cruel, but she's got a mean streak a mile wide. Like the magical world's version of Napoleon or something," Bridgette said. "She's only been queen for what, sixteen years? So you knew her growing up, right?"

Collum finished his tea and laid back on the soft grass. "Somewhat."

"Stop being so vague, Bundy. What was she like?"

"You must understand, Starshine, that Nehemi was thrust into her position without much training. In fact, because she was shrouded from us for her entire life until her parents' death, I'm not sure at all what sort of training and schooling she had," Collum said. "Queen Lalora was absent for years and had only very recently begun attending Samnung meetings and events again when she was killed. I'm assuming that whatever schooling and royal training Nehemi had, it was done in secret at the behest of Lalora. Kharis probably tutored her as well. He was the only one outside of the royal couple who even knew she existed, much less that she was the princess and heir.

"That day Kharis came to the Samnung to tell us what happened, and brought Nehemi and baby Cloa to us, was the first time we met Nehemi. She was *so* young, and suddenly was a queen and a single mother, with not only a babe to rear but an entire country and magical world looking up to her leadership. Because she materialized out of nowhere, there were only a few days for the Samnung to know her before she was officially crowned queen," Collum reminisced. "The Nehemi I met in those days was quieter, but just as cunning as she is now. There is an ice to her that I do not think can ever be fully thawed, and I do not know if it is a mask she wears or if it is truly her personality. King Hermann and Queen Lalora were not like her at all, but she spent decades locked up with Lalora in secret. Who knows what sort of behavior that wrought on her."

"And too," he continued, "I was thrust into the fyrdwisa position in those same few days. I had much more preparation for this role than Nehemi did for hers, but we were both fledgling leaders in our own rights. Endorsa has always been looked to as the leading country of Heáhwolcen, because it was the first to be founded. I think perhaps Nehemi learned to act older than her years as a way to fill this role expected of her."

"Oh," was all Bridgette could think to say.

Collum turned to look at her, observing her pensive position in the grass, ankles crossed with her arms wrapped around, pulling her knees to her chest so she could rest her head on them.

"You really don't like her, do you?" he asked.

"Do you?"

Collum spat out a laugh. "A fair question, Starshine. I'm not sure. I don't know that I was ever given a chance to like her, because she chose to dislike all of us almost immediately. That is a hard battle to overcome."

"I guess," Bridgette said. "I don't like her. At all. I think she's a total passive-aggressive bitch, and I think she's threatened by me. Why a half-Elf who can't do magic to save her life is a threat though, I couldn't tell you."

The next morning, Collum was off doing something before Bridgette woke, and she entered the kitchen to find a note in his spidery cursive telling her she was left to her own devices. Eloise would be stationed at the apartment gate while he was away, should she wish to venture out at all.

She sighed and rummaged through the refrigerator in search of the iced peach tea they'd let steep overnight. She'd need all the caffeine to function and focus today, the Elfling could already tell. Collum had been thoroughly perplexed by the concept both of iced tea and *sweetened* iced tea when he first saw them as menu options during his time in the southern states, and Bridgette finally convinced him to try making it. Thus far, they'd discovered success with a creamy Earl Grey blend, which had vanilla and bergamot, and peach was the summery variety she wanted to try next.

Bridgette poured herself a tall glass, then grabbed a muffin from the breadbox. Aurelias apparently not only grew strawberries that the Coffee Cauldron witches loved, but she could turn them into mean baked goods, too. The fyrdestre sent some home with the two before Lammas, and Bridgette was particularly pleased that magic allowed for preserving spells to keep them from drying out as quickly as they would have on Earth.

She took a large bite out of the treat and hauled over her stack of reports, her notebook, and pens. There were only two months of reports left for her partial year of getting to know Ulerion Mewt, and she was long ready to be done with this task and move on to something slightly more exciting than endless bookwork.

In July 2017, Ulerion and most of Palna seemed preoccupied with a coming "celestial phenomenon, the likes of which had not been observed in many decades." Bridgette rolled her eyes as she read Ulerion's excitement at the pending solar eclipse. She remembered this; had been at her university when it occurred in August the previous year. It *had* been pretty cool; she'd give it that. The student population at her college was relatively small, especially compared to the traditional university a few miles down the road, so to have thousands upon thousands of students and faculty, plus community members, gather in the blistering August heat and humidity was a rather unique experience.

They'd each been handed a pair of special sunglasses to wear, and brought blankets and beach towels to spread out on the campus green. The total solar eclipse meant that the moon was between the Earth and the sun — specifically the August new moon, per Ulerion — blocking its golden rays from fully dappling the planet. When people put on their special glasses and looked at the sun, all they could see for a few minutes was a black circle ensconced in a fiery crown. The Earth had gone from summer day to red twilight, to watery dawn and back again in a matter of minutes, making Bridgette wonder philosophical questions about space and time, about the interconnectivity of beings and Nature.

What an Elven set of thoughts, she chuckled to herself, remembering — and realizing. *Maybe I'm less crazy than I thought.*

Bridgette tore a page from her notebook and scratched out a reminder. She wondered if the rest of Heáhwolcen harbored the same excitement as Palna did surrounding this eclipse.

"It's not as if they're like, rare," she muttered. It did seem a little odd that Ulerion was so excited about something that happened pretty frequently. Although the American media had made quite a fuss about it, too. Something about the 2017 solar eclipse being a *total* eclipse and being visible during the day in North America, she vaguely recalled.

A few hours and a sandwich later, Bridgette grinned broadly as she beheld the *final* report in her first stack. There were still hundreds to go, of course, dating back as far as she knew they'd need to read, but this was a monumental burden about to be off her shoulders.

A Summation of Goings and Sights, as Reported on the 21st Day of the Eighth Month of the Year Two Thousand Seventeen
Prepared and Respectfully Submitted to Aristoces, Fairy of All Fairies, and the governing officials of Fairevella, by Ulerion Mewt

Tráthnóna mistéireach, ceannairí mine! I write to you my report in the early hours of this morning, as our Palnan colleagues and I make final preparations for the Nunta Alchimica. It is estimated we will be able to observe its effects at approximately 2:40 post-noon in the United States Eastern timezone, which is the local hour utilized by Palna for its timekeeping devices (as it is too for Fairevella, of course!). It is my understanding that the celebration and rituals will last all day, as it is most important for the energy to be maximized when the Nunta Alchimica reaches its peak. We are to begin with ceremonies in Düoria this morning and traverse to various other stopping points in the country, repeating the ritual ceremony at each. Ydessa and her advisors have been working non-stop toward this for an age now, and while I do not fully grasp the magnitude of her desire and anticipation, I am delighted to be both a participant and observer!

In this past week as the preparations became more hurried, I was able to glean more details about the Nunta Alchimica and its powerful energy correlations with these witches and wizards. This ancient magickal practice they plan to continue today honors the joining of the Sol and Lunaria as one, and for that brief moment when their union coats the worlds in darkness in the middle of the day, an astonishing energy is produced for both ultimate balance and chaos! Mine own magic is so very different that I do not, as I mentioned, understand how this can be, but I look very much forward to honoring and learning from these strange traditions surrounding the Great Celestia.

Sohli did not tell me if there was a certain attire expected for such a grand occasion, but I am doing my best to honor the union and energies. We procured a set of robes specially designed with wing flaps. They're made of truly the finest velvet I have ever experienced, and fashioned in such a way that the fabric glimmers both indigo and silver as the light catches it. Sohli is quite impressed with how they turned out and I would not be surprised if he arrives today in a similar set himself! The rituals we will be part of are complicated, from what I understand. I've only been part of such things done in Endorsa, so I am elated to see how Ydessa's rituals compare! I was tasked off and on these past months with assisting in making the elemental charms that will be distributed and worn by Palnan citizens during the festivities. They are lovely little things: glass vials on gold cord filled with select herbs and oils. So many of them have been made as keepsakes for this auspicious occasion!

Ulerion's report prattled on for several pages, and he seemed to repeat himself a lot, sharing how excited he was about this, that, and the other aspect of being part of the eclipse, or "Nunta Alchimica." Bridgette craved details he seemed to leave out: Why did the Tinuviels care so much about *this* eclipse, when surely there had been a zillion others in their lifetimes? What were the rituals Ydessa planned to repeat all day long? How could a people who weren't supposed to do magic perform a

ritual powerful enough to capture such energy? And, the
question that seemed to prick at her the most, *why* was it
necessary for this energy to exist?

She wondered if the ambassador either truly hadn't thought
to ask, so mesmerized as he seemed to be with Palna, or if he
wasn't permitted to say. The former seemed more likely, given
his flighty and eccentric demeanor. All seemed to be well for
him, this visitor of strange beaches and observer of illegal magic.

Bridgette skimmed the final page, excitement building in her
mind. She was almost done and could finally go to a new year of
reports, maybe even under Ulerion's predecessor. She had no
idea how far into the thirty years of his leadership her three
fellow researchers had read.

> A new time seems to be upon us in this country,
> not unlike the millennial celebrations of years past,
> though as you'll recall, there was less ritual then.
> I must sign off for now, ceannairí mine. A grand
> day of learning and magic awaits us as we
> commemorate the Nunta Alchimica and harness
> the energies of the Ballamúr!
>
> Respectfully yours and blessed be.
> Wy árung,
>   Ulerion Mewt

Ballamúr. Why did that word sound oddly familiar?
Bridgette read Ulerion's last few reports again, quicker this time.
She didn't recall reading that term anywhere else, but it played
with the tendrils of her sierwan gift, egging her conscious mind to
connect some scattered pattern of dots that she hadn't picked up
on. A third time she read that final paragraph.

"Ballamúr," she mused out loud, puzzling it out on her
tongue.

Her eyes went wide, and she dropped the pages on the floor.

~ 50 ~

"Eloise!" Bridgette shouted. She wasn't even sure the door had shut behind her, so fast had she bolted from Collum's kitchen. "Eloise!"

The Unicorn appeared calmly in her path, golden coat sheening. She was saddled, as she had been that first day they met.

"Liluthuaé, what is your hurry? Is something wrong?"

Bridgette didn't know how much the Unicorns knew of the Samnung's plan, of her and Collum's task to read more than a century's worth of documents, but she didn't have time to process the rights and wrongs of what she might reveal.

"Yes. Very wrong. I need to see Collum right now. It's an emergency."

All the Elfling could think about was how, even with as fast as the Unicorn could gallop, it would still likely take a couple hours to reach the fyrdwisa. And that was assuming he was in Eckenbourne. She wished beyond words she could fly straight to him — she knew it would be faster, harnessing the power of the wind beneath her invisible wings, than the ride they were about to undertake.

Eloise asked no questions, and lowered her head to allow Bridgette to climb on. She took off so fast the world around them was a blur as they sped through it, at the top speed her hooves could offer.

Come on, come on! Bridgette silently urged the Unicorn. And to Collum, on the off-chance he could pick up on it, she pleaded to him via the ísenwaer to find them. *Please, please, please, Bundy …*

She had no concept of how much time had passed when finally, *finally*, Collum could hear her and reply.

Are you safe? You're panicking, Bridgette, what's wrong? His thought-voice was concerned, even from however far away he was.

I know what happened in Palna and —

Eloise halted abruptly as navy dark whirls spiraled in the air in front of them. Collum appeared, jaw set, and extended a hand to the Elfling. "I'll take her, Eloise. I appreciate your sensitivity in this matter greatly."

The Unicorn lowered her head. "Do I need remain here, Fyrdwisa?"

Collum waved a hand, and her saddle and stirrups disappeared. "No. I thank you, annwyl. You are yours, and she is in my care now."

Whatever formal exchange that was gave Bridgette a moment to collect her indeed panicked thoughts. She watched as Eloise trotted away into the woods. No, not into the woods, out of, Bridgette realized. Collum had been somewhere in the woods. She hadn't noticed it with how fast they were going.

"What?" Collum asked, his blue eyes searching hers. They were wide, the opalescent flecks glittering intensely.

The wall. The Ballamúr. How long has it been up? Bridgette asked, mind-to-mind. Her heart was racing, both from the Unicorn travel and the anxiety of what she knew.

What wall? What is the Ballamúr?

Fuck, Bundy! The inner wall in Palna — it's called the Ballamúr — how long has it been up?

He looked at her, perplexed. *At least two decades.*

Who told you that? She needed him to figure it out, too. Partly so she could process this herself.

We knew of the Palnan barrier inside our own for years. I was still fyrdestre when that knowledge came to the Samnung, by way of our ... spies.

Bridgette resisted the urge to growl. Mohreen had indeed played a bigger part in this than she'd let on.

The last time anyone heard from Ulerion was August 21, 2017. Do you know what happened on that date? the Elfling asked him, mind-to-mind.

No ...? I was on Earth though, and Nehemi had largely cut off my communication at that time. I submitted my own reports, but got very few in return.

Collum. Bridgette's hands were shaking as they spoke mind-to-mind. *There was a total solar eclipse on August 21, 2017.*

The Elf still had no idea how any of this was connected, nor why it was sending the Bright Star on the verge of a panic attack.

I was on Earth for that, yes? he thought to her.

"Fucking fuck, Bundy," she said out loud, giving up on feeding him clues. "Ydessa Tinuviel harnessed the solar eclipse energy to activate the Ballamúr, to actually power the barrier wall, and bring magick back into existence in Palna."

"What —"

But Bridgette interrupted him. "Ulerion didn't disappear because he *actually* disappeared. Ulerion disappeared because that barrier is powered by Craft magic. Before the eclipse it was pretty much just a shield, but once it had power? It's like the Seolfurmúr in front of the Seledreám; that's how I figured this out. The fully powered Ballamúr cut off his ties to Aristoces, just like you and Trystane suggested had happened. Ydessa prepared for this for *years*. They knew," she groaned. "The Tinuviels *knew* that Craft magic could be reactivated under a total solar eclipse. I don't know how they knew it was possible. But that day, the day of the eclipse — Ulerion called it the 'Nunta Alchimica' — Ydessa went around the entire country and performed some ritual and each Palnan citizen was given a charmed necklace, a little glass vial full of herbs and oils and shit, as a keepsake. But it's *not* a keepsake, it was a way to collect and utilize everyone's energy to activate the Ballamúr at the exact right time when the sky went dark over Palna."

Her words made such stark, unexpected sense that Collum openly gaped at her, unable to decide what words he'd speak first.

"Craft Wizardry is powerful enough to take down the initial barrier," he said after a long moment. "They're going to wait until whatever moment they deem is right, and they're going to barrel right through the wall and overthrow the Samnung with magick we don't know how to stop."

Bridgette nodded. "And we won't know when. Or how."

He looked at her, dread filling his heart. "Until you go in and figure it out."

She squared her shoulders, and her eyes finally became her own again. "Until I go in and figure it out."

Trystane ran his hands through his ice-blonde hair, loosening it free from its usual braid. "This moves our timeline up significantly."

Collum nodded gravely. They'd convened an emergency Samnung meeting that night — "So much for only having to see Nehemi at Lammas this week," Bryten had muttered to Bridgette — and the fyrdwisa and Liluthuaé shared all they'd come to know in the past several hours.

"If the Ballamúr has only been … active, as you say, for a year or two, that is nowhere near time enough for an entire fighting force to be assembled," Nehemi said. She'd been notably quieter this evening, a silence further felt due to the absence of Cloa. Perhaps that exchange Collum witnessed between Nehemi and Bridgette had more of an effect than anyone realized.

"You're assuming, Your Majesty, that the Tinuviels are only just beginning to put such a military together," Corria Deathhunter said somberly. The Ifrinnevatt spirits in the corner of the chamber seemed to titter, as if they agreed.

No one said anything for a long, long minute.

"Ulerion's reports, the ones I read anyway, didn't mention anything about a military force. But if the Tinuviels thought he'd share that information with Aristoces, they probably kept it a secret," Bridgette said, breaking the silence.

Collum echoed her statement — none of the others recalled reading about anything of the sort either.

"What is to be your timeline, then?" Nehemi asked Bridgette.

The Elfling looked at Collum and Trystane. "We still have a lot of unanswered questions when it comes to Palna. I think we need to … maybe break off into groups for this. Y'all know that Collum, Aurelias, Njahla, and I have been reading Ulerion's reports. We should pause and instead look to the period that the Ballamúr most likely first went up. Ulerion does this thing when he writes, where he just kind of throws terms and names out there, as if whoever is reading his reports should automatically know what he's talking about. Those 2017 reports, for example, he's referencing someone or something that he reported on before. He just casually dropped the term 'Ballamúr' and like, if I wasn't a sierwan, I doubt I would have realized the importance of that word," Bridgette replied. "While whoever is reading and learning more about the wall, Collum and I need to go to Earth and find the Druids. We'll do that, then when I get back, I guess … send me in."

"No," Collum said sharply.

She shot him a serious look. "The hell do you mean, 'no'? We already went over all of this weeks ago."

"You're not going into Palna unprepared," the fyrdwisa said, his voice edged. "You aren't able to do magic, fine. But you at the *very* least need to know how to protect yourself from harm. You'll train with the Fórsaí Armada before you go, and I'll work with you daily on your mind-strength."

"Herewosa Donnachaidh will teach her himself," Nehemi volunteered immediately. "Arrange travel for the two of you to Earth. When you return, Bridgette, you will be a wígend."

"A what?"

The queen stared at her. "A wígend. A training warrior. Just like Collum, Aurelias, Aristoces, and Trystane."

Bridgette momentarily ignored the knowledge that Trystane and Aristoces were trained warriors, and her mind briefly felt as though it was ping-ponging between one revelation after another, too fast to keep up.

"I would feel more comfortable sending the two of you on this journey with an ambassador. Emi-Joye will accompany you," Aristoces said.

Bridgette's mind paused its ping-ponging.

"Why not the ambassador to Wales, since that's where we're going?" the Elfling asked, confused.

"As you already know her, it makes sense for her to join you. Apostine can manage the duties of office during your absence," the Fairy answered.

Bridgette's eyes shifted fast enough for only she and Collum to notice, but things were moving so quickly they barely had time to process a shared thought before the meeting continued: Aristoces was not being entirely honest with them, though the context eluded her sierwan gift.

Trystane volunteered himself, Njahla, and Aurelias to continue with the Palna research. Verivol and Bryten piped up to offer their aid.

Bridgette felt her panic begin to rise. She'd tamped it down so well for so long since returning to Heáhwolcen, but this day … it was eating her alive. *This is happening so, so fast, Bundy.*

He squeezed her thigh under the table. *We will do this, and we will do this well. We will not hurry.*

Aloud, he echoed his own words: "As Trystane said, this moves our timeline up. But I caution each of us to not attempt to hurry. Hurrying, making anxious preparations — these are all things that could easily alert citizens that something is amiss. There is still no need to cause panic. Bridgette, Emi-Joye, and I will make preparations to leave for Earth in the next couple of weeks, and we will return in time for Mabon. The Liluthuaé will train for several months, and continue researching with us, to prepare herself for Palna."

Collum turned to each of the four leaders. "We must prepare our own forces as well. The Guard, the Bródenmael, the Cailleach, the Mîleta, the Fyrdlytta, the Caomhnóir Feeric. It has been an age since all will come together as one. Not since the Ingefeoht have we needed all branches of the Armada, and we were unprepared then. We will not be unprepared this time."

Trystane stood, followed by Corria Deathhunter, Nehemi, and Aristoces.

"Nonóir es linne. The honor is ours," they said in stoic unison.

~ 51 ~

Aristoces remained standing while the other three resumed their seats. "I will speak with the ambassadora first thing in the morning and share with her the part she and Apostine will play in this."

Bridgette bristled slightly. She hadn't even seen the Fairy since her first trip to Heáhwolcen. She wondered, not for the first time, what Emi-Joye made of that strange meeting and her own abrupt departure.

The Fairy of All Fairies' announcement was met with nods from the full Samnung. Aristoces sat, then continued: "I am sure she, too, will request to know why we chose her to accompany you as opposed to Ambassador Whitby Lenoir, who is appointed to Wales. Emi-Joye is well-aware of the delicacy of your position, Liluthuaé, and will be as sworn to protect it as we are. I will ask her to glean what she can of Wales from Whitby, so as to best prepare all of you for this journey."

"Will you please ask her to glean information of the Druids? Specifically, who their leader is and how to find that individual," Collum piped up. "This will not be a sight-seeing trip, and it need not last more than a day or so. Perhaps three, in case we need some time to wheedle with the leader for the answers we seek."

The Fairy turn to him. "Would you like to join me in the morn, Fyrdwisa? You could explain precisely what you're looking for from the Druids, and pick up additional Palnan ambassador reports as well. I will instruct our historians to make available copies of the time period in question. That would be … the early to mid-1990s, yes?"

Collum did the math quickly in his head. "I believe so, yes. I would be glad to, Ceannairí."

She smiled at him. "And so it shall be."

Aristoces' summons arrived earlier than he intended the following morning. A warm tingling on his wrist woke the fyrdwisa from a restless sleep, and he blinked blearily at the stack of covenant bracelets. The one made of four bands of twisted metal, specifically the silver of Fairevella, glowed brightly. He took that to mean Aristoces was at the Seledreám and would see him at his leisure. Collum sincerely hoped she didn't think he'd be awake at this deity-damned hour otherwise; the sun had barely broken the horizon.

He dressed in somewhat professional attire — one of the tunics embroidered with the twisted golden "E" emblem of Eckenbourne — and snapped his fingers to set coffee brewing. Perhaps the earlier he left, the sooner her could come back. Early rising was not one of the Bright Star's chief attributes, and Collum felt her growing *so* distant these past weeks. They were both engrossed in their research, her especially, and he was still fyrdwisa with a job to do, houseguest or no. He never pried; never allowed himself to tune in to her mind; but the light and carefree Bridgette he met this past spring was changing. And he was not sure that he liked this change.

I harped so much on this task of hers, these responsibilities, and it's all becoming real, he mused, leaning against the counter as the coffee dripped its way into his earthenware travel mug. *She's losing herself, becoming so focused on this.*

With a start, he recognized exactly what Bridgette was doing, though he knew she might not realize it herself yet. The Elfling was acting just as he had when first appointed fyrdwisa: going so headstrong into his role after trauma that it consumed him whole.

That'll be a fun conversation when I get home. Seven fucking hells, this female. But he smiled in spite of himself, and evanesced to the Seledreám.

"Fáilte, Fyrdwisa!" one of the winged guards called out. "What brings you to the Seledreám at such an early hour?"

Collum laughed as he approached and raised his coffee in a mock toast. "Nonóir es linne, Caomhnóir Feeric. The Fairy herself summoned me."

"Be welcome then, Fyrdwisa," another guard said, waving him toward the Seolformúr.

As he walked through the gate, Collum tried to note if he sensed an aura, an energy — but other than its usual gentle tingle of existence as a magical barrier, there was nothing out of the ordinary. He ran his hand exasperatedly through his dark wavy hair and entered the hallowed hall of Fae.

This was assuredly a place Bridgette would gawk in wonder at. It pained him somewhat to know that, for now at least, she wouldn't be able to enter this palatial residence.

Like the travel portals, the Seledreám's interior had a clean, modern, and minimalist feel to it. So light and airy, with large windows everywhere to let in vast amounts of natural light during the day, and beautiful hanging chandeliers of patinaed metal that would emit soft pastel shadows of candlelight if it was dark out.

Where the Earth-bound Fairies had access to, and full expertise of, various technologies that were considered unnecessary on Heáhwolcen, the Seledreám was decorated in such a way that paid homage to Fae history without offering *too* cottage-esque an aesthetic. There were no closed doors in this building, just massive floral archways that could be shielded should privacy be necessary. The floors were a polished wood, tinted grayish-pink, that shone almost like marble. And the art!

Fairevella truly prided itself on art, and the entire Seledreám acted as a gallery for creatives of all sorts. The most recent installation in the administration wing was of three-dimensional mirrors either crafted directly from geodes, or arranged with frames of meticulously arranged crystals. Each had different colored mirror glass in it, and Collum had to remind himself briefly that he was here for work and not for browsing, so taken was he with the display. He made a mental note to find a way to show these to Bridgette, if he had to borrow them all and hang them himself inside the Caisleán.

We really should start doing something similar in Eckenbourne, he mused.

The largest and most striking of the mirrors, no surprise, was positioned outside Aristoces' quarters. It was a pair, one on either side of her archway, with crystals that replicated the deep orange and royal blues of her butterfly-like wings. In fact — he stood back and smiled broadly — each *was* shaped like a butterfly wing. It was breathtaking, and he said so when the Fairy of All Fairies greeted him a moment later.

"I do not like to select favorites, as we have such a variety of talented Fae, but these …" her warm voice trailed off. "These I do not want to see go."

"I don't blame you," Collum said. "I want to find a way to show them to Bridgette, if you'd ever like to share with your Elven brethren."

"That can be arranged, Fyrdwisa," Aristoces replied with a smile. "Come inside with me."

Emi-Joye and Apostine were both seated in the formal meeting room when they entered. The ambassadora looked the picture of her position, sitting straight backed on her stool, hands demurely in her lap, ankles crossed. Her smile was soft, but Collum wasn't fooled for a moment. This Fairy was no pet: she was a white tiger, waiting to pounce.

"Fyrdwisa," she said, tilting her chin down in acknowledgement. "Well met on this beautiful morning."

"Well met, now that the sun has risen and there is black fuel in my veins," he replied dryly. "Apostine, the same to you."

The Teif-Fae shot him a grin. He had a spunk to him, and Collum felt an unquestionable desire to introduce he and Aurelias. *That* would be a match for the ages.

"I'm sure you two are wondering why I've summoned you here this morning, along with our fyrdwisa," Aristoces said, waving an arm toward her archway to put up a sound shield. "This meeting is at request of the full Samnung, as is what Collum would like to ask of you. We are shielded in these quarters, and I would ask for delicacy in this matter. What the two of you are soon to be part of cannot leave this small group. Is that understood, ambassadora? Ambestre?"

The two glanced at each other, but nodded.

"Apostine, it is my honor to reveal to you now that among our number is the legendary Liluthuaé," the Fairy continued, and the ambestre's eyebrows shot up. "Her presence here is no secret, but her reason for being present *is*. I do not wish to explain that in its full at this time. Part of her task involves a trip back to Earth, to the country of Wales. Collum will go with her, as will you, Emi-Joye."

Clearly, this was not the news the ambassadora expected to hear just after seven-thirty in the morning. "Excuse me?"

"Apostine, during their time away, you will be acting ambassador. Is this understood?" Aristoces said, speaking over Emi-Joye, whose confusion was evident.

"I mean no disrespect, Ceannairí, but there is an ambassador to Wales," Emi-Joye said, eyes wide. "Would Whitby Lenoir not be a better guide for Bridgette and Collum than I? I've never even been to the United Kingdom; I wouldn't know where to begin!"

The Fairy of All Fairies regarded her for a moment. "It is imperative that as few beings as possible learn of Bridgette's true nature. As you are already familiar with her, it makes the most sense for you to be the Fairy to go with her. Ambassador Lenoir would be required to report her visit, whether or not he knew of her being the Liluthuaé, and I do not care for speculation to begin about why the fyrdwisa and an Elfling are traveling to Earth."

"That makes sense enough. But why Wales, though?" Apostine asked.

Collum answered this time. "Several of the Samnung believe that Druidic magic can aid us in strengthening the barrier wall between Palna and Bondrie. We have reason to believe that there is an interior threat in Palna that aims to creep its way out, and we'd like to prevent that, if possible. There *are* still Druids who reside in Wales. Bridgette and I call them 'True Druids,' because they live in complete isolation and secrecy from the greater Welsh society. Their existence is masked by the Druids Bridgette grew up knowing of. This is essentially a group of humans who practice a Druidic lifestyle, but are not gifted with the ability to use the Old Magicks. Bridgette and I have done enough research to understand that the leader of these human Druids is a gateway to meeting with the True Druids. Only the leader is aware of the masquerade and the part he and his fellow practitioners play in it.

"Our aim is to go to Wales for a few days, no more than three, I should think, to speak with this human Druid and find our way to the True Druids," Collum went on. "Then, we can ask our questions about using their magic to strengthen ours. Ideally they will acquiesce, and we will return to Heáhwolcen with either Druids or their rituals at our side."

The Elf gave the Fairies a moment to take that in. "We'll leave the fifteenth of September, which will put us back in time for Mabon. That will allow plenty of time for Bridgette and I to do additional research on the Palnan barrier wall. Geongre Akiko is aware of all of this, as is Geongestre Etreyn, so our travel will be fully arranged. Emi-Joye, your reports will be to the Samnung directly."

Apostine looked delighted. "Three whole days running the show? In the beginning of penguin hatching season?! I'm going to arrange some travel with Geongre Akiko myself, actually. This will be fascinating!"

"You'll have to tell me all about it," Emi-Joye said, and Collum noted an odd light in her icy blue whorls.

He outwardly feigned interest in Aristoces providing them further instructions, but his mind was split between the two young Fairies in front of him.

This is going to be the best *week. I can't believe it,* Apostine thought. *I'm actually going to get to see penguins hatching and I wonder if they'll let me use the antique camera set-up that Wylett brought back from his trip. How amazing will it be to capture modern photos on an old-school tintype? Maybe Aristoces will let me put a few on display —*

Collum shifted his attention away from the prattling inner voice of Apostine to its complete opposite. Emi-Joye was … there was no other description. She was pissed.

I would rather be ambestre, and I never thought I would say that, the ambassadora fumed. *How is it fair that Apostine gets to go in* my *stead, and I am shuttled to the other side of the world to some foreign country with Bridgette Conner? At least the fyrdwisa will be there; I rather like him. But if she brings up one more silly thing about that energy … and what if we feel it again, together like that? How do we begin to explain it when we never figured it out to begin with?*

The fyrdwisa blinked. *So Emi-Joye did lie to Bridgette that day. That's a fun revelation.*

He resisted the urge to question the ambassadora and out himself for prying, and instead tuned in to what was being said aloud.

"It is settled, then," Aristoces was saying. "Fyrdwisa, I appreciate greatly your presence this morning, and bid you farewell. I am sure you have a full day ahead, especially now that these are going home with you."

She flicked a wrist, and a tidy stack of papers appeared for him to grab. Unlike Ulerion's coded rainbow, these were all thankfully a yellowed shade of ivory.

"Thank you, Ceannairí," Collum said gratefully. "Ambassadora, ambestre, I'm certain I will see you soon."

He exited the archway, its sound-shield still in place, and evanesced immediately to his own kitchen, where a startled Bridgette shrieked and dropped her fork as he appeared in front of her.

"Fucking hell, Bundy!" she cried out. "A little warning would have been nice!"

Collum would never — or at least, not yet — say this to her face, but he privately adored when he stumbled upon her first thing in the morning, before she'd fully woken up. She absconded Elven sleepclothes for oversized shirts and athletic shorts, and there was something raw and tempting about her hair before she tamed it. She hadn't slept well either; he could tell by the visible tangles adding more texture than usual.

"My apologies, Starshine. I am somewhat surprised to return to find you awake."

"I slept like shit."

~ 52 ~

"Also, your coffee sucks this morning. What did you make, rocket fuel?" Bridgette grumbled.

He chuckled. "You are a true shining light in my life, Starshine."

"If I could do magic, I would command you to get me a caife calabaza right the fuck now."

"If you ask nicely, I will take you to get a caife calabaza."

She blinked. "Really?"

"Truly."

"It's a Saturnalia miracle!" Bridgette cried, quoting a silly line from her favorite television sitcom, a quote which was completely lost on her companion. "Give me … fifteen minutes."

It took twenty-five, but regardless, by the time Collum evanesced them in front of what Bridgette long ago declared her favorite place in both worlds, the Bright Star was much more animated than he'd seen her in weeks. This Elfling and her unearthly year-round obsession with pumpkin spice: he'd never really understand it.

They sat on the patio, soaking in the warm August sun. Both were grateful for the witch sisters' spelled cups that kept ice from melting despite the heat and humidity.

Bridgette tore off a chunk of peach cobbler honeycake and chewed on it thoughtfully. After a long moment, she asked, "What did you do while I was … gone?"

Collum stiffened, somewhat surprised. He was apprehensive about this question. Not that he didn't want to answer it, or wouldn't answer it. There was just a significant amount of backstory and context that was necessary to provide for her to fully understand.

"I invested time into myself," he said, choosing his words with care. "A lot of time, actually. I'd only just returned to normal life when you came back."

"'Normal,'" the Elfling laughed. "I still wake up convinced I'm in a dream half the time."

"I hope that it is at least a good dream," Collum replied.

She grinned at him, and sent a thought: *Oh, sweet Bundy, wouldn't you like to know.*

A feline smile in return, as he spoke aloud, "I very much would Starshine. Why don't we skip the government work today and have a little bit of fun?"

"Play hooky with the fyrdwisa?" Bridgette gasped in mock horror, her lilac eyes sparkling. "Why, I'd be honored."

Collum's eyes sparkled too, like sunshine dappling the ocean waters. "Then let us return home to change clothes. We are going to need something a bit more … rustic, for what I have in mind for us."

In true Collum Andoralain form, he told her naught of his plans. For once, Bridgette didn't press him, and dressed without question when they were back at the apartment. She traded her clothes for thicker leggings, a breezy sleeveless tunic, and her boots. She had an inkling of what their day might consist of when he tossed her a lined leather waterskin.

"Where are you sweeping me off to now?" Bridgette asked, stepping forward to take his hand.

"You'll see," he said mischievously.

He whipped them out of sight in that explosion of navy whorls, and they evanesced into the woods, on the outer banks of a large lake. There were swimming areas where families gathered, picnicking and relaxing. Bridgette could just barely make out a pier where beings appeared to be fishing, and there was a stand to their left where kayaks and, of all things, Kelpies and Selkies, could be reserved to ride through the water. Except for the fact that about forty percent of those around were definitely not of human descent, the lake didn't look much different from those she'd grown up visiting with her foster families.

"This is Loch Liath," Collum said. "It's one of three such lakes in Heáhwolcen, though by far the largest. And the only one with Kelpies and Selkies."

The horse-like and seal-like beings were basking in the sun, talking animatedly amongst themselves and the male witch who appeared to be in charge of the reservation stand.

"Are we going swimming?" Bridgette asked dubiously, glancing down at her definitely-not-water-safe attire.

"We are going hiking around the lake," Collum replied. "It's several miles, but fairly easy trails. Picturesque bridges and the like. The trailhead should be …" He turned around, eyes peeled for the well-hidden path. "Here. Follow me."

They walked in relative silence for a few minutes, listening to the younglings laughing at the swim banks behind them. Bridgette was reminded momentarily of the first day they'd met, when Collum came to the duck pond, and she had worried that her screams would be drowned out by the children's cacophony.

"I'm glad you chose to let me buy you tea that day," he murmured. He'd been listening to her inner monologue again.

"Not like you gave me much of a choice, punk."

The Elf flashed her a grin. "They do tell me I am very successful at my job, on occasion."

He let the grin fade as she chuckled. "You asked me earlier about what I did while you were gone. I was not very descriptive in my answer, and in truth, it is a subject difficult for me to share about. But I would like to, if you are open to hearing it."

Bridgette looked at him, brows furrowed. "Of course I am. Is that why you brought me out here?"

"Yes."

"Ha!" she laughed. "Alright then. Shoot."

Collum took a steadying breath, manifesting scents of birch and tobacco to calm his nerves. He did not always enjoy talking about his past, but wanted to be open with the Bright Star.

"Excellent. As we have many miles ahead of us, I thought this would be a beneficial way to spend the time," he said. Another deep breath. "I wished, intensely wished, two things in the immediate moments after you fled the Samnung chamber that afternoon. Firstly, I wished I'd stopped you. Secondly, I wished I'd begged a bargain with Trystane, to allow me to tell you far earlier about Mohreen."

Bridgette stiffened at her mother's name.

"That was … seeing you go, that was one of the most difficult things I have ever witnessed," Collum said. "It echoed, still echoes, in my head that I let you go. But we promised you the choice was yours, and we would respect the choice you made. I hoped you'd make a different choice — as you wound up doing — but you chose, and I could not break that promise to you. I admittedly also feared that if I came to Earth after you that I could not handle you saying 'no' again and closing the door to me forever. It is no secret that I have come to care for you a great deal in an immensely small amount of time, Starshine."

She smirked. "I guess I like you too, Bundy."

Collum punched her lightly in the shoulder, and continued. "I attempted to work. To go about my days as if the past *two years* hadn't happened, especially the past few weeks. It was a futile attempt. Aurelias will tell you, should you ask, that I lasted less than twenty-four hours before I had to just … go. Be alone, with myself, away from every being in every world. The thought of existing in my apartment, so empty, and in my own head, which was suddenly *very* empty, was excruciating. I have a bit of hubris, as do we all, so I did not want to admit what I saw as weaknesses of my mind to anyone, not even Trystane. It was best to escape.

"I have no idea how long I was actually on Hlafjordstiepel," Collum recalled. "Weeks, though. In the first hours you were gone, I came to the personal knowledge that I did not know how to appropriately process grief. Many years ago, when I was newly fyrdestre, my parents chose to cross into the spirit realm. Elves are, for all intents and purposes, immortal. But they are not immune to injury or disease, and if an injury or disease is strong enough, it can be fatal. My father came to have such a disease. To watch him, this former warrior of soul and pen, begin to waste away and wither … that was undoubtedly the hardest period of my life thus far. He and my mother were a perfect match for each other. Their love was eternal, and though as every partnership has its frustrations, theirs was as ideal a union as I could imagine."

The fyrdwisa's voice was pained. "Watching my father die for those long years was harder on my mother than on me. I had my duties to distract myself. She was a healer to begin with, and though she did not practice regularly by then — she preferred to hone her creative side after a certain age — felt it was her role to take care of my father. She felt she had to be strong for him, too, so that he would not despair as he saw himself wilt. But they both knew, deep down, there was nothing to be done."

The Elf took another deep breath, and felt wetness on his cheeks.

"As you may remember from our stories of Ylda, Elves and Fairies may take their destinies into their own hands and choose to transition to the next life at their leisure," he said. "It was I who convinced my mother that the two should cross into the spirit realm together. Trystane was always like an older brother to me, and he along with my fyrdwisa, promised to care for me. I think knowing that I wouldn't be alone was what finally freed my mother into making that decision. She waited as long as she felt comfortable, making preparations and whatnot. There were affairs to put in order; the ritual ceremony had to be planned. That sort of thing. When it was time, the ceremony was beautiful. It truly was. I'd never seen my parents so peaceful. I would not say they were happy, because of why they made the choice when they did, but they were at peace. I had a sort of peace too, knowing this of their departure from this life."

He paused and wiped the tears on the back of his hand. "But I saw grief, *emotion*, as a weakness. I was the fyrdestre! Second in command to the Fyrdlytta leadership, third in line for the Elven primarchy. I had to be *strong* for those who looked up to me. So I did not grieve. I buried myself in my work; became so fully immersed in my duties that I came to a point — which I did not realize until recently — where I defined myself not by who I was as a being, but by my job and success therein. I hid that grief for more than a century."

Collum stopped walking and looked at Bridgette. The look in his eyes wasn't painful, but his blue irises had more depth than usual. She stepped to him and put a comforting hand on each of his wrists.

"I realized I'd hidden it when you walked out that door," he said. "It hit me at the same time, that sense of immense loss. I still did not know, because I hadn't done it to begin with, how to process that loss in a public sphere. Thus, I wound up on the highest peak of our mountains for however many weeks that was. I did not lie to you when I said earlier that I invested time in myself. That was truth. I'd denied myself that time for so long though that it took a significant period to begin to work through it. There was much meditation, mindwork, physical exertion even. I'd become a mere shell with little substance. Being in your company, having this task to be your companion, had started to give me purpose again. So here I felt lost on many levels. Lost in my own head. Lost because I'd failed at this part of my job. Lost at knowing who I was *without* these things that had given me that sense of fulfillment for so long. I had to learn who I was again and become whole. I am still in that process, but I am getting better."

Bridgette was crying too.

"I hate so fucking much that you went through all that," she whispered. "With your parents, with feeling like you'd failed at your job, all of it. And I'm really, really glad you're getting better. I'm sorry that I contributed to that. But, Bundy, I swear that you have nothing to worry about anymore when it comes to me. I mean, I may do some pretty stupid shit now and then, and probably piss you off, but I'm not going anywhere unless you tell me to. Like I said, I knew I'd fucked up as soon as I left that room. I didn't want to deal with the humiliation and the failure feelings either, so I just kept going.

"And every damn second of every damn day I was back at my 'normal' life on Earth, I *worked* to bury you in my head," she continued. "If I thought of you all I wanted to do was to come find you. I couldn't face the idea that you might, like, shut the door on me, either. So it was easier to not think about you, until that day when I couldn't get you out of my head finally and I came running back."

Collum loosened one of his wrists from her grip and took a long drink from his waterskin. "And now your snide comments are back in my head, much to my absolute pleasure."

She stuck her tongue out at him playfully, sniffling as she

wiped her tears. "Fuck you, punk. You know you missed me."

"I very much did, Starshine."

They walked the trail around Loch Liath for hours upon hours. Some parts of the path were dirt, some flooded creekbed. Bridgette said something silly at one point and Collum leaned up against a tree to catch his breath from laughing so hard, disturbing a nest of stinging insects in the process. They bolted through a swarm of angry buzzing before collapsing in even more laughter a few feet away.

The two fell into step with a pair of foraging witches who showed them baskets of moss and mushrooms, wildflowers, and edible leaves, all of which they collected during their own walk that day. The path widened in some areas and tightened in others, leaving Bridgette and Collum to walk hand-in-hand behind one another — though he promised to shield her if she lost footing and started sliding into the water. There were camping platforms along one side of the lake with sheltered areas in which to spread hammocks or sleeping bags, along with what Bridgette said must be castle ruins, before the Elf laughed so hard he started crying and said they were simply stone fire pits for evening hikers and overnight campers.

She shoved him in mirthful retaliation, and he nearly lost his footing and fell into a creek.

~ 53 ~

Their waterskins ran out with at least two miles left to go along the trail, and by the time Bridgette and Collum reached a flowing spring to refill them, they were soaked in sweat. The Elf's wavy brown hair was dripping, and Bridgette's braid was frizzy and disheveled. Somehow mud was streaked up her bare arms, and they walked through so many spiderwebs along the way that their skin was shimmering and sticky with spidersilk.

"At least we didn't get stung," Collum said, watching as she dipped a palm in the water to vaguely attempt to clean off the muck.

"Yet."

"Yet," he agreed, grinning.

"You know," Bridgette began as she scrubbed her arm, "Your frihtri came true. Everything you told me earlier, about your parents, about me leaving … that stupid little fortune cookie told you it would happen."

Collum looked at her curiously, a half-smile on his lips. "I do believe you're right, Starshine."

She winked at him. "Must be magic."

The Elfling darted out of his reach, laughing, before he could retaliate her wordplay.

The sun was beginning its long descent on the horizon, and Bridgette pulled Collum out of the trees to see, to watch as the light sparkled and danced across the lake. "It's so beautiful here," she said.

Golden hour dappled through the trees as they continued the final leg of their hike, grateful for the drop in temperature. Bridgette didn't want it to end; didn't want to evanesce back to the apartment for piles of paperwork and the impending trip to find the Druids. It had been so needed, she thought, to be *away* from everything that was expected of her, and just spend this time with Collum. Like they used to do, that week she was first here.

I missed this, she thought to him. *Just … spending time with you. Not being fyrdwisa and Liluthuaé; not being these two co-workers, for lack of a better word.*

It was most refreshing, he agreed, mind-to-mind.

I wish it didn't have to end. I kind of would rather escape here with you than go save the world.

Collum chuckled. "It doesn't have to end, not really. Consider the next few weeks as a — minor inconvenience, to do some work before we return to the better things in life," he said out loud.

"I kind of like that perspective," Bridgette admitted. "So, since we're going back … what's for supper?"

The Elf looked at her, deadpan. "Do you *ever* stop thinking about food?"

"Nope."

He rolled his eyes. "I am rather hungry as well, though I admit I lack the energy to cook after this day's events. Perhaps we could venture to a restaurant."

"Perfect. You pick. I'm just famished," Bridgette said. "Plus I have no idea where anything is except the Coffee Cauldron and that shitty little tavern in Galdúr."

"Hmm," Collum mused, kicking at a pile of leaves as they exited the trail. "Do you enjoy fish?"

He evanesced them to a ramshackle wooden restaurant that specialized in just that. Since there were no oceans on Heáhwolcen — Ulerion's mysterious Palnan beach aside — it was freshwater fish and vegetation on the menu. When their orders arrived, Collum was so pleased with his grilled walleye and polenta cakes that he insisted on feeding Bridgette a forkful across the table.

"Damn, that is *good,*" she said, resisting the urge to ask for a second bite. Her own salad, made with salted kelp leaves and pickled vegetables, topped with spicy crawfish tails, was astonishing. Just like everything else food-wise on Heáhwolcen, it blew everything she'd eaten on Earth out of the water — pun intended.

They walked onto the streets after dinner, Bridgette longing still to prolong the evening. Lightning bugs flickered in the dark, and mysterious giggles seemed to fill the air.

"Pixies," Collum said. "Little rapscallions, they are. You'll rarely see them in the daylight; they rather like to hide and cause havoc after the sun sets."

"Oh!" Bridgette gasped, as something tweaked the end of her braid, followed by a cacophony of those shrill giggles.

"As I said."

He put his arm around her waist and evanesced them back to his living room. They were still dirty and icky with dried sweat and mud, thoroughly messy, but Bridgette hugged Collum tightly.

"Thank you," she said, meeting his gaze. "For today. For telling me … all of that. For just being you."

He smiled thoughtfully. "Thank you, then, I think."

The next morning, Bridgette pulled the covers over her head, wishing she could bottle up yesterday and relive it over and over. The thought of that stack of papers Collum showed up with after his meeting with the Fairies was overwhelming.

She freshened up and walked to the kitchen, a deep sigh escaping as she resigned herself to this "minor inconvenience" of a few weeks' more reading. The Elf was already awake, of course, perusing the newspaper.

"I hope this morning's coffee is more to your liking," he said, smiling, though he didn't look up from the article. "I'll make eggs in a few moments, if you'd like."

"I would like," Bridgette said, pouring the hot brew over ice. "I'm sore from all that walking yesterday. Who knew I'd gotten so out of shape from all this reading?"

He shrugged, folding the paper neatly on the table. "Unfortunately there is more reading to do."

"Trust me dude, I have not forgotten."

"Ulerion's predecessor was a Fairy named Garrin," Collum said. "I did not know him, but from what I know *of* him, he's more level-headed than Ulerion. And all of his reports were on the same color paper, thankfully."

Bridgette laughed. "Phew."

"I'm interested to see what we discover from him. We knew

of the inner barrier because of our spies, like Mohreen, not from the ambassador — which likely meant that it's common knowledge among the Tinuviels' circle, but was supposed to be kept secret from the Samnung and other citizens," Collum mused. He cracked eggs into the pan. "Fried or scrambled today?"

"Scrambled, please. Did Mohreen have to submit reports too?"

"Of a sort. Due to the nature of their assignment, they had covenants with beings including myself, the fyrdwisa, Trystane, etcetera. She could activate our covenant band and send thoughts through it. It was somewhat like the ísenwaer, like Magister Basira told us, but one that could only be used if you pressed a button to turn it off and on. When she had something to share, she would activate it briefly, to alert me. I would then respond in kind, and it was after she heard from me and knew she had my full attention that she would actually send things through our mind-bond," Collum explained. "But usually it was just a few sentences. A check-in, most of the time, to let me know she was alive and well. She had to be extremely careful not to alert anyone to what she was doing, thus most of our communications were exceedingly brief."

"So she told you the wall was up?" Bridgette pressed.

"She did, though I don't think she immediately knew what it meant. We didn't either, for a while. Mohreen overheard a conversation between Eryth Tinuviel and another being about the 'erected barrier' and how he hoped it would 'be the spark of something bigger.' Another line about it 'keeping their magic at bay.' She told me those things and I took them to the Samnung, suspecting that there was indeed something afoot the Tinuviels didn't want us to know about," Collum said. "After little bits and pieces of information of this nature, it was eventually suggested by one of the Samnung members that perhaps the Tinuviels were attempting to wall out the wall we'd walled them in with."

He salted the bubbling egg and butter mixture, then continued. "Our theory was confirmed when Mohreen needed out of Palna. When the spies were extracted, it was said there was a 'shield repair' ongoing. That piqued the interest of the Bondrie guards who were in charge of the transfer back into Heáhwolcen. One inquired of the Palnan authorities why the Samnung was not informed of the need for repairs on the barrier wall, as it was their responsibility to maintain it. The authorities hedged and gave a satisfactory enough answer that the guards barely thought to mention it when they gave their reports. It was months later when Master Swordsman Druan Heart of Stones, Corria Deathhunter's predecessor, happened to be reviewing reports and read that note."

"Since then," Collum continued, adjusting the stove's flame with a peculiar twist of his thumb, middle and forefinger, "the Samnung tried its damndest to find out why in seven hells their wall needed to be repaired. It wasn't until the death of King Hermann and Queen Lalora that solid evidence presented itself."

"Because that confirmed that maybe their barrier was getting too powerful?" Bridgette asked, trying to connect the dots. It plagued her that her sierwan gift could be so utterly unhelpful when she *actually* needed to put two-and-two together.

"Precisely."

"Okay. So fast-forward a bit," she said. "We know there's a second barrier, the Ballamúr. We know there are holes in the actual barrier wall that the Ballamúr magic can probably penetrate. Hell, the Ballamúr going up might have been what caused the holes in the first place! What we don't know is how to fix the holes."

Collum turned to Bridgette, her eggs in hand. "How many times are we going to go over this?"

"Until it sinks in exactly what we're going to do to solve the problem, punk. I just want to make sure we're going into this with clear heads and a plan. They're only giving us a few days to hunt down the Druids, then weasel our way to find the True Druids, *and* we have to then persuade said magical beings to give us spells that we can take back with us. We have a really short amount of time to do a fucking shit-ton of wheeling and dealing," Bridgette answered. Her words were trite, but the tone in which she spoke them was sincere.

The fyrdwisa sighed. "I'm sorry, Starshine. I don't mean to be short with you. On occasion I feel like I have the same conversation innumerable times with every being I come into contact with. I did not mention this yesterday, because in truth I needed that escape as much as you did, but I am immensely concerned about Emi-Joye coming with us to Wales. We need her expertise, most assuredly, but I had the pleasure of being privy to her inner thoughts during our meeting yesterday morning. She is — to put it mildly — a tad angsty that she is missing out on things in her territory. She also admitted she felt the aura."

Bridgette, whose mouth had been full of scrambled eggs, threw her fork to the table and shouted, "You are *fucking* joking with me!"

Collum chuckled. "I am fucking not, Starshine."

"That weaselly little *bitch* Fairy."

"For deity's sake, please play nice and do *not* call her that in the presence of anyone, save myself or perhaps Trystane."

"I want to know why she's lying to us about that," Bridgette fumed. She stabbed at her eggs. "And what's she so peeved about missing out on? Penguins?"

Her companion barked out his laugh. "Actually, yes."

"Please tell me you're kidding."

"I'm not," Collum assured her. "Apparently this is penguin hatching season, or the beginning of it, and she and Apostine were both supposed to travel to Antarctica to observe the proceedings. Apostine will still be able to, but she will be with us."

Bridgette shook her head. "This is asinine. We're going to save the worlds, and this chick wants to go play with *penguins* instead?"

"Apparently. Though I do not know Emi-Joye well, I have a feeling she is the type of Fairy who will do whatever she can to raise herself in Aristoces' eyes. She will not fail on this mission," Collum said. "She may resent having to join us, but she won't — as you say — 'half-ass' it out of spite."

"Well, cool, I guess," Bridgette muttered. She was still annoyed that Emi-Joye lied repeatedly about feeling the aura. "So now we read until the end of eternity. Again."

"A minor inconvenience," he reminded her quietly. "Let's read through these in my office, yes?"

She put her dirty dishes in the sink, and rose to follow Collum. "Whatever you say, Fyrdwisa."

~ 54 ~

When the time came for their trip to Wales, Bridgette was certain she'd never felt more unprepared for travel. Even coming to Heáhwolcen with a perfect stranger she initially thought was a serial killer was somehow less unnerving than what she, the said not-a-serial-killer, and Emi-Joye were set to embark on.

Collum evanesced the two of them and their luggage to the portal in Fairevella, where Emi-Joye would meet them. It was early evening, an intentionally chosen departure time to avoid crowds, questions, and recognition. Geongre Akiko herself was in charge of seeing to their travel documents — or lack thereof — and setting them off to Earth.

"You'll spend the night at Collum's home in Danvers," Akiko instructed them. "I suggest you not make it a late night of revelry. A car is arranged to pick you up from there tomorrow morning at five, and will transport you to the Boston airport. Your tickets are arranged in here for the flight to Cardiff. That departs at eight in the morning Eastern time, and you'll land in Amsterdam for a roughly eight-hour layover. It is imperative that you do not leave the airport during that time, in case of crowds at security checkpoints that could cause delays for you to get back in. The flight from Amsterdam will take you to Cardiff, where you will have just over two days' time to do the work you need. Then back to the airport you go, to repeat the same process in reverse. Am I understood?"

The three travelers nodded.

"Ambassadora, I implore you to glamour your wings before you leave the portal on Earth, and put these on," Akiko said, handing a folded stack of fabric to Emi-Joye. "Fyrdwisa, you know the drill, and Bridgette is already dressed for Earthly travel. You must blend in as much as possible."

The Fairy accepted the stack with a look of resigned annoyance. "Of course, Geongre."

Akiko turned to Collum and handed him the folder of documents. "The three of you are seated together on every flight. If you have any trouble whatsoever, in Amsterdam you are to dispatch immediately to the United States Embassy. In Cardiff, or wherever your travel in Wales takes you, contact the Embassy in London and alert them of your impending arrival. At either embassy, ask to see the special assistant to the ambassador, and tell them you are here on business assignment from Akiko Chidori. They will be able to get in touch with me and we will get you out of there immediately."

Her tone was serious and grave. Bridgette was struck then by the weightiness of their trip. Collum said it wasn't for sight-seeing, and she knew that, but the idea that they might have to contact the embassy made her stomach churn uncomfortably. She sincerely hoped they did not have to do that.

"Am I understood?" Geongre Akiko asked again. The three nodded. "Then may deity and spirit be at watch over you. Go well, ceannairí."

They portaled down at her instruction, Emi-Joye standing stoically in the white light while Bridgette pretended her heart wasn't about to beat out of its chest as she gripped Collum's hand. Upon their exit, Emi-Joye excused herself to change, and it was the Geongestre who attended to them. Bridgette thanked him again for his speedy response when she'd gone back to Heáhwolcen earlier that summer, as did Collum.

"I don't think I've ever seen anyone have such a way with the Unicorns as you," Etreyn replied. "Eloise was most delighted to come immediately to your aid. I did naught but ask."

Any further response was distracted by Emi-Joye's return, and the Elfling did a double-take. The Fairy reappeared without wings, wearing a pair of fitted white denim pants with a heathered gray T-shirt and braided gold sandals. Her hair was still up in its usual braided crown, and she wore gold-rimmed sunglasses to hide her eyes. Collum would do the same, Bridgette knew, as he had on the day they first met. But the ambassadora looked like a fashion model — tall and graceful, walking with such an ease as though she was gliding across the white marbled floor toward them.

"Are we ready?" Emi-Joye asked.

Collum nodded, and they said their goodbyes to Etreyn

before heading out into the waning sunshine. As they walked, he explained that a few days prior, he'd arranged to have the cottage fully stocked for their visit — he'd cook, so there would be no worries about restaurant waits that could affect their schedule. Bridgette privately thought that was a little silly, but accepted his explanation.

Mostly I didn't want the two of you getting into a fight in public, he thought to her.

You know, it's really rude to listen to people without permission, she thought back.

I wouldn't be half as good at my job if I had to do that! Collum's mind-speak was laced with sarcasm and amusement.

"You look quite passable as a human," he said out loud to Emi-Joye.

"I loathe having to banish my wings," she responded. "I do not do so out of enjoyment, but out of duty. I don't half-blame Baize Sammael for wanting to live in a world where Fae and magical beings can be themselves, without having to filter their existence through shams like glamour."

"I don't either," Collum said, and his response surprised Bridgette. "But the way in which he went about it was — and continues to have implications that are! — wholly inappropriate and wrong. We can do better, to achieve such an end goal."

Bridgette's eyes shifted, and she sent the thought to Collum: *The Liluthuaé is the balance.*

It wasn't a new thought; she'd had this knowledge before; but with his words came new context to the revelation. It was she who'd argued first to abolish the barrier in Palna and reopen the country. It was she who'd learned of the ill-intent that continued to drive Palnan leadership, but also she who cautioned against the idea that all citizens had such intentions. And it would be she who championed the cause he now spoke of: to one day build a collective existence without the need for subterfuge.

The Elf pondered that in the silence of their remaining journey. There was something missing, some knowledge and meaning that had yet to reveal itself to any of them. Collum had no doubt that his Elfling companion would indeed play a pivotal role in the future of magicks old and magic new — one day. But first, they must understand Palna as it stands in this moment in time. He breathed deeply, fighting the gnawing in his gut. The necessity of this trip, he did not question. The fear he had for the Elfling and her safety? He did not like how much it ate at him.

Perhaps once she learns to defend herself, I will feel less anxious for this situation, he thought to himself.

After a quiet dinner of salads at the cottage, Collum led the two upstairs and slipped into his bedroom, wondering how long before the two roommates would start shouting at each other. He knew Bridgette had been itching to question Emi-Joye about the aura. He also knew that she'd at least try to wait until he was out of earshot, and he thus tuned his entire mind and ears to hers after mere moments.

Sure enough, Bridgette gave Emi-Joye enough time for a bathroom break before hissing at her, "Why did Aristoces send you?"

"The Fairy of All Fairies explained her reasoning already," Emi-Joye said. "It is not my position to challenge her authority."

"Bullshit," Bridgette snapped. "That's bullshit. The same as when you said you felt *anxious* when we all were surrounded by that weird aura. The two of you know something and you're keeping it hidden. And don't come at me and try to weasel your way out of this. I may not know what you're hiding or why, but I know you *are.*"

"How intriguing that the Liluthuaé is accusing myself, an Earth ambassadora, and Aristoces, Fairy of All Fairies, of some sort of great conspiracy against her," Emi-Joye said mildly, not making eye contact. "As if she believes we are here to usurp her great position with the Samnung!"

"I'm not *accusing* you, I'm stating the facts," Bridgette sneered, looking over her shoulder at the Fairy behind her. "You're evading them. Plus, this has nothing to do with the Samnung. Just with you, and your ability to avoid the truth."

Something clicked in Collum's mind just as the Fairy retorted, "You are trying to connect dots that aren't meant to be connected!"

"Just because you don't want them to be connected, doesn't mean that they aren't," Bridgette said, rising to her feet. "You can stop fucking gaslighting me any time you'd like. I already know you're lying through your perfect white teeth."

The laugh that emanated from Emi-Joye was hollow. "What's your problem with me, Liluthuaé? Perhaps *this* is why the Seolformúr wouldn't let you pass."

Fuck, Collum thought at that insult.

The next thing he knew, before he could even process Bridgette's tumult of thoughts, Emi-Joye let out a scream. He bolted down the hall and found the two females grappling with each other against the wall, Bridgette fighting to get to her knife, her eyes so dark purple and unfocused they weren't even her own.

"Stop!" he commanded.

Emi-Joye looked at him, terrified, but it was as though Bridgette hadn't heard the instruction. She had a hand at the Fairy's throat, the other fighting off the two pairs of hands that were now attempting to prevent her from accessing the blade at her hip.

"Get her *off* me!" Emi-Joye choked out.

"Do not lie to me!" Bridgette shouted. She looked rabid. "Do not lie to me! I will know of your mistruths!"

Collum reached around her with both arms to try pulling her off, but the Elfling surprised him with a burst of strength as she twisted and elbowed him hard in the chest, not taking that hand off the Fairy's throat.

"Fuck!" he exclaimed, tripping backward.

Outward approaches clearly weren't calming her down, and he had no idea from where this sudden anger evolved. He sent scents of honeysuckle and vanilla — along with whatever Emi-Joye's sensory calmers would be — out into the room.

Starshine, come back to me, he pleaded, mind-to-mind. *Please stop this!*

It was as if he'd slapped her across the cheek. She froze, her eyes becoming their normal shade of lilac in an instant, and looked at the hand wrapped at the Fairy's neck.

"Holyfuckingshit," she cried, and jumped back, staring at the hand as though it had been bewitched. "What the fucking fuck was *that*?"

Emi-Joye hadn't moved from the wall. She breathed quickly and heavily, though Collum's scent-spell allowed her to ease somewhat.

"What. Was. That," Bridgette repeated, looking from her hand to Collum, from Collum to Emi-Joye.

"I think," Collum began quietly, "that we will need some coffee. We all have some explaining to do, and this may take time."

He walked them down to the tiny kitchen and set a pot to brew. Then he motioned for the two to sit. They did so, as far apart from each other as the table allowed. Collum positioned himself on the other end, forming a sort of triangle between them.

"I believe that Bridgette's sierwan gift allows her, to a certain extent, to detect when she is being lied to," he said. "I also believe that this stems from another sort of Old Magick, which I do not know enough about to even begin to try to explain. I do not know why it causes her to behave in such a way though — perhaps it is because sierwen are known for existing in times of war, they were utilized to extract truths from enemies."

"Okay, cool, so being a sierwan makes me able to flip a switch and become a master of torture chambers. That's exactly what I wanted my destiny to be," Bridgette said.

Collum ignored her and rose to pour their drinks. "A sierwan cannot lie about what knowings come to her. Emi-Joye, we have suspected for some time that there was more to the story about the auras felt between the two of you and Princess Cloa. We now have full confirmation that we are correct in that assumption. I ask you now to please explain yourself fully. We cannot go into this immediate journey of travel, nor the larger journey of the Palna situation and possible war, and keep secrets of this nature from one another. As your fyrdwisa, I command you explain yourself with full and utter sincerity. Leave nothing out unless you have sworn a word with Aristoces to not share outside of her confidence."

Emi-Joye swallowed hard. "It is … a complicated matter."

Bridgette glared at her.

The Fairy looked down at the coffee mug she now gripped between her hands, almost white-knuckled from the memory of being pinned to the wall by a suddenly strong, ravenous Liluthuaé. "During the after-soiree, when I approached you and Princess Cloa, all seemed fine when we were first speaking. But then I felt … *wrong*. I did not lie to you before, Bridgette, when I said I sensed the conversation must end. I would still not classify what I felt as an aura. More a, premonition, perhaps? A sense of knowing that something was at play, deeper energies than we would yet understand. It is very difficult for me to explain this, I hope you realize, because it was not a tangible feeling for me. Whereas for Bridgette it very much was."

She glanced at Bridgette, eyes soft yet wary. "I need for you to understand that I did not know what was happening. It was not something I hid from you intentionally."

Bridgette nodded curtly. "I believe you. But you pretended for *months* that it was nothing. What made you suddenly decide to change your mind?"

"Bridgette, Fyrdwisa, I did not ask to be put in this position," Emi-Joye replied, her voice trembling. "I wanted to be an ambassadora. That was my heart's greatest desire. To further the bridge between humans and magical beings! I did not want to be part of some great war or conspiracy. I did not want to have some role in magic at large. The idea that there was a connection between myself and *the* Liluthuaé was … abhorrent."

Bridgette again glared at her. "Abhorrent?"

The Fairy gritted her teeth. "Mayhap that was the wrong word choice. I did not want there to be a connection between us other than perhaps friendship. Because to be *friends* with the Liluthuaé? How amazing! More than that, however, implies taking on far, far more responsibility than I have any desire to. I decided it was better to avoid that possibility entirely. It is why when you mentioned this to me at the tavern, and then stormed off, I did not chase you. I truly at that time did not care to have a connection with you in the way the fyrdwisa does, where you are glued to each other as companions and warriors. I am not sure that I want that now, either, but I will serve my country as the Fairy Herself sees fit to ask of me."

Collum swirled his coffee. "Trystane and I are perhaps chasing ghosts, but we have an idea of what this energy might be. In due time, we are prepared to share our findings with the two of you, and the Samnung at large. In the meantime, the three of us have been tasked with this mission, and we cannot let trivial arguments drive a wedge between us. Emi-Joye, and Bridgette, I vow to work with you in complete honesty and transparency, unless an action or statement is protected by outside covenant. Will you swear the same to me, and to each other?"

The two females looked at each other, guarded expressions drawn, but nodded.

"Yes, Fyrdwisa," Emi-Joye said.

"Sure thing," Bridgette agreed. "Should we spit on it?"

Her magical companions gave her quizzical looks. She laughed. "Never mind. It's a human thing."

~ 55 ~

Their early departure from the cottage was without fanfare, and the trio successfully traversed the Boston-Logan airport and boarding. Collum sat himself between the two females, ostensibly to prevent the two of them managing to get into a mid-air fistfight, and was gladder than words could say when Bridgette slipped a pair of headphones into her headrest and put on some silly movie, ignoring the both of them.

She'd stepped away at some point in the airport to call her foster parents and apologize profusely for not being responsive to them for weeks — upon her surprise arrival in Heáhwolcen, Trystane and Aristoces arranged her cover story, delivered by way of a Fairy ambassador. Bridgette had gone away on an international study abroad to Europe, to study under a succession of trained violinists, the Simmonses were told.

Collum caught snippets of their conversation; overheard Bridgette tell them she'd taken on her first student, who was the son of a local shopkeeper, and she mentioned she was traveling to Amsterdam and Cardiff for the next leg of her journey. The Simmonses must have asked if this would impact her graduation, scheduled for that December, because Bridgette said she was taking a gap year to allow for this part of her studies.

Now on the plane, he thought perhaps she was upset with him, because she intentionally trained her whole focus on the movie in front of her, followed by three more, during the flight to Amsterdam. Emi-Joye was thoroughly engrossed in a series of books she'd picked up at a magazine stand, and Collum tried vaguely to sleep.

There was plenty to do to keep them entertained during their extensive stop in Amsterdam. Collum breathed a sigh of relief when Emi-Joye and Bridgette expressed shared glee upon discovering authentic stroopwafels at their terminal's coffee shop. He hadn't realized how pent up he was about the two of them getting along during the rest of the trip until they finally arrived in Cardiff. It was mid-morning, and all three were weary from the nearly day's worth of flights and staying awake.

Collum led them to the rental car kiosk to secure their transportation, and once the keys were handed over, he slipped into the driver's seat and gave the females a wicked, feline grin.

"Watch this," he told them.

A wrist flick and whispered phrase later, the car whirred itself to life and began its jaunt to their hotel, as the fyrdwisa casually tucked his hands behind his head, letting the steering wheel drive itself.

"This is *amazing*," Bridgette said, shaking her head with laughter. She was practically delirious at this point, having struggled to sleep on both their flights, especially the one from Amsterdam to Cardiff after indulging in a steaming cup of coffee with her stroopwafel.

All three companions were awed by the Welsh countryside that ambled past their windows as they drove the A483: Bridgette could *feel* the energy and magic, and it had nothing to do with her innate ability to sense unusual auras. She still didn't feel quite ready for this whole trip to unfold, despite plenty of research and planning. Out of caution, she and Collum hadn't revealed their full plan to anyone yet, not even Emi-Joye. That was item one on the agenda once they reached the hotel.

"This country is breathtaking," Emi-Joye said quietly, transfixed at the mossy mix of greens, blue-gray, and hazy fog. "I feel as though I can reach out my hand and touch our ancestors."

"I feel it too," Bridgette confessed. "Not the aura feeling, but just … like there's something more out here for us."

Collum didn't comment. He'd fallen asleep.

The fyrdwisa woke as the car slowed to turn into the hotel parking lot. They'd all share a room, with Collum in one bed and the two females in another. Room service was ordered for a late lunch, and they blearily sat down to discuss plans for the next two days before tucking in for a somewhat relaxing evening.

"We'll leave in the morning for Ynys Môn, the Isle of Anglesey," Collum said. He unfurled a map from his bag, pointing out an island just off the Welsh coast, perhaps an hour or two away. "Bridgette and I found out there are a number of Druidic organizations spread throughout Ireland, England, Scotland, and Wales, but the most history seems to stem from this place. We need to find the people in charge of the Anglesey Druidic Order, which we believe to be the oldest group in the world. If there are humans who know of the True Druids, they are most likely part of this order."

"What do we know of Druidry?" Emi-Joye asked.

"The basic beliefs and organizational structure," Collum said. "A bit of history. Shockingly, most of the history is quite vague, and only takes shape from the last couple of centuries when artists and poets began a Druid revival. Bridgette and I are of the belief that is the time period when the human Druids began to mask the True Druids."

"What if the True Druids aren't on this island?" Emi-Joye asked.

"Why are you so damn negative about this?" Bridgette muttered, a remark met with a scolding glare from Collum.

"Why is it considered negative to bring up points of information that I assume from your tone, you have not considered?" the Fairy snapped back, a brow raised in challenge.

"Why don't you trust our research?"

Emi-Joye opened her mouth to retort again, but the fyrdwisa hit his palms on the table.

"Will the two of you shut it?" Collum exclaimed, exasperated by their constant bickering. "I feel as though I've been sent to keep watch over a pair of younglings! Emi-Joye, to the best of our abilities in the timeframe we were given, we've researched most thoroughly the existence of human and True Druids. Our research led us to this island. Should we need to venture elsewhere, we will. The Bright Star has a point, though, that your frequent espousal of disbelief is most exhausting. And Bridgette, in the event our ambassadora chooses not to listen to me, please keep your thoughts to yourself if they're going to spark a fire I have to put out. I'm tired of listening to the two of you; I am going to bed."

He put the map of Wales back in his bag, then disappeared

to the bathroom to prepare for a night in with two females who had literally been at each other's throats twenty-four hours before.

Bridgette changed into sleepclothes, not caring if Emi-Joye thought it a crude move to do so in front of her, and slid under the covers. She shoved her face under the pillow and tried to meditate herself to sleep.

Collum emerged from the bathroom to see the two females on opposite sides of their bed, shoved as far to the edges as possible. He sighed and tucked himself in, prepared for a fitful night. His gift of thought-hearing was most effective when he was in close proximity to others, and given that he'd decided to intentionally tune into these two for the duration of the trip, he assumed this meant his head would be filled with the voices of Bridgette and Emi-Joye nonstop.

Listening during the night was his least favorite thing to do, and quite difficult: Collum nearly had to put himself in a trance to effectively rest while maintaining a conscious connection with the minds in his vicinity. If he fell asleep, there was a significant chance he'd pick up on dream-thought and struggle to separate dream from reality when he awoke. Or worse, he'd find himself inserted into the dream, where his mind would be trapped until the dreamer woke up.

He found Emi-Joye's mind to be full of angry and unsure thoughts, constantly reassuring herself that this was the walk she was meant to take, that Aristoces knew best and had Heáhwolcen's interests at heart. She thought of Apostine and considered silently activating their covenant to check in, since both were on Earth. Collum heard envy in her thoughts, wishing that she was with her ambestre to see penguins.

Having no interest this night in Antarctic wildlife, the Elf migrated his gift toward Bridgette, whose mind he found surprisingly quiet. She was stilling her mind, and he was pleased to know this. Collum sent a thought to her: *What are you thinking about, Starshine?*

Bridgette smiled despite the disruption. *Your office.*
Really?

Yup. I was *trying to meditate myself to sleep, until this nosy Elf I know stuck his mind in my head. Imagining myself in your office instead of this stuffy hotel room with Emi-Joye makes it easier. I was thinking of that first day I discovered it, when I sat next to that little bush and the butterfly came up to me.*

Collum shifted his weight to face her side of the bed. *The thought of this brings me much joy.*

Good, Bridgette thought back, peeking her head out from under the pillow to see him watching her, those blue eyes glimmering despite the only light being from the bathroom nightlight and clock on the dresser. She snuggled back under the pillow, and welcomed the sleep that overtook her.

The foggy morning they arose to was mythical and beautiful. The trio dressed and walked to the hotel common room, where a hearty English-style breakfast was being served.

"You know," Collum said conversationally, "When I found you, Bridgette, I swore I'd never eat another hotel breakfast ever again. I suppose one should never speak in absolutes about such things."

Emi-Joye reached for a croissant and a tin of chocolate-hazelnut spread. "I, for one, will not argue when the Samnung provides free accommodations for me."

"Sorry to disappoint you, Bun — Collum," Bridgette caught herself before she slipped up, again, with her promise not to use his nickname on official business. "Hold on. Isn't it breakfast? Why the fuck are there stewed tomatoes on this buffet?"

The Fairy shot her an annoyed glance. "You are *so* uncultured, Bridgette."

"I'm not uncultured," the Elfling responded. "I'm just a damn Yank."

Collum laughed so hard he nearly spit coffee on the breakfast station. "That you are, Starshine. But I do suppose we will keep you around for good measure."

Emi-Joye managed to crack a smile despite herself. "Just wait until you're handed haggis. During one of my first visits to the research station with Ambassador Malvarma, there was a group of researchers there from the University of Edinburgh who

BRIGHT STAR

thought it would be kind to make a meal for us all to celebrate the culmination of their data collection. I was handed a platter that included haggis and blood pudding, two very traditional Scottish dishes. I took one bite and then had to spell them when no one was looking to change the flavor so it was more pleasing to my palate."

"Seriously?" Bridgette asked. "You seem way too prim and proper to do that."

"Is it not prim and proper, as you say, to eat fully that which is given to me, without looking as though I may vomit at every nibble?"

"Oh. Well, when you put it that way …"

They smiled tentatively at one another, and Collum nearly put a fist in the air to celebrate. A shared smile instead of another argument? He'd take that as a victory.

Their drive from mainland Wales to the Isle of Anglesey was uneventful. Collum spelled the car again to take its own preferred route, and turned around to give a more detailed itinerary to the females. Bridgette knew most of the plan already, having helped put it together, but it would be new to Emi-Joye. The human Druids they sought had a headquarters in the city of Anglesey itself, but due to the age of books they were able to find at the University, it was unclear if the headquarters still existed in that spot, much less could they ascertain who the leader of the order now was.

"We'll ask shopkeepers and the like where we should go to find the Druid headquarters, just in case. Our cover story shall be that we are in search of a new spiritual path for ourselves, and we are interested in becoming part of a Druidic organization," Collum said. "I do not know yet if we should openly confess to the human Druids our true nature right away. I ask the both of you to please let me negotiate the breaking of our cover."

His companions agreed.

As it turned out, they didn't have to ask anyone where the Druid headquarters was. The car parked them on the side of the road in front of what looked to be a visitor's center and island museum, run by the Historic Anglesey Druidic Order.

"That's nice and convenient," Bridgette remarked. She followed Collum and Emi-Joye inside, where a middle-aged woman in a floral tunic sat behind the counter.

"Hello, ma'am," Collum greeted her.

"And a blessed day be to you three!" she said back. "What is it that brings you to the center? I have maps on that wall there, and the loo is out back behind the staircase. Tickets to the museum are eight quid apiece, though if you're a student we do offer a discount, so that'd be five quid if you've got your identification card on you."

"I'm not sure that the museum is on our agenda today," the fyrdwisa replied. "We are three friends in search of new meaning, and this search led us to the path of Druidry. We came from a fair distance to learn more about this form of spirituality, and hoped to speak with someone who could guide us."

"Ahh," the woman said. "Brilliant. You've come to the right place, you have. The museum will tell you much, of course, but I feel you have more intentional questions to ask of us."

Bridgette didn't miss the "us" in the response, but she let Collum continue talking.

"That we do," he said. "Is there such an individual here?"

"Not me," the woman responded. "But yes. There are many such individuals here. May I inquire as to the specific nature of your questions?"

Let me, Bridgette said to Collum, mind-to-mind. She felt her eyes shift. *This is a code, like how you ask for the archives at the Earth portal.*

She stepped forward and addressed the woman. "We would like to speak to the gatekeeper. His is the knowledge we seek."

"Then his is the knowledge ye shall have," the woman said. She rose and walked around Emi-Joye to lock the door. "Please, follow me."

They went through a door marked "Staff Only," and down a steep set of stairs into what had to be the museum basement. Dimly lit cubicles filled the room's center, and boxes and file cabinets lined the walls. Bridgette was reminded intensely of the attic space inside the Coven House of Wand and Sword.

At one of these cubicles sat a man, perhaps in his sixties, with close-cropped salt and pepper hair and an impressive length of beard. The woman walked directly to him and rapped a hand on the plexiglass barrier.

"Get on, Gary. We've got visitors."

"What is it that brings the three of yeh here?" Gary asked. He was gruff, with the thickly accented voice of someone who had smoked cigarettes heavily for a very, very long time. The woman told him they needed to speak with the gatekeeper, and he rose immediately from his cubicle to greet them.

They'd walked then to a bright café at the nearby harbor, arriving too early for afternoon tea, but not quite on time for lunch. Gary insisted on light sandwiches and a tea service anyway.

"They call you the gatekeeper?" Bridgette asked. Though her sierwan knowledge told her he was the right man to speak with, at least at this moment, she lacked concept of what the purpose of the gatekeeper was.

"They do," Gary said. "Yeh want to know wha' tha' is, I expect."

"Please, if you don't mind," Emi-Joye piped up. She sipped delicately at her tea.

"Yeh know this, I expect. We are Druids, o'course, but yeh know too tha' humans cannah do magic. Not as the Druids of old could," Gary said. He paused to stir more sugar in his cup. "My order is the oldest of 'em all, 'sides the Old Ones. We are the keepers of the ways. If yeh want to confer with the ways of the Old Ones, yeh have to come through us."

"Are the Old Ones … still alive?" Bridgette asked.

"They are."

"And they do magic?"

"They do."

"We'd really like to meet them."

"I expected yeh would. But yeh don't want to learn the ways, do yeh?" Gary asked.

Bridgette glanced at Collum, who answered for them. "Not quite. We would like to ask a boon of the Old Ones, as you call them. Where we hail from, there is trouble brewing, and we believe Druidic ways to be of utmost importance in helping end the malcontent."

"Tha's specific," Gary said. He raised a brow. "None of yeh are human, are yeh?"

"Negative, ghostrider," Bridgette said.

"I din't think so," their Druid host replied, offering them a knowing smile. "Humans don' ask for the gatekeeper. They ask the same queries over and over, wantin' to know if we can teach them magic or how old Stonehenge is. I won' ask yeh anymore abou' yeh're heritage; tha's not for me to know. Tha's between you and the Old Ones. I'm jus' here to protect the ways, but I can tell yeh aren' here to cause trouble."

Collum smiled back. "We are here to cause no trouble, sire. We are, however, in Wales on a very short trip. The day after tomorrow, we have a return flight and another long day of travel ahead of us. If it is possible, we would very much like to speak with the Old Ones sooner rather than later."

Gary sipped his tea. "I can take yeh. But tomorrow, not this day."

He pulled a cell phone from his pocket and keyed in a search phrase for a map. The trio gathered closer to see what was on the screen.

"The Old Ones are well-hidden," Gary murmured. "Their grove is here, by Shallow Falls, in Gwydir Forest Park. Tha's a few hours from here, and a decent hike once yeh get to the park itself. Meet me at this car park around 10 in the morning, yeah? Dress for walkin', not none of this fancy stuff. Sturdy shoes; it ain' an easy walk once yeh get to the Falls themselves."

They dressed per Gary's instructions the next morning, and purchased rain ponchos from a convenience store before departing. Gwydir Forest Park was part of a national forest system in Wales, and it was some of the most pristine, rustic scenery they'd ever seen. There was an air to their drive that morning that reminded Bridgette distinctly of Aelchanon, the Eckenbourne capital city, with its gently rolling hills and never-ending greenery as far as the eyes could see. The low-lying fog again gave the Welsh countryside an ethereal feel.

Gary was waiting, as he said he would be, at the parking lot — or car park, as he'd called it. He carried a thick, carved wooden walking staff, set with a dark garnet at the top. Collum noted the runes carved down its sides, and wished he'd bothered to remember what any of them meant after graduating the University. It looked more like a battlestaff than a walking stick, but he knew humans to be an odd sort, where they liked the idea of "witchy" things even if they didn't understand their full meanings or powers.

The path to the falls was uneven and narrow. The rocks were slick with fallen water, that of the sky and the trickle-down of the falls themselves, and so haggard that at times, the foursome was almost crawling. While Emi-Joye and Collum traversed it more easily, following Gary's lead, Bridgette had to keep a constant watch at her feet. She wondered at what point she'd grow enough confidence in her Elven heritage to trust her toes to find their own way as she kept watch over the scenery on the paths.

It seemed hours before they finally reached the crest of the waterfall, a torrent that cascaded down betwixt trees and shrubs, coating moss and rock with its life-giving force.

"Here is where we cross," Gary said simply. He stuck the strange curled-wood staff straight into the mouth of the waterfall, and as if the water was merely a curtain, parted the deluge.

A glamour! Bridgette thought in wonderment.

Collum glanced back at her and grinned. *I did not expect this at all,* he thought to her. *It is amazing the knowledge of magic that this human has, and how well he keeps our secret.*

That staff is spelled, Bridgette said to him, mind-to-mind. *It's a gift given to the one sworn to protect the secret.*

Collum recognized this as a sierwan knowing.

"Get on with it, if yeh don' mind," Gary said, and beckoned them forward with his free hand. Emi-Joye went through first, followed by Collum and Bridgette.

Though her companions had no concept of how strange and

otherworldly this was, Bridgette felt eerily as though the trio had stepped out from the modern age into an ancient past. The parting of the water led them into a cavernous tunnel that went under the river, Afon Llugwy, before opening on the other side into a brilliant green field, hidden from view by trees that seemed as old as the Earth itself. Scattered around the field was a series of roundhouses, some mounding up from the soil; others built up out of wood, peat and clay.

Gary turned to them. "This is Bywyd Derwyddon. I'll take yeh to see Heledd. He is the ovate adept of this Grove, the Ilwyn Gyfrinach."

This time, it was Bridgette who followed just behind Gary. The three of them said nothing out loud, but Bridgette used the isenwaer to send another sierwan knowing to Collum: *This is a Druidic commune. It is one of only a few of these to exist anywhere in the world, and Heledd is the over-arching leader of all the True Druids.*

A commune it may have been, but Collum was unnerved not to see a single being out and about in the vast field of dwellings. He wondered whether these Druids were entirely self-sufficient in their lifestyles, or if they depended on outside sources for food and materials. He also wondered how often they interacted with their human peers: being walked in upon by Gary with an Elf, an Elfling, and a Fairy in tow may be an unwelcome interruption, if Heledd was not used to visits.

Gary led them to the largest of the roundhouses, tall and stately despite its somewhat dilapidated construction. "Yeh can go in here."

"Aren't you coming with us?" Bridgette asked, suddenly wondering if Gary had given Heledd any sort of head's up.

"I am not," Gary replied, raising an eyebrow. "I don' meddle in the affairs of magical folk."

"Right ..." the Elfling muttered, and slipped past the door.

The Ovate Adept sat in a chair of boughs woven together with floral vines. No one else was inside the roundhouse — just him, at the very back opposite the entrance where Gary waited. Heledd was the oldest man any of them had ever seen. He had to be centuries old, so weathered and wrinkled was every papery fold of his pale, crepe-like skin. His hair was white-blond and wavy, reaching almost to his knees when he stood. The corresponding beard, which draped to his hip-belt, was braided below the chin.

Seeing the three beings walk in, Heledd stood and raised his hands outwardly in welcome.

"Tráthnóna mistéireach!" he called out, his voice echoing throughout the circular chamber. It was a strong voice, most at odds with his aged appearance; a voice of charisma that befuddled Bridgette when contrasted with his eccentric attire of long robes and ancient amulets dangling from the hip-belt. He carried a staff in one hand that looked like Gary's.

His traditional greeting, which was of magical origin, surprised Collum. The fyrdwisa wondered momentarily how much interaction Heledd had with the beings of Heáhwolcen — such a welcome wasn't common outside the world above the world.

"Deity Dhaoibh, Ceannairí," Collum said, deciding instantly to be truthful about their origins, since Heledd clearly knew they weren't human. "We are Collum Andoralain, Elven fyrdwisa of Heáhwolcen; Fairy Ambassadora Emi-Joye Vetur, and Bridgette Conner, Elfling born of Earth. It is our honor to be in your presence this day."

He bowed deeply at the waist. Emi-Joye curtsied with grace befitting a queen, and Bridgette flashed a thumb's up, earning a scornful smirk from the Elf.

"This honor is mine own," Heledd said. "Why has our gatekeeper brought you to Bywyd Derwyddon this day?"

"You are familiar, clearly, with the existence of Heáhwolcen, as I surmise from your usage of our traditional greeting," Collum said. He spoke slowly, considering his words carefully. "The world above the world is under threat from some of its own people, and has been for a lengthy time. Our leadership believed this threat was under control, but in recent years this has been shown to be less control than we thought."

"Oh?" Heledd said, resuming his seat. "Please do go on."

He waved his hand, and from the shadows of the roundhouse emerged three people in hooded robes, each bearing a chair for the visitors. As soon as the chairs were positioned, the hooded people retreated into the dark. The Heáhwolcen trio exchanged quick glances, then sat, letting Collum continue explaining.

"The country of Palna has been bordered off with a barrier that is strongly spelled and warded by our leadership. Those wards are supplemented with ritual and magics from other beings as well. It provides a generally strong combination of skills and intention," the fyrdwisa continued. "However, there seems to be some weakening of these wards in certain spots. We do not know why, but we struggle to fix them. Though our eventual plan is for all of Heáhwolcen to again be united, it would be best at this time for the wall to remain whole, until we are better able to plan for the re-integration of Palnans into greater society. It is our understanding that where our magics may fail at strengthening this series of wards, when combined with Druidic magicks, we may perhaps be able to address the weak spots."

Heledd cocked his head to one side.

"You wish for Druids to aid you in imprisoning our fellow beings?" he asked. Though the Ovate Adept's voice was calm, there was a deeper emotion decipherable in those words.

Oh boy, Bridgette thought. She spoke before Collum could resume digging their grave.

"Yes, and no," she said quickly. "I don't know how much you know of Craft Wizardry, but the short story is, it's a pretty shitty form of magic. It's been outlawed for good reason, for like, almost two hundred years in Heáhwolcen. But the Samnung, which is the government there, didn't want to kick all these beings back out into the world or to Earth. That seemed really dumb, so the compromise was they could remain safely in Heáhwolcen, free from the persecution against magic, so long as they kept to themselves and also did not practice Craft Wizardry ever again. About twenty, maybe twenty-five years ago, the leadership of Palna put up a shield wall of its own *inside* the ward-wall that the Samnung controlled. Then, you remember when that total eclipse happened, right?"

Heledd nodded. He seemed wary, but hadn't interrupted.

"So this eclipse took place, and according to our sources in the country, Palna's two leaders did some crazy ritual thing that harvested energy from all of its citizens and turned what was originally a random shield wall into a powerful magical object. They call it the Ballamúr and now that it is activated? One word from Ydessa or Eryth Tinuviel and they could blast through the Samnung's weakened wall, into Heáhwolcen and who the fuck knows where else," Bridgette said, her voice getting slightly louder with anxiety. Despite her casual vernacular, the gravity of what was happening in her beloved motherland was finally hitting now that she had to explain it to someone else.

She took a breath. "We don't want to go to war. We don't want to cause the rest of Heáhwolcen's citizens to freak out. We *do* want the non-crazy people of Palna to get out of being imprisoned in their own walls, because that is honestly so stupid of a place for them to be. Like, it's not every citizen's fault their country was founded by a murderous villain, you know? But the Tinuviels have to be out of power before that can happen, and we don't want to have Craft practitioners invade us while we're putting all of this in place. So we need the walls to hold, and we can't do that alone. Even though Druidic spells are similar to Elven magic, where they commune directly with Nature and the elements, Craft Wizardry wasn't developed to battle Druidic magick. We think that our powers combined is the only way to handle the situation."

The roundhouse filled with such silence that Bridgette wondered if anyone was even breathing. None of the three was about to rush Heledd into making a comment, much less into making a decision.

After a minutes-long pause, Heledd looked to Bridgette. "You are not who they say you are, Elfling."

She blinked. "I am an Elfling. I am of Earth."

"Ti yw'r Liluthuaé," Heledd murmured. "You are the Bright Star."

Bridgette nodded, curious as to how he reached that conclusion; how he even knew of the Elven legend. "You're right. I am the Bright Star."

"Y gwyr yn erbyn y byd: the truth against the world. You are Truth. Truth is Maylemaegus," Heledd said, almost to himself, and Collum had to stop from jumping in shock. Those were the exact words Trystane had said to him weeks ago, about those documents they hadn't bothered to look at yet, smuggled by Aelys Frost herself.

But the words meant nothing to Bridgette and Emi-Joye, who continued to sit patiently.

Heledd went on, "There are no Druids in Heáhwolcen. It is not a place for us. We belong grounded on this Earth, in these instances of space, time, and infinity. This is known. However, there is Druidic magic in Heáhwolcen. There has always been, and will always be. One does not have to be like mine kin and I to be its comrade."

Bridgette took a sharp intake of breath, her eyes shifting and glinting in the strange not-quite light of the dim roundhouse. "Artur Cromwell didn't just have Druid ancestors. He *was* a Druid."

Heledd's smile was confirmation enough.

"Should that not mean, Ceannairí Heledd, that Artur Cromwell's descendants will be Druid as well?" Emi-Joye asked.

"Ahh, an interesting inquiry," Heledd said, his smile growing bigger. "Though magic traverses the blood, to be a Druid is naught but a path of life. Our magicks are only different than yours in the sense that we live this path daily, bonding deeper with the celestial bodies, Nature, and the collective Universe, during every second of our existence. To be Druid is not to have an ancestry of such — to be Druid is to desire and hone connection between soil, sky, and sea; between that which is, that which was, that which will be."

"So Nehemi — the queen of Endorsa, who is descended directly from Artur Cromwell — can't do Druidic magick herself because *she* isn't a Druid?" Emi-Joye queried. "But given that Heáhwolcen exists because it is inherently imbued with such magick, does it not makes sense that a skilled witch could pick up the practice?"

"It is a path, not a practice," Heledd replied.

Bridgette understood, though she wasn't sure if it was common sense or her sierwan gift that put Heledd's meaning together. "Druidry is more than just spells, it's a deeper appreciation for existence, like Heledd's been trying to say," she explained to her companions. "So yeah, you're practicing magic, but that connection is really what's honed instead of skill with a wand. That kind of work gives a different level of strength and vitality to the spells when they're performed."

Heledd inclined his head. "Precisely."

"You won't come with us, and you're not going to send any of your followers to help. I can tell," Bridgette went on, her comment met with a curious glance from Collum. "But you also haven't said you *won't* help us."

She disliked this strange game they seemed to be playing, almost a chess match where the opponents were equally talented. Soft, subtle moves across the board, both feeling the other out for blind spots and potential risk.

Her heart went as cold as ice as she suddenly noticed their own blind spot, and spoke to Collum through the ísenwaer:
Throw your mind out and read the damn room. How many others are hidden in the shadows?

He whipped his head to her, forgetting momentarily that theirs was a shared secret. The fyrdwisa caught himself though, just in time. As he outwardly expanded his gift to the unseen beings, he spoke aloud to Heledd, "We have shared our purpose in coming here. What is it that gives you pause about aiding our cause?"

I haven't the slightest idea why I did not think to do this before, he thought to Bridgette. *There are seven others in this chamber beside*

Heledd — whose mind I will refrain from tuning into at the present moment. This chamber is spelled so I can only sense the presence of several dozen more minds out in the commune, waiting until it is deemed safe to emerge.

The Druid shifted his weight, not out of discomfort, but almost to see how the visitors would react. When they did not move themselves, he sighed deeply, resigned to answer the two questions given to him.

"The Liluthuaé is correct in her reasoning," he said. "Neither I nor those who follow the path will ascend to Heáhwolcen. That is not to say we do not feel for your need. But I do not know that we can help you any more than Druidic magick already has."

There was a hidden meaning in those words, Bridgette was sure of it. Something about the world above the world already being *of* Druidic origin in a way …

But clearly she was not yet meant to know the secret. Her sierwan gift did not show itself as she pondered what Heledd meant. When it was time, she would know.

"The magick we're looking for is already there, waiting to be found," Bridgette said aloud. "I get that. But none of us is a Druid. Can we at least have a hint as to what we should look for? How to find the Druidic spells or whatever?"

Heledd rose his ancient body again from the chair of boughs. "If you will follow me. I believe Gary is waiting to accompany us."

It was an instruction, not a request — nor an acknowledgement that the Elfling asked him a question. Collum stood, so his female companions did too. There was a rustling sound behind them, and Bridgette realized with a shudder that the seven Druids had emerged into the light, and they intended to go with Heledd.

They are the Guard of Eight, Collum thought to Bridgette in astonishment. *Eight is the number of energy flow, of balance and fulfillment. I did not expect the Druids to be so … truly like the beings of Heáhwolcen.*

What do you mean? Bridgette asked, mind-to mind, as they emerged back into the sun. He didn't answer.

- 422 -

Heledd stopped in the center of the clearing of roundhouses. He raised his hands, as he'd done when they first entered, and bellowed, "All are One!"

From roundhouses, from trees, from glamoured camouflage, more hooded Druids appeared in their midst. Heledd said nothing else, but continued walking toward the woods at the back of the field. The Druids who'd just appeared carried on with their daily activities, while the rest followed the leader.

They walked in silence, Bridgette and Collum not even speaking mind-to-mind. Whatever was happening here was beyond their control: there was a shared, unspoken acceptance that they would meet the day's events without question, no matter how strange or dangerous they seemed to be. The Druids did not seem prone to violence, and though Bridgette was not sure what their end goal was in coming here now, she was not afraid of them.

~ 58 ~

Heledd ceased the walk after what felt like at least an hour. He stopped abruptly at a parting in the trees, where the daylight shone directly onto a moss-coated floor. As he turned to face the group of followers, Heledd crooked his arms and staff in such a way that reminded Bridgette of someone about to practice yoga, or perhaps tai chi. In doing this, the very air around their group seemed to shimmer; the moss itself moved almost imperceptibly; a circle of twelve smooth stones emerged from the transposed forest floor.

The fuck? Bridgette thought to Collum, watching as the tiny plants migrated around their feet, re-positioning themselves to accommodate the sudden appearance of the stones. *Heledd didn't even ... do a spell, did he?*

The similarities of Druidic magick to Elven magic continue to make themselves known, was all Collum thought back.

What Heledd did made utmost sense to him, after hearing he and Bridgette explain the Druidic connection to Nature and the Universe. As Elves could commune directly with Nature, so could Druids, but the depth of that communication was of mind, soul, and spirit. Heledd had merely activated a connection channel and shared his mind with the lifeforms and Universal consciousness that surrounded them all, the latter part of which was untenable by any being Collum knew of in Heáhwolcen. But how to address the gap in connection? Collum supposed that once they figured that out, they could patch the Palnan border wards.

"Be seated," Heledd instructed them, taking a seat himself. Two of the Guard were instantly at his side, aiding the aged man onto the stone. He looked to the fyrdwisa. "You, Collum Andoralain, are aware of much in this space."

The Elf smiled. "I am, Ceannairí. I believe I have now understood your path, and why you brought us to this clearing."

"Do you see the way?" Heledd asked.

"I see the great path ahead of us, but know not where the trailhead lies."

It was Heledd's turn to smile. Bridgette and Emi-Joye exchanged a quick glance — the Elfling couldn't remember if the Fairy was aware of Collum's gift, and though he hadn't said a word about it, Heledd most assuredly picked up on it somehow.

She wondered if he could detect the ísenwaer.

"You were brought in this space to see where Druidry and magics new depart from one another," Heledd said. "To be Druid does not mean one is not a witch, an Elf, or Fae. One can be a witch by blood, a Druid by path. An Elf by birth, a Druid by path. A Fae by glimmering wings, a Druid by new wind-channel."

"The only way we can fix the wall in Palna is becoming Druids ourselves?" Emi-Joye asked.

"To become Druid takes many years of cultivating your path," Heledd said.

Another non-answer. Bridgette was getting rather sick of those.

"With respect, Ceannairí, I don't think we have many years," the Fairy replied. "I think we have many months, perhaps, with the knowledge that my fellow ambassador was able to provide us."

Heledd did not respond. He closed his eyes and turned his head to the streaming sunlight above them. The rest of the Guard, and Gary, did the same. The nine of them raised their arms in open embrace of the world around them, and chanted, "Seen and unseen, heard and unheard, known and unknown: all is One; one is All. Seen and unseen, heard and unheard, known and unknown: the all-mind is Universe."

They repeated this chant three times over, and without warning, the scene was frozen. Bridgette's physical form was seated on its smooth stone, but *she* was flying above them, looking down at the twelve bodies below her. She could see a wide-eyed expression on her own face, taking in the unusual ritual they'd unwillingly become part of.

The air around her was as a holographic film, shifting in shimmering pastels as she moved in the light. It was silent and yet not silent, but the sounds were ones she did not know; voices she did not recognize; whispers she could not make out. The gentle flap of birdwings and timed chirp of insects! Creaks of trees older than time itself as they inched higher into the sky! The scurrying of tiny creatures; what could be a flute played thousands of miles away. The core of Earth itself offered molten chords of cacophony, bubbling deep beneath the surface on which her body sat. The sounds and flickers of knowledge and context thrilled and terrified her; pulled her mind in millions of directions all at once, stretching further and further. She didn't know how to stop it, how to shut it off. For fuck's sake, she didn't know how to get back into the body that she could so very clearly see two dozen feet below.

Bridgette wanted to cover her ears and her eyes but as mere consciousness she *had* no hands, nor ears, nor eyes. It was a waking dream, a waking nightmare, her every essence flooded with the connections of each organism to ever have existed. Over and over again, she was pummeled with too many sounds and thoughts, and she thought her subconscious head might explode.

Then, as quickly as she'd absconded her body, she was whisked back into it, and the shock of having physical form again was too much. Bridgette swerved heavily where she sat, and fell sideways, passed out on the moss.

The entire episode had taken maybe a minute on Earth, but the time she'd been gone from them was infinite.

Emi-Joye gasped and Collum scrambled to her side, lifting her head from the grass. She was breathing, and he breathed a relieved sigh of his own.

"What is the meaning of this?" he asked, turning to Heledd. There was a darkness to those tidal pool eyes now. He sensed the magick in the ritual, unfamiliar tingles in the air and ground around them.

"A being goes to knowledge as it goes to war. Only when the mind is tranquil, at peace with its destiny, will an answer come," Heledd said. "The Bright Star has been given the answer which she sought. Gary will take you back now."

The Ovate Adept lifted a clump of moss from his stone, winked, and blew a puff of air. He and the seven other Druids disappeared instantly, the smooth stones the only sign they'd ever been there to begin with.

Emi-Joye jumped to her feet, furious. "Fyrdwisa! We cannot allow this to take place. We must go after them!"

Collum, who still held Bridgette's head in his lap, was torn between fury and anguish. "Ambassadora, we are unfit to do so, as the Liluthuaé is in this condition. I will wake her now, but I do not believe she will be of spirit to go anywhere except our lodging." He turned to Gary. "Could you tell us what just happened?"

"The Ovate Adept already told yeh," Gary said. "He gave the girl wha' she needed to know."

"But why did she lose consciousness?" Emi-Joye pressed him. "One moment we were sitting here, listening to you all chant that saying, and the next she's falling over!"

"Tha's because she got the knowledge yeh lot asked for," Gary replied. "Like I said, I don' meddle with the doin's of magical folk. We do tha' same ritual, but we don' have the magick for it to hit with the same intensity."

"Will you at least tell us what that ritual was?" the Fairy asked, her voice rising slightly. She, too, was tiring of these strange games the Druids played.

"Truth," Gary said. His tone implied he would not answer them further.

Emi-Joye gave Collum a frightened look. "Can you wake her?" she whispered under her breath.

He nodded, and whispered a word that resulted in the clearing filled with calming scents: vanilla and honeysuckle, for Bridgette; but the Fairy noted crisp gardenia and the smell of grass fresh from a midsummer rain.

The Elfling's eyelids flickered, and she stumbled out of Collum's grasp, landing on her palms and legs in the moss.

"What the *fuck* was that?" she shouted, looking first at Gary, then at the empty stones where the Druids no longer sat. "Where the fuck did they go? Did they just leave us?"

"Yes," Collum answered. "Can you stand?"

She pulled herself to her feet, swaying a bit as the blood

rushed back into her limbs. "What the —"

Before Bridgette could repeat her unanswered questions, Emi-Joye drew two fingers in front of her mouth, so swiftly Gary couldn't see. The Elfling could move her lips, but couldn't speak. She looked furious, but clamped her mouth together and turned toward Collum. He was ashen, anxious.

Are you alright? he asked, mind-to-mind.

Ask me that again when we get to the car, Bridgette answered likewise.

"Yeh lot, follow me," Gary said, deciding that it was time to leave the clearing. They followed him in the same silence as before, Collum trying to pick up on the man's thoughts as well as the presence of any Druids hiding in the trees and shrubs they passed. The Elf soon noticed they were not going back the same route they'd come, and tilted his head to instruct the females to walk in front of him. Should something come out of the bushes at them, he knew Emi-Joye could hold her own, but he wasn't sure about Bridgette.

I cannot wait for her to have feoht training, he thought to himself. *It would be nice to not be constantly worried about her physical safety.*

Gary took a back way to the parking lot, and though the trail wasn't well-marked, it was indeed a trail. The deceptively placed stones and trees appeared to be arranged to discourage anyone from believe its true nature. Another level of protection for the True Druids, Collum supposed.

They said nothing in the hours it took to walk back to their vehicles. Emi-Joye kept Bridgette's voice bound, though two miles into the trek she reached over to grab the Elfling's hand. She gave it a squeeze and mouthed "Sorry" with a pained expression. Bridgette responded with an eye-roll and a half-smile of her own.

Collum let his feet do the walking for him. His mind was elsewhere, flitting between listening to Gary and Emi-Joye, then back to scanning for curious beings who might be monitoring their movements. There was nothing to note, no threat he could detect. It was eerie, so eerie, to be unsure if the Druids were enemy or otherwise. He would not have thought they could be a violent group, but whatever their ritual had been, it caused physical harm to the Liluthuaé. The extent of this damage was yet to be known.

Their human guide watched them as they got into their vehicle. Gary did not say goodbye, just eyed them, making sure they indeed left. It was a few miles down the road toward the hotel before Emi-Joye removed the binding spell, and Bridgette clutched at her throat as her vocal cords tickled back to life.

"Holy shit, Emi-Joye. That is the *weirdest* feeling," she said, massaging her esophagus. "Ugh."

Collum turned from the driver's seat. "What happened in that clearing?"

Bridgette shook her head. "No clue. One second we were all there listening to the Druids chant, and then all of a sudden I'm up in the air looking down on all of us. There were all these sounds and smells and it was … it was just nuts. I couldn't even start to tell y'all what all was in my head."

"'Y'all'?" Emi-Joye asked.

"Oh. Sorry. I try not to say it because it's Southern slang. It means 'you all.' Everyone in Heáhwolcen is super proper and it seems stupid in comparison."

"You shouldn't apologize for using your language," the Fairy said gently. "We don't, and I'm sure you found it odd the first time you were called 'sigewíf.'"

Bridgette laughed. "I did, actually. I guess I won't filter myself so much. Who knows, maybe it'll catch on. But anyway. One minute I was up in the air, getting all of this crazy sensory detail, except I could still see myself sitting down there. It lasted for forever. Then I'm back in my body and I wake up and all the Druids are gone."

"You were sitting there for maybe a minute before you passed out," Emi-Joye reported. "But you say it was forever?"

"It felt like it." Bridgette shivered, though she wasn't cold. "Did Gary say anything about it?"

"He and Heledd said you were given the information you asked for, and Gary said it was a truth ritual," Collum said.

Bridgette raised an eyebrow. "I am pretty damn sure I didn't ask to hear the creaking of trees growing, but maybe our request was up to interpretation."

The three again ordered room service for dinner. They perhaps over-indulged, as at some point on the drive to the hotel, Emi-Joye remembered they hadn't eaten lunch. Once fully sated, and declaring they couldn't consume another bite, they took turns showering and preparing for bed. It would be another long day of traveling back to Heáhwolcen in the morning.

"Aren't we going to stay at the cottage again?" Bridgette asked Collum as she slipped under the covers.

"I do not plan to, unless our flights get delayed," he said. "We have much to do, and time is of the essence. Speaking of which, don't go to sleep yet. I need you both to do something for me, please."

The females regarded him with wary looks.

"We're not going to have a pillow fight," Bridgette said, grinning shrewdly.

Collum rolled his eyes and ignored her. "The Samnung will want full reports of this. I believe it would be best for each of us to share our perspectives of yesterday and today's experiences. That way, the Samnung can read multiple views of what happened, and we can see each other's as well. Perhaps one of us noticed something the other two didn't, and we will be able to put things together that haven't made sense yet."

Bridgette had brought her notebook full of Palna research, so she crawled back out of bed to fish it out of her suitcase. She stared at a blank page while the others scribbled away: *How the hell do I even start to talk about what happened today?*

"I'm going outside," she announced, not caring that she was in Elven sleepclothes. "I can't concentrate in here."

The Elfling walked into the hall without another word, then down to the lobby and outside. It was too dark to see the pages to write, but she didn't mind. She hadn't intended to journal anyway. She just needed clarity on whatever "truth" the Druids imparted to her. Bridgette closed her eyes and imagined she held her violin and bow, and began to hum the tune she'd composed during her time away. It took her deep into her own mind, and she added thrums of bass and gentle clinks of drumsticks on cymbals; a soft throb of guitar ebbing in the background. As she did this, creating an entire musical work in her mind, the sounds of the world began to join in.

She was above it all now, not separated from her body, but completely and utterly *aware* of every living thing. She could not hear thoughts as Collum could, but unmistakably could hear the outward sounds they made. Bridgette did not let their cacophony attack her this time: she could sift through the noise to filter out individual voices and sound.

The music played in the background of her mind, and she toyed with this new awareness. What did it mean, to have been gifted this? Or had she always had this ability, just been clueless as how to grasp it? The Druids said she was given the answers she needed — but how was the sound of wind through the treetops the same as knowing how to fix the Palnan barrier?

Her eyes shot open, and she spoke mind-to-mind to Collum. *I know what to do.*

Bridgette raced back upstairs and the door swung open to let her in. Emi-Joye was thoroughly confused, still writing her own summation. "What's wrong?" she asked.

"Nothing's wrong!" Bridgette cried. "Well. That might not be totally true. But I know what to do to fix the barrier. Except … ugh, I'll get to that. First things first, I can, sense the Universal consciousness."

Collum and Emi-Joye were giving her astonished looks.

"I know that sounds crazy! For real though. All those bird sounds and the creaking trees, it's the voices and sounds of every single living thing. It takes Druids years and years to be able to do that, but since I'm the Liluthuaé, apparently it's part of the whole shebang. You're the Liluthuaé, you're a sierwan, also by the way you can meditate yourself into hearing the whole world existing at once. Super weird party trick," Bridgette continued.

"How exactly will that help with the barrier?" Collum asked.

"Because it's basically Druidic magick at its finest," Bridgette said. "Being able to fix the barrier means I can use that connection to collective conscious to strengthen the spells the Samnung places."

The Elf chewed the inside of his cheek for a moment. "Bridgette ..." he began cautiously, "You cannot do magic."

She smiled painfully. "That would be the problem part."

"The only way to strengthen the barrier wall is to do so via Druidic magick. The one being who has been gifted the ability to enhance spells in such a way cannot actually perform said spells," Emi-Joye muttered. She looked up at her companions, a titter of fear flickering across her features. "Thus, there is no way to fix the barrier wall."

Bridgette's painful smile grew. "And that, my friends, is the truth part."

~ 59 ~

The knowledge that nothing could be done to prevent Palna from making its eventual move on Heáhwolcen sat heavily on the trio's spirits. They said little on the flights back, another layover in Amsterdam providing some respite from the cramped airplane cabins. Bridgette was again engrossed in movies, trying to avoid letting her mind wander to her new-found ability of connecting to the Universe without really trying. Collum decided to teach himself Welsh using a language guide purchased at the hotel gift shop, and Emi-Joye sped-read through the first two books in a fantasy trilogy, making notes in the margins criticizing what she called the "utterly illogical" representation of certain beings by the author.

"Really, this just gives more credence to the idea that Baize Sammael wasn't *entirely* off-kilter with his ideals," she scoffed as they took their seats in a hired vehicle. "Think of it! If humans knew what Fae and Elves were like, how much better their literature would be! Verivol would be horrified at the concept of what this human considers *vampire*."

"Wait until someone shows you the movie," Bridgette replied, noting the titles. "I think Verivol would forgive the shitty representation because the main vampire is *hot*."

Collum gave her a bemused look. "Could we perhaps not have a discussion on the physical characteristics of males you two find attractive? At least not while I am in the same car?"

The females laughed, and their fyrdwisa couldn't help but breathe a sigh of relief. Just a few days ago they were ready to kill each other, and somehow ... somehow they bonded during this bizarre trip across the globe.

It was late evening when the car dropped them off at Endicott Park, where Etreyn again waited for them to privately portal up. He joined them, and the four were greeted by Geongre Akiko. She ushered them into her office, giving Emi-Joye fresh clothes so she could again be her winged self, and looked to Collum, expecting some sort of report.

He smiled. "Geongre, this needs to be presented directly to

the Samnung first. I am sorry that I cannot share it with you directly."

"Worth a try," the Fairy replied, smiling. "Do the two of you require transportation?"

"I'll evanesce us, and Emi-Joye can fly herself back."

As if on cue, the ambassadora emerged, returning the Earthly fashions back to Akiko. "Thank you, Geongre."

"Emi-Joye, I plan to call an urgent Samnung meeting at noon tomorrow. I would like you to be there, for obvious reasons, and Apostine as well. Geongre, should your schedule allow, I'm sure Aristoces would appreciate your presence," Collum said.

Akiko's face lit up. "If I can make it, I certainly will. The three of you be careful, will you?"

They assured her they would, and went their separate ways.

"It feels so stinking good to be back in this bed!" Bridgette said, throwing herself on top of the comforter at the apartment a short while later. "I hate hotels."

"They are not my favorite," Collum agreed, sitting on the edge of her mattress. "That was most certainly a trip, was it not?"

"Yeah, a fucking acid trip. Not like I've ever done acid, but I think it would be like that," Bridgette replied, propping up on her elbows to face him. "I still don't know how to tell the Samnung what I felt and saw while I was up there in the conscious infinity."

"I suppose beginning your report by telling them the Druids sent you 'into the conscious infinity' would be an auspicious place to start," Collum replied slyly.

"I just feel like I'm about to let the whole country down, you know?" Bridgette said. "Like, here I am, this mysterious, legendary heroine of the Elves, supposed to come figure out how to save the world, and uh — Houston, we have a problem; she *cannot* save the world due to being physically unable to perform the assigned task."

"Your negativity is thoroughly refreshing. I might have to start calling you Emi-Joye."

"Punk."

"I'm not wrong though, am I? You being unable to patch the barrier does not mean you're not living up to what has been forebode of you. It simply means this is not the way in which the Liluthuaé will serve her purpose," Collum said gently.

"I guess," Bridgette muttered. "It's so frustrating though. We went through *all* that work just to find out that this *won't* work. I'm not exactly excited to waltz into Endorsa tomorrow and tell Nehemi that we're shit outta luck in terms of fixing the barrier wall."

"She will come to terms with that knowledge," Collum responded. "It may not be easy; we perhaps pinned too many hopes on this trip to Earth. But you will still go to Palna. You will still train with the Fórsaí Armada. You will still find out what we need to know, and how to move forward. This is just another minor inconvenience."

The Elfling sighed dramatically. "Fiiiine. Fine. I'll stop complaining. Tomorrow's a new day, right?"

"That's the spirit, Starshine."

It was pouring rain the next morning. Bridgette hadn't experienced a stormy day in Heáhwolcen yet — they were rare, given that the continent was above most of the cloudline — and the gods were giving their all to make up for insufficient rainfall the past few months. Rainy days made the Elfling want to burrow under her covers, not be out and about. Much less be out and about doing something she already dreaded.

But Collum coaxed her out of her bed and into a fresh pair of leggings and one of the new tunics she'd bought on Lammas. After a breakfast of vegetable omelettes, scones Aurelias sent during their absence, and an entire carafe of iced breakfast tea with cinnamon to aid in the post-travel sleep deprivation, the two were finally prepared to discuss their findings.

Collum evanesced them into the foyer of Cyneham Breonna, but that was a horrid mistake: due to the recent lack of rain, Nehemi had ordered that the foyer windows be open so the plants could be watered naturally. That message did not make it through to the fyrdwisa, though, whose navy whorls deposited he and the Bright Star smack in the middle of a deluge. They were soaked, and would only get wetter during the walk across the room to the stairwell.

This is off to a fabulous start, Bridgette thought to him sarcastically. *I can see the headlines now: 'Drowned Rat Claims to be the Legendary Liluthuaé; Yet Professes Inability to do Her Job.'*

Collum punched her shoulder. "Come on, you. We'll dry off upstairs."

The spell he cast had indeed almost dried them off by the time they reached the chamber. Lucilla was there, having moved her desk out of the way of the interior rainshower, and she offered them a simpering smile.

"I'm *so* sorry, Fyrdwisa. I must have forgotten to send you the notice to evanesce into the chamber hall," she simpered, the apology feigned.

Bridgette fought the urge to stick her tongue out at the witch, and instead leaned slightly into Collum, while staring straight at Lucilla. "Thank you for drying me off, Fyrdwisa. That was *so* gentlemanly of you."

The Elf groaned and pulled Bridgette into the chamber before she and Lucilla could start something he'd have to finish.

You vile thing, he thought to her.

Apostine wasn't there, nor was Geongre Akiko, but Emi-Joye sat at a stool along with the Samnung. Cloa was also notably absent, something Bridgette attributed to the meeting being called on an unusual day. There was a tense atmosphere in the room: Collum wondered if Emi-Joye had already spoken to Aristoces.

Nehemi rose to call the meeting to order, and almost immediately turned the floor to Collum. "We will begin with your report and findings, and move on to a luncheon. The Samnung is most intrigued to learn from your meetings with the human and True Druids."

She sat and looked pointedly at the fyrdwisa.

"First, allow me to express gratitude to the travel Fairies who put this agenda together on such short notice, and were able to follow the plan most efficiently and confidentially. We had no troubles on our flights or with any of the arranged transportation, and our lodging in Wales was quite efficient. The breakfast options far exceeded my experience in the past with American hotels," Collum began.

He told them of finding the museum and meeting Gary, then with help from Bridgette and Emi-Joye, described the interaction with Heledd and the True Druids. When the trio described the truth ritual, Nehemi's eyes narrowed and Trystane's nostrils flared.

"Can you tell us, exactly, about by your vision?" the Elven leader asked.

Bridgette nodded, surprising Collum. "I'd rather … show you. Can we all go in the hallway, and maybe send that witch downstairs?"

They did so, Lucilla obviously annoyed, and Bridgette arranged them in a circle. "Please close your eyes. I recently learned that my sierwan gift lets me share visual knowings, so I'm going to do my best to uh, show y'all what it was like. Not all of it, but just a taste."

She silently instructed Collum to open his mind and keep track of everyone's reactions. Bridgette was curious to know if anyone knew of what she experienced.

Their reactions were a mixed bag: Emi-Joye was miffed that Bridgette hadn't shared this with them while in Wales; Aristoces and Trystane, both of whom knew of Maylemaegus, digested the vision with terrified interest; Verivol *did* cover their ears; Corria Deathhunter wanted to, but chose to brave it out as Bridgette had been forced to. Bryten and Kharis stepped out of the circle as if they might be sick. Only Nehemi did not have a strong emotional response to seeing, hearing, and knowing the full cacophony that accosted Bridgette in those moments.

"What does all of that mean?" the queen demanded, opening her eyes. She led them back into the Samnung chamber, Verivol in a daze.

As they resumed their seats, Bridgette took a deep breath, and Collum squeezed her thigh under the table.

You can do this, he thought to her.

"It means that I have the ability to access infinite consciousness, the Universal collective and Nature, like a Druid does," Bridgette said. "It means I can use Druidic magick to strengthen the barrier wall spells."

Elation was the first response to cross the table. Until Trystane spoke up: "Except you cannot perform magic, Bright Star."

"Right. That's the hiccup," Bridgette said.

There was a long moment of silence.

"What does *that* mean?" Nehemi asked, leaning across the table. There was a cold, cold look in her golden eyes. Fierce, like a lioness about to pounce on a mouse.

The Elfling fought the urge to run.

"It means we can't fix this," she said. "Not unless one of us decides to spend nineteen years on Earth to become a Druid, then defy the rule that doesn't let Druids come to Heáhwolcen, to portal back here and patch the wall."

That news was met with predictable groans, anger, headshaking, and a defeated pound of her fist on the table from the Bondrie master swordswoman.

"I'm really sorry," Bridgette said. She was on the verge of tears. "That wasn't the report any of us wanted to bring back, but it's the truth. If there's a way to stop Palna, or really stop Craft Wizardry from rejoining the greater world, it's not going to be through fixing the barrier wall."

Aristoces laid a gentle hand on Bridgette's. "You went through a great ordeal to find this information for us, Liluthuaé. For that, we are grateful."

She smiled at the Fairy, thankful that at least she had one non-Elven ally in the government.

"However," Aristoces continued, and Bridgette's smile faltered, "This places greater impetus on your journey into Palna. You have been found to have this new, even more unusual gift. Perhaps it will be a boon to this leg of your destiny. We can prepare you to the best of our ability by continuing to research the country's culture and recent past. You will also begin your physical training here tomorrow. Your Majesty, is

Herewosa Donnachaidh prepared for his new student?"

Nehemi looked to Kharis, who nodded.

"I will ensure he is aware, Ceannairí," the wizard said.

"This is most excellent," Aristoces acknowledged.

"I do not think our previous timeline is sufficient," Nehemi remarked. "That plan was forfeit the moment Bridgette learned she could not perform the spells needed to fix the wards. If there is imminent risk to Palna's perhaps-army flooding through the barrier at any given moment, we cannot afford to procrastinate sending her in."

Verivol shot her a look that clearly indicated their disapproval, and Collum made a mental note to thank the Sanguisuge later.

"We cannot send her in unprepared, Your Majesty," the Elf said carefully. "It will do as much harm to place an untrained wígend in a battle as it will to risk waiting until the time is perfect to strike."

"She will not be unprepared. Herewosa Donnachaidh will train her, and a more adept mentor you could not ask for," Nehemi retorted, insulted. "The Bright Star doesn't need to be a fully trained warrior before going off to pretend to be a college student, for deity's sake. The basics of combat will suffice."

"*The basics?*" Collum was nearly seething. "Do you have any idea —"

Trystane interrupted before the queen and fyrdwisa went into a shouting match. "Your Majesty, what is the timeline you'd like to see?"

"Four weeks' time."

Bridgette blanched. *A month?* she thought to Collum. *I mean, I didn't think we'd be dragging this out for too long, but just one month? Is Nehemi crazy?*

Collum didn't respond to his companion, but rather fixed his gaze on the Endorsan queen. "I caution you, Your Majesty, against making an ill-informed mistake."

"Bridgette is to report to Minthame by eight o'clock tomorrow morning, Fyrdwisa. Do not be late. Is that understood?" Nehemi instructed, choosing to ignore his warning.

~ 60 ~

Bridgette barely touched her dinner that night. Collum made a rich, protein-heavy meal of roast chicken, fresh field peas, and sweet corn, and though it smelled delicious, the Elfling felt sick to her core after the Samnung meeting.

Four weeks. One month. That's all the prep time she would get before they would send her into Palna. So much to do; so little time to make it all happen. She got up from the table and rummaged for a gingewinde bottle to soothe her jittery nerves and stomach.

"How did we go from months of training to one month?" Bridgette asked.

Collum had already decided the whole apartment would be scented in honeysuckle and vanilla for the next month, and sent Aurelias on a venture to procure everlasting wax candles that could be placed in Bridgette's room and bathroom. Whatever he could help keep his Starshine calm and focused, he would, no matter how silly his fyrdestre thought him.

"Nehemi is worried," Collum said simply. "The full Samnung is. And has been. I think she made a hasty decision, and it was in poor taste to make such a declaration without consulting us all. It was as if she knew nothing could be done — or perhaps has such little faith in us that she resigned herself to that fact many moons ago — and therefore made her own plans."

That didn't help to comfort Bridgette. She went to take a bath, her stomach grumbling in an odd gurgle of part hunger, part desire to vomit everything she'd eaten her entire life.

Meanwhile, Collum set the dishes to wash, feeling defeated. Not that he wanted Bridgette to know this: he hadn't lost belief in her, not at all. The fyrdwisa had no doubt that Bridgette Eileen Conner could battle Baize Sammael himself and win, provided she had the proper training. But he was concerned that their warning to not hurry was not being heeded. He was concerned that there was a larger *something* at play, that Nehemi perhaps suspected, but hadn't shared with anyone else.

He slipped two fingers underneath one of his covenants, and summoned Trystane. If anything could help him sort out his depressing thoughts, it was an evening spent with his "brother" and a glass or seven of that liqueur.

The Elven leader rapped sharply on the door several minutes later, already holding a crystal goblet out to Collum as the heavy wooden barrier swung open.

"Your summons sounded like you needed this," he said.

Collum accepted the drink gratefully. "Thank you, Trystane."

"Mine pleasure, Fyrdwisa," the Elf said in mock formality. "What's on your mind?"

They sat on opposite ends of the sofa. "I have no doubt that Bridgette will fulfill what was forbode of her," Collum began. "None whatsoever. But I'm wary of Nehemi's new plan, for a number of reasons. Firstly being the safety of Bridgette's now-rushed training before she goes to Palna. I don't expect her to get attacked by sword-wielding Ealdaelfen the moment she crosses the barrier walls, but I do worry that she'll find herself in some sort of scrape and have to go on the defense. I'm worried four weeks is not enough time for her to be sufficiently versed in her cover story and past life. You of all beings know that when we send an operative in, they are prepped for at least a month on that alone! Furthermore, if Ulerion *is* still in Palna and is unable to submit reports to an official government body, how in the seven hells is an Elfling who can't do magic supposed to secretly send information?"

"These are all excellent questions, Collum," Trystane said. "I do not think Nehemi has considered any of them."

"Neither do I," the fyrdwisa agreed. "Which begs the additional question of what she's hiding."

That caused Trystane to sit straighter. "What do you mean?"

"This whole … everything! None of it reads right," Collum said, frustrated. "It goes back two years, to when there was the complete lack of communication about finding Bridgette to begin with. As if Nehemi didn't want there to be a Bright Star. I found that to be vanity, at the time; perhaps she was afraid of being usurped in popularity. She's never respected Bridgette, who in turn refuses to respect her, and *that's* always fun."

"To be fair, none of us really respects Nehemi," Trystane laughed.

"True," Collum admitted. "She's still the queen of Endorsa though! Should that not come with this expectation of mutual respect?"

"It should."

"But that is beside my point," Collum went on. "I do not understand Nehemi's reluctance to search for Bridgette, followed by her insistence that since Bridgette is the Liluthuaé, now it's perfectly okay to send her into a country that only two, perhaps three Fairies have set foot in during the last two centuries. When and why did this switch of thought occur? Does she still question Bridgette's validity and authority, and is doing this in the hopes it will kill the Bright Star?"

"I do not know," Trystane replied quietly. "Nehemi is, and always has been, an enigma to us. I do not understand her methods of leadership, only realize that her citizens adore her for being the long-awaited for child of their beloved former king and queen. You know I don't agree with her on this. I think she's out of her mind to expect Bridgette to be any sort of prepared after merely four weeks of training."

"Why did you and Aristoces not speak up?" Collum asked. He didn't want to blame this situation on them, but it irked him mightily that the only one who'd stood up for Bridgette in the meeting was he.

"Do not read into that as a personal affront, Collum," Trystane chastised him. "Nehemi is, by birthright, the Spreca. We do not tend to recognize her as such, in part due to her youth, in part due to her lack of commanding respect despite her dominating personality. But no new Spreca was elected after her parents died, and though Aristoces took up the mantle and wears it well, Nehemi is technically the leader of the Samnung, the one whose voice is final. That being said, if we get a week or two into Bridgette's training and it does not appear to be going well, I will be the first to tell my fellow ceannairí that a month isn't near enough time."

Collum processed those words. He could accept that, and could do so from his role as fyrdwisa — not as Bridgette's friend and companion. For this moment, he hated having to draw such a line.

"We are on the same page, brother," Trystane said. "I adore the Bright Star as much as you, and have concern over her safety, too. This will work out as it is meant to. Do you recall what Emi-Joye said during her ceremony, about the foighne agus grásta?"

Collum shook his head.

"It is the concept of patience and grace. To know what will be, but to accept that the timeline is out of your control, and in the hands of deity and spirit. That is where we are now with Bridgette. I have chosen to go this route, though it is unfamiliar in its entirety," Trystane explained. "I suggest you do the same."

The Elven leader was gone by the time Bridgette finally emerged from her soothing bath. She found Collum still on the sofa, though he'd switched to a bottle of elixir instead of brandy.

"I'm nervous about tomorrow," she confessed.

He padded the seat next to him, inviting her to sit. "Don't be. You'll do great, Starshine. Everyone has a rough first few days, myself included. My advice? Do not expect to leave after lesson one as an expert in hand-to-hand combat. Do not expect to leave any lesson with Herewosa Donnachaidh as an expert in combat. Even the greatest warriors of old could still learn, practice, and sharpen their skills. You and I are no exceptions."

When Bridgette and Collum arrived at Minthame, the home of the Fórsaí Armada, the next morning, she was dressed in what was probably the Elven equivalent of workout leggings and a sports bra. Both were fashioned of lightweight leather; thicker than what she normally wore, but thinner than full fighting leathers and armor. Those would come later — *much* later, Collum assured her.

Herewosa Donnachaidh, however, was dressed in what Bridgette assumed to be traditional battle attire for the Fórsaí

Armada: leather from head to toe, with protective metal pieces over the shoulders, elbows, and knees. His metal was the bronze of Endorsa, and she knew him then to be part of the Cailleach — the witch and wizard warriors equally skilled in combat and Cath Draíochta. Donnachaidh stood a foot taller than Bridgette, and from the little she could see, his fair skin was covered in both freckles and tattoos. He had short-cropped hair dyed neon orange, with a geometric design of arrows shaved behind both ears. Though he was distinctly of human descent, the wizard's eyes were as bright green as Trystane's, albeit more kelly than emerald. The Elfling wasn't sure whether to bow or tremble in his presence.

"Bright Star," he greeted her, his voice gruff and professing the same semi-brogue as Collum. "Welcome to Minthame."

"Thank you," she said weakly. "Um, I've never fought before."

"I did not think you had. Her Majesty instructed us to begin at the beginning," Donnachaidh replied. "And so we shall. It does not matter how much force you put into a punch, a kick, a weapon swing or stab, unless you are punching, kicking, swinging, and stabbing from the right positions. We will start with proper footwork for these next two to three weeks."

Bridgette tried not to let her disappointment show. That was nearly the full time she was allotted to train! She'd been looking forward to learning the ins and outs of hand-to-hand combat, and while she figured day one wouldn't involve a Braveheart-style longsword … multiple weeks of footwork seemed unnecessary and tenuous.

But she nodded. "I'm here to learn, Herewosa."

He smiled, in such a way as if he *knew* she was dreading footwork, and turned to lead her into the main training building. Minthame was a massive complex, Collum had told her. It included not only the barracks and grounds, obstacle courses and fighting circles, but magically protected acreage of different environments to teach and test how various spells and techniques would perform in assorted climates.

Bridgette followed Herewosa Donnachaidh toward the

central-most area of fighting circles, outlined in white chalk on the dark soil, hardened by centuries of warriors using it to train. They were surrounded by pairs, foursomes and even one group of twelve — fighting in uneven distribution, all of whom seemed fully focused on their opponents.

Her instructor picked a circle, then turned to face the apprehensive Elfling.

"Stand with your feet shoulder-width apart," Herewosa Donnachaidh instructed her. "You're right-handed, yes? Now step your right leg back so that it is at approximately a forty-five degree angle from your lead leg, which should be facing forward. Fist your right hand out by your cheek, your left in front of your jaw. Loosen your shoulders and your posture. Stand up a bit, not on your toes, but the balls of your feet, keeping your ankles loose. As if you're ready to spring at a moment's notice."

So many instructions, Bridgette thought, but did as she was told. A few adjustments later, and she was ready for lesson one in footwork. The basic step was to move forward and back, right and left, focusing on maintaining the same distance and angles between her feet at all times. Going forward or to the left, she led with her left foot. Back or to the right, she led with her right foot. Herewosa Donnachaidh had her do patterns: three steps in each direction, a box inside the edges of the circle, as she moved around the fighting ring.

Bridgette's bare feet, unaccustomed to both the texture of the grit and the weight of supporting her body in a new position that stretched her hips and calves, began to blister angrily. She started to go off-balance, and wrenched her core strength to hold her upright — and her mental strength to push past the raw wounds now open on the balls of her feet and toes.

For a solid hour, nothing but this. At some point she realized Donnachaidh left her to her own devices, and was out of her line of vision. She paused her relentless steps long enough for one deep breath before he reappeared behind her.

"Do not stop. You have twenty more minutes today, and then we will rest before a few rounds of putting this into practice," he said.

Bridgette was already so exhausted she could barely nod. She picked her stance back up, noting that it already seemed a more natural feeling to have her hips and legs in such a way than it had when she first arrived. These were some of the longest twenty minutes of her life, and when a bell next to her finally rang, it was all the Elfling could do not to collapse and never move another muscle.

Donnachaidh handed her a leather waterskin, and she chugged the entire thing before coughing out a thank-you.

"Holy shit," she gasped out. "This is absolute insanity."

"Your body will become accustomed to the motion, and you will grow stronger. And you're an Elfling: you have an inherent ability to develop muscle faster than those of us with human ancestry," the instructor said.

He gave her a few more minutes' rest, then told her to get back into position. Donnachaidh stood across from her and showed her how to use her lead and dominant hands to jab forward — a "one" and "two" punch, respectively. He slid thick pads onto his forearms and held them out for her to practice hitting, going slow at first to perfect how the entire body needed to move for maximum power behind each.

"I understand that at first, we have limited time together. As such, we will concentrate on the basics. From now on, an hour of footwork, followed by an hour of punching rounds," Donnachaidh said to her when the lesson was over. "When you return from your excursion, we'll build into kicking, kneeing, and defensive moves, and as time progresses, add weaponry and weight. This is the same combat training we all do, no matter what branch. Elves fight from the ground, and Fairies can, as do our other non-winged magical brethren. You're training to be one of us, Liluthuaé."

He practically murmured the last sentence so no prying ears could overhear.

"Well, hopefully it sticks better than any other extracurricular activity did," Bridgette said, laughing. "The only thing I'm good at really is the violin, so who knows, maybe I can at least hold my own as the Elven equivalent of a drummer boy."

~ 61 ~

Bridgette could barely get out of bed the next morning. Everything, save her fingers, ached from the feoht training. Her joints felt stiff and unused; her calves were so tight it was difficult to stretch them out enough to put her feet flat to the floor to walk. Even a task as simple as twisting her doorknob activated sore muscles in her torso and arms she didn't know existed. She would kill for some of Collum's salve. This was worse than her body being on fire after flying the first time.

The scent of buttery biscuits was the only thing that motivated her to ease her miserable physical form out of the guest wing and into the kitchen. Bridgette winced with pain as she stepped nearly tip-toe down the hallway: her feet seemed permanently formed to footwork position.

"How do you feel?" Collum asked, observing her from the table. He was trying hard not to let the corners of his mouth turn up in a bemused smile.

She looked daggers at him and practically growled, "The bottoms of my feet are living blisters. My back, my abs, shoulders, and arms feel like I tried to grow wings and fly, but failed miserably and wound up catapulting straight back to the ground to crash-land flat on hard clay. How the fuck do you think I feel, Bundy?"

"You're so sweet to me, Starshine."

"I cannot fucking walk. I'm hungry and I want to go lay in a bath of liquid ibuprofen until I die."

He did grin this time. "Welcome to the Fórsaí Armada, Liluthuaé."

"I have to do this every day for how long, again?"

"Until you can defend yourself from potential physical threats."

"Cool, so forever, then."

Collum laughed. "That is indeed why the Fyrdlytta trains daily, no matter the threat."

"I didn't think I'd be so grateful to only have four weeks of this shit," Bridgette replied. "Hand me that coffee?"

She was embarrassed to limp into the practice ring for her lesson that day, but Herewosa Donnachaidh assured her it was to be expected. He offered her a salve similar Collum's, specifically to address the feet and their accumulated blisters. Bridgette pursued her footwork slowly that day, carefully placing her toes and the balls of her feet instead of rushing through as she had the day before. She paid more attention to the angles of her positions, particularly as she jabbed forward and from the side when it came time to throw punches. Her body throbbed, but she insisted on fighting through it.

No pain, no gain, she thought vaguely to herself. She threw one- and two-punches on command, aiming at the empty air, then at the pads on her herewosa's arms and legs again.

After what seemed like endless combinations of stepping, punching; punching, stepping; her two hours were up. Bridgette nearly collapsed again on the hard-packed earth beneath her.

"I'd like you to stay a bit longer this day, Bridgette," Herewosa Donnachaidh said, kneeling next to her. She looked up with a grimace, and he chuckled. "Not to teach your physical form, but to teach the mind. The fyrdwisa requested you learn more of the Armada's history, particularly as it pertains to the Ingefeoht."

Bridgette chugged from the waterskin he handed her. She wasn't in the mood for a history lesson, but if Collum requested it, she'd humor him now and berate him later.

"Follow me," Donnachaidh instructed her, and she struggled to her feet, tip-toeing behind him deeper into the Minthame complex. He led her past fellow wígend in more fighting circles, beyond the barracks and cookhouses, into what looked to be the administration wing. Up a spiral flight of stairs, down a marbled hallway — Bridgette hadn't put shoes on; the cool stone felt wonderful underneath her aching feet — and into a completely black room. Donnachaidh shut the door behind them, and the two were in utter darkness.

She heard him whisper a word and realized immediately it was a spell. The room slowly came to life, and Bridgette found herself not in the extensive home of Heáhwolcen's warriors, but in the middle of the woods. She heard shouting and screaming, and turned to the right to see a young girl bolting toward them. The girl was chased by humans in period dress, brandishing flaming torches and pitchforks.

Bridgette looked to Herewosa Donnachaidh for explanation. Should they run?

"Thousands of years ago, long before Artur Cromwell was born, magical beings already existed on the Earth that you called home," the instructor said. "Though some humans revered them, most feared them, as I am sure you know. Scenes like this were common. Too common, when a human mob would chase after *children* and *younglings* because they were different. After a time, each of our individual species of magical being assembled fighting forces to fight back. Witchcraft practitioners like my ancestors developed the art of Cath Draíochta, enabling them to fight with hand, weapon, and word. It was incredibly dangerous for witches and wizards to fight humans though: Many times, as I understand you know from the Salem Witch Trials, it was innocent humans who were being persecuted as well as witches. For our ancestors to out themselves as actual magical practitioners was to put their lives, families, and livelihoods at risk. Yet time after time, they did."

The scene in front of them altered, and a group of men and women in long robes stepped forward from the trees. One woman scooped up the screaming girl as the rest of the assembled magical beings banded together to cast spells upon the mob. Bridgette watched as trees moved to block them, as additional beings high in the trees shot arrows and threw rocks at the humans. When a human's torch hit dry timber, a witch was quick to put it out.

"It was not just the witches who chose to do this. Simultaneously during these periods of time, the Elves and Fae were attacking similarly," Donnachaidh continued. "Elves did not join the public much, as it was hard to blend in and not be caught as *other*, but Fairies could banish their wings and glamour their eyes to be human if they chose. Or if this life was chosen for them, as it was with our founder Galdúr. All around the world, magical beings were uniting to protect their heritage and young. Even the Sanguisuges, whose history has been the most co-opted for human consumption, established their own fighting force. It is there from which vampires were accidentally created: One can be born a Sanguisuge, but if a Sanguisuge bit a human and the human did not die, it became an entirely new being. So much of that happened throughout the centuries that vampires became magical creatures in their own regard, though they are quite different from their predecessors that Ylda designed and sent into the world."

The images of fierce Elves and Fae, both European Fairies and African Aziza, entered the scene in front of the two wígend. The Elves carried swords and arrows, the Fae quivers with daggers at their belts. A hoard of bats dangled from a tree limb. Dwarves, which were rare in Heáhwolcen, and Gnomes walked proudly at the feet of their taller magical brethren. All around Bridgette in this room, the spirits of hundreds of thousands of felled magical warriors made themselves known. They had been prepared to die, and their sacrifice was what made her beloved new home possible, so many centuries later.

As Donnachaidh's story moved forward, the room went pure white, then suddenly Bridgette recognized the Minthame complex in front of them. But the vision was older; it clearly wasn't modern-day Heáhwolcen.

"When Heáhwolcen was more fully established, specifically once a significant number of Elves and Fae joined my ancestors in the world above the world, it was decided to form a cohesive government," Donnachaidh said. "The Elves wanted to keep to themselves, and the Fairies were already considering their passion for goodwill betwixt Earthly and magical beings. Thus was the formation of the Samnung, with an old Artur Cromwell and Galdúr at its helm, leading Endorsa and Fairevella. Aelys

Frost, of course, represented the Elves. It is not known at what point other representatives were invited to join, though it was the three country leaders who truly ran the show. With government came the formation of a united front of warriors, and combat and weaponry became skilled careers. The Cailleach of Endorsa features a host of spell-workers and Cath Draíochta practitioners. The Míleta became our flying force, though Fae were trained equally in land combat should their wings be injured, or an enemy spell make the sky dangerous. Your Fyrdlytta are the most skilled in combat, and some Elven warriors have the ability to shift the terrain to our benefit."

Bridgette tucked that nugget away in her brain — it meant that if things came to war with the Ealdaelfen, they could likely do the exact same thing.

"When Baize Sammael ascended to Heáhwolcen, he was an anomaly," Donnachaidh went on. "None of our leaders knew his age, but all recognized his great power and charm. Though it is seen now in hindsight as a master ability to manipulate, at the time Baize Sammael was considered the future of magic. He presented Craft Wizardry in such a way that beings flocked to learn from him, to add this new form to their own skillset. He traveled to Earth to spread the word of this new magic with other beings, and they came to Heáhwolcen in numbers not seen since Artur Cromwell himself was alive."

The most beautiful man Bridgette had ever seen emerged from the doors of Minthame in the scene. He was tall and trim, though heavily muscled, as though body fat was simply a thing that didn't exist on him. He was dressed in high-waisted leather leggings in a shade of aubergine, with a black top tucked into the waistband and a printed set of fitted robes worn over it. Baize Sammael had coppery-gold hair that waved in the breeze, its gentle curly texture giving him a distinctly Greek sculptured look. He had the straightest nose, most even features and chiseled jawline. In fact, the more Bridgette looked at this memory of a man, the more she believed he *was* a Greek sculpture come to life. He carried a beautifully carved white ashwood wand in his left hand and twirled it absentmindedly between fingers as he walked toward the fighting circles.

Before Bridgette could ascertain any further detail, the scene abruptly shifted, and Baize Sammael was in fighting leathers not dissimilar from those Herewosa Donnachaidh wore now, with a metallic purple helm hiding his face. He was shouting commands, and there was acrid smoke and sweet smells of death permeating the air. Bridgette was hot and cold all at once, her heartbeat racing as it took in the sights, sounds, and scents of war.

"This was the Ingefeoht," Donnachaidh said quietly, taking in the scene himself. "Baize Sammael was given Palna. An entire country for those who wished to follow him. It wasn't just witches and wizards, either. There are plenty of beings within those borders. At the time, there were not Fairy ambassadors to the other countries in Heáhwolcen. It seemed unnecessary, as their leader was part of the Samnung. A great lesson was learned though: Baize Sammael never intended to assimilate into Heáhwolcen. He wanted every single human dead, along with the magical beings who desired to protect them. He saw no middle ground. And because he himself was a Samnung leader, he could tell his fellow ceannairí what he wanted them to know, and he gleaned much from those meetings. He knew where the Fórsaí Armada was weak. He had his own warriors training there, of course, but there was subterfuge. They were there to pick out when and where to strike.

"The day that war first came to Heáhwolcen, it began here. Here at Minthame. To this day we are unsure what the spark was decided to be, but in the middle of a large training session, the Palnan fighters espoused a stunning spell powerful enough to freeze their opponents in the fighting circles. They ran from Minthame back to Palna, some carried by Fairies, some evanescing long distances at a time. They joined battalions in the mountains; sympathetic recruits from Fairevella, Eckenbourne, and Endorsa picked up arms with them. By the time the spell wore off on the rest of Minthame, Palna was marching and we were scrambling," Donnachaidh said. "It was a massacre."

"But Heáhwolcen won," Bridgette replied.

"Heáhwolcen did win. But it was terrible, and it was bloody," her instructor said quietly, his voice nearly drowned out in the din of the battle scene they watched unfold. "We'd lost a large portion of our fighting force, because it was Palnan warriors and those they brought to their cause. Each branch of the Armada was training new wígend every day. Fairy ambassadors portaled down weekly to Earth, attempting to bring more beings to our cause. However, America was in the midst of its own Civil War, and so it was a time when more beings than usual wanted to exist in secrecy. A few came. But not many. Baize Sammael was very, very powerful. And none of our other leaders understood Craft Wizardry. Half of our spells were useless against it. It wasn't until several years of fighting had occurred that one of the Samnung thought to weave together the magic of witchcraft, Elven magic, and Fae magic with the land-wards of Heáhwolcen itself that we came up with a solution strong enough to hold our own."

The battle scene morphed to show a massive collection of beings in the largest ritual gathering Bridgette had laid eyes on, larger even than the crowd at Lammas. The number of color changes and sounds she picked up on reminded her of the moments she spent in the infinite consciousness.

"Whatever was happening in this ritual was bad news bears for the Palnan army," she said.

Herewosa Donnachaidh smiled. "That it was, Bright Star. This particular ritual we view now, though, was not that which ended the war. But it brought fear to Palna, and Baize Sammael made a crucial mistake. He bewitched a Unicorn to be his annwyl, an act that defies the balance of magic itself. The Unicorns would not fight for Palna. They would not fight for Craft magic. Baize Sammael and this Unicorn led the remainder of his army through the night into Heáhwolcen's encampment at the river delta in Endorsa. Our own force of Unicorns was the first to alert us of impending danger, and it was they who noted the commander's steed."

The room went dark again, and Bridgette heard the distinct braying of alarm coming from somewhere to her left. Fae light and blue flame bobbed gently in the distance on the other side of the room, showing from where Baize Sammael approached.

"The commander of the Unicorn forces called for charge. None of them was armored, save the one on watch, as it was night," Donnachaidh said. "Still, forth they came, and fought hoof and horn for Heáhwolcen. Baize Sammael had not brought enough spell-casters with him that night to fend off the horde of Unicorns. And he had not been learned in Unicorn lore: it is utterly forbidden for these beings to fight against each other. His Unicorn stopped. Simply stopped, and would not move against those who charged them."

Bridgette understood what happened. "Baize Sammael was stabbed with a Unicorn horn."

"Precisely."

"And that killed him?"

The scene shifted to show a pure white Unicorn, armored in that same purple metal as Baize Sammael's helm, standing in the middle of a battle, surrounded by fighting Unicorns taking down beings at a fierce pace. Coming at their rear was the remainder of the river encampment, brandishing weapons and flickering electricity between their fingers. And the shouting! So, so much shouting.

"Baize Sammael's body was trampled in the fray," Herewosa Donnachaidh said. "This was the final battle of the Ingefeoht: Once it was known he was dead, the forces were chased back to Palna. It had already been decided by the Samnung how to *handle* these beings. Our leaders had not expected the good fortune of Baize Sammael actually being killed. He was the most powerful Craft wizard, the only one who could unravel their spells. His body was burned and the ashes thrown off the edge of the world. There was no room in Ifrinnevatt for the likes of his spirit. To this day, I hope his soul is suffering the very worst the nine circles of the seven hells could provide."

The Elfling shivered. The room again dimmed to darkness, though she detected the sounds of cheering. The war was over; Heáhwolcen had won.

Yet somehow, here we are, about to do the same damn thing, Bridgette thought to herself.

~ 62 ~

For the first time in ages, Bridgette and Collum evanesced to Maluridae Wood that night to fly. He hoped she wouldn't need to show this gift during her time in Palna, but both of them decided it would be better for her to have a handle on it just in case. The Elfling could ascend and descend easily, and fly off in other directions, but still found it difficult to control her speed unless she was going straight up and down.

"In a battle, should you need to fly, you're going to need to be able to use your arms to fight," Collum called up to her. "You need to figure out how to direct your flight using the most minute of movements and your mind, without needing to put your whole body into it."

"That's probably why they call it fight *or* flight, Bundy," she replied, grappling in midair to hold herself still enough to shoot an imaginary arrow at the ground. "This is probably way easier to do if you're a Fairy. All your flying is in your wings and the rest of you is free to fuck around."

"Deity bless, please don't ever let me hear you say that in front of a Fairy," Collum scolded, shaking his head and laughing despite himself.

"I can't make any promises!"

They practiced for hours, until long after sunset. Bridgette was so sore from her first two days of feoht training that she could hardly move, which didn't make her in-air fighting any easier. But she pushed through, hoping Collum's salve would do its job when they returned to the apartment. Her body already found itself a healing rhythm: the footwork from today had caused a low, aching soreness instead of sharp pains at every muscle flex. In time, she knew she would be able to practice and train with minimal discomfort.

She was right. Two weeks into training, Bridgette no longer ached constantly from morning to night.

"If I'm supposed to be part of the Armada, what kind of

fighting will I get to learn?" she asked Collum one night as he massaged the salve into her shoulders, where tight muscles were visible under her skin.

"Since no one in Heáhwolcen needs to know you can fly, you'll be trained in the arts of combat and weaponry," Collum said. "Hand-to-hand, of course. Sword and shield, probably archery."

"Why do most Fairies fight with daggers instead of swords?" she asked, remembering the scene Herewosa Donnachaidh showed her.

"Fairies fight with swords," the fyrdwisa answered. "It's personal preference. Emi-Joye, for example, finds knives far more satisfying than a longsword. But Aristoces! She is one of the most adept swordswomen I've ever encountered, Fae or no. You should see she and Corria Deathhunter practice together."

"Excuse me?" Bridgette winced as she flipped over to face her companion. "Aristoces and Corria Deathhunter have Samnung sword fights?"

"That they do, Starshine."

"Fuck, what I'd do to watch one of those. It might be worth going to war with Palna."

Collum continued to work the salve into her back, preparing her for another long day of training followed by a protein-packed meal and reading Garrin's reports. Those were significantly less entertaining than Ulerion's. Garrin was meticulous in detail, but where Ulerion offered insight into culture and daily life, Garrin preferred to give reports on snippets of conversation and meetings.

In fact, Bridgette had looked up from one of his reports once and asked deadpan if all Garrin did was sit in a palace meeting room, waiting for news to come to him.

The memory set a smile to Collum's face. He wasn't ready for Bridgette to leave again, even though this was voluntary and necessary. They had less than two weeks left to prepare her to the best of their ability, which largely fell to him and Herewosa Donnachaidh. It wouldn't be nearly enough preparation.

"Tell me your cover story," he told her.

"Again?" Bridgette complained. "We've done this already yesterday and the day before."

"We will do it every day until it is cemented in you that this is who you are," Collum chided her.

Bridgette closed her eyes. "I am Bridgette Roberts. I was born on Earth to a human mother, Erin, who married my stepfather Paul when I was a baby. Erin was a college student along with a dude who she later found out was an Elf, and he was on Earth studying as part of one of Heáhwolcen's study abroad programs."

Collum interrupted her. "Stop calling her 'Erin.'"

"Right. *My mother* was a college student along with a dude who was an Elf. He knocked her up, but didn't want to stay, and she didn't want to leave my grandparents to move to Heáhwolcen with him. So I grew up being the weirdo with purple eyes and funky ears, and eventually my mother came clean about who my birth father was. We never told Paul, or anyone else, and I didn't believe her at first. It was only when she showed me the one photo she had of the three of us, which she kept locked in her jewelry safe, that I believed her," Bridgette said. "When I was old enough, she told me how to get to the portal. She never told me his name, though. Roberts is Paul's last name. He adopted me when they got married. My mother said if I wanted to, I could come up to Heáhwolcen and learn about my Elven heritage. And I finally did, so here I am."

"And why are you in Palna?"

"I enrolled in University classes for a secondary degree," Bridgette replied. "My bachelor's from Earth is in history and I decided to study that here, too. I begged and begged to go to Palna to learn directly from its archives, because the history that interests me most is stuff like World War II and Hitler being a total manipulative douchenugget, and the Civil War. I was fascinated by the idea that this country had a civil war too and wanted to learn more. My program thesis is going to be about how technology influences the outcome of battle, and since science and magic are so inter-related, that's going to have a big part in it."

"You sound like you're repeating this from rote memorization," Collum remarked. "You need to believe this about yourself. We cannot risk raising suspicion immediately upon you entering the country."

"Ugh. You're right," Bridgette groaned. "It's just so hard to imagine this whole other entity as *me* when I've only just begun learning about my actual history."

"What has Herewosa Donnachaidh planned for you next?" Collum asked, changing subjects.

"Probably more footwork," the Elfling groaned. "And jabbing combinations."

The Elf gave her a sly smile. "I'm going to bring a guest along tomorrow. She could do with some training herself."

About halfway through Bridgette's lesson the following day, Collum evanesced with not one, but two guests — Aurelias and Emi-Joye. Apostine flew in behind them a few minutes later, looking gleeful.

"Oh, I can't wait for this!" he called out, coming to land next to a very breathless Bridgette. "It's always the quiet ones that are the most to be feared."

She glanced at the Tief-Fae, then back at the Fairy and fellow Elfling. "What are you talking about?"

"We're going to watch our ambassadora fight," Apostine replied. He snapped his fingers and of all things, a cardboard box of popcorn appeared in his other hand. "Care for refreshments?"

The kernels glittered with edible gold. Bridgette helped herself to a handful, and the two sat on the outskirts of a fighting ring. Herewosa Donnachaidh called for a Fairy wígend Bridgette didn't recognize, a male with bluish gossamer wings. The ambassadora wasn't in fighting leathers or even training leathers. She had on a sleeveless shift dress with slits that reached high up either thigh, and a hip belt from which hung a dagger sheath.

A small crowd gathered, eager to view the proceedings. Bridgette couldn't hear what the two opponents said to each other, but suddenly, the male pushed Emi-Joye, a feline grin on his face. She staggered back a step, regaining her footing almost instantly, and pulled the dagger in the same moment. Bridgette watched as the two paced each other. The ambassadora twirled the dagger between her fingers in the same manner Baize Sammael had done his wand in the vision-room.

Emi-Joye broke the pace first, darting forward and feigning a jab. As the two went for each other, they summoned invisible shields held in their lead fists. They masterfully switched weapon hands as they stepped forward, back, side to side, changing lead sides of their body depending on how the other moved. Emi-Joye whirled out of the way of some punches, and leapt briefly into the air to avoid kicks aimed at her legs and lower abdomen. They slashed at the air in front of each other, throwing uppercuts and body punches that made the other wince. There were cheers when the male Fairy put an elbow up and knocked Emi-Joye in the jaw, a move quickly followed by the ambassadora rainbow-kicking him to the ground, using her wings to provide additional lift and force. She pounced on his prone form, and held her dagger to his throat, its blue steel blade gleaming in the midday sunshine.

A cold, icy smile grew from her lips. "Muerte," she announced, and stood.

Minthame filled with applause at the show, and Apostine was practically jumping with joy for his comrade's victory. Bridgette was shocked. She couldn't believe that Emi-Joye was this skilled with a knife. She also couldn't believe that for someone so skilled with a knife, an unskilled novice Elfling was able to choke her against a wall.

My thoughts exactly, Collum's voice came to her mind. *Emi-Joye should have been prepared to hold her own that night. She was not. She will not make that error again.*

When Aurelias entered the ring next, it was Bridgette to whom she beckoned to join her.

"Are you joking?" Bridgette hissed. "You're going to kill me!"

"The fyrdwisa would have my head!" Aurelias laughed. "I'm not going to hurt you, I'm going to teach you."

She lunged at Bridgette without warning, who stepped backward and assumed her fighting stance, muscles protesting the sudden movement. They moved slower than the Fairies had, but intentionally. Where Herewosa Donnachaidh held punching targets up for her to hit, Aurelias taught Bridgette to watch for signs her opponent was about to perform a certain punch or kick. After getting knocked down six or seven times, Bridgette finally picked up on some cues that kept her whirling out of the way, or throwing an offensive punch of her own that made Aurelias pause or retreat.

"That was *excellent!*" the fyrdestre praised her, once she called a cease to their battle. "You pick up techniques very quickly, Bridgette."

"Thanks," Bridgette replied, surprised at the compliment.

"You're going to be quite the fighter, I can tell. It will be most exciting when you return from your assignment and are able to pursue your training at full force!"

Her assignment.

The unforgettable, looming future she would face in thirteen days. Bridgette shuddered.

~ 63 ~

The day before her departure to Palna, a Wednesday, finally dawned. Bridgette was asked to attend one final Samnung meeting of preparation. Though she had no desire to be anywhere near Nehemi and the potential for another spat with the queen, it was not the end of the world for her to miss out on feoht training.

Bridgette hadn't been this nervous about a Samnung meeting since March. Thankfully, there was not a surprise visitor in their company this day, just the regular crowd of Aristoces, Trystane, Corria Deathhunter, Nehemi, Kharis, Cloa, Verivol, and Bryten. Not even spirits graced the chamber.

She and Collum took their seats, and he slipped his hand under the table to give hers a reassuring squeeze.

"Liluthuaé, are you ready for your departure tomorrow?" Nehemi asked.

"Nope," Bridgette answered honestly, causing a snort from Trystane. "Not at all. I am pretty damn terrified, actually."

"You will do well, Bright Star," Corria Deathhunter said. She rose to her full height, chrome armor clanging slightly as she moved. "The fyrdwisa will bring you to Bondrie in the mid-morning. You are to pack lightly, bringing only unmarked Elven clothes — your boots are fine; they will aid in your cover story being believable. The Bondrie Guard have alerted the Palnan government that you are coming."

"How?" Bridgette asked, unable to stop herself. "If Ulerion can't send reports out, how can the Bondrie Guard send communications in?"

"We can communicate through our own barrier," Corria Deathhunter replied. "In truth, we cannot be sure the message was received. We do not know how the Palnan wall itself is monitored on the other side."

Her unspoken words hung in the air: the Samnung also wasn't sure that Bridgette could get through.

The Elfling grinned. "I can make it through. I know I can."

They accepted this sierwan knowing without question, and

Verivol let out a deep breath.

"That is most excellent knowledge indeed," Corria Deathhunter said. "Once you are through, you will be in charge of securing your own lodgings, in the event the Tinuviels did not receive our communication. You will be provided a salary of coin and paper, as we cannot be sure either how goods and services are paid for. You will remain in Palna for two weeks, learning as much as you can about how the government operates, how the citizens feel about Craft magic and Heáhwolcen. You will find ways to learn about Craft itself, if possible. After two weeks have elapsed, you are to return to Heáhwolcen by way of the wall. Your findings will be thoroughly reviewed, and you need to be prepared to return as needed. Is this understood?"

"Yes, Ceannairí," Bridgette said.

"I will open the table now to discuss any specific things we would like the Liluthuaé to research while she is in Palna," Nehemi announced.

The Ealdaelfen, Collum thought to her.

Obviously, Bridgette responded in kind. He tapped at her foot under the table.

"Knowing the whereabouts of the Elusive Grimoire might be nice," Trystane offered.

Nehemi shot him a look. "As you well know, Trystane, that is well-hidden in my own borders."

"Are you sure?" he replied, taking a long sip from his ever-present glass.

"Of course I am sure. It was placed here following the Ingefeoht and hasn't left. You know it is so well-hidden that I myself cannot find it," Nehemi snapped back.

"Okay, so finding the Elusive Grimoire is not a priority; got it," Bridgette said quickly, hoping to diffuse the tension. "Anything else that is important?"

"We need to know what sort of forces they're amassing," Bryten piped up, a suggestion met with murmurs of agreement. "We don't even know what kinds of beings remain in Palna. If they have a Fairy aerial force, for example, that would be good information indeed to have."

"What do I do if the Tinuviels or someone starts to suspect that I'm not who I say I am?" Bridgette asked.

"You lie, Bright Star," Verivol said, smiling. "You lie, and you believe that lie until you are living it fully. We are not changing who you are. We are changing a few names and details of your past. That is all, yes?"

"I guess," she replied. "And what if I fuck up and have to get out of there like, as soon as freaking possible?"

"Get to the border wall. You are the only one of us who can cross over it, Bridgette. The moment you step over that threshold, your path is out of our sight and control," Trystane said. His words were blatant truth, but his tone was not unkind.

The longer they sat, discussing potentials instead of specifics, the more anxious Bridgette became. She was starting to question herself again, starting to feel as she had during that last intensive Samnung meeting before she ran away back to Earth.

Tell me what's wrong, Collum urged her, mind-to-mind. *You look as though you're going to be ill.*

I think I might puke, Bridgette thought back, closing her ears to the discussion happening around them. *I'm trying to keep myself from running out of here again like a fucking coward.*

He bit his lip, unsure how to ease her anxiety. *You are not a coward, Starshine. You are a light into the world. You have done much, much more in far less time than any of us could ever begin to fathom. You will enter Palna with gifts and abilities that we cannot, will not share. You will see and know things we otherwise would not. You will be our eyes and ears, and be the voice to us of Palnan citizens who wish to be rid of Ydessa and Eryth. You have much riding on you at this moment, yes, but you are* not *a coward. You are made for this.*

She stood up, interrupting the conversations she'd been tuning out. "I think this is enough chatter, y'all. I need to pack. And I'll … see you in a couple weeks, I guess."

The word "see" made Trystane remember. "Bridgette, your eyes," he said. Her sierwan gift had to be glamoured.

"Will it hurt?" she asked apprehensively.

The Elf laughed. "Not at all. You'll still be able to feel them shift, but they will remain as lilac as they are right now to anyone who's watching," he said. "Nehemi?"

Bridgette turned to the witch queen, who bade the Elfling keep her eyes open, and to glance upward. Nehemi asked Kharis to lift the chamber wards. She hushed her fellow Samnung members, and said,

"To save the vision of she who Sees,
Hide the eyes against those who peek.
Oscuro for now, and in the weeks to come,
Until her task is said and done.
By the power of three times three,
As it is, so mote it be."

The air in front of Bridgette's eyes clouded but for a moment, and the Elfling blinked. It was done.

The Samnung rose around her, even Cloa with Arctura clutched in her arms.

"We believe in you, Bright Star," Verivol said. "Thank you for your bravery."

"Thank you for coming back to us," Bryten added, earning a sideways smile from his Sanguisuge friend. "We'll miss your smart retorts while you're gone, but I promise that the two of us will try to keep these meetings entertaining."

Nehemi let out an uncharacteristic chuckle. "I do not look forward to that."

Aristoces took Bridgette's wrists in her hands. "Emi-Joye has asked to accompany you tomorrow, to the barrier. Is that an agreeable task?"

Bridgette nodded. "I'd be honored," she said, and meant it.

"Be well in your travels," Kharis offered, and the princess nodded vigorously. Arctura let out a loud purr, and jumped from Cloa's arms to circle Bridgette's ankles. She froze, not sure how to handle that sign of affection.

I'm telling you, this thing is not a normal cat, she thought to Collum as the feline leapt onto the table, where Cloa again scooped him up.

Before Collum could reply, Trystane was between them,

wrapping Bridgette in a very unprofessional hug. "We'll keep the fyrdwisa occupied. We're grateful for you, Bridgette Conner."

He let her go. The companions stepped from the Samnung chamber, and evanesced back to Aelchanon.

"As much as I'll miss you while you're away, I will not miss constantly having to feed you," Collum joked that evening, watching her eat two sandwiches in less time than it had taken to cook them. "If regular Bright Star has an appetite, wígend Bright Star is that times ten."

"Oh, shut up," Bridgette mumbled through a mouthful of meat, cheese, and toasted bread. "I can cook too, you know."

He raised a skeptical brow. "I watched you attempt that potato chowder last week. You got distracted and let the milk curdle to burning."

She chose not to respond. Instead, she asked, "Can we have one more night in your office? Tomorrow is just, so soon."

It had arrived sooner than he'd thought possible, Collum mused. They'd spent the past few weeks compiling all sorts of notes on Palnan life, on what little they could glean of Craft magic. Collum hadn't yet found his father's war journals from the Ingefeoht, and he wished they'd had those as a resource before Bridgette left. He hoped those heirlooms, both to him personally and for Heáhwolcen at large, had escaped harm in the centuries since, and would be discovered soon.

The plan was for her to spend two weeks in Palna, and she would return earlier if needed. The Elfling was disappointed to be missing Mabon, which had been hyped up as the largest food festival known to both man and magical being. The week-long celebration was slated to begin the day after she left, and no one was sure if it was celebrated in Palna. Since Bridgette's portion of Ulerion's reports ended in August, she didn't have a clue about it, and because Mabon wasn't out of the ordinary, it hadn't made anyone else's notebooks. Bridgette *was* promised an incredible holiday for Samhain, however, and assured that there would be many Mabons to come for her in Heáhwolcen.

Collum had his own assignments while Bridgette would be away. He would resume the search for his father's writings, and he and Trystane planned to take a deep dive into the Aelys Frost documents. He told the Elven leader about Heledd's knowledge of the Maylemaegus, and added that he suspected the Druids knew more about Heáhwolcen than anyone realized. Perhaps it was due to their inherent connection with the Universal consciousness — or perhaps, Trystane warned, someone else had traveled to Wales long before they had.

In addition to yet more reading and researching — which made Collum joke that by the time Palna was defeated again, he should earn a third University degree — there was a physical charge to take care of. For the first time in almost two hundred years, the full Fórsaí Armada would soon be practicing together.

The Samnung planned to move all its troops to Minthame, which would require a barracks expansion as well as additional protective wards around the complex. They did not want word of this reaching anyone else, and would be taking somewhat extreme measures to keep their preparations for war a secret.

The Elf was brought out of his reverie by a concerned Bridgette, who waved her fork in front of his face. "Hello? You alive in there, Bundy?"

"Yes," he smiled, swatting at the utensil. "I was lost in my own mind."

"I noticed."

They walked around his office paradise in silence for a time, letting Bridgette soak in every memory that she could of this place. It would be what calmed her when her anxiety inevitably caused her heart to race faster than she could fetch it. She knew it was only two weeks, perhaps a few more intermittent visits that would follow, but it was so surreal.

Ulerion liked Palna, she reassured herself. *It can't be all that awful. Just the Tinuviels are a couple of assholes, along with anyone else who might be illegally practicing Craft magic.*

She reached up to pluck a vibrant green apple from a tree in front of them and took a large bite. Its sweet tang hit her tastebuds with the intensity of a thousand Earth apples, all at once, and she wondered if Palna was able to cultivate food such as this. The tree had a crook between two branches, and

Bridgette lifted herself into the sky, settling there with her treat.

"Starshine, I need to ask you something that probably should have come up in a previous meeting, but has not yet. It has rather been an elephant in the room, so to speak," Collum said, catching the just-picked apple she tossed him. "Why do you think you'll be able to get through the Ballamúr, when the Seolformúr barricaded you?"

Bridgette flipped herself over from her perch in the tree, hanging off a thick, gnarled branch by the bends of her knees.

"The Seolformúr keeps Craft blood out," she answered nonchalantly, ripping another large bite from her own apple. "The Ballamúr is meant to keep it *in*."

Collum sat on the edge of the bed, watching Bridgette pack her bags. This was in a way worse than when she'd simply left: it was as if the Universe forced him to drag out the farewell.

All the clothes she'd bought on Lammas went in. Her training leathers, just in case. Socks and undergarments. Several sets of sleepclothes, and she started to tuck in the toothbrush Collum had saved, but he stopped her.

"Leave that here, please," he said. It was silly, he knew. Silly, like the idea of constantly filling the air with honeysuckle and vanilla. But comforting, too, and he needed that comfort right now more than he wanted to admit.

Bridgette didn't question him, and took her human toothbrush instead.

"I don't want to go, Bundy." She nearly whispered the words. "I want to live here, to be here in Heáhwolcen, and I want the people of Palna to get to experience this place like I did. But I don't want to be the one to break down the wall, and I don't want to be the one to unify the continent again."

His heart thudded. "Do you remember what you said when you came back?" Collum asked her.

".... Uh?"

"You said you no longer wanted to be the person who defied her destiny."

"Oh, right. Maybe I was being a little facetious," Bridgette said, smirking. She shook her head in defeat. "But I guess I did make a promise here, and I really feel guilty when I break those."

She barely slept that night. The same strange dreams that plagued her the first night she met Collum came back to haunt her, though this time, the unmistakable form of battle-ready Baize Sammael traipsed through them, taunting her. She dreamed she couldn't get through the barrier; dreamed she was stuck in between Heáhwolcen's wall and Palna's inner sanctum. Trapped in a no-man's land, a giant circle that went between two countries that were supposed to be of the same world.

Dream-Bridgette flew through the sky unseen, though she saw much: looked down upon burning lands and heard screams, both of victory and of pain. A child-like witch entered her mind, its face becoming contorted like the evil queen in grotesque fairytales. At one point, the Bright Star sat straight up in bed, coated with a cold sweat, unable to recall what sent her into such a state.

She checked the marked hourglass that sat at her bedside table, squinting in the dimness of early dawn to see that it was barely after six in the morning. The sun wasn't due to breach the horizon for nearly an hour, but Bridgette knew she'd never get back to sleep.

The Elfling lay on her pillow, counting the minutes as they trailed through the sand. Collum would be up with the sun, though she wasn't sure she could stomach eating anything before they left. She felt like she was waiting for her death to come.

Why couldn't Collum be the damn Liluthuaé? she wondered. *Or Trystane. Or someone else in the Fyrdlytta, who would already be trained. Why me?*

The Universe did not answer.

She dressed slowly, unable to remain in bed quietly any longer, and made her way to the kitchen table, where Collum was just arising to make coffee and get the day's newspaper. He was surprised to see her up and offered up a mug with ice for her morning beverage. They did not speak to one another, but she accepted with a blank, grateful smile.

"I wish we had time to show you Bondrie before you left," he said quietly, after a while of sitting in silence. "It is the most fascinating, to me, of all our countries."

Bridgette jumped at the chance to distract her mind from impending doom. "Herewosa Donnachaidh showed me in this like, vision-room thing, all about the Ingefeoht and the old-school warriors fighting on Earth. But the vision ended after the war, and didn't talk about Bondrie at all."

"Bondrie was not created until a few years after the wall

went up," Collum said. "Its founding citizens were all here already, though they were spread out mostly in Endorsa. A few chose to reside in the mountain ranges. More chose to come from Earth. The Samnung leaders at the time were considering amassing a branch of the Armada specifically to keep an eye on the wall, and to aid the Fairy ambassadors crossing to and from. The Cailleach was the most obvious choice, but its numbers sustained many losses during the Ingefeoht. One group that ascended the portal in this period had been estranged from their human companions, who at one time had embraced their abilities. But humans are ... human, and over time, their feelings toward magic influenced those who previously worshipped it.

"Those were warrior peoples, whose beliefs I find quite similar to those of the Druids, in many instances," Collum continued. "They found companionship with others who had come from such situations. Many were descended from indigenous peoples in the Americas, and brought their forged customs of magic and ritual to us. They also presented a new form of combat, which was far heavier on the physicality than much of what even the Cailleach could do. And so, the people of Bondrie became our guards. Of course, not all in Bondrie are of indigenous descent. There are plenty who aren't, but who embrace this form of life and culture. They differ from admirers on Earth in that they are active participants, not ones who appropriate the heritage of Bondrie's citizens and use this to laud themselves over others. Those who behave in this manner are unwelcome there, and find a better home in Endorsa."

"It sounds fascinating," Bridgette said. "I would definitely like to spend more time there, and with Verivol and Bryten. There's so much more about the beings of Heáhwolcen that I want to know. I guess it's a good thing Elflings live pretty long lives, huh?"

"That it is, Starshine."

Two hours later, they stood in the apartment doorway, Bridgette clutching her bag so tight she thought her fingers might shatter of their own accord. Her heart was beating so loud Collum could probably hear it as they evanesced to Bondrie, where they found an animated Emi-Joye making friends with two Bondrie Guardsmen. Corria Deathhunter looked on with amusement.

When the master swordswoman noted their arrival, she called the guards and ambassadora to her.

"We will walk you to the wall, and Collum and Emi-Joye will accompany you through," she said to Bridgette. "They will be unable to pass through the Ballamúr, but will see you safely until that moment."

The Bright Star gulped heavily, nodding. She couldn't speak. It was like the day Emi-Joye had bound her voice, except this was her body's own doing. They began the long walk to the wall, a silvered column shimmering off in the distance. There was a desert-like feel to the ground they walked on, with cacti and reddish soil covering the land between the woods they'd appeared in and the border with Palna.

Emi-Joye reached over and grasped Bridgette's hand reassuringly. Collum put his arm around her shoulders, the three of them following Corria Deathhunter and her Bondrie Guardsmen. Each step was like a weight, growing heavier and heavier.

The closer they got to the wall, the more Bridgette could feel its presence. It felt like a giant magnet, pulling them closer and yet repelling them simultaneously. Constant force fields at work to prevent those who should remain inside from coming through it. But the feeling wasn't the same as the physical illness of the Seolfurmúr, nor was it the wrongness of the aura that surrounded Bridgette, Cloa, and Emi-Joye. It was a true physical barrier, protected with the spells of almost two hundred years' of Elves, witches, Fae, and more. She wondered what it looked like in the spots that needed patching: Did they shimmer the same, or was the silver hue tarnished?

When they could go no further, and the electricity was nearly static around them, the Guard stopped. Corria Deathhunter turned to Bridgette and drew her sword. She knelt at Bridgette's feet, placing the sword up in a gesture of fealty.

"You have chosen to sacrifice your happiness to follow that which was forebode of you," she said. "I cannot speak for the Samnung, but I speak for Bondrie. Upon your return, we will follow you."

The Guardsmen joined her on their knees, presenting her own swords, and Bridgette felt tears starting to well in her eyes. They put *so* much faith in her ...

As the Bondrie folk rose and stepped back, Bridgette reached a hand to each, thanking them for their belief in her. She was crying openly now and welcomed the tears. They meant this crazy adventure, this whole unbelievable story, was real. And in the next few weeks, when she was supposed to pretend to be someone else, to have that reality was of vital importance to cling to.

"Here," Collum said, when the Guard walked out of earshot. He reached for Bridgette's left hand, slipped a bracelet around her wrist, and fastened it permanently with a word whispered so quietly, the Elfling couldn't hear. It was made of two braided bands, one lavender and one navy, each studded with silver beads.

"What —"

Collum held his wrist next to hers. A matching bracelet was now amongst the dozen or so he had stacked along his forearm. "I can't just let you go into Palna without some way to get back out. This is our covenant, and I vow to never let it go unanswered. Should you need me, hold your band and summon me. I will do the same for you."

"Will it work, far away like that?" Bridgette stammered, fingering the bracelet. There was no end to it now; it was perfectly sized to fit her slim wrist. A never-ending circle of bond between them. "Won't it be cut off, like Ulerion and Aristoces' covenant was?"

"We cannot know for sure, but we believe theirs was ended because he was already in Palna when the Ballamúr was activated, breaking the bond of communication. And, Starshine ... the strength of a covenant is largely based on the bond between those who hold it between them," Collum said quietly. He lifted Bridgette's chin upward to meet her eyes. "I have a feeling this one will work over many more miles than it is from Eckenbourne to Palna."

She chewed the inside of her cheek, fighting back a different sort of tear she didn't want to let free. "Thank you."

The fyrdwisa pulled her close then, and Bridgette found herself pressing her face against his chest. They wrapped their arms around each other in embrace.

I'm so scared, Collum, she thought to him. *What if this doesn't work?*

Then at least we will have tried, he thought back, squeezing her gently. *You know I'd never let anything happen to you or hurt you if I can help it. I am but a summon away, always.*

Will you stay with me?

Until the very end.

She remembered what he said to her, so long ago — the ask for patience; the gentle reassurance that one day, her forever would be there with her. Bridgette closed her eyes and held him tighter, confident in that moment that what was destined for her would come to pass. She took a minute more to breathe in every scent and feel of him that she could, then stepped back to meet his gaze. Her lilac irises twinkled, and a half-smile was forming on her mouth as she looked deeply into Collum's tidal pool eyes.

"Ready to go kick some Craft wizard ass?"

Collum's wicked grin lit up his face. He linked one elbow with Bridgette, and the other with Emi-Joye. "I thought you'd never ask."

The trio evanesced through the wall into an explosion of navy dark, unsure what they would find when they emerged on the other side. Perhaps nothing at all. Perhaps much worse than they feared. But no matter: it was in the hands of deity and spirit now.

The era of the Liluthuaé had begun.

THE MERIDIAN TRILOGY

~ Phonetic Pronunciation & Other Notes ~

Please note the below pronunciations are based on the English pronunciations, unless they are specifically words derived from other languages.

Bridgette Eileen Conner *(Brih-d-jet Eye-leen)* — your protagonist

Sorts of Beings

African Aziza *(Ah-zee-zah)* — A species of Fairy that originated in Africa, known for having wings of insects including beetles, moths, and butterflies

Baetalüan/Baetalü *(Bay-tah-loo-ahn / Bay-tah-loo)* — Magical species with human-esque builds and limbs, who have simple, small horns growing from their heads

Celtic Fae — A species of Fairy that originated in Europe, typically with gossamer-look wings, though rare Fae are born with bat-like wings

Ciguapa *(See-gwah-pah)* — Magical being found in the Dominican Republic, known for appearing as female humans with backwards feet and long, dark hair

Druid / True Druid *(Drew-ehd)* — The magical beings and human "masks" who practice a specific lifestyle that furthers the bond between sentient being, Nature, and the Universal consciousness; only the True Druids are able to perform magic utilizing this bond

Dwarf — A small, heftily built type of being known for residing in and around mountainous habitats. Rare in Heáhwolcen.

Ealdaelfen *(Eel-dehl-fen)* — The legendary sect of "dark Elves" that haunt bedtime stories of magical younglings

Ealdgecynd *(Eel-d-geh-send)* — An old term for Elves, used before the Ealdaelfen sect formed, describing them as beings who are One with Nature

Gnome — Similar to Dwarves and markedly different; another small-built being not typically found in Heáhwolcen that prefers a life of solitude and underground habitats

Kelpie *(Kehl-pee)* — A water-dwelling shape-shifting being of Scottish origin, able to take human or centaur-like form, but in Heáhwolcen typically stay as its horse-like shape

Merfolk *(Murr-folk)* — Humanoid sea-dwellers with fish fins and tails; none reside in Heáhwolcen due to its lack of ocean waters

Obeah *(Oh-bee-uh)* — A loose term used to describe some forms of spiritual healing and practices developed among enslaved peoples in the West Indies, and used among witchcraft practitioners as a descriptor for those who practice these methods

Sanguisuge *(Sayn-gwih-sooj)* — Magical being that requires only meat and blood to survive and perform magic, known for the healing powers of their own blood. Accidentally created vampires by biting humans who did not die, but instead were infected with Sanguisuge blood and became a new type of being entirely

Selkie *(Sell-kee)* — Seal-like shape-shifting beings that can become human by shedding their skin, and alternately can be enslaved if their seal skins are stolen, trapping them in human form

Tiefling *(Teef-ling)* — Solitary beings with horns like those of a ram, very adept at magics of subterfuge. Rumored to have been related to "demon races" at one time due to a characteristic pointed tail many Tieflings have

Vampire — Humans bitten by a Sanguisuge, or another vampire, thus becoming immortal beings themselves that thrive on blood alone

Witch / Wizard — Humans with magic in their veins, able to harness powers and elements by way of tools such as wands, staffs, and guiding words

TITLES

Ambassador/Ambassadora — Titles for the lead Fairy liaison between Fairevella and the various countries of Heáhwolcen and Earth

Ambestre *(Am-beh-stray)* — Second-in-command Fairy to each ambassador or ambassadora

Ard Rialóir *(Arrd Ree-ah-lohr)* — Head of the Elves in Heáhwolcen

Borhond *(Boar-hund)* — The witch king or queen's lead advisor

Ceannairí *(She-an-air-ee)* — Both a generic title for magical leader, and a specific title that can be used when addressing a magical leader, similar to "Your Majesty"

Fairy of All Fairies — Leader of the Fairies in Heáhwolcen

Fyrdestre *(Fuh-yord-es-tray)* — The Elves' second-in-command to the Fyrdwisa, and second in line to succeed the Ard Rialóir

Fyrdwisa *(Fuh-yord-wee-sa)* — The primary Elven spy and military leader, first in line to succeed the Ard Rialóir

Geongre *(Gay-awn-grey)* — Lead Fairy travel deputy

Geongrestre *(Gay-awn-greh-stray)* — The Fairies' second-in-command travel deputy

Ilwyn Gyfrinach *(Ill-wen Guy-frih-nahk)* — Also known as the Ovate Adept, the title of the leader of Druids

Iontach an Chéad Cheannaire *(Eon-tack ahn Chay-d She-an-air-ee)* — A title Fairies use when referring to the founding Fae of Fairevella

Liluthuaé *(Lih-loo-thoo-aye)* — A mythological Elven being

Master Swordsman/Swordswoman — Warrior leader of Bondrie

Raisarch *(Rye-sark)* — Leader of the Ealdaelfen, the mysterious and legendary "dark Elves"

Sigewíf *(See-jweef)* — Title of respect for a female/feminine being

Spreca *(Spreh-ka)* — Lead voice of the Samnung

Thighearna *(Thee-gar-nah)* — Title of respect for a male/masculine being

THE SAMNUNG (SAHM-NUN-G)

Arctura *(Arc-tuhr-ah)* — Princess Cloa's mysterious and ever-present cat

Aristoces *(Ah-rihs-toh-sees)* — Fairy of All Fairies, leader of Fairevella, and wisest being in the Samnung chamber

Bryten *(Brighten)* — A Baetalüan elected to represent horned beings and the more "minor" populations of magical folk in Heáhwolcen; frequently absconds shirts

Cloa *(Cl-oh-ah)* — Sixteen-year-old princess of Endorsa, addled by an unusual lack of mental presence that causes frequent discomfort during meetings

Collum Andoralain *(Call-uhm And-or-ah-layn)* — Elven Fyrdwisa and Bridgette's stalwart companion

Corria Deathhunter *(Cor-ee-uh)* — Master Swordswoman of Bondrie, quiet but quite adept at her gifts of leadership and warrior arts

Kharis *(Care-ihs)* — Nehemi's right-hand wizard

Nehemi *(Neh-heh-mee)* — Witch queen of Endorsa, haughty and proud

Trystane Eiríkr *(Tryst-ayn Air-ih-kur)* — Ard Rialóir, leader of Eckenbourne; Collum's best friend and symbolic elder brother

Verivol *(Veh-rih-vole)* — A gender nonbinary Sanguisuge chosen to represent the coteries of their kind. Loves fashion and immediately brings Bridgette into their fold and heart

BEINGS ON EARTH

Anglesey Druidic Order *(Ayn-gleh-see)* — The oldest group of Druids on Earth

Agustín Muños *(Uh-goos-teen Moon-yohs)* — Chilean leader of the human Antarctic delegation

Aroha Te Rauna *(Ah-roh-ha Te Rah-oona)* — New Zealand leader of the human Antarctic delegation

Catalina Quiroga *(Key-roh-gah)* — Argentinian leader of the human Antarctic delegation

Charles Brady — British; the United Kingdom's leader of the human Antarctic delegation

Dagmar Nilsen *(Dahg-mahr Nihl-son)* — Norway's leader of the human Antarctic delegation

Élodie Jacquot *(Eh-loh-dee Shack-whoa)* — French leader of the human Antarctic delegation

Gary — The Druids' human gatekeeper on Earth

Heledd *(Heh-led)* — The ovate adept, or Ilwyn Gyfrinach, of the True Druids

Jamie and Wade — Bridgette's co-workers at the diner in Nashville

Martha and "Doc" Joel Simmons — Bridgette's most-present foster parents

Noah Irwin — Australian leader of the human Antarctic delegation

BEINGS OF ENDORSA

Artur and Felicity Cromwell — Witch founders of Heáhwolcen in the 1690s. Escaped persecution in Europe to journey to the Americas, but after getting caught up in the Salem Witch Trials, the Cromwells chose to move forward with creating a safe space of their own for beings of magical origin and blood

Galdúr *(Gal-durr)* — Heáhwolcen's co-founder, an enslaved Black Fairy who became free after the king who imprisoned and sold him died. Joined with the Cromwells and provided the missing key spell that created Heáhwolcen

Herewosa Donnachaidh *(Hair-eh-whoa-suh Donna-key)* — Cailleach wígend and Cath Draíochta practitioner. Bridgette's feoht trainer

King Hermann *(Her-mahn)* — Former king of Endorsa, killed when errant magic from Palna overtook his carriage

Lucilla *(Loo-silla)* — Witch who acts as the Samnung's secretary, though her actual employ is to Queen Nehemi and Princess Cloa

Lymerian *(Lie-meer-ian)* — Sanguisuge owner of a crystal and ritual shop

Magister Basira *(Mah-jihs-ter Bah-see-rah)* — A professor and scholar at the University in Heáhwolcen, studying mind magics

Magister Ephynius *(Mah-jihs-ter Eh-fin-ee-yus)* — The foremost magical historian at the University in Heáhwolcen

Murthel, Teale, Avengeline *(Muhr-thel, Teal, Ah-vehn-jeh-leen)* — Members of the Endorsan Modern Kitchen Witch Society, sisters, and owners of the Coffee Cauldron

Queen Lalora *(Lah-lohr-ah)* — Former queen of Endorsa, killed when errant magic from Palna overtook her carriage

Sheridan *(Share-ih-den)* — Male witch barkeep, friend to the Fairy ambassadora to the Antarctic

Zurina *(Zuh-ree-na)* — Witch stewardess on Earth airplanes traveling on official Samnung business

BEINGS OF ECKENBOURNE

Aelys Frost *(Aye-lihs Frost)* — The original founding Elf of Eckenbourne

Aurelias Parvhin *(Arr-ee-lee-us Pahr-ven)* — Elven fyrdestre, of Tiefling and Elven heritage

Eloise *(Eh-loh-ees)* — Golden-hued Unicorn annwyl of the Liluthuaé

Ethros *(Eh-thros)* — A seordwiph and friend of Collum's

Mithrilken *(Mih-thrill-ken)* — Black Unicorn annwyl of the fyrdwisa

Mohreen Conner *(Mor-een)* — Mysterious Elven figure

Njahla *(En-jah-lah)* — Trystane's right-hand Elf, without whom he'd be lost

Starkardia *(Star-car-dee-uh)* — Ethros' daughter, the first youngling Elf Bridgette meets

Beings of Fairevella

Akiko Chidori *(Ah-key-koh Chee-dor-ee)* — Geongre for Fairevella

Apostine *(Uh-post-een)* — Fairy ambestre to the Antarctic, the first Tiefling-blooded being to take such a prestigious position

Emi-Joye Vetur *(Eh-mee – Joy Veh-tuhr)* — Fairy ambassadora to the Antarctic

Etreyn *(Eh-trey-en)* — Geongrestre for Fairevella

Frosset Malvarma *(Froh-set Mahl-vahr-ma)* — Former Fairy ambassador to the Antarctic, now serving as its ambassador-emeritus

> *Family members* —
>
> Esmerina Malvarma *(Ehs-mare-een-ah Mahl-vahr-ma)*
>
> Siofra Malvarma *(See-oh-frah Mahl-vahr-ma)*
>
> Ilayda Malvarma *(Ill-aye-duh Mahl-vahr-ma)*

Garrin Fitzhugh (Gah-ren) — Former Fairy ambassador to Palna, deceased and succeeded by Ulerion Mewt

Hafiz *(Hah-feez)* — Fairy guard and warrior

Luthus *(Loo-thuhs)* — A Fairy travel deputy

Marcallus Gaccio *(Mahr-callous Gah-chee-oh)* — Fairy ambassador to Italy and good friend and mentor to Emi-Joye

Skyanna Elixabete *(Sky-anna Eh-licks-ah-bet)* — Heáhwolcen's poet laureate

Seamund *(See-mund)* — Fairy ambassador to Eckenbourne

Tula & Johannes Vetur *(Too-lah, Yo-hahn-ess Veh-tuhr)* — Emi-Joye's mother and father

Ulerion Mewt *(You-lair-eon Meew-t)* — Current Fairy ambassador to Palna, who disappeared without a trace in August 2017

Whitby Lenoir *(Whit-bee Leh-noor)* — Fairy ambassador to Wales

Beings of Bondrie

Druan Heart of Stones *(Drew-an)* — Former master swordsman

Beings of Palna

Baize Sammael *(Bay-ze Sam-eye-ehl)* — The late creator of Craft Wizardry and founder of Palna; deceased in the Ingefeoht

Eryth Tinuviel *(Eh-rehth Tin-oo-vee-ehl)* — Current male witch leading Palna along with partner Ydessa

Sohli *(Soh-lee)* — Unknown figure whose name appears repeatedly in Ulerion Mewt's ambassador reports about the country

Ydessa Tinuviel *(Ee-dessah Tin-oo-vee-ehl)* — Current female witch leading Palna along with partner Eryth

Geography and Architecture in The World Above the World

Heáhwolcen *(Heh-uh-wall-shen)* —
Literally "continent in the clouds," a magical continent hidden above the cloudline over North America. Includes the countries Endorsa, Eckenbourne, Fairevella, Bondrie, and Palna, as well as the spirit realm Ifrinnevatt

Bondrie *(Bon-dree)* — Borderland created between Palna and the rest of Heáhwolcen. Its citizenry largely includes witches and warrior beings descended from indigenous peoples of North America

Eckenbourne *(Eck-en-born)* — Elven lands of Heáhwolcen

> Aelchanon *(Aye-ehl-cannon)* — The capital city and main region of Elven business and government
>
> Caisleán *(Case-lee-ahn)* — Elven capital building
>
> Estmereamel *(Ehst-meer-ah-mell)* — Elven city of water
>
> Faustdúnleshire *(Fao-ust-doon-leh-shur)* — Mountainous region
>
> Feormeham *(Fey-ohrm-hum)* — Rural, farming region of Eckenbourne, where Collum's apartment is located
>
> Hlafjordstiepel *(Lah-fyord-shh-tee-pehl)* — Tallest peak in the mountains of Heáhwolcen

Lisweald *(Lihs-wehld)* — Beautiful wooded, natural garden area of Eckenbourne that is primarily inhabited by Nature itself

Loch Liath *(Lock Lie-ahth)* — A recreational lake in Estmereamel

Maluridae Wood (Mah-luhr-ih-day) — Secret grove in Faustdúnleshire that can only be accessed by Elves who know of its existence

Endorsa *(Ehn-door-sah)* — The original country of Heáhwolcen

Coffee Cauldron — Magical coffee shop frequented by Bridgette

Coven House of Wand and Sword — Similar to Maluridae Wood, a glamoured shed that serves as the meeting space for the most prestigious secret society in Heáhwolcen

Cyneham Breonna *(Chin-hum Bree-oh-nah)* — The governmental offices and administration building for Endorsa and the Samnung at large

Deu Medgar *(Due Mehd-gar)* — Residential palace for the ruling family of Endorsa

Galdúr *(Gal-durr)* — Capital city of Endorsa, named for Heáhwolcen's co-founder

Mimea Botanicci *(Mih-mee-uh Boat-an-ee-chee)* — Magical botanical garden in the capital city

Minthame *(Mint-haym)* — The training complex of the Fórsaí Armada

Prifysgol Grantabrych Draíochta *(Riffs-goal Grahn-tah-br-eye-k Dry-och-tah)* — The full name of what is colloquially known as the University

Taberna Körtz *(Tah-behr-na Courts)* — an old, original tavern that Emi-Joye and many other magical beings frequent, where Sheridan serves as barkeep

Fairevella *(Fair-eh-vell-ah)* — Home of the Fairies

Çeofilye *(Seoh-feel-yeh)* — Capital city of Fairevella

Maremóhr *(Mah-reh-moor)* — Performance and ceremonial venue

Seledreám *(Seh-leh-dree-am)* — The Noble House of Fae

Seolformúr *(Say-ohl-for-myur)* — Gate at the entrance to the Seledreám; the most powerful magical object in all of Heáhwolcen

Ifrinnevatt *(Eh-frihn-eh-vat)* — The spirit realm considered part of Heáhwolcen

Palna *(Pahl-nuh)* — Baize Sammael's country founded to study and teach Craft Wizardry, walled off from the rest of Heáhwolcen following the Ingefeoht

Ballamúr *(Bah-lah-myur)* — The name of the inner wall in Palna

Düoria *(Due-or-ee-ya)* — Palna's capital city

Larivuria *(Lah-rih-vur-free-ya)* — An unmapped oceanic city

Geography and Architecture on Earth

Bywyd Derwyddon *(Buh-wihd Duhr-wihd-on)* — The Druids' grove

Gwydir Forest Park *(Gwih-duhr)* — Welsh national forest where the Druids live

Torridon Wood *(Tohr-ih-don)* — The original location of the Celtic Fae homeland, on which the Seolformúr originally stood

Whipple Hill — A spot in Old Salem Village, now Danvers, Massachusetts, where Puritan girls spied witchcraft taking place, and on which the original Earth portal was located

Ynys Môn *(Oon-es Mahn)* — The Isle of Anglesey in Wales, where Collum and Bridgette traced the Druids

MAGICAL FOOD AND DRINK

Brimlad *(Brihm-lahd)* — Dried, seasoned strips of meat, similar to South African biltong; venison and beef are most common

Caife calabaza *(Cai-fey cah-lah-bah-zah)* — A spiced coffee beverage developed from pumpkins

Caife mokka *(Cai-fey mocha)* — A milk chocolate-based coffee beverage

Frihtri *(Frih-tree)* — Enchanted Fae version of fortune cookies

Gingewinde *(Jinj-eh-wihnd)* — Healing, soothing beverage made from ginger, similar to human ginger ale

Honeycakes — Dessert or breakfast pastry made of lightly sweetened, fluffy dough, somewhere between a doughnut and cinnamon bun

THE FORSAI ARMADA AND ASSOCIATED TERMS

Fórsaí Armada *(For-sai Ahrm-ah-dah)* — Heáhwolcen's united battle forces

Bondrie Guard *(Bond-ree)* — The armed guard charged with watching over the Palnan border wall

Bródenmael *(Broad-en-mayl)* — Bondrie's most elite on-the-ground warriors

Cailleach *(Callie-ack)* — Endorsa's skilled combat fighters and weapons experts

Caomhnóir Feeric *(Cahm-noor Fee-rick)* — Fairevella's winged fighting force, specifically trained in swordsmanship and knife-fighting

Cath Draíochta *(Cah-th Dry-och-tah)* — The art of spellcasting as part of battle

Fairy Mîleta *(Mih-leh-tuh)* — Heáhwolcen's aerial attack force, primarily skilled in archery and spellcasting from the sky

Feoht *(Fey-oht)* — General term for fighting and battle

Fyrdlytta *(Fyord-light-uh)* — Elven fighting forces, including the Unicorn calvary

Ingefeoht *(Eeng-fey-oht)* — Heáhwolcen's civil war, which took place approximately around the same time as that of the United States in the late 1850s and early 1860s

Wígend *(Wee-gehnd)* — A singular and plural term referring to trained warriors

Magical Origins

Ceannairí Álfar *(She-an-air-ee Al-far)* — The original magical being

Demiurge *(Deh-mee-urge)* — Origin of the world before the worlds existed

The Fyrst *(Fy-urst)* — The first group of magical offspring produced following Ceannairí Álfar's procreation rituals

Ylda *(Eel-dah)* — One of the Fyrst who was charged with designing and creating other magical species and creatures, including the Liluthuaé

Fae Holidays

Ostara *(Oh-star-uh)* — The Spring Equinox

Lammas *(Lah-mahs)* — The first harvest, a granary festival

Mabon *(May-bon)* — A celebration of the bounty of the summer and fall seasons

Samhaim *(Sow-ihn)* — The time when the spirit world and Earthen planes are no longer separated by a veil of shadows

Traditional Sayings and Other Words of Note

Annwyl *(An-wull)* — A Unicorn chosen to be bonded with an Elf as its steed

Beannaithe a Bhieth *(Bee-nay-thuh ah Bee-th)* — "Blessed be that [or that which] should come to pass"

Craft Wizardry — The powerful magic of ill-intent hawked by Baize Sammael

Dúnaelfen *(Doon-ayl-fen)* — A group of Elves that follow a selected leader

Diety Dhaoibh *(Dee-ih-tee Doh-b)* — Nondenominational form of "god or goddess bless, honor us"

Elusive Grimoire *(Grih-m-war)* — Baize Sammael's long-missing books of Craft Wizardry lore, spells, and history, hidden for more than a century somewhere in Endorsa for safekeeping

Fáilte *(Fayl-teh)* — "Welcome"

Foighne agus grásta *(Foyn ah-guhs grah-stah)* — "Patience and grace," a philosophy based on the idea that by understanding and accepting the timeline in which your existence is carved is only under the Universe's control, you shall grow into the prosperous life, future happenstance, or mission you were charged with leading and know is coming for you

Grudai *(Groo-dye)* — The season's first grain harvest

Hyldájj *(Hihll-dahssh)* — An oath of office for magical leaders

Indryhtu Sciccel *(En-dry-too Sih-shell)* — The mark of an office, such as the capes worn by Fairy ambassadors or the embroidered "E" present on Elven leadership's clothing

Ísenwaer *(Eye-sehn-wayr)* — An ability for two people to speak mind-to-mind with one another

Leódrúne *(Leh-oh-droon)* — A witch specializing in the craft of divining through tarot, palmistry, bones, etc.

Matla *(Maht-lah)* — The mighty power of the ancient ones

Maylemaegus *(Male-eh-may-guhs)* — An old term for Universal knowledge and power

Nonóir es linne *(Noh-noor es lihn-eh)* — "The honor is ours/mine"

Nunta Alchimica *(Noon-tuh Al-key-mee-kah)* — A magical term for the total solar eclipse, referring to the union of sun and moon

Palnan sympathist *(Sihm-pah-thist)* — Citizens in greater Heáhwolcen who believe in Baize Sammael's teachings and argue Palna should be a free country

Rídend *(Ree-dehnd)* — An Elf, Elfling, or other magical being of high rank and friendship to the Elves who is allowed to be bonded with a Unicorn

Seordwiph *(Say-ord-weef)* — Swordsmith, bladesmith

Sierwan/Sierwen *(See-er-wahn / See-er-when)* — The singular and
plural terms, respectively, for a gifted Elf who receives
knowledge from the Universe and is able to connect dots
others cannot

Téitheoir *(Teeth-oor)* — Healers

Ti yw'r Liluthuaé *(Teh yeh-r Lih-loo-thoo-aye)* — "You are the
Bright Star"

Tráthnóna mistéireach *(Trahth-no-nah Mih-stee-ryech)* —
Traditional greeting; "A joyous and fair day to you"

Wilgiest winedryhtenen *(Wihld-geyst wine-dry-teh-nehn)* —
Ceremonial greeting; "Be welcome, friends and comrades"

Wy árung *(Why ah-ruhng)* — Traditional signature; "With
regards/respect"

Y gwyr yn erbyn y byd *(Eh gweh-r ehn er-byne eh beh-d)* — "The
truth against the world"

~ Acknowledgements ~

"Bright Star" and "The Meridian Trilogy" would never have come to life — outside of my hand-written journals and long-neglected Word documents, that is — without a few very important folks. This is a non-exhaustive list of a few.

My family, first and foremost. My mom, from whom I developed my ability to write and tell stories, and my dad, who gifted me unending creativity and artistic ability. My test readers, who gave me feedback, pointed out grammatical errors I missed, and hyped me up when I was feeling lost between chapters. My cats, for being my constant cuddly companions.

To the fantasy authors and creators who inspired me in various phases of my life and writing career, including: Christopher Paolini, Mercedes Lackey, Sarah J. Maas, Charles DeLint, J.R.R. Tolkien, J.M. Barrie, Anne Rice, Amy Brown, cosplayer Erin White, yarn dyer and designer Trysten Molina of Dragon Hoard Yarn, vlogger + Fiberomancer Meghan Britt, the cast of Classless Characters podcast, and the various humans who got me sucked into D&D and Warhammer lore — you are gems, and I am grateful for your work and tireless pursuit of turning fantasy into reality.

To my main "coven" who encouraged me without fail, from start to finish.
I love you all: Chera, Lynsey, Liz, Elyse, Whitney, Trysten, Marissa, Meghan, Annie, Carlie, and Donovan. A special thanks to Annie for writing the poem immortalized by Skyanna Elixabete during Emi-Joye's installation. I cried the first time I read it, and it adds so much to that moment in the story.

To a few particularly important teachers I had in my life — You were some of the first to encourage me to write and create, and I would not be the author I am today without your guidance … and for a few key backwards check marks.

Cecilia Powell: North Columbia Elementary
Sandy Woods + Leslie Wright: Greenbrier Middle
Kim Buchanan, Sharon Florence, Carrie Brooks, Tracy Roden: Greenbrier High

But mostly ... to you, friend. For taking the time to read this story, and to consider adding the rest of "The Meridian Trilogy" and its associated novels to your bookshelves. I am honored to be in your midst.

— RETURN TO HEÁHWOLCEN —

The Story Continues November 2023

Ink-black midnight swirled through the air surrounding Heáhwolcen. It was a temperate night, not quite the balmy warmth of Southern summer eves, but the sort of night where windows were left cracked open to let fresh breezes waft in, bringing with them gentle scents of emergent springtime and promises of warmer weather ahead. The sort of night pregnant with promise, when witches of old would have stirred from their beds and wrapped themselves in lightweight cloaks before converging on Whipple Hill to praise the Spirits for this sign of good tiding.

Indeed, Nehemi wore a lacy wool shawl around her shoulders. The knitted stitches sparkled in the hints of starlight, for the yarn held the barest amount of milkfiber in its blend, which offered pearlescent sheen to the peacock feather pattern they adorned.

Peacocks, the witch queen thought to herself, huffing aloud. *Artur Cromwell and his deity-damned peacocks.*

They were all over Endorsa, and by default, Heáhwolcen. They had been, for centuries longer than she'd been alive. The beautiful birds held such symbolism for the ancient, long-dead founder of her world. Every ruler of Endorsa since the 1700s had worn their own one-of-a-kind peacock crown and livery at official events. These late hours of the night were the only times Nehemi would be caught without hers on. It didn't make sense to wear her crown at midnight.

And, supposing they *did* go into this war with Palna ... she smiled to herself. A rueful smile; Nehemi rarely ever truly smiled.

Only a fool wears a crown into battle, she remembered someone once telling her.

No, she would store her beloved peacock crown at Deu Medgar, the royal residence of Endorsa, should combat ensue. There were other ways for the wígend to know who in their midst was the mighty witch queen.

She shivered. *Mighty witch queen.* Nehemi knew what others called her, replacing the middle word with a more sinister rhyme. She did not balk from the insult. It was an honor to wear this crown, to represent and lead these beings, and she would not take that honor lightly. All her life she'd been raised to be "mighty". Her mother made it so — "princess lessons," they'd called her childhood. Every day, every night, she was tutored in the ancient arts of being a courtier. Endless years of manners, history — both of Earthen and magical realms; religion and spirituality, spellcasting and ritual, mathematics and business. The latter two, King Hermann told her once, were essential if one was to run a kingdom, not just a castle.

But it was the side lessons she learned from Queen Lalora's handmaiden, Naomi, that Nehemi used most often. Not just how to handle a state dinner for visiting dignitaries, which Heáhwolcen got quite a lot of ever since the Fairies began their ambassador duties again, but how to hone in and listen to what the dignitaries said. How to tell lies from truth. How to question *everything* without seeming to question anything. The art of being a servant was an artform indeed.

Before she was named queen, Nehemi would use this knowledge of Naomi's to sneak out of the palatial residence, and the other temporary residences that Endorsa held in neighboring nations. She'd not been to Earth though — until *the accident* happened, Nehemi had been deemed too young to accompany King Hermann on international visits. Queen Lalora and Naomi never went.

Going to Earth was something Nehemi still wanted to do. Yet somehow, in the nearly seventeen years since she'd been thrust into the role of queen, the time to do so eluded her. She was always doing something. There was always some group that wanted her to preside over a ritual, always a Samnung meeting, always responsibilities; not to mention practicing her magic, the constant honing of skills and learning. And … Cloa.

Blasted, *blasted* bloody Princess Cloa of Endorsa. Sometimes Nehemi hated the girl. She scowled, annoyed that thoughts of the princess invaded her peaceful midnight walkabout. Even the air seemed to have stilled at the scowl on the queen's face. She heaved a deep breath, forcing herself to calm down. To think about something other than the daft girl she wound up raising. The girl who would one day succeed her, take over everything she'd —

NO, a staunch voice inside Nehemi's head said. *You know what Lacnestre Pompié said.*

Normally the queen would have been attended to by a lacnian, one of the head healers. But Pompié was different. She wasn't much older than Nehemi, perhaps her senior by fifteen or so years, and was one of the first of the lacnestre to choose to study mind-health. Pompié spent months at a time on Earth for her training. She would be the first lacnian of mind-health, Nehemi knew. The healer was one of the few blessings Nehemi came across in her years of life thus far. Without Pompié's expertise, and constant obsession with learning, the queen wouldn't have a clue how to run her own life, much less oversee the lives of fellow government leaders and deity forbid, all of magickind in their world above the world.

The burden of this was overwhelming. It was why the witch queen stole from her bedroom in the middle of the night on a regular basis, wrapped in this shawl that Queen Lalora commissioned for her. The shawl, of that shimmering yarn dyed a glimmering burnished bronze, had been presented to Nehemi the day of *the accident*. Queen Lalora was rushing about, chiding Nehemi over her "dealings" with Dominus and telling her for the umpteenth time that no, she couldn't accompany them that day. It would be a long journey with several stops, and the first official day back for Lalora after decades of being out of the public eye. Lalora needed to be seen out and about, but she wasn't ready to reveal her motherhood yet. Something they had all chosen to keep very, very secret.

For good measure, as it turned out. Nehemi knew the whole of Heáhwolcen shuddered to think what would have befallen Endorsa had she and Cloa been in the carriage that day, too. No one knew what would happen to the warded wall around Palna if one of those who wielded the magic … *died*. Especially without an heir whom the ritual would then fall to.

And despite all the wary envy she had of the princess, the animosity she felt toward the next heir … at least she had this. This one, pivotal role she could play for Heáhwolcen, which all must be grateful for: Keeping threats at bay, her powers combining with those of Eckenbourne, Fairevella, and Bondrie.

Now that the Ballamúr was powered though …

The queen wondered how long their defense would continue to last.

Though Galdúr was hundreds of miles from the Palnan border, Nehemi paused by the bay window in the upper landing and gazed east, imagining she could see it. See that mythical barrier surging up from the magical soil on which their world was grounded; rising higher than the eyes could see, higher than Hlafjordstiepel even, a constant throbbing power source that walled Craft Wizardry in and protected the rest of the worlds from the evil that could be wrought from its raw energy.

She squinted. Something caught her eye in that distant east. Something coming her way, at a rather quick pace. Whoever was venturing westward was being pushed forward via magic. Fairies would fly. Elves and Sanguisuges would run too fast for her eyes to make out the — Nehemi squinted again — bobbing light as they came toward her. The longer she watched, the more corporal a form the figure took. She tilted her head and watched as it came closer: a figure on horseback, perhaps Unicorn-back, carrying a witchlight lantern. She knew it was witchlight because the gleam inside burned a pale acid green.

As the figure drew nearer, the witchlight illuminated its form. It was definitely a horse, she'd have seen the Unicorn horn glow by now. The figure was clad in gray leather, with chrome armor atop its shoulders and a matching helmet on its head. The helmet's face mask was lifted, but the face beneath cast in shadow.

A Bondrie guardsman, Nehemi realized. Her eyes widened. *Why in Hecate's name is a Bondrie guardsman galloping toward Endorsa at midnight?*

The queen pulled her wand from her houserobe pocket and flicked it slightly to the left,
whispering "Cíegan Kharis" as she did so. A moment later, the wizened old man evanesced to appear by her side, in sleeping clothes as well.

"Majesty," he said, bleary-eyed but awake. Nehemi rarely used a summoning spell for her hand. Their covenant bracelet sufficed unless she didn't feel like waiting on him to answer … or unless it was an emergency.

"Come," the witch queen told him. "We have a guest."

Kharis' brows raised. "At this time of night? Who?"

"A Bondrie guardsman, from the look of him."

The wizard's brows raised somehow higher. "With Corria?"

She shook her head. "He comes alone. And quickly."

Nehemi led Kharis down the staircase she'd just walked up, past the sitting room and formal tearoom to the front entrance. As they walked, she activated a thin cuff of Endorsan bronze on her left wrist, alerting her own guards to join them. By the time the queen and hand reached the doors to the residential entrance of the palace, they were flanked by guards of their own.

"Majesty," the Endorsan night commander addressed her.

"There is a Bondrie guardsman approaching," Nehemi said, all dreamy airiness gone and replaced with a tight air of authority. "There is no scheduled meeting. We do not know for what reason he is visiting."

Her face was set, and she hoped her eyes did not look too worried. She hadn't seen an uninvited member of the Bondrie Guard in Endorsa in almost seventeen years.

It seemed like an eternity, but perhaps it was only a few minutes between the time Nehemi arrived at the front door and the guardsman reached the gate. She heard the horse's hooves on the cobbled drive, nearly a half-mile away, galloping as if lives depended on it. Perhaps they did.

There was the thud and clank of armor as he dismounted, followed by synchronized steps of the Endorsan guards as they stepped between the unannounced visitor and the front doors.

"I am here to see the queen," they heard him say, his voice thickly accented — the 'th' sounded more like 'zuh'.

The Endorsan night commander looked to Nehemi for permission. She nodded to let the man in, hardening her expression in anticipation. The commander rapped on their side of the door, which opened heavily as the Bondrie guardsman darted in and nearly tackled the queen in the midst of his panicked entrance.

"I do not mean to affront, Your Excellency," he stammered, realizing who he'd run into. The man's eyes, visible now in the dim flicker of candlelight, were wild. He was coated in a thin film of sweat from the inhumanly fast ride.

Royal "princess lessons" would have had her offer him a glass of water, perhaps a seat somewhere more comfortable, before accosting him. But those were roles of queens who had the privilege of being married to kings. The mighty witch queen, whose might was questioned by none as often as herself, did not have such a privilege.

This was her kingdom. She wanted to know this man's business, right this moment.

"Quite alright," Nehemi said in polite forgiveness, though her tone was curt. "Who are you, and what is your business at Deu Medgar at this time of night?"

The Bondrie guardsman met her eyes, and she saw terror there. He opened his mouth to reply, swallowed deeply, then spoke:

"They know."

Lightning Source UK Ltd.
Milton Keynes UK
UKHW020749241022
410994UK00016B/933

9 798985 012125